THE MAN FROM NOWHERE

The men were so close Johnny could pick out their words....A wave of flaring pain rippled hotly up his leg. He set his teeth to keep from crying out and sank prone into the chilly water. Only his head surfaced. Then the mucky bottom fell away in an abrupt dropoff and Johnny, a poor swimmer, grabbed frantically at a log, wrapped his arm around its smooth bole, and hung on as it slid into midchannel. Suddenly he felt a powerful drag as the mainstream caught the log and swept it along like a cork....

BITTER GRASS

They rode along the upper creek to a line of spindly cottonwoods. Jonathan chose one with a thick limb of convenient height. He and Chino slung their ropes across the limb; Chino's falling noose grazed the Mexican rustler's face and he jerked his head away and began screaming.

Chino said in Spanish, "Be still, boy, you disgrace us," and gave him a cuff across the cheek. The shock of the blow, not the words, silenced the Mexican; he sat shaking, mumbling, as Chino adjusted the noose.

Creech sat still-faced, but he was sweating. "Look. Maybe we can talk about paying you for them."

"Talk all you want," Jonathan said. "You'll pay all right." He slipped the noose over Creech's head and kneed his horse around behind them. He lashed at the speckled rump of the Mexican's horse and it walked away, letting the man's full weight drop and swing. He kicked and writhed and slowly strangled.

T. V. OLSEN

THE MAN
FROM NOWHERE
&
BITTER GRASS

LEISURE BOOKS   NEW YORK CITY

A LEISURE BOOK®

January 1995

Published by special arrangement with
Golden West Literary Agency.

Dorchester Publishing Co., Inc.
276 Fifth Avenue
New York, NY 10001

THE MAN
FROM NOWHERE

CHAPTER ONE

At first there were five of them. Five who rode up from
the south, into the foothills of the Wyoming Absarokas.
Five stony-faced, weather-stained men who rode slack and
easy in the saddle like all men bred to horseback, but
whose eyes were narrow-tense and hard and skin-crinkled
at the outer corners from a long habit of watchfulness. All
were alike in these ways, although in age they ranged from
white-haired Bowie Samse's fifty-eight to the twenty-odd
years of "the kid," Johnny Vano.

They'd ridden for a long time through drought-parched
country, but it was a day for ducks when they hit the
foothills. All morning swift clouds with dark swollen
underbellies scudded the drab sky. Shortly after the noon
stop the rain began, catching the five riders in the open.
Four of them wanted to find shelter, but their leader, Sam
Vano, inexorable, absolute, and always sure, kept them
heading north into pale, slashing torrents of water that
whipped in windlashed gusts against the leaning forms of
horses and men. No brief blow, and they rode it out. A
day-long siege of it.

Even in high-buttoned slickers, they were soaked, miserable, and ugly-tempered when, toward evening, a densely-

timbered rise of ground loomed ahead and Sam Vano called a halt. They put their horses directly toward the heart of the scrub oak stand, and broke into a wide clearing. Sam looked around and dismounted with a grunt of satisfaction. They'd be well-hidden here, which was all that concerned him. The mutinous, surly grumblings of the others couldn't make Sam bat an eyelash; he knew his men, knew that they'd be lost without him, and that they knew it too.

They made a cold, wet camp—a misery camp. The rain had begun to slacken away into a gray drizzle. Young Johnny Vano threw saddle, saddlebags, and canvas-wrapped blanket roll from his sorrel, and lugged them over to the leeward side of a looming granite outcrop. Where the rock had checked the blast of wind and rain it was reasonably dry. With a saddle-weary grunt, Johnny dropped his gear and sat down on his bedroll, stretching this thin arms. He didn't rest long, for shortly Sam Vano was yelling for him to build a fire.

What with, and how? Johnny wondered sourly, but knew better than to question his father's orders aloud. A full-armed slap of a hard-calloused palm was Sam Vano's wordless reply to filial rebellion. Resignedly Johnny got stiffly to his feet and made a circle of the clearing, limbering his legs and arms.

When he chanced to glance over at his rock, he saw that his cousin, Jesse Norcross, was kicking Johnny's gear out into the rain, appropriating the lee side for himself. Johnny's hands balled into fists and he started across the clearing, choking, "Damn you, Jess!"

Jesse's long-limbered, cat-lithe body swung to face him, with the bubbling laugh that showed chalk-white teeth and never reached his eyes. He whipped off his hat, batting the wet felt against the shining wetness of his brush-chaps and tossing it on his other gear. The rain matted Jesse's crisp black hair, roached like a mule's mane, and he ran a hand over it in a slicking-back motion, handsome face still laughing.

"You don't like it, tiger, you know what to do."

Jesse was several years Johnny's senior. Fast with his fists and guns, faster with the women, he knew just how to needle the kid and always tried.

Choked with rage, Johnny dived headlong for the slim, mocking figure, and Jesse made a fluid sideward step and Johnny burgeoned past and plowed on his face in the littered gear. Instantly he lunged to his feet, whirled, went after Jesse again, and Jesse danced away, taunting him. "That's it, tiger, let's see your teeth."

The other men watched disinterestedly. Johnny bored furiously in, swinging wild blows which didn't connect. His boot skidded on the wet loam and his feet, aided by the awkward reactions of his long, gangling body, flailed the ground away and piled him on his face again. He lay there, sobbing in torn breaths. Jesse prodded him tentatively in the side with a boot, laughing. "Come on, tiger, you can do it. No?"

Johnny didn't rise, even after Jesse walked away, whistling, to the rock shelter. He knew that a fight with his cousin would end like all their others; he'd be pummeled to a pulp and Jesse would take what he wanted anyhow.

Finally he pushed himself up on his hands and knees and then to his feet, avoiding the looks of the others. Wet socks squishing in his boots, he walked from the clearing, pushed into a dripping oak thicket and hunkered down there to be alone with his present shame and the memories of a thousand others. He rested his arms on his knees and set his teeth into his slicker sleeve, tasting its oiliness, and listened to the rain pock the leaves above his head.

From the clearing he heard the mildly chiding voice of Bowie Samse. "You hadn't ought to let Jesse maul the kid that way, Sam."

"Growing-up medicine," was Sam Vano's terse reply. "Kid's got to learn to take knocks like the rest of us. No business for cream puffs, this." He lifted his voice. "Johnny! You fetch wood, build up that fire now, hear me?"

Johnny got to his feet and plunged through the brush, heedless of the wet lash of back-whipping branches, till he found a rotten deadfall. With furious energy, he kicked out great chunks of its tinder-dry heart. As he bent to scoop them up, bootsteps thunked solidly across the sodden ground. He looked up at Bowie Samse.

Bowie's slicker hung in loose folds on his shriveled body; there were feverish spots of color in his wasted cheeks, and one clawlike hand smothered a racking cough. Bowie was consumptive. He looked twenty years older than he was, a shadowy ghost of the big, vital man Johnny remembered.

Swift concern touched Johnny. "You're in a bad way."

Bowie gave a dry chuckle. "I'll live." His hollow tone doubted it. He squatted with a grim face, reaching trembling fingers. "Here, I'll help you."

Johnny dug his chin into his collar, said gruffly, "Never mind." He piled up an armload of the rotten heartwood. Bowie rested on his heels. He reached out and tapped bony knuckles against the hard shell of the log. Another dry chuckle. "Sort of like Jess, ain't it? Sound on the outside, bad at the core."

Johnny grunted uneasily. *Watch it*, he told himself; *he's making more fool talk*. Sam Vano would say in one of his rare streaks of almost humorless humor, "Damn Bowie plumb missed his calling. Should've been a sky-pilot."

Then Sam would add, more meaningfully, as a plain warning. "Maybe you're gettin' too old for the game, Bowie?" Sam and Bowie had ridden together for twenty years and more; that gave Bowie some room for liberties that hardbitten Sam Vano wouldn't tolerate from the younger men—but beyond a point, even Bowie didn't step. That line marked Sam's iron-fisted domination of his men; it made dangerous tampering.

Bowie was moodily twirling a twig between his fingers, frowning at it. "I said it before, kid," he told Johnny. "Get out of this rat race before it's too late. You're cut from a different cloth."

"Like you ain't?" Johnny jeered softly. "Like Jesse, Lopez, and Sam ain't? Hell, Bowie, I'm Sam's son. I ain't ashamed of it."

Bowie glanced at him swiftly, scowling, and opened his mouth, then shook his hawkish head as though he'd decided against saying something. But he did grunt, "Difference is, the rest of us, Sam included, all decided long time ago what we'd make of our lives. We had a choice. Being born to it, you never did. Think back once, son. What do you remember. . . ?"

Johnny's busy hands held motionless. He rocked back on his heels, studying on it. A thousand camps like this one, some colder and wetter. Some dry and hungry. Days and often nights of far-ranging, grueling rides in rain, snow, blazing heat, till you'd never known anything but the rocking and jolting back and forth in a sweaty saddle. Weeks stretching into months of holing up in a desert rendezvous or a mountain hideaway, where boredom hung like a dead weight. Riding alone into a hundred towns from Rio to the Canadian border to fetch supplies for the gang, with the feeling that a thousand unseen eyes were boring at your back, expecting any time to feel the heavy hand of a lawman clamp your shoulder. Ten thousand days and nights in company with taciturn, haggard-eyed men who jumped at a sound, hands dropping to well-worn pistol grips. Men who came and went, whom you never got to know and didn't want to.

That was Johnny Vano's life.

"Make good studyin', son?" Bowie broke his thoughts softly.

"Damn it, Bowie," Johnny burst out, "you hush that talk! You know Sam don't—"

"I now Sam a sight better'n you, youngster," Bowie Samse cut him off with a harsh abruptness. "Come on, let's be toting this stuff into camp."

In silence, they trudged to the clearing with armfuls of the crumbling punk, dumping it on a dry place under the widespreading boughs of a gnarled oak. Johnny's mind was an angry turmoil. He wondered if Bowie knew how deeply he'd scored. His words had forced Johnny to face the nameless yearnings that had begun to gnaw in him more and more frequently. Things he had to cover with rough words or surly silence so the others wouldn't see. The trouble was, having known no other life than this, he wasn't sure what his hidden urges amounted to, or how much they meant.

Biting his lip in frustration, he ground a handful of the heartwood between his palms to make a small heap of loose tinder. Over this he built a wigwam of dry twigs he'd gathered from under the log. He reached inside his slicker for the oilcloth-wrapped packet of matches, fumbled one out, struck it alight on a dry patch of his pants, and cupped the orange flare in his palms. Smoke threaded from the tinder, then a spoon of flame which caught the twigs. When he had a steady blaze, Johnny piled on chunks of the rotten wood.

Jesse came across the clearing at a swinging stride, whistling cheefully, carrying the battered coffee pot full of canteen water. Before Johnny had time to wonder why Jesse was doing a menial chore with a cheerful air, Jesse reached the fire and bent as though to set the pot close by. It tilted in his hand; a stream of water gouted over the meager blaze. The fire sizzled and died in a thin mushrooming of steam and smoke. Johnny came to his feet, no uncertainty in him.

"You did that a-purpose."

Jesse's black brows lifted in the blandest shrug of innocence. "Why tiger, I was trying to help."

Sam Vano strode heavy-footed across the clearing, an emphatic anger in his swinging arms. "Jesse, you're goin' to far, damn it!"

The sodden smack of his fist froze each man in position, except Jesse, who somersaulted backward. He rolled over once and landed on his back. He shook his head. Handsome face distorted, he ripped open his slicker, clawing for his holstered gun.

CHAPTER TWO

Both Vanos, Sam and Johnny, were covering Jesse Norcross with leveled sidearms before he had his clear of its holster. He lay on his back, crafty-bleached eyes gauging his chances and rejecting them, behind those eyes a silent fury still walled, biding its time now.

Sam Vano slammed his gun into its sheath with a contemptuous grunt. Standing well over a bull-shouldered six feet, Sam Vano's face was bone-gaunt, craggy as a mountain, the mouth a thin slash of brown granite. Just the look of him had made more than one hardcase think twice.

"You know better than to brace a man on your back, Jess. Since you're feeling so raunchy, git some more wood and make up that fire. You can cook supper too."

Jesse maneuvered cautiously to one knee, then straightended up, baleful eyes following Sam Vano's broad back as he stalked away. Jesse wiped a thin trickle of blood from the corner of his mouth. He stared briefly at Johnny, but didn't say anything. He picked up his hat and walked from the clearing.

Johnny was conscious that he still held the gun. The grips slippery against his palm. He sheathed it slowly. He was realizing that though he and Sam had gotten their slickers open at the same time, that they'd made the draw within a fraction of the instant, his gun had been pointed and cocked while Sam's was still swinging to level. For a moment he felt a wild exultation; long hours of unstinting practice had paid off. He had at last beat Sam, who had a broad reputation with a hand-gun.

Then he noticed that Bowie Samse and Chino Lopez, silent observers, were both watching him steadily from a few yards distance. Lopez had just come from tending the horses, his special detail. He was a Mexican-Ute half-breed, a wolf-gaunt, loosely built man in his middle thirties, whose turgid, ink-black eyes surveyed Johnny stolidly. But Johnny saw Bowie shake his head, very slightly, before he turned away.

Johnny hunkered down against the oak trunk, his back to the wet bark. Bowie's look had the effect of changing his moment of triumph into a gray sense of failure. It was a feeling for which he wouldn't account. Who had he failed, he wondered. Not Bowie, for Bowie was a dying man, full of regret, but past caring about success or failure for his own dwindling days. Himself, then? In a groping, elemental fashion, Johnny reasoned that Bowie saw that ready gun-draw as only another factor that would stand against Johnny if ever he tried to escape this life.

But he thought: *Bowie's a talky old fool. Even if you wanted, there's no turning back.* Sam had said so many a time. His name was known to half the sheriffs and territorial marshals in the West, together with the rest of the Vano gang. *What the hell are you thinking of, letting old Bowie get under your skin with this sky-pilot stuff? Get rid of it!*

It was much the way Sam Vano himself might have rebutted Johnny's thoughts, had he known them. Johnny had never quite understood his own feeling about Sam.

Oddly, he rarely thought of the elder Vano as his father. He did admire Sam's rough-and-ready way of tackling a situation, his iron dominance of the men who rode with him; he used Sam's rough judgments of life as his own criteria. He made a hard, even brutal, parent; but Johnny, knowing no other, and with no memory of a mother whom Sam had never mentioned, saw nothing amiss in that. He and his father were not close, yet he'd never questioned the fact of his unswerving loyalty to the man.

Jesse tramped into camp, bearing an armload of dry wood. Without a word he set to building a fire. His hands were shaking with the residue of his fear and fury. Johnny wondered uneasily how wise it had been of Sam to strike Jesse, even to maintain authority.

Jesse, the bastard son of Sam Vano's only sister and a gambler named Ned Norcross, had been with the gang for eight years. With his own peculiar sense of familial obligation, Sam had taken on the orphaned boy when his mother, Norcross's shill, had died from a stray bullet in a gambling table shoot-out in Abilene. A more purposely aimed slug had taken Ned Norcross's spotty life. As the youngest men of the gang, Johnny and Jesse had been thrown together in a sort of spit-and-claw companionship; there'd been only bad blood between them from the start.

Johnny had long known two things about Jesse: he was a natural bully, and he never forgot a slight. Long since, Sam Vano had earned the ebullient Jesse's resentment with his utter lack of sympathy; tonight Johnny had watched that brimming resentment turn abruptly into deep hatred. Sam had struck him hard, but the lightest of cuffs would have produced the same reaction from Jesse. So Johnny was watchful and uneasy.

The meal was a good one, for Jesse, though hating work, took a perverse pride in doing any job well. He had a magic touch for the crudest of camp fare; even under tonight's miserable conditions, the usual coffee, beans, bacon, and biscuits had never tasted better.

Squatting on their heels around the fire, the men wolfed their food in silence. The drizzle had died away. Numb and chill from hours of cold, beating rain, the men held their hands to the fire and began to dry out. Their mood warmed with their bodies. Bowie told a joke in his dry way, and all, even Jesse, grinned.

Sam Vano stripped off his slicker and rubbed his ham-like hands together. His chipped-rock features had a fitful, ghoulish quality in the flickering light. "Let's get to business."

"Good," growled Bowie Samse. "We ride clear up from Sonora on your say-so that there's a big job waiting in Wyoming, but you don't breathe a word of what it's to be."

A muscle twitched momentarily at the corner of Vano's vise-like mouth—the closest he ever came to a smile. He clapped Bowie's thin shoulder lightly. Sam's spirits always mounted before he brought a job off, Johnny knew.

Almost a year ago the gang had hit a Texas rancher's herd along the Rio, then had fled south of the border where there was no fear of pursuit, driving several hundred head of the Texan's cattle ahead of them. They'd sold the herd to a *haciendado* in Sonora who asked no questions, then settled down in Hermosillo for a long wait, while the hue and cry back in Texas died down. It was a familiar routine for Sam Vano, one he'd always followed. Hit, and vanish where they can't reach you. Across the Mexican border, or the Canadian, sometimes into the wild back-reaches of mountain country in the U.S. states and territories.

The men enjoyed the enforced leisure, giving them a chance to drink and gamble their danger-won gains away.

Also the black-eyed *senoritas* were obliging. But Sam Vano always chafed restlessly under his own steely restraints. During the long months that followed, he'd learned that Texas Ranger patrols were watching the border for his return. Only when the Rangers had relaxed their vigilance had Vano moved.

During the weeks they'd ridden north; in the saddle by night and holing up by day in the more populated country, the leader gave the others no hint of his plans. Johnny knew only that a fat letter, datemarked two months earlier in Rutherford, Wyoming, and frayed and dog-eared from many miles of different hands, had been delivered to Sam a week before they started north. But that was Sam's standing policy: keep them in ignorance of a job till the last minute so no one would have time to crawfish out.

Now, with his first touch of jubilance in many months, Vano grunted, "Bowie, it was worth it. You'll see." His eyes—bullet-gray, with a bullet's impact—moved over the others, then fell to the ground between his feet. He picked up a charred twig from the crumbling embers and began to sketch in the dirt. "This's the Little Muddy River, which we crossed this mornin'. It takes a wide bend around the hills here, and circles the town of Rutherford, just west of where we are now. This town supplies ranchers for a big area. Been a prosperous year for those ranches. Exceptional spring round-up. Town's got one bank. It's still loaded with local cattlemen's stock income." He looked at them, man by man, and said flatly: "We're taking it."

Bowie started to speak, but his words dissolved in a raw, retching cough. When the spasm ended, he got out breathlessly, "How you know all this? You ain't had time to size up the layout."

Sam Vano reached in his shirt and drew out the thick

letter which Johnny had just glimpsed back in Sonora—now more grimy and dog-eared than ever. "This here letter's from Mort Huggins. You remember Mort."

Johnny remembered Mort Huggins—a cadaverous-looking outlaw who'd joined briefly with the gang in the Tonto Rim country about three years ago. Bowie nodded. "Good man, Mort."

Vano read the letter aloud, frowning and stumbling over the tersely-phrased scrawl. Mort had written that he'd been contacted by a young clerk in the Rutherford bank—Emmett Gorman by name—who had been losing heavily at faro in a local gaming room, to the tune of nearly two thousand dollars. The dealer held his I.O.U.'s for the entire sum. Gorman had succeeded in wheedling off payments for six months, promising to pay in full at the end of that time.

At first he'd had the idea of embezzling that amount by minor degrees from his own teller's cage, but a shortage couldn't be covered indefinitely, and a full investigation would eventually find him out. He had to find a way to cover the loss. So he looked up Mort Huggins and made him a proposal. It was well-known that Mort rode on the shady side of the law, but there were no warrants out for him at present, and he was keeping to the open.

Gorman's proposition was this: he would give Mort Huggins the complete layout of the bank, including the combination to the big vault and any other pertinent information. The day before Mort pulled the job, Gorman would quietly remove two thousand dollars from the vault—a loss that would be assumed by bank officials to be part of the holdup loot. It was a tempting offer, but Mort refused, telling Gorman that it would take at least four men to pull a sure-fire daytime bank job in a town of Rutherford's size. Besides, the sheriff of Rutherford County was Leonard Wolfe, one of the shrewdest and most relentless lawmen in the territory, and Mort wanted no truck with him.

However, Mort Huggins had made Gorman a counter offer: one that would involve no personal risk for Mort. His friend Sam Vano enjoyed a calculated risk. Sam and his gang were in Sonora, last Mort had heard, but for five hundred dollars he'd contact Sam and put it up to him. Gorman agreed to remove enough from the vault to cover Mort's fee, if Mort were willing to wait. He was and he lost no time in composing the lengthy letter to Sam.

Mort added that he intended to leave for up north so he wouldn't be connected with the job. Later on, he'd return to collect his five hundred. Therefore Sam was not to waste time trying to contact Mort when he reached Rutherford, but to get directly in touch with the bank clerk, who would give them all the necessary details to bring off a smooth job. Gorman lived in a room at the hotel.

"That's the story Mort gave me, I liked the sound of it, and here we are," Sam Vano concluded, folding the letter between his scarred, stubby fingers.

"Here we are," echoed Bowie, dryly. "It occurs to you this could be a law trap?"

Sam Vano gave his spare, humorless side-flick of a smile. "Ain't but a chance in a thousand a square lad like Mort would side with the law to get Sam Vano in a jackpot."

Lopez, legs scissored under him tailor-fashion, leaned forward, mahogany-sphinx face polished by firelight. "W'at about thees *Senor* Gorman. Could not he, how you say, string along the Mort Huggins?"

"Use Mort to toll us into a trap? Maybe," Vano grunted, "but you been with Sam Vano a while longer, Chino, you'll learn he rides into nothing blind." His lead-gray eyes moved to Jesse, then to Johnny. "That's why you two roosters are going to handle the spadework for this job."

Bowie groaned, started to object, but a lift of Sam's hand cut him off. "You boys will ride into town, register at the hotel. If anyone asks, you're trail hands from Texas, just finished a drive from Montana, and are headin' back. You'll see Gorman on the quiet. That's important. Ask him questions, get all the dirt we need. You'll ride out of town in the morning—south toward Texas, in case anyone sees you go—then swing back and meet us here. Now— Bowie?"

"I was goin' to suggest," Bowie said sourly, "that you send just one man, a more experienced head. Like me. There's bad blood between these two; they might tip our hand with their private feud."

"That's why I'm sendin' 'em," Vano said, his eyes very flat and hard on Jesse and Johnny. "Time they had more know-how, plannin' and organizin'. Also to learn to keep their spurs tucked in. Can't have this personal grudge stuff in the gang. In Rutherford, they'll have to get along or dig their own graves. But they'll dig 'em without the rest of us."

Both boys stared sullenly at the fire. For a moment there was a ponderous silence broken only by the thin moan of wind through leafy oak branches, as Sam let his statement sink home.

"All right," Bowie said mildly. "But what about this Wolfe? I've heard of him; he's smart and tough as they come, no jackleg John Law. He's like to spot these two greenhorns."

Sam was already shaking his head. "That's just it. Wolfe's an old-time lawman, likely to spot a pair of old hardcase birds like you or me right off. Fact, he knows my face from long ago, back in Texas. These two smooth-faced young 'uns would stand a better chance of passin' with Lenny Wolfe, posin' as a pair of lone riders.''

"Long riders, don't you mean?'' growled Bowie. He drew his shoulders in, shivering in spite of the fire's roasting aura.

"Quit worryin','' Sam said irritably, "Swear, you're gettin' worse than an old squaw.''

"Can't help it. Got a bad feeling about this job . . . that's all.''

Jesse cleared his throat. "When you want us to ride to town, Uncle Sam?''

Sam swung his gaze to Jesse, curtly answering his question: "Tonight.''

CHAPTER THREE

Following Sam Vano's directions, Johnny and Jesse rode due northwest through the foothills, full gear on their saddle to heighten the impression of two drifting cowhands. Sam had known this country from years ago, and his mental mapping was flawless. In fifteen minutes, as he'd predicted, the two young men hit a wagon road. This they followed due west through rugged pine timber till they came out on a denuded ridge. Here they paused to blow their horses and listen to thunder rumble thinly across the peaks to the north.

"More rotten-mean weather coming," Jesse commented sourly. Johnny didn't answer. He'd resolved to say nothing to Jesse that didn't need saying; they couldn't afford a quarrel on a crucial mission. But Jesse himself appeared to be taking this seriously; unusual for him, he'd hardly spoken since leaving camp. Johnny peered through the darkness at Jesse's slim silhouette, slack-easy in the saddle, wishing he could see his cousin's face. Somehow his very silence made Johnny uneasy. Of what was he thinking? The job ahead? Or was he still brooding on how Sam had knocked him down, hating in silence like an Indian?

They took their way along a right forking of the road,

following the ridge south for five miles. They descended into a dip where the main tributary of the Little Muddy roiled tumultously, swollen by the day's heavy rain. Crossing a rickety bridge, they rode down a densely timbered slope and broke at last into the open flat between the hills where the town of Rutherford sprawled.

It was plain that Rutherford was no ordinary backwoods cowtown. On the outskirts they rode through a substantial residential section of big, prosperous-looking houses with rambling verandas and gingerbread trim. The streets were bordered with hedges, picket fences, and giant shade trees. Johnny felt a hungry resurgence of the old yearnings as his eyes eagerly took in the comfortable homes with their warm sprinkling of window lights. Once he glimpsed a couple standing in the shadows of a broad veranda, and a girl's spritely laugh carried clearly.

The subdued mutter of thunder was louder now. It began to rain again as they turned down into the mud-rutted main street. Doors and windows were all closed, except for one open doorway where a bulky figure leaned. A tortured rope of lightning writhed across the sky, bathing the buildings in burnished white. Just then Johnny was looking at the man in the doorway; the flickering light picked out his face, staring straight at the two riders, and above his head, a lettered sign: *Sheriff's Office*.

They rode on. Johnny heard Jesse's breath release sharply. "So that's him. He *is* a watchful bastard."

"And he was watchin' us."

"Don't start cryin' before you been bit, tiger," Jesse gibed. "Hell, he can't know us."

They rode to the livery barn and stabled their horses, asked for and received permission to leave their saddle gear there, then slogged through mud and pelting rain to the hotel, a two-storied sturdy building with the legend

ROOMS over the entrance nearly weathered away. The dimly lighted lobby was deserted except for the night clerk and a drummer snoring in a plushly leather chair, a newspaper over his face.

Jesse and Johnny registered under the false names that Sam Vano had directed them to use. With a bare glance at their rough-printed signatures, the night clerk selected a key from the wall rack. "Number 102, gentlemen. Second floor, second room to your right. That'll be a dollar apiece in advance."

Johnny was unbuttoning his slicker to reach his wallet when Jesse nudged him in the ribs and jerked his head at the door. "Checking on us already," he murmured.

The bulky man had just pushed through the door and was crossing the lobby, heavy body rolling from side to side with his lumbering walk.

"If anything happens now, he'll know our faces," Johnny whispered.

"Keep your mouth shut," Jesse murmured. "I'll handle this."

The sheriff came to the desk, his shabby, rain-spotted coat stretching taut across his wide shoulders as he hunched over to scan the register. There was a deceptive aspect of a sleepy, shaggy bear about him. The cloudy ruff of sparse light hair around his big head gave an impression of tired benevolence as did the half-lidded pale blue eyes that now swung on the two young men.

"Evenin'," Jesse said, with a civil bob of his head. "Night for ducks, eh?"

"Evenin'." The sheriff's drawl was deep-chested and booming. "Pete Lacy and Tom Brooks of Valverde, Texas, eh?"

"That's right, sir. I'm Pete, this's Tom. Just drove a feeder herd clear to Montana, headin' home now."

"Leonard Wolfe." The sheriff shook hands with both. "What part of Montana?"

"Northwest corner."

"Mmp. Reckon you Texas boys felt right at home on all that rollin' prairie."

"No, sir," Jesse said glibly. "That part's near solid timber—yellow pine, white pine, fir, hemlock. Some hilly grazing land. Mighty pretty country."

"My mistake. Staying over to see the elephant?"

"Gettin' an early start south in the mornin', sir."

A curt nod of Wolfe's heavy head. "Pleasant trip." He said to the clerk, "Night, Bill," and left the lobby at his tired bear roll of a walk.

Jesse slapped a silver cartwheel on the desk. "Suspicious law hereabouts."

"Keeps his eyes open is all, stranger," the clerk said. "That's why he's one of the best, even at sixty-two."

They ascended the creaking stairway to a narrow, dirty corridor. Jesse unlocked their door and stepped into the room with Johnny following. Jesse dug out a match, lighted the lamp on the dresser. It was a meagerly furnished cubbyhole with a battered commode, an iron bedstead with most of the paint flaked off, a chair which would never take a man's weight, and a cracked pitcher and basin.

Jesse flung his hat on the bed with an explosive laugh. "The clever bastard! Trying to catch us with that Montana business. Good thing we holed up in them woods a couple winters ago."

"After the hold-up, he'll remember our faces," Johnny said.

Jesse shrugged out of his slicker with a disgusted sound. "Hell, knock off that tack. Chances you take are part of the game." He flopped on his back across the sagging bedframe, grunted luxuriously, and tilted his hat over his eyes.

"We better see Gorman right now," Johnny said.

Jesse groaned, swung hs long body to a sitting position, and ran his hands over his hair. "Hell. What room did Mort's letter say?"

Johnny shucked off his slicker and tossed it across the chair. "One-oh-four. Two doors down."

They eased quietly from the room and moved on tiptoe to 104. A pencil of light flowed from the crack beneath the door. Jesse tapped his knuckles softly on a panel. A chair scraped back in the room, and the door opened. A sandy-haired, balding and bespectacled young man stood blinking at them. He wore a black suit of old-fashioned cut. In muted lampglow, his face looked sallow. There was a nervous tic in his left cheek.

"Well?"

"You Gorman?"

"Who are you?"

"You want a bank robbed or not?" Jesse asked amusedly.

The young man's jaw sagged. "You're Sam Vano?"

Jesse prodded a thumb against Gorman's stocky chest and moved him gently backward. "Let's talk inside."

Gorman bolted the door behind them with feverish haste. Jesse swung the single chair around, straddled it, settled his arms on its backrest, and watched Gorman's nervous precautions with a deepening amusement. "I'm Sam's nephew, Jesse Norcross. Sam's son here, 'Tiger' Vano. Sit down, fella, before you fall down."

Johnny put his back to the wall, folded his arms, and watched Gorman sink onto the edge of the bed, twisting his hands like a pair of damp spiders. Johnny guessed at the measureless strain under which the clerk had labored: it could tear the guts out of man.

Emmett Gorman took a folded paper from an inside pocket of his coat and handed it to Jesse. "Here's a floor plan of the bank. What else do you want?"

Sam had rehearsed them both to the letter on the information he needed, but Johnny let Jesse do the talking, and Jesse was thorough. Consulting the floor plan pressed smooth on his knee, he grunted off terse questions about what hours the bank's business was slackest, which employees were likely to play heroic, and so on. Finally, tucking the plan in his pocket, Jesse stood up, yawned, and gave Emmett Gorman a cheerful nod. "Real thorough, Mr. Gorman. You'd have made a hell of an owlhoot."

Gorman stood too, round eyes feverishly eager behind the thick glasses. "Tomorrow morning, then? The job, I mean? I'll need time to get my money from the vault before you come."

"Likely. But Sam'll set the time." Jesse chuckled.

"What's that for?"

"Just thinking. I never saw dollar signs in a man's eyes before."

Ruddy rage beat through Gorman's face; he took a step toward Jesse, his hands knuckling into fists.

"Don't get feisty, prissy Alice, or I'll pull your pigtails," Jesse drawled, as he lounged toward the door. He shot back the bolt, opened it a crack and surveyed the corridor. He looked back at Gorman. "One little thing, counterjumper. The total head money on Sam and the rest of us comes to maybe five thousand dollars."

Gorman stared at him with undiluted hatred. "What's that to do with me?"

"Only this," Jesse said gently. "That's considerable more than you'd planned on taking out of this. Tip off the sheriff, and you stand to collect a lot more, *inside* the law—with a ready-sounding excuse for your own part. So tie to this: if anything goes wrong tomorrow, even five thousand won't help you run far enough."

He nodded to Johnny and the two returned to their room. When Johnny had closed the door after them, he turned to Jesse hotly: "That was smart, putting it in his head about the reward money!"

Jesse was sitting on the bed, tugging off his boots. He said easily, "Just a word of warning to the man, tiger. He's hungry, you noticed, real hungry." He laughed. "Fancy that mousy runt running up a two thousand dollar gambling debt . . . just goes to show you can't tell about some folks." He rolled onto the bed and lay with his back to Johnny, saying unconcernedly, "Blow out that damn' lamp and let's get some sleep."

Johnny glared at his back, then deliberately stripped off his shirt, poured some water into the basin, and began to sponge off his bony upper body. He stared at himself in a shard of cracked mirror held by bent nails to the wall over the commode. His rib-lean body, narrow as a lath. His young face, sunblackened and gaunt-angled, his straight hair bleached past its natural blondness. The wariness of a man on the dodge showed in his deep-set amber eyes, making them older than his years warranted. *What're you looking for?* he asked the image silently. *What the hell you expect to find, anyhow?*

Over on the bed, Jesse stirred, grunted impatiently. "You hear me about the lamp?" Johnny toweled himself dry, blew out the lamp, pulled off his boots and rolled in, back to Jesse.

Rain rattled against the window. The lower sash was open a crack; a rain-scented draft fingered the dry, musty air of the room. A woman's raucous laugh drifted downstreet from a saloon or crib-house, carrying with it a lifetime's disillusionment. It was a familiar sound. Johnny thought of the buoyant, life-loving laugh of that girl in the shadows of the big house, coming into town. The bitter frustration came back to him.

Jesse's sleepy voice startled him. "Caught the way you pulled that hogleg on me, back in camp. Faster even than Sam."

Johnny didn't reply. He folded his arms behind his head and stared ceilingward, at darkness, at nothing.

"Yessir, you're gettin' to be some shucks, tiger," Jesse murmured sleepily. "Only you want to counterweight that butt so's the barrel won't throw so hard. Next time you might not be lucky enough to brace me while I'm flat on my back."

CHAPTER FOUR

The bad weather had not lifted by morning. Johnny and Jesse woke to a gray and dismal dawning, checked out of the hotel, and claimed horses and gear at the livery barn. Mist hung in the air like a thin, wet powder, sleekly burnishing slickers and horses' hides. As they rode past the sheriff's office, Johnny saw Wolfe watching them through the single dingy window. Jesse gave the sheriff an audacious salute of parting, and Wolfe replied with a curt nod.

"Now," Jesse chuckled, "we'll head south on the wagon road like a couple of cowpokes moseying back to Texas, then cut off and circle 'round back to camp."

A mile from town, they loped off from the road, cutting at right angles into thick timber. Then they sloped in a wide circle through deep hills.

Sam received Gorman's map from Jesse and scrutinized it while he rattled questions at the two. When he was satisfied, the leader said, "Pay attention now, all of you."

With a twig, Sam sketched on the wet ground in the lee of the big rock. Working only from his knowledge of the country and his memory of Rutherford's layout, he made

lines and squares to represent two streets and key buildings. He drew the wavering course of the Little Muddy,
and worked in lesser streams and tributaries. He drew in
roads and locations of prominent landmarks. While he
sketched, he talked, naming or describing these matters in
detail. He timed and placed each separate movement of
each man, from where they'd leave the horses and who
would hold them to which roads each would travel—for
the gang would separate and scatter after the job, then
converge on a single rendezvous later: another of Sam
Vano's personal earmarks for confusing pursuit. They'd
hole up in rough country for a couple of weeks till the
searching posses were discouraged, then travel out of the
country by easy stages.

Sam went over it three times, then rapid-fired questions
at them to make sure each man was thoroughly briefed on
his part. Afterward they dispersed to break camp.

The five men rode in silence, dark-slickered forms without identity in the slanting rain. Occupied with his thoughts,
feeling nothing but the beating water against hat and slicker,
Johnny rocked emptily with the motion of his horse. He
hardly glanced up till Sam Vano said curtly, "Hold it."

Johnny saw buildings take dim shape through the storm.
They'd reached the outfringe of Rutherford. "String out,"
Sam told them. "We'll ride in one by one and go into the
bank together. Bowie, you'll watch the horses—and Lenny
Wolfe's office. Have your saddle gun ready. Plug him if he
steps out."

Bowie said nothing. No great shakes with a hand-gun,
he was the best rifle shot in the gang. Only Johnny, and
maybe Sam, guessed how this life had begun to pall on
him with encroachment of death in his shriveling body.

"You hear me, Bowie?"

"I hear you, Sam."

"I'll go first," Vano said. "Bowie next, rest of you follow. Time it a minute apart."

Sam spurred away, slowed as he neared the first building, and finally vanished down a residential street. They sat in the rain, waiting without talk. Bowie dipped a scrawny hand inside his slicker and took out his big turnip watch, consulting it more as a gesture than anything. "Luck, boys," he said, and kicked his horse into motion.

"Your turn, tiger," Jesse said in a faintly jeering voice.

Johnny hesitated, needled by something in Jesse's tone, by Bowie's communicated reluctance, by his own uneasiness. Then he heeled his sorrel hard, heading into the side street.

He turned onto the main street at the intersection and hauled in his fiddlefooting animal, then peered through the wet murk toward the bank, a block down. There were Sam and Bowie on the sidewalk, their horses tied at the front rack. Johnny's gaze raked along the tie rails opposite the bank, at the saddle horses standing hipshot there, wet rumps shimmering softly in the rain. An unusual number of people in town, considering the weather. . . . Johnny took passing notice of this, then roweled the sorrel downstreet.

As he swung down, ducked under the tie rail, and moved up on the walk by Sam and Bowie, Johnny realized that Bowie was arguing quietly and that Sam was nodding in agreement. The leader's bleak eyes threw darting restless glances up and down the street. "Maybe you're right," he murmured. "I must need spectacles. Too damn' many horses. . . ."

"There," Bowie said quickly, nodding toward the hotel diagonally across from the bank, and Johnny caught it too—a swift flicker of movement behind a second-story hotel window. "Know what?" Bowie asked softly. "Bet you there's men watching us from each of those windows across the way.''

"Won't give you odds,'' Sam Vano said impassively, and Johnny, in a swift grip of panic, made an impulsive step toward the horses. Sam's steely fingers caught his upper arm with bruising power. "Easy, boy. They'd cut us down like flies, in the street. We'll break when I give the word. . . . Here comes Lopez. Wait'll we're all together, we'll make a rush for that alley alongside the bank. We'll take to the timber.''

"On foot? They'll ride us down in no time,'' Bowie prophesied grimly.

"I know this country,'' Vano said. "I know places no horse can follow. They come after us, they'll have to do it on our terms.''

Now Lopez had reached the tie rail. The half-breed dismounted and began to step around his horse. Suddenly a man in town clothes burgeoned out the hotel door. Johnny saw him swing a shotgun to level, pull both triggers. The double blast bucketed racketing echoes down the street. It caught Lopez just as he stepped into view from behind the horse's flank, flinging him backward, rolling him into the hoof-churned mud where he sprawled like a broken rag doll.

Buck fever took Johnny by the throat and shook him; for a moment, his brain refused to function. Sam Vano dropped to one knee, blazing away at the townsman. The fellow dropped his shotgun, reeled away, clawing at the clapboard siding of the hotel, and fell in a sodden sprawl across the board walk.

It was the signal for the men in the windows to open up. Bullets gouted chocolate geysers in the muddy thoroughfare, ripped in screaming ricochets off the brick front of the bank. *"Run for it!"* Sam Vano bellowed, leaping for the alleyway. Bowie took a step after him, then saw Johnny frozen there.

"Johnny-boy, come on!" His clawing grip tore at Johnny's slicker, tugged him into a stumbling run. He heard the impact of lead thudding into flesh, heard Bowie's retching, lung-torn gasp, felt Bowie's falling weight tear away his hold on Johnny's arm.

"*Bowie!*" It shocked Johnny to life. He dropped on his knees by Bowie. Sam glanced at Bowie's gray face, said sharply, "He's cashed, kid. Let's grab our horses, ride through these soft-bellied counterjumpers, pick Jesse up as we head out. . . ."

While he was still speaking, Sam had grabbed Johnny by the shoulder, half-lifting him, hauling him in a dragging run under the tie rail, clamping Johnny's hand over his stirrup before he swung to his own horse. The feel of the stirrup was enough to galvanize Johnny's tense-tight muscles to the automatic reflex of mounting. As he hit the saddle swell, a bullet smashed the horn, another whipped the skirt of his slicker. The townsmen were rattled and shooting wild. Johnny quartered around and spurred headlong after Sam.

The gamut of gunfire fell behind them. *We're making it,* Johnny was thinking, when a man appeared in a doorway to fire at the passing riders. Sam Vano's oxlike form rocked to the impact of a bullet. Seemingly it was a minor graze, for Sam instantly twisted in his saddle without cutting pace and returned the fire. The man spun under a shoulder hit and staggered into the shop. Then they veered around the block, up the side street, a corner building cutting them off from random fire.

"Now ride like hell!" Sam grated. "That's why they had them horses ready, case any slipped out of the ambush. . . ."

Wind whipped at Johnny's face, tearing his words away. "Jesse? Where is he?"

"Must've cut and run when he heard the shooting."

The town began to fall behind. Only a few outskirt houses remained before the street petered out on the twisting wagon road. Johnny, squinting and blinking at the pouring rain, didn't at first react to the sight of a barely seen figure running out through a picket gate into the street.

"Daddy?" It was the frightened voice of a small girl. That was all that Johnny knew, except that he was frantically reining in his horse, yelling thinly, "Sam, the kid, look—"

Sam Vano didn't slacken his headlong pace, didn't pull aside. Johnny saw the big black pound past the small, crumpled form.

Johnny quartered his horse around, body tensing to swing down, when a door opened beyond the picket gate. A woman's scream knifed the lashing storm.

Johnny drove in his spurs; his horse reared, bolted after the black. Sobs tore his chest as he quirted the animal with his reins, savagely, viciously, and not caring.

CHAPTER FIVE

They lined onto the wagon road, rolling ahead of them like a dark brown ribbon. Johnny was just behind Sam Vano, the leader's broad, slickered back filling his blurred vision. *He must have seen that little girl,* Johnny's thoughts ran numbly. *I did. But he rode right over her like he didn't hear me—or didn't give a damn. Only maybe he didn't see her, coming on top of her that way, maybe he couldn't hear me for the damned wind—*

Sam was slowing to a trot, his granite-etched face turning to Johnny as he swung his arm around toward a high ridge shouldering away to their left. "We'll cut off, head up there. Won't be looking for us to leave the road till we're well away, figurin' we'd put plenty of fast distance between town an' us."

They pushed their horses into a plunging, stumbling lunge up the long boulder-strewn incline.

Soon a posse of men poured around the bend that cut off their view of the town. At least thirty men. The roar of churning hoofs diminished in the wailing storm, and they were gone.

Johnny glanced at Sam. Vano's hatbrim whipped suddenly back in a wind-driven gust, and Johnny saw the stony face beneath white and strained in a vivid flare of lightning. Sam began to bow forward across his pommel, his weight sloughing sideways. Then his lax hands clenched into fists over the horn and held him in the seat. *More than a graze,* Johnny thought in panic: he was hard-hit.

Johnny half-fell out of the saddle to reach Sam's side. The slate eyes stared dully into his. "All right, kid. You'll have to get us both out of this." The effort to speak cost him an agonizingly drawn breath; for a moment he gulped air, then pulled erect, calling on some untapped reserve of iron vitality. "You take my reins, I'll direct you to a place I know of . . . never find us there. . . ."

It was a nightmarish journey for Johnny. He plodded through sheets of falling water that drove in solid masses against face and body as though to smash him back, to drown him. When he looked over his shoulder, Sam Vano's bulk was only a spectral shape rocking back and forth; his reins clutched in Johnny's half-frozen fist the only thing connecting them in the storm's fury.

East . . . high stony bluff . . . was all Vano had gasped before he lapsed into a half-coma; only a superhuman effort of will keeping him in the saddle. All Johnny could do was hold to a due southerly route in the teeth of the raging elements. If there was one bright spot, it was this: not even an Indian could trail them after this storm.

Johnny came upon the bluff and then worked south till he found what he sought: a shallow cave eroded into the base rock and nearly concealed by a tangle of low-growing brush. Johnny dismounted and hobbled at a cramped and stiff-legged gait to the mouth. He had to crouch low and worm through the brush to get inside. He found the cave dry and spacious, though so low-roofed he was obliged to bend almost double. Thanks to the dense foliage crowding

the mouth, a man could spot anyone sneaking up long
before they could be sure of his position.

He returned to the horses and led them to a brushy
covert close to the wall, where the high liprock would
also afford some shelter. He ground-hitched the animals
there. Sam was almost wholly unconscious now; he didn't
respond by a twitch to Johnny's voice or tugging hands. It
took all Johnny's strength to unpry the leader's death-grip
on the horn. As Sam's limp hulk toppled sideways, Johnny
braced himself and somehow kept his feet as he caught
Sam's full weight and eased it to the ground. He tried to
lift the leader across his shoulders and, in his own sluggish exhaustion, failed. Finally he grabbed Sam under the
arms and dragged him across the stony ground into the
cave. Then he lugged their saddles and gear inside.

Sam's tough hide had been scored with a good deal of
lead in a lifetime; he still carried some of it. But the
leader's bluing lips and shallow breathing told him that
this time Sam Vano had crossed the narrow margin between life and death: an ordinary man would be dead by
now.

The first raw shock of realization left Johnny oddly
steady. He tore up a fairly clean shirt he found stuffed
inside Sam's blankets and made a fresh compress and
bandages. He tied the wound tightly and wrapped the
unconscious man in his blankets. He coldn't afford to
think of what this would mean, he had to keep his hands
and thoughts occupied. He left the cave and scoured up
some dry dead brush. He built a small fire that made a
clean, smokeless blaze in the mouth of the cave, and
crouched over its warmth, palms extended, to thaw his
chilled, soaked body. Then he took off his clothes and
propped them on sticks near the fire, afterward wrapping

himself in a blanket and settling down with his back to the rough wall and his gun in his fist.

He dozed on and off through the remaining hours of daylight, jerking to wakefulness at every least sound and scrambling to the entrance to stare out at empty, rain-lashed distance, though he knew there was only the barest chance that even an organized posse would find them while the storm lasted. Probably the searchers had long since broken up and returned to town.

When some of his jitters had worn off, he relaxed at last into full sleep only to be brought out of it by Sam's voice. The leader was awake, his gray stare clear-eyed and rational on Johnny. "Made it, eh? I'd like a drink."

Johnny was reaching for a canteen when Sam said dryly, "There's a pint of J. H. Cutter in my saddlebag," and when Johnny hesitated, he rapped harshly, "Give it here!"

Johnny dug out a half-empty bottle of whiskey and silently handed it to him. Vano gulped most of the remaining contents before he leaned back, gasping, and told Johnny flatly, "Finish it. You need the heat."

Johnny choked on his first raw swallow, but drained the bottle. A stove-like glow spread through his belly.

"Reckon we both know it's up with me," Sam said calmly. Johnny said nothing. Vano's rock-hewn face didn't alter as he went on, "That little kid—"

Johnny's head lifted swiftly. "You saw her?" Something constricted in his chest like a closing fist.

Vano's thin lips twitched. A thing close to emotion shaded his opaque eyes. "Funny thing," he mused. "A man spends a lifetime killing, robbing, it never touches him. Things was always black or white to me, no grays, no shadings. I was always a funny owlhoot that way, went into it with my eyes open. Just never gave a damn. Liked doing it, was all. But this mornin', when I saw that kid run in front of me and didn't bother to pull aside—'' He shook his shaggy head, let it bow on his chest. ''Funny. That six-gun of mine must have orphaned a dozen kids and it never meant anything. But that little girl keeps coming back. All the way here, I was rockin' out of my head in the saddle, and her ridin' with me every foot of the way . . .''

''Sam—''

''Let me talk, kid. Haven't much longer. Things you have to know. I'm bad, bad all through. Always knew it, but it never got me till now . . .'' He lifted his head, glaring feverishly at Johnny. ''You hate this life. Bowie saw it, and he wanted you to clear out. I saw it, and was too twisted up inside to give a damn. Bowie was right, kid . . . get out of it.''

''Get out of it,'' Johnny echoed bitterly. ''Just like that. Who was it always told me there was no turnin' back?''

Sam stirred an impatient hand beneath the blanket. ''Lots worse characters than you started over clean. Your name's known to the law, but not your face.''

''Sheriff Wolfe knows it—after last night.''

''He can't connect it to you, though, not unless he got a good look at you today, and that ain't likely . . . If you don't want to risk a fresh start in the states, there's Canada, South America, even Europe. Man can work his way before the mast.'' His hand shot out, caught Johnny's wrist, fevered eyes yellow-tinged in the firelight. ''You go straight from here on. Promise!''

''You're my father,'' Johnny yelled, his eyes suddenly smarting. ''All my life you pulled me your way. Top of that, I'm your blood. Supposin' I want to, how can I change things now?''

''Because you want to,'' Vano said harshly. ''That's all you need. Me, I don't know if there's anythin' to this business of bad blood runnin' in a family. My folks was

strait-laced Ohio farmers. Other hand, my sister turned out
no good, Jesse's her boy, he's pure coyote. But this don't
apply to you." He fell back in his blankets, hauling sterto-
rous breaths. "You ain't my son, Johnny."

Johnny watched him numbly.

"There was a Ute massacre of an emigrant train just
below the Canadian River, twenty years ago. My gang and
me came on it a day after, found a toddler bawling in the
sage near a wrecked wagon. Injuns missed you. You must
of walked out of the wagon after it was over. It was
Bowie's crazy idea that we raise you, and I agreed if we'd
pass you as my son. I had some fool notion that a son
would be useful for taking the reins when I got too old to
handle the men. I raised you tough and mean to that end."

"My people," Johnny said huskily.

"All gone, wiped out, whoever they were."

"Don't matter where I came from," Johnny muttered.
"It's what I got to be."

"Listen, you fool kid. I raised you rough as I could and
still couldn't stamp out an idea you always had of changing. Difference between a man and an animal is, a man
can choose. I know. I chose—wrong. Only thing a man
can't choose is bein' born in the first place."

Johnny edged to the mouth of the cave and squatted
there, huddled in his blanket. Bright slashing torrents of
water cascaded in twinkling streams off the high rimrock
and poured past his face in miniature waterfalls. When he
spoke, his hunched back to Sam Vano, it was a barely
audible mutter. "All right, Sam. I'll try."

Sam Vano grunted, "Good," and closed his eyes. After
a while he murmured, "That Gorman bastard, you think?"

Johnny humped his shoulders in a shrug. "Who else?
Jesse shot off his mouth in front of Gorman last night
about the head money on the Vano gang."

"Damn him," Vano said tonelessly. "Damn that clerk."

"I been thinkin' of doin' more about that," Johnny said in a too-soft tone.

Vano jerked upright, then toppled back with a groan. "Now damn you, listen to me! You got a chance, don't risk it by going after Emmett Gorman."

Johnny had lied: he'd hardly thought through these long hours of Emmett Gorman, but abruptly Gorman gave him a badly needed sense of direction for his own pointless life, for the rage, hate, and frustration that had come to a boil inside him. Thought of revenge on the treacherous clerk provided a relief that was almost overwhelming. So now he lied again: "All right, Sam, just as you say."

"Good boy," Sam Vano mumbled. He was beginning to slip back into semi-consciousness. Shortly afterward, he began raving, about long-ago names and happenings that Johnny had never heard. Finally he fell into a silent, burning fever.

For all that Johnny could do, Sam Vano died before the desolate day had spent itself.

CHAPTER SIX

After dark, the rain stopped at last. A night wind wailed down from the flinty hills, driving the banked storm clouds before it, chilling with a marrow-bite. Johnny left the cave and stepped into a dripping, starlighted evening. He'd made up his mind. Paying back Emmett Gorman's betrayal was something he had to do, even if he used up his last chance.

He tried to tell himself it was because of his three dead fellows, but that didn't ring true. Lopez, a recent addition to the gang, he'd hardly known; the sullen halfbreed had won rapport with no one. The bullet that had blasted away Bowie Samse's life had really been a mercy to a slowly dying man. Sam and Johnny had never been close, and now he'd learned that Sam was not even his father.

True, Sam had given him a chance for life on that long-gone day when he'd picked up a waif survivor of a butchered caravan . . . but what sort of life was this? An endless pilgrimage that kept him one jump ahead of the law . . . with a future of the same stretching drearily ahead. Bowie's and Sam's argument that he could change held no conviction for him; he'd never really believed there was an out beyond his daydreams. Dimly, he understood that this was the real sum of his hatred for Gorman, but he couldn't change the way he felt.

Johnny returned to the cave. With his hands he scooped a shallow trough in the floor and rolled Sam Vano's blanket-wrapped body into it. He filled the grave, then methodically went over Sam's gear for any articles that might be useful. He buried the rest, afterward spreading the sandy floor to pristine smoothness. He stamped out the fire, kicking its smoldering remains into the earth. He dragged dead brush to the cave and piled it across the entrance, obscuring it from a casual observer.

He fetched the horses and threw on his own rig. Then, mounting his own, he quirted Sam's animal, hoorawing it into a run. He sat listening till the sound of hoofbeats died away and turned his horse toward the west, guided by the stars.

He wondered if the sheriff's posses were still combing the countryside. Likely they'd not stay out long while the bad weather held. But tomorrow, if the rain hadn't resumed, they'd be searching for fresh signs of the fugitives. Jesse had doubtlessly made a clean getaway, and was well out of the area by this time. *And you'd be smart to do the same,* he told himself, knowing he wouldn't, though. An old fox like Wolfe would have the roads covered. He'd have his posses organized into far-flung, yet close-knit cordons that a rabbit couldn't break through. And he could send word to other towns in his district, telling his deputies to assemble search parties to head off the fugitives.

He rubbed his palm across the thin, youthful rasp of his week-old beard. How to reach Gorman? Why not play it bold and open? The citizenry might be keyed-up enough, after the morning's excitement, to shoot at a skulking figure, but not at a casually incoming stranger. They'd never conceive of a bank robber crazy enough to ride back into a town which had driven him out in a hail of gunfire.

When he passed the sheriff's office, he let out a held breath when he saw the darkened window. Dogged, tireless lawman that he was, Wolfe was still out scouring the hills where the robbers would be likely to hole up. He dismounted by the hotel, tied his horse, and sent a roving glance up and down the street before moving to a lobby window. The same clerk who'd been on duty last night was dozing in his chair behind the desk. *Suppose he was in that deadfall this morning and saw my face?* Johnny thought warily. Unlikely, though, that anyone had caught more than a distant, fleeting glimpse of him. . . .

Johnny opened the door and stepped quietly inside, hoping to make the stairs without waking the clerk, but the man came instantly awake as the door opened. Johnny crossed the lobby to the desk, casually brushing raindrops from his slicker. "Evenin'."

"Hoddy." The clerk stood, yawning, giving him an idle once-over, and some of the tension left Johnny. "Say, ain't you one of the fellas was going to Texas?"

"Uh-huh. My pard went on, I decided to stay awhile. Rode around the country today, like the looks of it."

"Oh." The clerk's bored gaze sharpened. "Say, you meet any of the posses on the road?"

"Posses?"

"That's right, you rode out this mornin' early. hell, they was a lot of excitement later on. . . . Sam Vano gang rode in this mornin' to hit the bank. Lenny Wolfe had an ambush rigged, got two. He's out lookin' for the others."

Johnny whistled softly. "Vano, eh? No, I didn't meet nobody. I hung to the road most of the time; reckon they'd hit for the deep brush."

"Reckon. Everyone in town, just about, joined the search. Bastards rode down a little kid, Jenny Carpentier, when they left. Got the town madder'n a nest of riled hornets."

Johnny's heart thudded almost to a stop. "Kid bad hurt?"

The clerk spread his pale hands. "Ain't sure she'll pull through, that's all I heard. You want a room?"

Johnny said yes, signed "Tom Brooks" to the register, gave the clerk a dollar, received his key, and tramped up the shabbily-carpeted staircase. He'd wanted to ask the clerk if he knew who'd tipped off the sheriff about the robbery, except that might stretch a successful bluff too far. *Hell*, he thought, *you know who.* . . .

At the head of the stairs, he paused in the gloom to unbutton his slicker. He slipped his .45 from its holster, checked the loads, and moved on tiptoe to Gorman's door. A board creaked under the boot, and he stiffened. He could hear the pen scratching on paper in the room—and now it stopped. Realizing that Gorman had probably bolted the door, Johnny thought fast, then spoke, imitating the night clerk's high-pitched nasality:

"Message for you."

Gorman's voice cracked with nervousness. "Slide it under the door."

"I'm supposed to get your answer."

He heard Gorman cross the room, heard the bolt shoot back. Johnny wrenched the doorknob and pushed into the room, sending Gorman reeling. Johnny kicked backward, slamming the door, and jammed his gun into the bank clerk's soft belly, doubling him with wheezing pain. "Sit, Gorman."

Emmett Gorman sank into his creaking chair, his face chalky. His eyes jerked uncontrollably. "What do you want?"

"You know what happened today?"

"I had nothing to do with that,"Gorman said wildly. "Don't be a young fool, Vano! Why should I—"

"Because it's like Jesse said. You could make more money this way, with no danger to your own rotten hide. The other way, if anything went wrong, if any of us were caught, you knew we wouldn't cover for a rat like you. Five thousand dollars, Gorman . . . blood money you'll never spend. Think about it, because you ain't got long."

The clerk's quivering hulk almost slipped out of the chair. He grabbed for the support of his small writing desk, his whisper a strained gasp. "I swear I didn't breathe a word. Look—look here, I'm in plenty of trouble, I took that money from the vault early this morning, and the robbery didn't come off to cover it. Don't do it, Vano, don't kill an innocent man!"

Unsteady rage dug at Johnny; the gun shook in his fist. "You were ready and willing to cheat your own bank, and you want me to—"

"Yes—because it's the truth!"

Backed to the wall, a coward like Gorman could easily lie with a vehemence that was convincing, Johnny knew— yet he was shaken. *Get it over with before you think about it,* he thought. He cocked the gun and Gorman jerked as though the bullet had already slapped his flesh.

But Johnny's finger never tightened. He knew then that he couldn't do it, and it had nothing to do with Gorman's guilt or innocence. Many things passed through his mind in a breath-hung moment. He'd always had a fatalistic feeling about his blood-tie to Sam Vano, and knew now that it had never exited. That fact was beginning to sink home, leaving him with a curious sense of freedom. Even Sam himself, a cynical hardcase dying in a lonely cave, had been humanized and full of regret. And what had Sam said? *A man has a choice.* And now Johnny Vano, having a choice, meant to shoot a man in cold blood and cement himself for good into a life he hated. . . .

His face showed nothing, and a sick glaze had come over Emmett Gorman's eyes, tensed for the shock of a bullet. Then Johnny holstered the gun, saying quietly, "Don't follow me, Gorman," and turned to the door.

Behind him he heard the clerk's sobbing gasp of relief, but he'd never expected what happened next. He heard Gorman yank open a desk drawer, and he swung quickly around. Goaded by a reaction of rabbity bravado after his sudden reprieve, Gorman had snatched out a nickel-plated .32.

As he swung it to bear, Johnny drew and fired with the reflex of long practice. Gorman buckled at the waist, his white shirt staining red. He stared at Johnny with a sort of stunned reproach, took two steps forward, fell to his knees, and then full length with his face plowing the splintery floor. Johnny stood rooted, hardly believing this. Gorman's outflung hand touched his boot, and he pulled it back quickly. He heard the thunder of feet on the staircase.

Spurred by a dismal urgency, his eyes swung to the open window, curtains bellying inward on the wind. He stepped to it, thrust his head out, seeing the dark gulf of an alleyway beneath. He swung a leg over the sill, then the other. He drew a deep breath and dropped into the darkness just as the door crashed open.

Johnny hit the muddy ground on both feet, but his boots instantly skidded away and flung him on his hip and shoulder. He got his legs under him, driving like pistons. He flung a look over his shoulder as he achieved the mouth of the alley and his waiting horse, and saw the night clerk leaning out the window, mouth opening to yell: "There he is! Get him!" Johnny twisted a backward look, saw the man's gangling figure burgeoning out of the lobby at a jerky run, swinging a pointing finger. There were scattered shots as a few men with six-guns opened up. But they were shooting blind, for Johnny was almost at street's end now, the lighted section behind him, the empty wagon road rolling clear before him.

Then, coming abreast of a darkened doorway, a lone pedestrian, no more than a dark shadow among the shadows, swung up his arm: Johnny caught a gleam of pistol steel. He tried to swerve, to confuse the fellow's aim. The pistol spoke.

A burst of pain knifed through Johnny's left thigh, and he cried out hoarsely and leaned low in the saddle, his face bent into the whipping mane.

CHAPTER SEVEN

Johnny hit the road and lined into a steady, hoof-thrumming pace that was torture to his leg. There had been the first tearing blow, then a numbness that was already receding into rhythmic hammerstrokes of pain. He set his teeth against it, banishing throbbing hurt from his mind. With the icy clarity of a man with his back to the wall, with the savage cunning of a lifetime on the dodge, he assayed his chances. Under the double handicap of a game leg and a fast-tiring horse, he must not only thwart the pursuit from the town that would soon be breathing down his neck, but also break through Wolfe's posse cordons which he now felt certain would be strung out ahead of him.

He reined aside and cut into a skimpy aspen grove bordering the road. He swung down and held his trembling horse, clamping his hand over its nose and mouth. "Quiet, boy. . . ." He stood in immobility, listening, not even shrugging in annoyance when a cold dribble from a water-laden branch ran into his collar and down his bare spine. Soon ten or more townsmen thundered past, dark, eager-spurring shapes of fresh, straining mounts.

He stood for another frozen moment as the sound of their going receded down the road. In less than no time

they'd have overtaken his faltering horse. In a few more
hours it would be light enough to dissipate the off-trail
shadows that now concealed him. He must use the remaining darkness to best advantage. . . . He unslung the saddlebags which held his provisions and threw them off. He
untied his suggan-roll and let it slide to the ground. Of his
saddle gear, he kept only his canteen and rifle. *When
you're pressed for your life, don't quibble over shedding
trifles,* Sam had always said. *Pound of gear might slow
you by just enough.*

In his mind's eye, he reviewed the map Sam had scratched
in the dirt nearly twenty-four hours ago (it seemed like
years) . . . *Little Muddy River . . . curves around hills
mile east of town. . . .*

Get lost in unfamiliar country, Sam used to say, *follow
the rivers. They'll take you out.* That was an advantage
these men had: they knew the country. The river was
Johnny's best bet, and water would leave no trail.

He wound a pocket bandanna around his blood-welling
thigh, knotting it tightly. That was his greatest fear—that
bloodloss would slow his reactions and muddy his thoughts
to a gray ebb.

He mounted again, then had to hold dizzily to his
pommel for a moment, sickened by the cost of effort to his
used-up body. His still-damp clothes were clammy rags
against his feverish skin. A cold needle of fear lanced him,
alerting to the danger-signs of his waning strength.

He pushed due east, feeling the ground rise beneath him
momentarily. He headed up a pine-mantled ridge, into
thick timber where a springy needle carpet deadened hoof-
falls. He moved through starlight-dappled glades, whose
air was pungent with the pitchy pine smell, where the faint
soughing of wind in high boughs made a comfortable
break in the brooding stillness, thinking how very fine it

would be to lie down . . . dream all this away. . . . *Damn that hot poker in his leg*.

The timber ended abruptly in a straggle of stunted trees as he broke onto the western end of the ridge, a bald, exposed promontory. He stopped to blow his horse, feeling the animal's flanks heave like bellows. He would have dismounted and rested except for a cold conviction that if he left the saddle he might not be able to make it back. His leg was stiffening on the chilly air, and his questing hand located the dark wet soaking of his pants: his improvised bandage could not stop the fresh pumping of the wound with each movement of thigh muscles.

Far beyond and below he was aware of a deep rush of sound which he'd at first attributed to the wind. Now, he strained his eyes, finally picking out where a deep, wide gulf bisected his downslope of the ridge. He caught the gleam of water flashing in a silvery torrent, and his heart sank. He would not be riding this river, swollen by rain, even if he could descend the steep walls which confined it.

He blinked his blurring eyes and ran a hand over his wet face. *All right, one way's as good as another. Follow it upstream, maybe it'll widen and shallow out. Maybe . . .*

Shortly the ridge tapered off into low banks. But the water was still too swift and deep to ride the river-bottom, and Johnny had to fight his way through tangles of willow and cherry thickets which choked the banks to the water's edge. Finally in the first gray overcast that hinted at false dawn, he picked out the pale blobs of sandbars, ahead where the river broadened to three times its downstream width. Injected with sudden hope he plunged down the bank, splashed through the shallows toward the nearest sandbar.

Suddenly an orange glow staining the solid black woods not fifty feet to his right and ahead brought him up sharply.

A fire. . . . *Posse camp,* he thought, wings of panic beating in him. The fire was well-hidden, pocketed in a heavy timber belt: Johnny had spotted it only because he'd come on it from the water instead of the brush-obstructed shore. Wolfe was no fool; he had the river covered, probably at regular points with guards to patrol them. There might be a dozen men lying in concealment almost anywhere. Johnny sat his horse in the shallows, hardly daring to breathe, eyes whipping the thickets and timber along the banks. Cautiously he kneed his horse toward shore, then abruptly kicked it into a lunging climb up the bank. He had to get out of the open, into the timber. . . .

As they topped the bank, a rifle shot sent shattering echoes across the river. It killed the sorrel on its feet; it relaxed in death as it sloughed over sideways with Johnny somehow kicking his bad leg from the stirrup, and rolling free of the falling animal. With an impact that smashed the breath from his lungs, he hit the sloping bank and kept rolling, sliding into the water with a shallow, almost noiseless splash. The misery of the icy river shocked his paralyzed senses to renewed life.

The unseen rifleman shot again, and yet again, but he was firing at shadows now, Johnny knew. He heard the excited voices upstream, and shrank inwardly at Sheriff Wolfe's bull-chested boom, shouting a question.

He let his head sink on his flexed arm in a sick, tired despair, thinking, *Can't dog it any further. Can't run. Can't swim. . . . No use trying any more.*

He could see the smoky flare of bobbing torches moving down the bank only yards upstream; the murky water and shadows concealed him now, but they'd be on him in a few minutes. Wearily, he reached out his arm, grabbing for a rough protuberance to drag himself from the water. His hand closed over a dead, barkless limb; as he pulled, a great log attached to the limb rocked with a gurgling sound and slowly settled back.

A new thought jerked life into Johnny's veins; water peeled from his slicker as he staggered to his feet and climbed over the log. He propped the knee of his bad leg against the bank and with the foot of his other leg lunged his whole weight against the huge timber. A wave of flaring pain rippled hotly up his leg. He set his teeth to keep from crying out. The log had stirred. He placed his weight again, shoved, and the log, freed from clogging brush and oozing muck moved out of the shadows.

Johnny waded out, tugging at the massive cylinder of driftwood. It scraped bottom at first, but gained buoyancy as it coasted into deeper water, Johnny finding to his relief that it wasn't waterlogged. The men were so close now he could pick out their words. ". . . swear it came from right here."

Johnny sank prone into the chill water, only his head surfaced, giving the log silent momentum with the drive of his feet against the mucky bottom. Then the bottom fell away in an abrupt drop-off. Johnny, a poor swimmer, grabbed frantically at the log, wrapped his arm around its smooth bole, and hung on as it slid into mid-channel. Suddenly he felt a powerful drag as the mainstream caught the log and swept it along like a cork.

Eddying to left and right, rudderless with the vagaries of the current, the log, with its half-conscious burden, gave itself aimlessly to the river, to the night.

CHAPTER EIGHT

Johnny Vano dreamed he was in hell. He and Sam Vano were squatting on a bed of glowing coals. Sam was wearing a pair of horns and a barbed tail and was saying, *Hell is something folks make up to help 'em keep rules they break anyways.*

But ain't this hell, Sam?

Kid, hell is where a man happens to be. . . .

Johnny groaned and twisted with burning pain. Scenes shifted kaleidoscopically and swam hazily together. And always, at its worst, a cool hand on his head and a woman's voice soothed away the pain till it eased into a vast ocean of peace. That was the part that puzzled him. The girl. Her face was never more than a swimming blur bent over his, and always it receded into the chaotic blur of past memories till he couldn't distinguish reality from nightmare.

Finally, though, he slept. Slept through a long gray interval that was dreamless. . . .

When he woke, the girl was there by his bedside. He was in a bed—that startled him. Bright sunlight from an open window checkered the flowered counterpane, and he stared at it for an uncomprehending moment. He remembered an eternity of storm and wetness. No sunlight.

"How long . . . have I been here?" The words husked from his throat in a broken whisper.

He looked at the girl, seeing her eyes widen, her lips part. She was tall, in her late teens, wearing shapeless men's trousers and a hickory shirt which didn't hide the supple lines of her young body. Twin blonde braids were pinned in a coronet around her high-held head; her features were regular, strongly angled, handsome rather than pretty, holding a knowing competence beyond her years.

She touched his forehead. "Fever's down," she murmured.

Johnny felt irritation, despite his lightheaded weakness. What in hell did she think he was, a colt with the colic? "I ain't a baby, lady."

She straightened, rocking on her heels and shoving her hands in her hip pockets. "No? You're as full of questions as a two-year-old, though." She raised her voice. "Mike. Lee. He's awake and sassy."

A man and woman entered the room. Father and his two daughters, Johnny guessed. He warily braced himself for an onslaught of questions as the man moved to the bedside. He was great-framed, slightly stooped, in his early fifties. His graying blonde hair fell in a boyish cowlick over a ruddy, strongly boned Celtic face, gray-rimmed brows frowning over chipped-ice eyes that were clear, bright azure, like the blonde girl's.

He laid a heavy hand on Johnny's shoulder. "Glad to see you poco-poco, boy. You're at my ranch, Tulare. Name's Mike Murphy. My daughter Nan, here, and my wife Leonora."

That was all. No questions, no accusations. Johnny swallowed the knot of panic in his throat, and looked from one to the other. A point of frontier courtesy. Waiting, rather than asking for information. He looked at the tall young woman by the door. Not Murphy's daughter, but his wife. A child-bride, maybe, but she didn't look it. Her skin was soft and pale against the raven mass of hair clubbed at the back of her neck. There was compassion in her face as she regarded Johnny, but its faultless sculpture was accented by an inbred aloofness, marred by a deep shadow of discontent. She wore an expensive dress of watered silk. She didn't fit in with this rough-hewn rancher and his tomboy daughter.

Johnny met Murphy's patient gaze. "Billy Barnes," he said. "Fellow upriver shot me for my poke. Dumped me in the river. All I recall."

Murphy glanced at Johnny's hands on the covers. "Puncher?"

There were plenty of rope-scars on Johnny's hands—from hazing stolen cattle. "Off and on," he said. "Just drift, mostly."

Boots scraped the floor as a man came swiftly into the room. His clothes were colorless with caked dust; he batted a dusty Stetson against his chaps.

"Boze Hendryx, my foreman," Murphy said. "He's the one hauled you out of the river. Boze, this is Billy Barnes."

Hendryx nodded, drawling, "Hoddy." He was a sparely built man with saddle leather for skin and a long, gaunt face like that of a faithful horse. His jaws, silvered with stubble, clamped on a reeking cob pipe set between his stained teeth. His faded eyes held a kindly, hard-won wisdom that made Johnny uneasy. All of these people made him uneasy; he'd never known their kind. He guessed he hadn't deliriously babbled of his past, for they appeared to accept his story. That was something. But he'd have to watch himself.

"Trouble, cap'n," the foreman said now. "Looks like the Hornes used the bad weather to cover their drivin' off more of your prime whitefaces."

Mike Murphy's face darkened; his hamlike fist lifted. "The Hornes! Those spalpeens. Mountain scum! Wait a bit; I'll change clothes, ride back with you." He gave Johnny a jerky nod, saying curtly, "Boy, get some sleep, get your strength. We'll talk later."

He pivoted on his heel and followed his foreman from the room. Johnny struggled to get his elbows under him. "Look, just fetch me my clothes. . . ."

Nan Murphy placed a strong hand on his chest and shoved him back on the pillows. She straightened, setting her fists on her hips, a humorous glint in her eyes. "Look at you. Weak as a cat. Ganted up like a deer-hunting dog. You're not going anywhere, buster. You heard the man. Get some sleep."

The bedridden two weeks that followed laid a heavy tax on Johnny's strength. Then he was giddy and light-headed on his feet. But it was mostly a shaky aftermath of nervous exhaustion; the wound itself, despite bloodloss, wasn't too serious, the slug having embedded itself in the outer fleshy muscles of his thigh. A medico from the nearby settlement of Cedar Forks had removed the lead, and healing was quick and clean.

While he mended, Johnny liked loafing around the bunkhouse while the crew was on-range. It was a typical high country bunkroom, with eight sets of double bunks, but the thing that puzzled him was the many unused bunks. The crew now numbered nine men. Despite its prosperous sprawl of labyrinthian barns, sheds and corrals, Tulare ranch was plainly becoming slowly impoverished.

It was Nan Murphy who told him why, while they were sitting on the washbench by the bunkhouse, where she'd joined him. He felt an unspoken pleasure in her company which he couldn't define, for she'd shown him nothing but a cool face and a tart, flippant tongue. He wondered if he'd imagined the gentle care she'd given him when he was sick and out of his head with fever. Johnny Vano knew little of girls, but he sensed that Nan softened toward something only so long as she felt a strong advantage over it.

Just now they were silent, letting their gaze range across the pine-stippled backbones of the foothills. Tulare headquarters was situated on a meadowed slope tucked snugly between two rolling, timbered ridges. The rambling main house, set upslope from the working part of the ranch, was a well-weathered frame building.

The girl broke the silence, nodding toward the purple-heighted scarps to the north. "Pretty, isn't it? Wouldn't think it means ruination for the Murphys, would you?"

"Rustlers?" was Johnny's token reply.

She nodded, an angry edge to her voice: "The Hornes. A bunch of rawhiders from the Ozarks. They squatted on Tulare years ago. Mike ran them off. So they found a valley back in those peaks, a regular walled-in fortress where no one could get at them, and hit our herds off and on, driving small bunches back into the canyons to butcher for beef. About a year ago, someone started heavy, organized raids on our cattle—and they're the logical suspects."

"Gettin' back at your dad, eh?"

"Obviously. They've hardly touched the other ranches, while our cattle are vanishing in droves. The only thing those simple-minded hill folk can remember is a grudge.

Feuding is their way of life. But why they suddenly went in for organized cattle-stealing is a puzzle. Where can they market branded beef without bills of sale? How can they drive it to a respected rail outlet without being spotted? The ony railhead hereabouts is Rutherford, the county seat, and no cattle thief in his right mind would try to market right under Lenny Wolfe's nose.''

"Wolfe?'' Johnny said guardedly. "Sheriff, ain't he? How come he doesn't stop 'em?''

She tossed her head, a bitter smile tilting her lips. Sunlight tangled in her crown of spun-taffy braids. "You *are* a drifter, aren't you, buster? This mountain country is a crazy-quilt. Trying to intercept every isolated raid, or searching these mountains for lost beeves, is worse than useless. Both Mike and the sheriff have taken posses out, but they've lost every trail over rough country.''

Johnny glanced at her. "Sounds like some smart fella's usin' these Hornes' old grudge to break your dad.''

She frowned. "But who? Mike didn't build this spread by climbing roughshod over other men—not without a good cause. With the Hornes, he had no choice. They're trash. Their kind squat on a good range and bleed it dry.''

Johnny was silent, thinking that it was a hell of a thing for a man of Murphy's caliber to lose the fruits of a lifetime's sweat and blood. Because of his large debt to the Murphys, he had the strange conviction that their troubles were his. Because an owlhoot was trained to look out for number one, he tried inwardly to shrug off this sensation, and failed.

Leonora Murphy came out on the veranda of the big house, and restlessly walked its length to the railing at the east end. She shaded her eyes and peered across the heat-dancing flats, then walked back inside, banging the door.

"Poor Lee,'' Nan said softly.

"Pardon?"

"My stepmother. She's from a fine Boston family. Mike met her on a trip East a year ago. I guess she was bored with parties, the social whirl, smooth-talking dandies. When she met my father, she was taken with his rough, outright ways. They practically eloped, after her family objected to him on general social principles. But it hasn't worked. This big ranch, with the nearest neighbor ten miles distant, is the opposite of everything she knew."

Johnny said hesitantly, "Your ma?"

"Died when I was fourteen," Nan said shortly.

Johnny, sensing that he'd touched a sore spot, didn't reply. With a sudden insight, he understood Nan Murphy. A grown woman's responsibilities had been forced on her in her early teens. To find her place in a big ranch's lonely men's world, she'd taken on a man's bluff manner. She could talk to a man easily enough, but she'd be lost trying to approach him as a woman. He reckoned that she'd sought his company to talk the loneliness out of her system with someone near her own age. He knew how that could be.

She grinned at him and stretched in a yawn, unconscious of how the arching movement tightened the man's shirt across her small, firm breasts. She straightened her arm and idly rubbed her palm along his cheek. "You don't look so mean without the fur, buster."

Johnny felt hot color rise in his face. He'd shaved off his scraggly beard that morning, and his mirror had showed him a bony, hollow-eyed face beneath a tan turned to sickly saffron. He looked like a curly wolf, sure enough. He thought she was laughing at him now. He said deliberately, "How old're you?"

"Goin on nineteen."

"I'm older'n you. Call me 'buster' again, and I'll pull your pigtails down and tie 'em under your chin."

She flushed angrily; sparks of temper flickered in her eyes. Then, surprisingly, she laughed. "I had that coming."

Then as their eyes continued to hold, something deep and disturbing touched her gaze. The merriment left her face for an expression almost of bewilderment. Johnny understood it no better.

The moment was broken by Mike Murphy's cheery shout. He was riding up from the corrals in a spring wagon, hitched to a pair of splendidly matched copperbottom bays. Johnny knew then that Mike had seen the look that passed between them, for the cheeriness of his seamed, stolid face was replaced by a sudden scowl, his twinkling eyes becoming glacial. Just for an instant. Then his rugged features were composed, his voice normal: "What's the conference?"

Nan laughed. "Mr. Barnes was mad at me, Mike."

"Don't blame him," Murphy growled. "You're a bothersome baggage. Billy, you feel well enough to ride to town? Cook needs a lay-in of grub. I could use an extra pair of totin' hands."

CHAPTER NINE

Jogging along by Mike Murphy's wagon, letting the coolness of the morning work through him, Johnny wondered if it were wise to show his face in Cedar Forks. It was too near Rutherford. Yet he couldn't have objected without arousing Mike's suspicions. So far the rancher had no cause to think that he was other than what he claimed to be, and Johnny meant to give him none.

As they followed the wagon road connecting Tulare and the settlement, Mike talked, his cold cigar bobbing in his mouth, pointing out landmarks and telling their historical tie-ins. Yonder, on his south range, was Murphy's Pass, where Mike had come through the mountains to catch his first glimpse of the basin which he had pioneered. Yonder was the spot where he and Boze had slapped the first Tulare brand on a spavined cow.

"There's the Little Muddy Boze picked you out of," Mike stabbed a horny finger. "All west of the river, far as you can see, is Tulare; east is Miles King's Moon."

"Big spread, Mr. King's."

"Biggest in two hundred miles, except mine. Soon's we cross the river, we'll be riding Moon land almost clear to Cedar Forks."

63

As they neared the river's flood-swollen onrush, they spooked up bunches of cattle ranging along the riverbottom, heavy bellies surfeited with water after weeks of near-drought. Among these, Johnny noted, were a few Tulare head; the bulk bore the earmarks and crescent-moon brand of Miles King.

They crossed the crude bridge and drew near the turn-off which led to Moon headquarters. As they neared the road junction, Johnny saw two riders coming briskly along the turn-off from beyond a rolling swell. Mike hauled up the team, bracing them to a stop in the raw mud and giving the horsemen a neutral nod as they cantered up.

"Morning, Murphy." The man who spoke was in his early thirties. His ox-chested frame was clad in black suit trousers stuffed into fine-tooled boots, a white broadcloth shirt with string tie, and an embroidered Mexican *charro* jacket, giving him an affluent, well-fed look. His golden, curling hair was close-cropped under a neatly blocked Stetson. Behind his almost foppish grooming and bored airs lurked a vicious and prideful arrogance which he took little trouble to conceal.

"Howdy, King. New hand, Billy Barnes."

"Looks sort of puny to work cattle, 'less you use him as a fence rail." This from the other man, a lean-lobo type with a bony clown's face. A small waxed mustache was his one affectation. His well-worn range clothes were stiff and black with grime. He wore a gun in a low-slung, thigh-thonged sheath, which, with his double-rigged saddle, peculiar hatcrease, and drawl, stamped him as a Texan. His shiny black eyes rested with strange amusement on Johnny, and Johnny, with a sickening pound of his heart, knew why.

"Tole Sayrs, likewise new," King said pleasantly.

"Murph, you used to be pretty zealous with a smoke-pole, from all I've heard."

Mike shrugged. "You don't build a spread like Tulare without rousting a share of troublemakers along the way. Unless," he added meaningly, "you have the money to buy the land and cattle to start off in a big way."

"Tole, here, throws a fast equalizer himself," King blandly passed over Mike's comment. "Just for the hell of it, wonder if you could match it?"

Mike shifted his bulk impatiently on the seat. "Sounds like damned foolery to me, King."

"Just a thought. You're packing a side gun. Figure you and Tole could shuck out your shells, no harm done." King paused, then jeered mildly, "Afraid of the past rep?"

Mike glared at him and without a word shrugged out of his coat, broke the loading gate of his pistol and spilled out the loads. He barely looked up as Tole Sayrs did the same. Johnny felt his shirt cling to his back with a crawl of cold sweat. Keened to such things, he sensed the deliberation behind this. Yet he sat his horse and said nothing as Mike swung down.

Sayrs stepped down, tossed his reins to King, and paced off a distance from Mike. When they faced each other, squared away, King said, "I'll count three. First to pull trigger wins."

Mike wiped his palms on his trousers. "Ready."

"One . . . two . . ."

The bucking roar of a gun drowned King's voice. Dirt erupted between the two poised men. "Billy," Mike bellowed. "What the hell!"

Johnny's gun was leveled on Sayrs, holding the man frozen. "Mr. Murphy, I know this man. He's a gun-tipper. Hires out his iron for pay. You pull against him, you're dead."

"Are ye daft?" Mike sputtered. "You saw us unload!"

"I saw both of you chuck five shells. That figures, man who does a lot of riding keeps his firin' pin on an empty chamber. But I seen this dodge pulled before. Wager you Sayrs's hammer is restin' on a live shell right this minute. Man like him don't draw a gun in play, not ever."

The cold, dead certainty of his words made Mike hesitate. King spoke dryly. "Didn't know Tulare was hiring wet-eared gunslicks."

Mike shuttled his glare to the man. "I might say the same."

"Rot! I suggested an innocent contest, and this fresh-mouthed— "

"Easy to settle," Mike said grimly. "Let's see your gun, Mr. Sayrs."

The man stared at him unblinkingly. He scuffed his feet in the brown earth. "I don't give my gun to no man."

Mike kept walking. His deepening brogue was soft and even. "Ye'll give it me, spalpeen, or I'll break your damned head and take it."

Sayrs's loose-hanging right hand twitched. Johnny's gun crashed again; Sayrs's hat spun from his head. "Let him take it, Tole!" King's wrathful shout came on the heel of the shot.

Sayrs stood in stone-faced immobility as Murphy lifted his gun from leather, broke it, twirled the cylinder. "Aye," he breathed.

"A mistake," Sayrs said thinly.

"Mistake, hell!"

King's voice was silk over steel. "Can you prove it was anything else, Murphy?"

Mike's meaty fist with Sayrs's gun fell to his side. He set his teeth on his storming rage and after a moment spoke in a normal voice. "I reckon I cannot. And it would be too easy to kill either of you with my fists. But this will be remembered. Only *why*, I'm asking. Why, King?''

King's face and voice again held the smooth blandness of utter self-possession. "Didn't Tole say it was an accident? On your horse, Mr. Sayrs.''

Jerky-striding, Sayrs retrieved his hat, moved to his horse and swung lankily up. He and King gigged their animals into motion along the road to Cedar Forks. Mike climbed to the seat again, took up the reins with shaking fingers. "With two witnesses, the law would have had to call it an accident. But why in hell would Miles King rig a thing like this? We scrapped some, sure, two adjoining ranches our size are bound to, but—" A sharp lift of Mike's head bore his gaze to Johnny. "You said you knew Sayrs before?''

"I knew him," Johnny Vano said, tight-lipped. "Gun-handy.''

"But you, Billy, you just made the handiest draw I ever saw.''

Johnny didn't reply.

Mike said now, slowly, "It'd be a small thing for me to ask the why of that, after you saved my life—a smaller thing for me to tell Leo Shallis—the deputy sheriff at Cedar Forks. But I might do it.''

"Will you?" Their eyes locked fast, and Mike's were the first to slide away.

"No," he muttered. "In very fact, I'd ask ye to fork that horse now and ride while the way is open to you, save that I'd do you a worse disfavor askin' you to run than otherwise. Besides," he added roughly, "I now owe you the sanctuary of my roof as long as you want it.''

"You hauled me out of the river," Johnny said stiffly. "We're square." He started to rein his horse around.

"Hold on." Mike scowled, chewed his lower lip. "You

stay, Billy Barnes. I ask you in friendship, not as an
obligation. Whatever you've been, you have the will to do
right. I'll take a chance on that, and gladly. Later, we'll
see what's to be done. You stay, Billy.''

Cedar Forks drowsed in the morning as they cruised
down the main street. The only commotion was caused by
a brown and white dog who yapped back and forth at the
rear wheels as they pulled up at the hitch rack in front of
Perrin's General Store. A few loafers lounging on the
boardwalk stared incuriously as Mike tramped into the
store's spicy coolness.

The long-faced proprietor rounded the counter and shook
hands with Mike, then Billy as Mike introduced them.
"Howdy, son. . . . Say, Mike, I think Leo wants to see
you."

"He say what about?"

Johnny's heart thudded sickeningly as Abe Perrin an-
swered, "Something about that hold-up try up in Rutherford a couple weeks ago."

Mike's thick brows lifted. "News to me. Haven't been
off Tulare for near a month."

"Hell, man, whole country's been talking it up. Lenny
Wolfe got word that the Vano gang meant to try for the
bank. Had an ambush laid for 'em. Nailed two right on the
street. Two others got away, one old Sam Vano himself.
There was another known member of the gang who didn't
show—Jesse Norcross, Sam's nephew. He's dropped out
of sight, as has Sam. Lenny threw posses out over the
area, got the fella who was with Vano. Shot his horse on
the riverbank, but he got away in the water. Blood on his
saddle leather. Must have been hard-hit. Drowned, more'n
likely. Lenny figured the river'd take his body down as far
as your spread. Asked Leo to ask you. Course if you'd

found a body, you'd of brought it in.'' Perrin chuckled.
''And you know Leo. Hates to budge from town. Hard to
find a horse that'll carry him.''

Breath held, Johnny watched Mike inspect the tip of his
cigar. Murphy did not even glance at him, only said
casually, ''Who would this fellow be?''

''Lenny reckoned he was Johnny Vano, Sam's son.''

''The devil!'' Mike breathed.

''Gospel,'' Perrin said dryly. ''Even the devil won't
want Sam Vano's breed. Sam and his kid rode down a
little girl when they made their break out of Rutherford.
She lived, but barely. Later, the kid rode back and shot a
young bank clerk named Gorman in his hotel room. No
one knows why.''

Johnny felt coldness ball up in his guts like a chunk of
lead. He watched Murphy, seeing him slowly pale beneath
his weather-burned ruddiness. Yet his voice held an utter,
casual calm: ''Guess I better see Leo.''

''Yeah. He can supply the details for you.''

''Here's the cook's list. See it's filled, will you, Abe?''
Only now did Mike look narrowly at Johnny Vano. ''Billy,
you can start loadin' the wagon.''

Mike left the store. Johnny's muscles jerked with the
impulse to run, to jump on his horse and ride. Murphy's
talk with the deputy would resolve any lingering uncertainty into conviction. Perrin's voice broke into his wild
thoughts. ''Step back to the storeroom, young fella. You
can start with a barrel of flour. . . .''

Johnny wrestled the heavy keg onto the tailgate of the
wagon, throwing constant, wary glances at the deputy's
office across the street. *You're a sucker*, he told himself
cynically. Yet after his first impulse to run, he'd had no
doubts about what he'd do. He'd put his trust in Mike

Murphy. The rancher had a solid, rooted-in-the-earth strength that commanded trust.

By the time Mike returned he had the wagon bed high-heaped with supplies. The man's face told Johnny nothing. "Should have let me load the heavy stuff," Mike growled, surveying the piled goods. "That everything?"

"That's it."

Johnny didn't breathe easily till they were on the road with the town well behind them. Beyond his clipped query, Mike hadn't said a word. Now he spoke, quietly, flatly:

"I talked to Leo Shallis. Now I want your side of the story, Johnny Vano. All of it."

Johnny talked in terse, dogged phrases as they rode, till the picture filled in for Mike.

The rancher was silent when he'd finished, and Johnny said, shooting him a wary sidelong glance, "You don't figure it happened the way I said?"

"I believe you, Johnny," Mike said kindly. "But the law demands proof. Suppose you could convince a jury that it was Sam, not you, who rode down the child— according to Leo's information, she's crippled for life. You'd still have to prove you killed Emmett Gorman in self-defense."

Johnny stiffened. "Gorman died?"

"Leo said so."

Johnny reined in his horse. "End of the line, then, and too late to jump freight. Innnocent man hangs as easy as a guilty one."

Mike spoke to the horses, sawed them to a halt. He knuckled his chin in a thoughtful, rubbing gesture. "Yeah. Give yourself up with no witnesses to back you, you'll put your head in a noose sure."

Johnny stared across the brown, rolling land to the

serrated rim of misty-purpled mountains. "I wanted to stop. Had a crazy feeling this might be the place. . . ."

"Maybe it can be, Johnny. You said that this Sayrs rode with your gang awhile, that's how he knew you. Any chance he might give you away to the law?"

"Not much, without cutting his own throat. There's a few warrants on his head, too."

"Then only Sayrs and me know who Billy Barnes really is. We'll tell my foreman, too. Between the three of us, I think we can work out this notion that's sticking in my craw."

"You mean—"

A faint smile traced Mike's mouth. He spoke to the horses, putting them in motion again. "What I said a while back, I meant. You could have run out a few minutes ago. You didn't. I got no reason to change my opinion."

CHAPTER TEN

The horse was a sorry, ganted crowbait and the dilapidated hull that Johnny was cinching on matched the animal. But both horse and gear had seen hard usage, and that was in careful keeping with the plan that Johnny, Mike, and Boze had discussed last night into the small hours.

Finished, Johnny swung to the saddle and rode from the maze of corrals across the ranchyard, stopping by the main house where a single saddled horse waited.

Nan Murphy stepped onto the porch, not hiding the vexed concern in her young face. "Boze will be out in a minute," she said, and then, flatly, "I don't like this, Johnny Vano, any of it. I wormed the whole story out of Mike and Boze, and I don't like it."

"Sorry you feel that way," he said thinly.

She stepped off the porch, shaking her head impatiently as she laid a hand on his bridle, looking up at him with clear, grave eyes. "I don't mean it the way you think. I'm glad that you're getting this chance. It's just that it's so dangerous. If there's any other way at all—"

"There isn't."

She bit her lip. "I don't think it's right, sending one man—"

73

Johnny voice was unintentionally harsh. "Look, missy, I had to act a grown man by the time I was eight. No choice. I ain't meanin' to brag, but there's few men could handle this game like I can."

"I know," she said. "I'm not saying what I mean to. I—just wanted to say, please be careful. Be very careful, will you?" She reached up a hand to cover his, swiftly, almost shyly, then wheeled and went into the house, half running.

Johnny slowly rubbed his hand where hers had rested and let it fall back to the saddle leather, a flatly denying gesture, thinking, *Don't get ideas*. Several times he'd noticed the hard-drawn tightness of Mike Murphy's ruddy-burned face when he and Nan were talking. The rancher, for all his bigness, didn't want his daughter palavering with an owlhoot, and Johnny did not blame him.

Boze and Mike came out of the house. They shook hands solemnly, without words, and Boze moved over to his waiting horse. Mike moved off the porch and extended his calloused hand to grasp Johnny's. "Good luck, son. We'll be watching for word from you."

The afternoon sun was kind to the buildings of Cedar Forks, mellowing their harsh and warp-walled outlines. It was Saturday. The rigs and saddle horses of farmers and one-loop ranchers lined the tie rails.

Mike Murphy had said that the Horne clan rarely left the mountains, and then only the men, singly, or a few at a time, never in a body. Town held few needs for them: they lived off the land by hunting, fishing, a little hoe-grubbing, butchering Tulare cows. Garth Horne, old man Horne's eldest son, was the only one who came to town regularly.

You could set a watch by the time Garth rode in every Saturday on his herring-gutted roan till snow clogged the high passes. He followed a branded ritual, buying up the family's meager wants—accommodating nearly fifty Hornes for a week—and packing them back to the mountains on his saddle. Before he left, he always dropped into the Alhambra Bar and bought a water glass of whiskey which he nursed along for an hour, listening to the talk but minding his own business.

Boze fished out his watch as they reined in at the main street. "Hold it right here. Don't want to be seen together. If we timed it right, Garth'll be hittin' the Alhambra about now. . . . Sure enough, that's his horse racked in front."

The two dismounted at a tie rail, and Boze's hand tightened over Johnny's arm as he tied up. "Soup's in the fire, son," he said in a low voice. "Your last chance to back out. Mike's hunch might not pan. And if Leo Shallis should chance to spot you before you leave—"

Johnny shook his head, an impatient negation. "Let's get to it. Give you ten minutes?"

Boze nodded, then angled across the street. Johnny watched him push through the Alhambra's batwing doors. Then, crowded between the horses, he bent his head to hide his face from passersby and pretended to fiddle with his cinch. When he calculated that enough time had passed, he jerked his hatbrim low and crossed to the Alhambra.

He entered a narrow, high-ceilinged room with a bar running down the length of the east wall. The air held a dim coolness that was pleasant in spite of stratified tobacco smoke and an odor of sour whiskey that clung to it. Some farmers were drinking and talking at a rear table. The bar was unoccupied except for Boze bellied against one end and at the other, a tall, thin man of about thirty-five, in buckskins ingrained with dirt and grease drippings.

This was Garth Horne. A tangled black beard hid his face. His eyes were the bleak neutral shade of a fogged sky. There was the untamed look of wild places about him. A tough customer to reckon with, Johnny judged, yet Mike had described Garth as "the soundest apple in a bad bushel," opining that it would be easiest to deal with the Hornes through their least suspicious member.

The fat bartender leaned against the backbar, scanning a soiled, tattered *Rutherford Weekly Journal*. Sweat glistened on his cue-ball head. He looked up with a grunt. Johnny lifted two fingers, then merely stared moodily into his glass after his drink was poured. The pressure beginning to edge his nerves made him wary of drink befuddlement.

He waited for Boze to make the play, and it came soon. He glanced up as Boze moved to his side, simulating a wobbling walk. In a slurred voice: "Kid, have a drink with me."

"Got a drink," Johnny said coldly.

"Have another. Give the kid another, Charley."

Johnny put both hands on the bar and shoved away from it. "Look, mister, he said softly, "just tend your own affairs."

Boze stared at him. "Fresh squirt. Got a mind to take Charley's towel and dry you behind the ears."

"You do that."

Boze didn't reply, just swayed unsteadily. Johnny reached slowly for his glass and sipped it, watching Boze over the rim. "Empty barrel makes the most noise, but it's still empty."

Boze eyed Johnny up and down as if he were making up his mind, then he laughed and lurched away. Out of the tail of his eye, Johnny saw Garth Horne watching, stillfaced. It would establish Johnny's surly enmity toward the Tulare foreman in Garth's mind.

Boze banged his glass on the bar. "Come on, Charley, fill me."

The bartender silently re-filled Boze's glass, and Boze maneuvered along the bar till he reached Garth Horne. He jabbed the man with a sharp elbow. "Hey, Horne, how many Tulare cattle you get last raid?"

Charley said hastily, "Boze, do me a favor—"

Boze gave him a red-eyed glare. "Do me one, Charley. Crawl in one of your bottles and pull the cork in tight. I asked you a question, Horne."

Garth Horne said stonily, "I got no quarrel with you, Hendryx."

"You only think you ain't!" Boze yelled. "Old man Murphy's had me workin' the draws down till dark to find them damn' cows. On your account!" With a jerk of his hand, he sent the contents of his glass into Horne's face. Garth Horne stood stock-still, paling above his dripping beard. Finally he slowly lifted a hand and wiped a sleeve across his face.

"Can't rawhide you to a draw, eh?" Boze bellowed. "Well, I ain't waiting."

He swung from the bar, clawing for his holstered gun. Johnny made an easy draw, the sharp cocking of his .45 freezing Boze's arm before he cleared leather. "Buckskin fella ain't armed, Mr. Loudmouth," Johnny said softly. "Reckon you saw that."

Boze stared at the gun in Johnny's fist, then staggered away from the bar and toppled into a chair, letting his head fall limp on the table. A farmer's chair scraped back in the silence. "I'll get Leo, Charley."

"You stay set, sodbuster," Johnny snapped. "No one's lighting a shuck till I say."

The man stared, his lower jaw falling at something he saw in Johnny's wolf-lean look, then he dropped loosely into his chair. Johnny sheathed his gun and deliberately turned his back on the farmers. He nodded at Horne. "Buy you a drink?"

Uncertainty flickered in the pale eyes. Horne nodded, emptied his glass. Johnny carried his drink over by Horne, waited till Charley had filled Horne's glass, then said mildly, "Happen you might be kin of Jubal Horne?"

"My old man."

"That a fact." Johnny lowered his voice confidentially. "It true you folks'll hide a man for a price?"

Johnny was playing his main hand on Mike's suggestion. Half-savage haters of organized society and its laws, though they'd never openly run afoul of that law till their recent raids on Tulare, the Hornes were rumored to have given sanctuary from time to time to not a few of the West's most notorious outlaws. From the swift wariness that touched Horne's bearded face, Johnny knew that the hearsay was true.

Horne asked slowly, "Who are you?"

"Name Vano mean anything to you?"

Horne nodded, grunted. "Though gossip, plenty. Hear tell Sam Vano and most of his gang got it when they rode into an ambush up at Rutherford, two—three weeks ago."

"I'm Sam's son," Johnny murmured.

Horne's eyes widened, narrowed to cautious slits. "Yeah? He had only one son, Johnny Vano. I got it the kid was shot and drowned way up the Little Muddy."

Johnny shook his head. "I can show you the hole in my leg. But I made the far shore after I lost my horse, picked up another and some grub at a farmhouse, hid out in the hills."

Horne said narrowly, "Town's a bad place for you then."

"Got tired of lean rations, talkin' to myself. Came in for a drink and to see some faces. Stroke of luck, runnin' across you. Figure you can hide me out till things cool down? Don't want to take a chance, even if the law's got me dead.''

Garth Horne scowled darkly, fiddled with his glass between thick fingers.

''Look, I got money.'' Mike had provided him with a well-stuffed moneybelt.

''Ain't that. Just have to be sure you're who you say. Otherwise the old man'll buzzard-bait me.''

''You want me to go slap the sheriff's face?'' Johnny asked angrily. Mike had warned him that he'd have to convince the Hornes of his identity, and Johnny was steeled to meet any test that Garth might demand.

''Just remembered,'' Garth said then. ''We have a fella up there who rode with the Vanos . . . he can vouch for you. I figure you're on the level, just have to satisfy the old man is all.''

Johnny shrugged. A lot of men had ridden with Sam Vano, any of whom could identify ''Sam's brat.'' He drained his glass and set it down. ''Let's start, then. My back gets crawlier longer I stand here.''

CHAPTER ELEVEN

Riding beside Garth Horne, putting the last building of Cedar Forks behind him, Johnny could afford to draw a long, deep breath. The first step was past. The rigged byplay between Boze and himself had duped Garth Horne: from here, Johnny was on his own. . . .

They rode northwest, mounting a vast tableland rolling away to distance-blued mountains.

Johnny had been too busy placing landmarks in his mind to realize how far they'd come; now he saw that the westering sun had crowned the far peaks with rose tinge, the land was beginning to fall into a black outline.

"We come a piece," he told Garth. "Will we make it before sunset?"

"Not quite. But don't worry. I can find our way in the pitch dark."

Shadows of horses and men lengthened into grotesque black specters. The swift twilight had already faded into a soft gray mantle of deepening dusk when they descended the ridge at its opposite end. Now Johnny saw ahead what appeared to be a solid, sheer-faced scarp forming a solid wall against their ingress. Nearing it, he saw that a great, eroded fissure wound tortuously into the rock, and without pause Garth put his horse directly into one of these narrow pockets. They rode single file, shod hoofs clinking ringing echoes along the precipitous walls yawning away to either side.

Suddenly a shout drifted down the canyon from high above. Garth pulled up. A man stood with ready rifle on the lip of the rimrock, skylined as a lone and seemingly faceless figure int he pooling twilight. Garth hailed a reply to the challenge. Satisfied, the sentry pulled back from sight and they rode on.

"Lookout?" Johnny asked.

The dark shape of Garth's head bobbed. "Always one of the menfolk on duty up there. The old man's orders. Takes just one man to hold off an army from that rim. Riders can only come one at a time through this here canyon, in plain view of our man all the way, where they can't get a sight of him. Way the echoes carry, even an Injun couldn't sneak through by night."

Johnny said nothing more, thinking of the impregnability of this mountain refuge. The frowning ramparts tapered gradually lower as they continued, until a sudden turn in the pass debouched upon a rolling, rock-strewn slope falling away from the cliffs to flats of dimly squared fields and meadows: primitively tilled acreage in a wild mountain range. They picked their way down the slope through the growing dark, across a narrow belt of meadow, and into a scattered grove of pine. They rode into a wide, brush-cleared area where a number of small log cabins nestled haphazardly. A door opened; a lank, scarecrow-like man appeared against the firelight.

"Take our hosses, Clem," Garth called. "I got to see Pa."

Johnny swung down, his leg aching with a dull, stiff hurt. He stood flexing it as cabin doors opened and the

Horne clan boiled to the doorways to survey the new-comer. Houndtooth-lean men, slatternly moon-faced women, many obviously related by blood to a degree of near degeneracy.

"Come on," Garth told Johnny, and, supplies slung from his shoulder, led the way around a dense hedge of trees that cut off a little nook from the settlement proper. Here was set a lofty log house much larger than the others. Johnny followed Garth inside, blinking at the flickering glare from the stone fireplace. Four men crowded in crude, hand-carved arm-chairs around the shallow oasis of heat and light. Three were lean, dark, younger copies of Garth.

The fourth man was past seventy, but, even slumped loosely in his chair he was well over a great-boned six feet. Age had lean-strung his muscles, stooped and rounded his shoulders. A full, snowy beard hid half his face and spilled like hoary frost over his burly chest. It lent him a benign and patriarchal air that belied the crafty alertness of sharp-blue, still-young eyes. He was shirtless, his gray, cotton underwear grimy. "You git my 'baccy, Garth?" The wheezing voice was like a bucksaw ripping through ironwood.

Garth fumbled in the flour sack. "Here, Papa."

Jubal Horne took the plug, took a clasp knife from his pocket, sheared off a wad, and stowed it in his cheek. Johnny felt himself targeted by the sharp, old eyes. Jubal Horne said nothing, just chucked a thumb at him.

"This here's Sam Vano's son, Johnny," Garth said. With spare phrases, he told of their meeting.

"Easy to prove if he's who he says," old Jubal husked. "Remember that feller your brought here awhile back, Garth? He was a Vano man, proved it with a reward dodger he had of hisself. Bije, you fetch him here. Jump now."

One of the sons stood, stalked wordlessly from the room. Old Jubal gummed his plug with a contented grunt. "Sit down, young Vano. Bije'll be back directly. Meet my other boys, Buck, Eli. You got money?"

Johnny pulled out his shirt and untied Mike's leather money belt cinched around his bare midriff. "Just give it over, son," old Jubal said pleasantly. "I'll keep it safe till you leave. Lot of light-fingered younkers in my family."

Without objection Johnny passed over the belt with all its money, knowing that he'd seen the last of it. It was a small price for acceptance by the clan, and he couldn't afford to antagonize its leader at the offset.

Shortly Bije's gangling figure pushed through the door, followed by a slim man who moved with feline grace. Behind Johnny, a flame-curling log collapsed in the fireplace with an ash-muted *plop*. It sent up high-flaring sparks and threw a diffused, rippling glare across the room, catching on the man's laughing face. Jesse Norcross' voice was a light mockery:

"Fancy meeting you here, Tiger."

Johnny was up at first light of day to inspect the valley. From the pine bench its vast rolling floor fell away in terraced flats, till cut off by the almost perpendicular cliffs that ringed the valley. Even from the bench, Johnny could assure himself that those distant, rugged walls, though bisected laterally with broken shale ledges, would defy the most experienced climber. Yet he felt strongly that there was at least one other exit besides the outer canyon trail. If the Hornes were holding Tulare's stolen stock anywhere, it was plainly not within their home valley.

But for all his hours of keen-eyed exploring, he could not locate the hidden passage in the cliffs which he was now certain existed. Three times he'd watched from his cabin window while Jubal Horne's sons saddled up in the gray twilight and rode from the valley. Always they left by the regular canyon exit, and always they returned from the opposite end of the valley, riding up the teraces around mid-morning.

He was sure only that there was a passage and that it was well camouflaged from even a close observer. He considered waiting by the cliffs some morning to watch for the returning raiders, but there were two solid, rambling miles of the northern ramparts, and one man could not cover all points.

His perseverance paid off on the sixteenth day. He was trekking along a high, shaly bank which flanked the plunging course of a stony stream bed appearing to have its origin somewhere along the boulder-littered base of the escarpment. Johnny hadn't followed it this far before, and now he heard a hollow roar which grew in volume as he advanced. Rounding a place where the stream curved torrentially around the shoulder of a rocky buttress, he saw the white, curving sheet of a narrow waterfall which apparently emerged from a huge crevice at a height of some fifty feet on the sheer wall. It dashed to the rocks below, creaming to wild foam, and here the stream had its source.

With the growing excitement of a sudden realization, Johnny stared at the tumbling cataract.

Scrambling over spray-slippery rocks, he reached a deeply scored niche adjacent to the falls. Standing within the niche, he could see into a gloomy cave. A narrow shelf, just wide enough to accommodate a single horseman or man afoot provided precarious footing between the rock face and the wall of water. He edged along it, till he stood on the white sand floor of the water-hollowed tunnel. Johnny conjectured that two underground streams had once rushed through the wall, working through quake-convulsed cracks, one above the other. The lower one, after ages of pounding out its eroded passage, had gone dry, probably through some change in the upper stream bed. Far down, he could see a distant glimmer of daylight pale the walls.

This was it.

That night, standing by his cabin window, Johnny watched a tight-knit little group riding away toward the canyon exit. He counted five of them. All of Jubal Horne's sons, and Jesse Norcross, too. Another night, another raid.

Only this one would be different, Johnny thought grimly, because he'd be waiting when they returned with their stolen beef. Once he knew where they were holding the cattle, his part would be done. Against the night chill, he shrugged into his ducking jacket and headed for the fenced pasture to get his horse.

CHAPTER TWELVE

Nan Murphy had been cooking and house cleaning most of the day, and she felt begrimed, sweaty and tired. All this trouble for a ranchers' meeting. A day of making the place immaculate for a score of men who would shortly be crowding in, boisterously tramping mud over the carpets and dribbling ashes on freshly swept floors.

Her stepmother had been little help, as usual; Leonora's preparations consisted of spending hours making herself as beautiful as possible. Leonora enjoyed being on exhibit, Nan thought sourly: it was her sole function in life. Nan understood well enough the difference between the world in which she and Lee had been reared to feel sympathy toward the older woman's inability to adjust, but tonight she was tired, irritable, and out of patience.

She stood in front of her mirror, adjusting the white collar of her plain dark dress, thinking of the young outlaw called Johnny Vano as she often had in the days since he'd left Tulare. Long days, during which no word had come out of the hills. He might have changed his mind and decided to throw in with the Hornes: no doubt, their loose, happy-ignorant way of life had its primal attraction.

She remembered how she'd eagerly questioned Boze

Hendryx, upon his return from Cedar Forks after seeing
Johnny safely in the confidence of Garth Horne. "You
should of seen the lad put it over," Boze had said. "Talent wasted. Should of gone on the stage. Me, too." His
sharp eyes had quested her expression. "Plenty worried
about him, ain't you?" Yes, Nan thought angrily, of
course she was worried . . . sending a man alone among
that cutthroat clan. She'd tongue-lashed Mike smartly on
that score. "You and your damned maternal eyes," Mike
had chuckled. "Hell, Nan, Sam Vano's boy can give
those Hornes kings in toughness and draw aces. Don't
worry your head about him."

Mother-hen-clucking. Maybe that was it. But hadn't
there been something more? She tried to deny it and failed.
Johnny Vano's hungry, brooding look had made her feel,
for once, like a woman. The moment by the bunkhouse
before Mike had interrupted kept returning with its memory of the new, exciting feeling that had swept her.

Leonora entered through the connecting door between
their rooms. The older girl wore a white satin gown that
left bare the ivory whiteness of throat and shoulders, clinging to the fullness of her upper body and narrow waist
before it belled into a full skirt. Beside her, Nan felt thin
and angular, and it deepened her resentment.

Leonora said languidly, as she ran a brush through the
jet-black shining swirl of her hair, "Would you like one of
my gowns, dear?"

Nan eyed Lee's full-blown figure and said dryly, "Thanks
just the same."

Abruptly Leonora's lips trembled; the hand with the
brush fell to her side. "Can't you try to like me—a little?"

Nan's irritation rose. "Lee, everyone on the ranch has
tried to make you feel at home here because we knew it

was all different for you. We tried. Don't blame us. What
can you do for weakness except pity it?''

Lee bit on her lower lip. ''That's cruel.''

''It's fact. You had everything. Beauty, wealth, gentle
breeding. With all that, a person would expect character.
Instead, you flit back and forth like a pretty moth. When
you were bored with Boston soirees, you married my
father for a pleasant change. But marriage is permanent,
Lee. We could forgive your being spoiled and useless;
your background made you what you are. But no one ad-
mires spinelessness. Mike must have seen something else
in you, or thought he did. Enough to marry you. But so far
I haven't caught a sign of it.''

Leonora dabbed at her eyes. ''How can you!''

Nan shook her head resignedly and walked to the window. From the darkness beyond came the sounds of creaking harness, of men's deep voices. ''The men are arriving.
You'd better hurry. The moth to the flame, you know.''

''Stop it!'' Lee's voice carried a sharpness Nan had
never heard, and she glanced in surprise at Lee as she
arranged her hair into a high, gleaming coiffure, her fingers swift and angry. *I'll be switched*, Nan thought, *I
struck fire*.

Maybe that was what Leonora needed . . . antagonism,
not sympathy. Everyone had bent over backward to be
nice to her. It was possible that a real ordeal might shock
her from her pampered shell. . . .

Side by side they walked to the parlor and paused in the
archway watching the men throng into the big room. All of
them had come directly off round-up; it showed in their
run-down boots, dust-caked clothes, and sun-boiled faces.

Mike Murphy stood by the door, the span of his shoulders wedge uncomfortably in his tailored suit. His greetings and handshakes were cordial, until the last man entered.

Mike didn't offer his hand; hs voice was cool. "Glad you could make it, King."

There was a sardonic twitch to Miles King's half-smile as he gave the women a slight, but courtly-perfect bow. He was dressed fit to kill, his Marseilles waistcoat of white silk and bottle-green frock coat tailored perfectly to his blocky upper body. His boots were of finest morocco leather, polished to a glow. A new pearl-gray Stetson was geometrically angled on his ruggedly handsome head. Nan sensed that King and her father had had a serious falling-out recently, though Mike hadn't spoken of it. But this meeting was important enough for Mike to forego personal feelings: he could not afford to exclude the second largest basin rancher.

"There," Leonora murmured loftily, "is proof that a man can be a real man and a gentleman too."

"King?" Nan laughed softly. "That dress suit with a head on its shoulders?"

Leonora flushed angrily and walked away with a silken rustle of skirts. She began to talk and laugh with King, lightly flirting to show her pique. No one else paid attention, but Nan saw a deep crimson stain lift to her father's face. Mike's stolid Irish Catholic forebears had bequeathed him the firm belief that a man's home and family were sacred beyond even playful tampering, and for a moment she feared he'd explode and throw King out bodily. But after a moment he turned to one of the ranchers and spoke casually, and she relaxed.

Presently Mike turned to the room at large and said loudly, "Sit down, boys."

There was a concerted movement toward chairs. Some of the men leaned against the walls. An impatient one said, "Let's get to it, Murph. You called this meeting, and it better be important to take us away from round-up."

Mike sat on the arm of a big leather chair, hands on his knees. "Tell the truth, Tom, the notion just come to me. More I thought about it, better I liked it. But with round-up almost over, there's no time to be wasted. Would have been simpler to sound you out individually, but the thing I have in mind is a joint effort." He grinned. "That's a bad word to you boys, but I hope you'll see its reasonableness in this instance."

There were a few appreciative chuckles and a good many stony faces. Nan leaned in the archway, her arms folded, smiling a little as she thought, *He's really grabbing the tiger by the tail.*

Each man in this room owned and ran his own spread. Their ranching statuses ran from wealth to near poverty. Mike himself employed a fifteen man crew; belligerent Tom Davisson, who'd first spoken, worked his own one-loop outfit. If all had one characteristic in common, it was the stubborn independence of backwoods individualists. Mike's statement sounded nearly revolutionary. Nan knew that his real reason for taking this step was his own ignorance of Johnny Vano's fate. He'd expected to hear from Johnny days before, and he could not afford to wait longer and give the Hornes their chance to strike the main blow that would smash Tulare.

"We'll hear you out, Murph," Tom Davisson said gruffly.

"Coming from you, Tom, that is a concession," Mike said dryly; this time most of them laughed. "I'll lay it on the line. . . . We know our heards are being hit by a gang operating from the mountains. Reckon we all know the Hornes are first suspect." There was a general mutter of agreement. "All right. Until such time as we can get evidence and means to stop the Hornes, we'll have to take measures to protect ourselves.

"We work together twice a year as a rule, on fall and spring round-ups. We cut our stock, each man holds his own herd, makes his own drive to Rutherford. . . . So far, the Hornes have made small pickings, though these add up. But once our beeves are assembled, they'll likely see a chance to make a bold killing. They could raid a bed grounds, kill the nighthawks, and make off with a whole herd. Something like that might be more than they could handle, but it'd be prime bait, maybe too tempting to pass up."

Nan glanced at Miles King relaxed in his chair as he listened, squinting slightly against the up-furling smoke of his cigar. A faint, enigmatical smile traced his lips.

Nan's deprecating comment about King had been for Leonora's benefit: she did not underestimate the man. In spite of his present prestige, the owner of Moon had come to the territory only five years before and had established himself as a ranching power within two years. His past, the source of his wealth were unknown, though the accepted rumor was that he'd been a Mississippi gambler who'd reaped a small fortune over swift-riffled cards in smoky riverboat salons. It tallied with his slick airs. Maybe, though, her instinctive distrust of King stemmed simply from the fact that she didn't understand men of his dandified cut, of his devious, secretive nature. . . .

"What I propose," Mike was saying, "is that with fall round-up almost over, we pool our herds, riders, wagons and trail gear, and make a concerted drive to market. We'll station armed outriders as flankers, like the military does, and they'll be on shifts around the clock. Every man jack of the crew will be armed to the teeth. No jayhawkers would dare hit an organization like that. Outside Rutherford, we'll split into our own outfits again." He paused. "That's the gist. It leaves a lot of details to smooth out. Just now I want your main reaction."

King lifted his hand a couple of inches. "The idea's all right. Only whose protection will it insure?"

Mike stood, his massive torso blocking out the lighted lamp behind him. "What you implying by that?"

"Nothing, man, nothing." King spread his hands. "I only mean that the rustlers have hit you the hardest by far. For the rest of us, it totals a very minor loss. You'll not take offense at an obvious fact?"

"What about that, Murph?" Davisson demanded.

"I expected that," Mike said grimly. "All right, none of you have been noticeably hurt—yet. But the longer they hit me, the biggest basin rancher, successfully, and get away with it, the bolder they'll become. They'll start to hit oftener and heavier. They may break me. And when they have, d'ye think they'll give up a good thing, once begun? Oh no. Then it'll be your turn. Then it'll be too late to get together and fight back. Alone, each is a sitting duck." His fierce eyes swept them. "Are ye with me?"

"Dammit, yes!" Tom Davisson said. "I like a man who ain't afraid to shoot off his mouth." There was general laughter. One by one the ranchers assented, none eagerly and most of them with reluctance. They began to discuss pros and cons: the joining of herds could be completed in a day . . . the drive begun the next day.

"We'll drink to this," Mike said, "for it's a pact."

"If anyone wants whiskey," Nan put in, "he'll step into the next room. You're not messing up these rugs."

"Hey, Nan," called a young rancher, "how about a walk in the moonlight?"

"Go ahead," she told him tartly, the men roared. They thronged into the dining room, where Nan had earlier prepared a tray of glasses. Mike raised his, toasted the loose partnership, and they drank.

Both women fitted into the man-gathering with rare

ease, but in striking contrast. Where Leonora exploited her feminity with flirtatious vivacity, Nan joked and talked with the men as one of them. Behind her easy banter, Nan considered this with irony. Strange how she pitied her stepmother on one score, and was beginning to envy her on another. Stranger still that her own lack of ordinary womanly coquetry had never troubled her before. Not until Johnny Vano had come along. In the face of the realization, she told herself that it was foolish, hopeless, yet she couldn't dislodge the simple fact.

King set his glass down and patted his mouth on his handkerchief. "Strong stuff. I could use a glass of water."

Lee smiled at him archly. "There is water in the kitchen."

She led the way through a side door, King following. Nan heard their bantering voices, and Lee's trilling laughter. Mike, always too bluff to hide his feelings, wore a fixed glare until they returned, both laughing at something that King had said.

But Nan detected a faint, harried impatience in King's face, and her wonder deepened when King turned abruptly to Mike and said quickly, "Good idea you have, Murph. I'll go along with whatever your fellows decide. Hate to leave so soon, but I got some business hanging fire at the ranch. See you tomorrow at round-up."

He pivoted on his heel before Mike could reply, clamped on his Stetson, murmured to Leonora's startled question, "No, ma'am, I really have to leave. I'll see myself out. Good night, gentlemen, ladies."

The broken-off talk resumed as the front door closed behind King. "What'n blazes is so important at Moon that it can't wait?" Tom Davisson muttered. "That dude rancher always was an odd duck."

CHAPTER THIRTEEN

Johnny blew on his hands and rubbed them. He yawned again. He'd been waiting for two hours. He had easily located the tunnel behind the waterfall with the help of moonglow, and had followed it to its end, coming out in a long-dry wash which he traveled for two miles till it met a high-walled gorge that bit deeply through otherwise inaccessible terrain. On the floor of the gorge Johnny had found much recent cattle sign. He knew that his was the pass through which the Hornes drove their stolen beef, and a moment's thought had persuaded him to wait till the returning raiders came this way, and follow them. In daylight he could have tracked the old cattle sign, but at night the trail could be easily lost in any of a hundred intersecting canyons. By the roundabout ascent he'd mounted to this promontory from which he could command a wide view of the gorge.

He chewed some cold jerky from his knapsack, washed it down with a swallow of canteen water, and sat in chilled tiredness while the minutes crawled by.

At last the distant hooraws of riders drifted faintly downcanyon. Johnny strained his eyes to pick out the specks of cattle and riders against the dark ribbon of gorge. Within minutes they would be out of sight. He caught up his reins, vaulted into leather, and put his horse carefully down the slope.

Shortly, as Johnny had anticipated, the men hazed the cattle up a cross-canyon. He slowed now, picking his way carefully because the narrowly confined walls carried in ringing echoes the clang of horseshoes against rock. This canyon terminated at the brink of a rushing mountain stream. Johnny knew that there must be several such on their backtrail: water left no sign. The riders had driven the bawling animals into the swift, shallow current and were working them downstream.

To spare the risk of being spotted, Johnny left the direct route of the drive and mounted a spur ridge fringed with scrub pine, hoping he could follow unseen along the summit of the ridge. He was in luck, hitting a game trail twisting erratically through the timber.

As the general terrain heightened he left the ridge. His chilled body warmed with the rising sun. Distantly, the faint bawling of massed cattle carried with pine-soughing wind. Feeling a a nudge of mounting excitement, he roweled his horse forward and pulled up suddenly almost at the rim of cliffs where sheered steeply off into a yawning gulf. Shading his eyes against the thin sunlight which washed in a bright shimmer against his eyes, he found himself overlooking a vast park tucked within the mountain heights. Below hundreds of cattle grazed a sun-drenched meadow that unrolled like an emerald carpet to a far periphery of rocky precipices. Almost to the base of the cliffs, flourished a heavy grove of lodgepole pine, and through the feathery yellow-green foliage he made out the gray roof of a cabin.

Then he saw that the Hornes were pushing their horses toward the little cabin. Soon the grove hid them from view,

but in a few minutes he saw a wisping of smoke spiral from
the chimney. After the night's work they'd rest awhile and
have a hot meal before returning to the home valley.
Johnny kneaded his reins between his fingers, biting his lip.
Get close to that cabin and he might get a slant on their
plans.

With Johnny thought was action. He pulled his horse
back from the bald summit of the cliffs and ground-haltered
him out of sight. He moved through the dense trees, lifting
and setting his feet down with silent care. Around the
building trees and brush had been cleared away for a dozen
feet. He stopped at the edge of the clearing, poising for a
short swift run that would take him to the single small,
high window on the near wall of the cabin.

Then the door began to scrape open. Johnny settled on
his haunches behind screening foliage. Bije Horne stepped
out, his whiskers parting in a yawn. He stood for a moment, shoving a hand inside his dust-grimed shirt to scratch
his ribs, while his idle gaze circled the clearing. He yawned
again, picked up a bucket by the door and headed down a
narrow footpath that straggled off through the trees, evidently to fetch water.

Johnny's palms were sweating. He parted the shrubbery,
ducked his head, and ran across the clearing to crouch
below the window. He pulled off his hat and cautiously
lifted his eyes till he could see over the sill, through a dirty
pane. Garth, Buck, and Eli were lackadaisically playing
cards at the table in the center of the single log-walled
room. Jesse Norcross was occupied at the stove.

Garth's lips moved; fragments of speech carried faintly.
"Raid . . . King . . . one big drive . . ."

Johnny's skin tingled; his heart thudded dully. Was
Miles King's Moon their next major target?

A boot grated behind him.

Johnny started to turn. Bije Horne was there. Sunlight streaked along the barrel of a down-arching six-gun. Johnny threw up an arm, too late. There was a single bursting flare of pain which trailed into numbing darkness. . . .

Consciousness and feeling returned by aching degrees. He lay on his back in a jumble of harness in one corner, tied hand and foot. Johnny sat up by painful degrees. Over by the table, dark-eyed Bije said, "Shoulda been more careful, Vano. Seen you in the bushes when I come out."

Johnny lay on his back, staring at the sagging roof. A tight sickness gripped his stomach. He'd played a rash and ill-considered game, coming in by the cabin. Now he faced its bitter consequences.

There was a sound of coming horses. The Hornes were on their feet, crowding to the door, their guns out. "Two riders," muttered Garth. "Slack off, boys. It's Papa."

"Will you look who's with him," Buck said. He chuckled.

Horses reined into the yard; men's voices reached Johnny, a creak of leather, the clink of bridle chains. The Hornes moved back from the doorway as their father shouldered through them. His white hair was awry; as his pale-glaring eyes swung to find Johnny, he gave a surprised grunt. He called "Here's your man, hogtied like a lamb."

Johnny's swift thoughts snagged on an astonished blank. Miles King stood in the threshold, slapping a silver-tipped quirt against his gloved palm. His once-immaculate clothes were dusty and wrinkled; his red-rimmed eyes jumped with a harried impatience. He said slowly, "So you caught him. How?"

Garth told him.

"Good work, boys," King said, his color returning with his bland equanimity. "I rode half the night to tell your father; he had the camp searched, and couldn't find a trace of Vano. We reasoned that either he'd left the valley to see Murphy, or else was tracking you boys here. We rode hard to warn you . . . but this is better than I'd hoped for.''

"Don't reckon we follow you," Garth said slowly.

King pointed his doubled quirt at Johnny. "He's a spy for Mike Murphy. He's Sam Vano's son, all right, but getting into your valley was a rigged play to let him circulate freely among you—collecting evidence that could hang us all.''

"How d'ye know this, Mr. King?''

King gave Garth a pointed look. "Never mind. The important thing is, he knows. Can't take a chance he'll tell . . . now can we, gentlemen?''

CHAPTER FOURTEEN

Hunched over the table with the Hornes, King sketched his plan. Johnny listened carefully, wondering in the back of his mind what good it would do.

Murphy had persuaded the basin ranchers to throw their round-up herds together and post a rotated guard detail till they reached railhead. King said that wasn't important in itself; he hadn't intended raiding the market herds. The end he had in sight (Johnny wondered what that was) would have come about through slow, calculated decimation of Tulare stock by small periodic raids, and King was satisfied to wait.

But Mike Murphy, without knowing it, had played into King's hands with his notion of tying the herds into one body. Suppose the Hornes could hit the big herd, stampede them back into the hills? The ranchers would recover the majority of course, but meanwhile the Hornes would be rounding up and working small bunches back here. They'd score a *coup* that would shave months off King's projected plans, and more than double the Hornes' present tally of stolen beef.

Old Jubal cleared his throat. "What about them guards, sir?"

King replied that they could toll off the herdsmen by a ruse. Today the ranchers would assemble the big herd; tonight the cattle would be held on a bedgrounds. A number of basin ranch buildings could be fired simultaneously. In this country, bucket brigades were the only counter to a serious blaze, and bucket lines absorbed a lot of men. Fires would be seen from the round-up camp and bedgrounds; men would rush for horses and ride to offer help. The few remaining nighthawks could be easily taken care of.

"Prime opportunity," old Jubal's shaggy head bobbed approvingly. "Take a sizeable crew to hit that hard, though. Need men to set the fires, too. So far just my boys and Norcross have been able to handle the raids."

"You have the say-so with your clan. Draft every able-bodied man. I can join you with my crew of tough nuts."

"Reckon that'll do. . . . Tonight, then. And now, sir, I'd planned a rough tally of the head we've already got."

"Good," King said. "We should get an approximation on how badly we've nicked Murphy so far. That meeting he called proved he's coming to the end of the rope—and tonight should turn the trick. Bring your boys and we'll spread out and take a general count. Then I've got to get back to round-up before my fellow ranchers get suspicious." He moved toward the door, his eyes slanting at Johnny. "What about him?"

"He'll keep," said old Jubal, adding ponderously, "This thing has to be, but it's a dirty job, damn if it isn't. Least we can do is give the lad a time alone, to make his peace."

"Don't wait too long, Mr. Horne," King said softly. "Waiting doesn't cleanse a dirty job."

"I said he'll be taken care of," old Jubal growled, "and I'll not renege."

After they'd gone, Johnny lay on his back, trying to think over the battering ache of his skull. *No time to lose your grip. Your last chance; use it.* Setting his teeth against a grip of nausea, he rolled onto his belly, craning his neck upward. On the clay-chinked wall, about waist-high to a standing man, he saw a rusty spoke-long nail sunk halfway into the timber. The tangle of harness on which he sat must have been slung carelessly over it and had fallen off.

With the wall as a support for his back, Johnny maneuvered by painful degrees to his feet. He snagged the tightdrawn turns of rope confining his wrists across the shank of the nail, giving the strands a tearing jerk across the square, sharp edged head. He lost count of how many times he did this: it was the work of long, aching minutes, tension-strung muscles cramped from his half-bent position and limited orbit of movement. Once he gashed his palm on the nailhead and had to govern his frantic nerves to a harder, steadier pace. Finally he pushed away from the wall, gathered his shoulder muscles, and gave a violent twisting pull that parted the remaining strands.

It was a matter of a minute to free his feet. He stepped to the doorway and halted; a lift of voices told him the men were returning. Johnny lunged through the doorway, across the clearing, running low for the brief shelter of the grove. He heard Jesse Norcross's angry yell. Johnny burst through the dappled glade onto the open meadow and made a beeline for the cliff. A crash of gunfire. Bullets volleyed the tall grasses. He half-turned in his full run. The Hornes, Jesse and King had been making for the shack; now they'd veered their horses to cut him off.

Johnny changed his line of flight to a zigzag run. He reached the ruptured ramp in the cliffs and scrambled to its upper end. From there it was a few seconds to his waiting horse. He hit the saddle in a sprawling leap and kicked the animal into a bolting run. Looking back, he saw the pursuers pouring up from the gully with old Jubal in the lead, his silvery mane streaming, looking like a white haired centaur.

He heard a shot blast its racketing echo from high away to his left. The two who'd cut off had swarmed over the summit of a ridge and were pushing their horses recklessly down a pine dotted slope, directly athwart his path. Johnny swerved, cut south into the deep ridges. Suddenly he found himself sloping down into the converging walls of a broad cove, which tapered till they dwindled into a deep canyon. With his lead narrowing, he had no choice but to spur into the canyon.

They'd deliberately maneuvered him into this canyon, so it must pinch off somewhere: he was boxed. His rope might get him out of it. Quickly he untied it from his pommel and slipped its coiled length over his shoulder, then slid his rifle from its scabbard.

The men had almost reached the canyon; they opened up with a blistering volley. Johnny's horse shied; he grabbed at the reins and missed as the animal bolted like a released arrow from the canyon. The Hornes' exultant yells rose as his riderless mount pounded past them.

Johnny opened up with his rifle. The men pulled up hurriedly, piled from the saddles and sought shelter. Johnny moved deeper into the canyon at a dogged run. The Hornes followed, but kept their distance, hidden by the twisting walls. He could hear the murmur of their voices, the rush of their boots. They were in no great hurry; they were sure of their quarry.

Suddenly he dug in his heels and hauled up. He knew now: he wasn't boxed, but he might as well have been.

The canyon ended on the lip of a precipice, falling away

from his feet for a sheer hundred feet. A hundred feet of smooth, bland sheets and crumbling blocks of rotten shale, eroded by water-burrowed tunnels.

Johnny dropped on his hunkers behind a low, squat out-cropping, watching downcanyon, rifle ready for the final rush. It did not come. They could afford to wait—and to laugh . . . his only way out was straight down. Even with the aid of his fifty-foot lariat, he could negotiate only half of the precarious descent . . . and simple matter for the Hornes to cut the rope before he could get that far.

The minutes passed, and still the Hornes did not close in. They had water and shade. The sun beat heavily on Johnny's exposed back. Flies buzzed in lazy ovals around his head. He licked his cracked lips and clamped an iron control on his panicking nerves. A wrathful determination took its hold on him . . . a man could only die trying.

On his belly he wriggled to the rimrock and looked down. A great rounded buttress of smooth rock whose lower surface curved inward cut off the immediate view below. There was the barest chance that if he could let himself down by rope past that bulge he could find enough broken irregularities to furnish hand-and-foot holds to the bottom . . . and the bulge would cut off fire from above.

He slipped his rope from his shoulder and looped the noose-end over the thick outcrop that had sheltered him. He shook out the coils over the brink, the end dropping out of sight. He let himself over the edge, his body moving down the rope in brief jerks.

He was past the outermost thrust of the bulge then, and was hanging clear of the cliff-face, nothing but a slender line of well-worn hemp between him and nearly a hundred-foot fall to the stone littered base. Less than a yard from his clinging body, nestled in a deep nook beneath the bulge, he saw a broad, projecting shelf of solid rock. He shifted his weight, giving his body the motion of a pendulum. Above, the rush of feet, and Miles King's harshly recriminating voice:

"Damn' fools, he's got away!"

Jesse's excited yell; "He left his rifle. And here's his rope . . . it's jerkin'. He's down there!"

King swore. "Who's got a knife? Here, let me . . ."

Johnny's swinging body was almost touching the ledge now: he gave a violent thrust of one leg against it, swung far out, and then, arching back, let go the rope and dropped on his hands and knees within the nook.

The rope parted; he saw it fall in a long, graceful loop. With swift presence of mind, he scrambled over to a loose boulder balancing on the shelf-edge. One long straining push sent it over, bounding down the escarpment, setting up a miniature avalanche of broken shale. There was a shattering crash below, and the residual rattlings of falling rock died away.

Buck's hesitant voice carried from above the overhang: "Think we ought to go down there?"

"Why bother?" King asked. "Even if he's alive, he's too broken up to move. Let's go. We've wasted enough . . ."

Retreating footfalls. Voices died away. Johnny sank slowly on his back, letting out his inheld breath.

But there was little time to rest. Get off this cliff. Find his horse. Reach Tulare before nightfall and tell Murphy about the scheduled raid . . . things that had to be done, and any one of them looked near-impossible.

Beneath the ledge, the walls out-tapered slightly at about a ten degree slant. He began to work down, twist his gaze downward to ferret out every crevice or protuberance where he could next put hand or foot. Twice his rope-burned hands slipped from inadequate holds, luckily firm footing saved him. Once a ledge crumbled under his boots and he swung by his arms from a slender pinnacle. He kicked at rotted shale till he secured fresh foothold, then resumed the descent.

When he stood at last on the bottom, his palms were shredded and bleeding. He tore up his ragged neckerchief and knotted it around his hands in a way that would leave his fingers free. Afterward he started a long trek along the cliffs till he found a long-collapsed slide area where he could climb to the rim. Taking his bearings from the sun, he circled north, up and down one high ride after another, forging in a wide circle at a steady, grueling pace till he reached the canyon entrance where his mount had bolted. Hoping against hope that the Hornes hadn't picked the animal up, he began his search.

It was late afternoon when he found his horse grazing in a well grassed pocket. Staggering with weariness, Johnny carefully approached the animal, softly cursing him in a soothing, cajoling tone. He paused long enough to check the girth before dragging himself into the saddle and kicking the animal into motion. Now . . . find the cattle trail. Follow it out of the mountains.

Warn Mike Murphy.

CHAPTER FIFTEEN

It was well after dark when the lighted windows of the Tulare main house came into sight. Johnny approached the ranch layout from the rear, not wanting to be picked up by one of the crew or by a ranch dog. He had to see either Mike or Boze, and both might be on round-up now. But Nan would surely be home. . . . He cut through a night-shrouded grove, through a cavernous blackness pocked by scattered patches of dappled moonlight. His horse plodded with lowered head, its breath whistling, on its last legs, he knew. He wondered if his own rubbery limbs would take his weight. Hot food, coffee, a warm bed, swam tiredly through his mind.

He broke from the grove where it bordered a stone-floored patio at the back of the house, illumined by a soft spill of lamplight from windows and the open rear door.

He heard a soft, choked sob. Disbelievingly, he reined in and listened. A woman crying. Then he saw her, huddled alone on a stone bench in the shadows. Her startled face turned toward him. It was Nan Murphy; she lifted a hand to her mouth as if to smother a cry. Johnny realized that she didn't recognize him—small wonder. His drooping horse's once-groomed hide was fouled with dirty lather;

his clothes were stiff with dust, his body loose-limbed with exhaustion. A dirty growth of whiskers blurred his lower face below eyes that he knew were red-rimmed and glaring. He must be a hell of a sight.

He swung painfully down, croaking, "Me, Miss Murphy."

The small cry left her then, and he saw her sway forward, then she was close against him, sobbing into his shoulder. Johnny put his arms around her gingerly and awkwardly patted her back, trying to think of something to say. The clean fragrance of her hair filled his nostrils, and all he could think of was that he'd never thought to see this tough-minded girl with her defenses broken.

Suddenly she pulled back, and her voice was steady. "I'm sorry. I guess I was holding too much in. It just broke out—and then—seeing you—"

"Set me back a little," Johnny said lamely. "Never figured you for the cryin' type."

"Neither did I. The trouble in our family . . . I was worried about you. A lot of things."

"Something important Mr. Murphy has to hear."

"Sit down a minute. You're tuckered." Her hand on his arm guided him to the stone bench. Her breath sucked in swiftly as lamplight fell full on his face. "You've been hurt—and your hands—!"

Johnny felt his pulse quicken with the heightening awareness of this girl. She was wearing a simple calico that shaped her slim body, making her look soft and feminine. He edged uneasily away, not trusting himself. "Tell you about it later."

"What are you afraid of?"

He didn't answer. Her flesh lay warm against his arm. "Johnny," she whispered. He felt his throat thicken as he reached for her, felt her parted lips sigh against his before their mouths met, her pliant strength straining against his body.

They were breathless as they came apart. He said huskily, "No good. Forget it. It just happened."

"You don't believe that. Listen, Johnny Vano. I'm a bossy, aggressive female. I guess—after Mother died, there was something empty in me that dad couldn't fill. And that's why I tried to fill it another way, pretending it didn't exist. I never thought I'd feel like this about anyone. If I can, in spite of everything, then it's good, Johnny. It'll last. . . ."

She drew away with a shaky laugh. "I guess I've said enough for now. Mike and Boze came in off round-up for a hot supper. Boze rode on to town to fetch his best gun from the repair shop, but Mike's here. Let's see him."

Mike Murphy was in the parlor, relaxing with an after-supper cigar. He greeted Johnny with surprise and pleasure, afterward listening with deeper surprise to his story.

"So King is behind the operation," he mused. "It explains a number of things. If we can get the ranchers organized before those curly wolves come tonight, we'll spike their guns before they know what hit them. As soon as Boze gets back—"

Hoofbeats of a fast-coming rider hit the yard, and a moment later Boze charged breathlessly into the house. Seeing Johnny, he hauled up with a chagrined stared, saying, "Boy, you picked a hell of a time to ride in!"

"What is it, man," Mike snapped.

"Cap'n, I was drinking in the Alhambra when I heard the talk. Some of our crew were in town the other night, and a bartender overheard 'em talking about 'Billy Barnes,' how he came sudden to Tulare and left just as sudden."

"Should of warned 'em to keep it quiet," Mike grated.

"Too late now. They didn't know who Billy Barnes was. But Leo Shallis was in there, and he put two and two together and sent for Sheriff Wolfe. Wolfe got here tonight, and he's organizin' a posse of townsmen. They're like on their way here now. Wolfe'll want to question you. Even if we hide Johnny—''

Mike was already on his feet, reaching for his hat. "We won't be here. Something important's come up, Boze; tell you about it as we ride. Nan, you'll have to stall Wolfe. . . .''

It was after midnight when they reached the round-up camp. Mike Murphy assembled the ranchers and their crews and in hard, flat tones told them who Johnny was and what he'd been doing on their behalf. They accepted the news incredulously, many with outright suspicion.

But because all were basically men of action, they responded with alacrity when Mike called for volunteers. In addition to a reception committee for the Hornes, another group was dispatched in pairs to each valley ranch as a home guard, since there was no way of telling which ranches the rustlers would attempt to fire in order to draw off the herders.

The handiest approach from the Hornes' stronghold was a wide pass through the hilly country north of the bedgrounds. At a point where this pass broadened into a natural bowl, flanked by great slabs of rock and rank chokecherry thickets, Mike dispersed the cowmen. The strategy was simple: stationed in outflanking concealment, they could catch the rustlers in a blistering crossfire. Mike had little hope that it would tide over without gunplay; nevertheless, he warned no one to open fire till the Hornes had been given an opportunity to surrender.

Hours went by, and the cattlemen began to grumble about squatting here half the night on the word of an outlaw brat. Already the night was waning; shreds of gray rifted the eastern sky, the rim of mountains standing out starkly like a ridged black backbone. From the bedgrounds, the distant stirrings of a vast herd carried through the stillness.

A man grumbled nearby, "Wonder where'n hell Miles King and his boys are. Rode out before midnight hell-afire." The ranchers hadn't been told of King's alliance with the Hornes; it would overstrain their credulity.

Boze, positioned to Johnny's left, whispered, "Hist!"

Johnny listened, straining his ears to a sound of muffled hoofs, a creak of saddle leather. Now a spasm of movement in the dimness, a fitful gleam of rifle metal. Next the shadowy forms of riders, emerging like a body of gray ghosts out of a solid bank of darkness.

Mike eased to his feet, sucked a great breath into his lungs, and lifted his cupped hands to form a megaphone. His breath released in a bellow. "You, Hornes! You're surrounded by forty men with rifles! Give up, throw down your guns."

As the last word left Mike's lips, he dropped prone behind his rock. Instantly a shot smashed the silence, ripping air where he'd stood. It was as though the one had set off a fusillade. In the near-dark, it was difficult to place shots with accuracy, but the close-crowded riders made a massed target for ambush guns. Their demoralized return fire was futile; they couldn't break for cover without riding into the teeth of flying lead.

'Every man for himself! Scatter!" Old Jubal's stentorian roar lifted above the roll of gunfire. Johnny picked out his huge upper body straining low over his horse's withers as he wheeled and streaked back down the pass, a handful of others in his wake. He caught Jubal's back in his sights, then deliberately lowered them to the horse's haunches. He pulled trigger, saw the animal's hindquarters collapse. Those behind piled into it and went down in a tangle of harness, kicking horseflesh, and screaming men. Johnny saw at least two riders hurdle the squirming pile and vanish in the fast-graying darkness.

Some of the raiders were already flinging down their guns and throwing arms high in token of surrender. A small group had taken a stand behind a flint outcropping. But it left them inevitably exposed on one side to bullets which poured down like slanting hail.

"All right! Quit! We quit!" Garth Horne stepped away from the outcropping, both hands lifting his rifle above his head. Gunfire died away.

"Let's see all those hands high," Mike Murphy ordered, "and no guns in 'em." With the slow compliance of the raiders who could still raise a hand, the ranchers and their men moved from shelter and came forward to collect their prisoners. Men lay groaning on the ground, unable to stand. Others sprawled silent and grotesque.

Of the Hornes, Buck and old Jubal had not survived the ambush. Eli favored a leg broken in two places by bullets. Garth and Bije stood off to one side, supporting Eli between them, their faces tight-lipped and expressionless. They had made their gamble and had lost.

Boze, rifle snugged in the crook of his arm, fell into step beside Johnny. "Warbag's all laced up, looks like," he said. "No one bad hurt on our side. . . . King was with 'em, all right; we got some of his men."

Johnny came to a dead halt. "Not him?"

Boze grimly shook his head. "Few broke out of the trap. He must of been one."

CHAPTER SIXTEEN

King smashed his fist against his knee. How had they known? How *could* they have known? . . . No matter. It was finished. And at the moment, it was little matter to him if he escaped, only to live with a memory of defeat. Until it killed him. And it would kill him, for the inner, overbearing arrogance that was the mainstay of his life was the one thing that all his disillusioned cynicism had never destroyed in him, and now that had received its fatal blow.

With vicious intensity his thoughts veered to Mike Murphy. In a blink concentration of hatred, he fixed all the blame on Murphy. He'd recognized Murphy's voice, calling for a surrender, and it must have been he who'd set up the ambush. King's fingers caressed the cold steel of his pistol. Just one bullet could wipe out the shame in his mind. . . .

He started nervously as a lean figure approached through the mist. It was Tole Sayrs, returning from the summit of a rise where he'd gone to reconnoiter.

Sayrs hauled up before him, his lean, clownish face strangely placid. King felt an envious anger at the way the gunman thrived on danger, and it roughened his clipped query:

"Well?"

"I made out a body of riders movin' east," the Texan drawled. "Reckon that'll be the ranchers, headin' for Cedar Forks with their prisoners. Leaves the way open for us to clear out. But we better hustle. They'll be lookin' for you shortly."

"Not yet, Mr. Sayrs," King said softly, "not yet. First I have to kill a man."

Sayrs' eyebrows cocked quizzically. "Murphy?"

"Murphy . . . a simple matter to cut across country to Tulare headquarters—and wait for him there."

"A damn-fool matter, too," Sayrs grunted. "Allowin' for your feelin's, we'll do best to get while the way's open."

"Do as you please," King snapped. "But I'm also thinking of the Murphy women."

"Come again."

"His wife and daughter, you fool. They'll make prime hostages to see us safely out of the country."

Sayrs grinned toothily. "Sure."

King stood up, "Let's not waste time, then . . . wait!" He palmed up his gun and cocked it. "What's that?"

A shod hoof clinked on stone. A slow-pacing horseman took shape from the swirling mists. He stopped, a few yards away. "King?"

"It's Jesse Norcross," Sayrs said.

Norcross swung to the ground in a lithe movement and moved toward them. His reckless, chalk-white grin was genial, but his eyes held a hint of bridled viciousnes that kept King sharply on guard. "So you got away too," King said.

"Figured I'd stick with you, King, You know the country, I don't. You sort of got me into this . . . thought it'd be nice if you saw me out of it."

"You thought wrong, fellow," King said tightly. "I suggest you get on that horse and . . ."

"You do, eh?" Norcross's easy grin hardened as he moved back a step, his thumb caressing light along the worn leather of his gunbelt.

King said through set teeth, "Sayrs."

Norcross's eyes shuttled to the Texan. He said softly, "You sure you can take me, Tole?"

The gunman showed his small, icy smile. "Any time. But hell . . ." He shrugged one shoulder and looked at King. "Three guns're better'n two."

"All right, all right," King said impatiently. "But he'll ride with us under my orders."

"That's understood," Norcross grinned mockingly. . . .

The three of them hunkered in the timber above the Tulare ranch house, watching the front veranda. A body of townsmen sat in the yard, while a big, gray-haired man, one foot resting on the bottom step, talked to Nan Murphy. She wore a gray wrapper and leaned on a fluted porch column, her head shaking in quick negation to something the man had said.

"That's Sheriff Wolfe," King whispered. "Those men must be a posse . . . but what the hell are they doing here?"

At his elbow, Norcross said with an amused malice, "Maybe looking for you?"

King shook his head emphatically. "They couldn't know we'd come here . . . and the bunch that ambushed us were ranchers, not townsmen. They have to be after someone else."

The sheriff's voice, harshened and heavy, bore faintly up the slope: ". . . All right, Nan, I can't wait any longer.

But there's something fishy here. When Mike gets back,
you tell him to come in and see me, understand?''

He stumped angrily over to his horse, climbed labori-
ously into the saddle, and rode away with his posse. King
noticed only now that one man rode between two guards,
his hands lashed to the saddle horn, and he recognized one
of his own crew: the man who'd been dispatched to Tulare
to fire one or more buildings. Somehow, Murphy had
known of that phase of the plan, too, and had no doubt
planted men at all valley ranches to foil each would-be
arsonist. It was fresh fuel on King's smoldering fury. He
said thickly:

"We'll leave the horses here, work in on foot."

With Norcross and Sayrs close on his heels, he stumbled
down the slope, keeping a meager screen of timber between them and the house. At a hard run, they crossed the
yard that lay open to the veranda. King tramped up to the
door and banged on it with his gun-butt.

Nan Murphy opened it, her hand brushing back a straggling wisp of hair. The hand froze, her eyes widened in
shock as they rested on the gun thrust almost in her face.

"Move back," King snarled, "before I blow your head
off."

Nan pulled aside to let the three men shoulder past. She
faced King unflinchingly, saying coldly, "What do you
want?"

From the tail of his eye, King caught a movement in the
archway at the opposite end of the room. He swung his
gun toward it. Leonora stood there, hair spilling in an
ebony mass over the shirred collar of her quilted wrapper.
Her face was sleep-flushed, her lips sulky and pouting.
"What's all the—Mr. King! What are you—"

"Be quiet," King grated. He jerked his gun at the
horsehair-stuffed sofa. "Sit, both of you."

Nan obeyed, walking across the room with her chin high, and Leonora followed automatically, watching King with dazed eyes.

Norcross's light gaze flicked from one to the other, admiringly. "Nice." He chuckled. "No wonder you wanted to come here."

"Just shut up," King said shakingly. His rage dug in deeper at the unsteadiness of his voice. He glared at Nan. "What did Wolfe want?

"Don't you know?"

He took a step toward her, his gun lifting. "Don't bandy words, my girl. I want a straight answer."

"He was looking for Johnny Vano."

Vano! King's brain rocked with the words. Somehow, Vano must have survived that fall . . . and tipped off Murphy and the ranchers. No wonder they'd been able to intercept every facet of his scheme. "How'd you capture my man?"

"My father sent two men to guard the ranch. They took him."

"I see they did. And those two men?"

Her lips compressed, a twitch of contempt at the corner of her mouth. "You're safe, King. They left with the sheriff's posse."

King considered that. "Just how much," he said slowly, "does Wolfe know?"

"Nothing, except what I told him. That the man tried to fire our house, and that my father would tell him the rest of it when he was ready to." Nan smiled faintly, letting him see the full sum of her contempt. "I'm afraid it didn't satisfy him. He's liable to be back. You'd better make tracks, mister."

"Oh no," King said softly. "We're waiting. Right here. Till your old man comes."

He felt a savage satisfaction at the swift flare of alarm in her face. His words seemed to shock Leonora from her half-daze. She came quickly to her feet, putting out a faltering hand. "Mr. King, you can't—"

Something tension-born snapped inside King. He shifted his gun to his left hand; his right palm whipcracked across her face. "Don't tell me I can't!"

With a low cry, Leonora fell back onto the sofa. She stared up at him, whimpering softly as her fingers touched the thin line of blood from her lip.

Nan said very quietly, "There's your fine gentleman, Lee. A real man, too."

CHAPTER SEVENTEEN

As full, rose-gold daybreak tinted the sky, a loose-strung group of men dropped out of their saddles at the Tulare corrals. The other ranches' crews had stayed at the bedgrounds with the herd while Mike Murphy and his men formed a guard detail to escort the Hornes and the renegade Moon crew to Cedar Forks and Leo Shallis's lockup.

Leo hadn't been there; the old jailer he'd left in charge told them that Leo and Wolfe were on a search for an escaped prisoner. Deciding that this was as good a time as any to turn himself in, Johnny Vano had begun to speak up—but Boze had given him an elbow nudge and a quick shake of his head. Later, as they rode toward Tulare, Boze had said, "You wait. You're beat out. Give yourself a few days' rest at Tulare, then the boss and I'll ride in with you to see Wolfe. He can lock you up if he wants, but he'll sure-hell hear the straight of your story."

At the corrals the crew quickly off-saddled and headed for the bunkhouse to catch a few hours' sleep before returning to the routine of round-up. Mike, Boze, and Johnny tramped up toward the house.

"Presently," Mike was saying, "we'll take some men up to remove the Horne families, the women and children, from that valley. We'll drive our cattle out of the other valley . . . few charges of giant powder'll make certain no one uses them passes that way again.''

He glanced at Johnny. "Why so quiet, lad?''

"Trying to figure how to tell you something,'' Johnny said tonelessly.

A slow frown furrowed Murphy's face. "I think I know. Knew it when Nan and you came into the parlor last night. I know my daughter pretty well.''

"All right,'' Johnny said patiently.

A dry smile flicked the rancher's mouth. "Well, what more is there to say? I know my daughter too well to argue. If it's wrong, she'll have to find out for herself. You too.'' He paused, rather uneasily. "Just meant to say, you're both pretty young. Do an old man a favor, wait a while. Be sure. Do that?''

Johnny answered him bluntly. "All right, Mr. Murphy, but it won't change anything.''

Mike glanced at Boze's long, grinning face, then said humbly, "No, guess it won't. And I guess, at that, I ain't sorry.'' He hesitated. "You be good to her. She's all—'' He broke off then, saying gently, "I reckon you know, son.''

They reached the veranda and tramped onto it, self-consciously stamping dirt from their boots against womanly injunctions. Johnny's pulse quickened at the knowledge that in another moment he would see Nan. . . .

Mike reached for the doorknob; it turned before his hand closed on it: the door yanked open. A gun gleamed in the hand of the man who stood there. His urbane tones grated with an inheld tension. "Come in, by all means do, gentlemen.''

Like stunned automatons, the three men shuffled across the threshold, past Miles King who stepped back to let them enter, his gun on-cock and ready. Though it was full daylight now, a lamp burned unnoticed on a small table. Johnny felt a tug at his hip and half-turned to meet Jesse Norcross's flashing grin. Jesse rammed the six-shooter he'd lifted from Johnny's holster into his own belt, giving Johnny his old, cocky salute. "Howdy, tiger."

Jesse here!—with King. . . . Numbly, Johnny stumbled against the wall, propelled there by Jesse's rough-prodding gun in the small of his back. There was Tole Sayrs, too, lounging against the fireplace, one arm hooked over the mantelpiece, the other hanging loosely at his side. A cold twirly dangled from his lips; his ice-calm face showed nothing at all. He hadn't troubled to pull his gun, and Johnny, remembering Tole's ability with a sidearm, understood his composure. Even with his Colts in leather, Sayrs was the one to watch if gunplay started.

King took Mike's gun, and Boze's, and pushed them over beside Johnny. Johnny turned to face the entire room now, seeing Nan and Leonora huddled together on the divan. Nan seemed composed, her only mark of tension a restless movement of hands; she managed a smile for him. Likely she'd been comforting the older woman. The color was drained from Leonora's tear-streaked face. Johnny wondered narrowly if either girl had been manhandled: Leonora's lips looked cut and swollen.

Mike's blue-bright gaze ranged from his wife to King. He began thickly, "Damned divil, if you—"

"You'll do nothing," King said wickedly, his pistol centered on Mike's chest. "You're holding aces and eights right now. I'd hate to end it so soon—but I can. Any time."

Mike's weight, forward poised on the balls of his feet, settled back onto his heels, his breathing gusty and hard drawn.

"That's better. I'd hate to finish it now when I can watch you sweat a while. Time doesn't matter much, now. It did, of course. The sooner you were dead, the better. Later, as Tulare went under from continued rustling losses, your daughter and widow would be eager to sell out, cheap."

Boze cleared his throat gently, his voice surprisingly mild: "This Sayrs fella was to finish Mike?" Johnny glanced quickly at Boze, caught the foreman's eye fleetingly: Boze was stalling for time, and now Johnny sensed his unspoken message: You're younger and faster than me, son. Think of something, but think fast. When you make your play, make it good.

King grimaced, "I hired Tole for that purpose . . . a killing which would seem like an accident. The first chance we got. But when it came, Vano, there, saw through it." Moving on to Johnny, his eyes looked cruel, yellow-sheened by the lamplight. "Vano is too smart for his own good."

Boze persisted, "All along, you were really after Tulare?"

King laughed with an unsteady timbre and began pacing the room back and forth. ". . . Sure, but not solely for the ranch itself. Hell, I'm a gambler, not a cattleman. And no gambler ever played for higher stakes. The Hornes' mountain set-up tied in perfectly; with their help I could have kept hitting the lowland ranches indefinitely. My own problem was where to ship the cattle. Rutherford couldn't be risked, even with clever job of venting the stuff to my Moon brand and forging bills of sale, and I'd have to drive across this basin to get there.

"Railports to north and east are hundreds of miles away, across the ruggedest mountain terrain in the territory . . . out of the question. But Murphy's Pass, on Tulare's south range, cuts deep and wide through the bad country and would give me access to far southern railroad towns, where I could market without suspicion because the basin ranchers always drive to Rutherford, a lot nearer. From that strategic point I could bleed the basin dry.''

Boze nodded calmly. ''Ahuh. You had to have Tulare first . . . that's why the Hornes were hitting us nearly exclusive. Spliced in neat with their old grudge against Mike. You used them, they used you.''

King shrugged indifferently, looking restlessly away. Johnny sent a swift sidelong look at the still-burning lamp on its table: that might be the answer, if he could edge nearer.

''Still don't know how you learned about Johnny,'' Boze added.

King laughed. ''Why, Murphy's little idiot of a wife. Who else?''

Mike's face darkened with a lift of tidal blood. He took a step toward King, saying softly, ''You blackleg liar.''

''No, Mike,'' Leonora cried. ''It's true.''

''What!''

''I didn't mean . . . I didn't know. The other night, when King and I stepped into the kitchen, he asked about the reason for your calling an abrupt meeting. I knew you'd cautioned me not to breathe a word about Johnny Vano spying out the Hornes, but I was mad at Nan and I—I wasn't thinking. And I couldn't see the harm in telling King. He—he—''

''Yes,'' Nan interrupted, ''he seemed like such a gentleman. I'd badgered Lee about that . . . and I guess I'm as much to blame.''

''Touching,'' sneered King, ''this familial loyalty . . . very.''

Johnny shifted his feet with seeming restlessness, a side-stepping movement carrying him a foot nearer the lamp. Jesse lounged over and rammed his gun muzzle into Johnny's short ribs. "You act sort of skittish, tiger. Best stand easy. Wouldn't want you to keel over of heart failure before I do the job."

"You want to kill me, Jess?"

Bantering mockery fled Jesse's face, exchanged for a cold, killing hatred. "Still in the dark, are you? Still think it was Gorman who tipped off that bank job?"

Johnny's flesh chilled as though a wintry draft had swept the room. *"You?* You, Jess?"

"Me." Jesse's face pinched with a long-stored malignancy. "Sam Vano was rough on you, but he was groomin' you for the leadership. Heard him tell Bowie so, once. And Bowie was your friend. For me, nobody ever gave a damn, not ever. You know what my ma and pa was. The gang had got to be a habit, that's why I hadn't broke away before. Only that night before the job, when Sam hit me, that tied it. I was through, and I was goin' to make him and the damn' lot of you pay. When you and me was in Gorman's room, I planted the hunch in your head that he might cross us for the head money—so in case the ambush failed, the gang would put the blame on him. Later, when you were asleep, I sneaked out of the hotel and left a note under Wolfe's office door. Oh, make no mistake, Tiger . . . I'll enjoy killin' you."

"Don't talk, Norcross, do it," King put in harshly. He steadied his gun on Mike. "Tole, you take Hendryx."

Boze said in a tight, quick way. "Shots'll bring the whole crew up here on the run. You overplayed it, King."

"On the contrary. Our hostages will see us safely past your men."

"Hostages?"

"Why yes," King grinned tightly. "Our hostages will be our hostesses. What do you think of—"

"Why you damned—" It left Boze on an explosive breath. His lean body launched in a low-driving tackle at King. The man flinched back involuntarily, then pulled trigger. The gunshot, confined by four walls, crashed deafeningly. In mid-lunge, Boze was hammered back in a twisting fall.

Instantly, Johnny moved. With a cuffing swing of his arm he sent the lamp flying from the table, crashing in the center of the room. A reeking flood of kerosene sprayed over the carpet; a tiny flame caught, sent a broad sheet of flame ripping across the floor with a wildly diffused flare of brilliance.

Already Johnny was flinging himself sideways into the startled Jesse, hitting him solidly, grappling him around the waist, gun hand pinned to his hip. The impetus carried them both into the little table, and it gave under their weight and crashed to the floor with them, Johnny on top. Pinning Jesse's elbows with his knees, he yanked his own gun from Jesse's belt and clubbed the fisted weapon to his jaw. Jesse's muscles strung hard in brief protest, then went limp.

Johnny scrambled to his feet, pivoting to face the room. He saw that Mike Murphy must have moved almost as fast as himself, for he'd caught Miles King around the chest in a crushing bear-hug, the hand with the gun twisted up behind him at an agonizing angle, contorting King's face with wrenching pain. The two men swayed back and forth between Johnny and Tole Sayrs—the only thing, Johnny knew, which had kept Sayrs from gunning him as he was occupied with Jesse. That, and the high-leaping swath of flames which blocked Sayrs off, his back to the fireplace.

Then a violent heave of King's body carried him and Mike burgeoning away, crashing into the wall with an impact that shook the room. It cleared the space between

Sayrs and Johnny. The Texan's hand blurred down, slapped pistol grips and whipped to level. Automatically, smoothly, Johnny swung his gun up, thumbed the hammer and fired, aiming with his eyes. The recoil smacked the butt against his palm. Sayrs grunted in pained surprise, and started to reel forward. He got off a shot which slammed wide of its mark. Then he dropped his gun and toppled forward, straight-stiff as a felled pine, across the blazing carpet.

Johnny's gaze flicked on to Murphy and King. Two big men wrestling for a gun which sawed dangerously back and forth between them. Their struggles carried them in tussling, turning confusion across the room and back, making it impossible for Johnny to help Mike. Suddenly the gun exploded. Mike stumbled away, and Johnny saw that he held the gun. King was bending over, his fists doubled against his belly, an expression of utter disbelief filling his face, pulling his mouth into a lolling slackness. Then the face went blank and he dropped to his knees, pitched full length on his face.

Johnny caught a glimpse of Nan on her feet, her fists clenched at her sides, and he shouted hoarsely for her to stand aside as he reached a far wall, ripped up an edge of carpet and with a desperate heave of strength that carried the furniture before it, flung the end he held over the burning part, folding back on itself to smother the flame. Clouds of smoke mushroomed out, lifting pungently, blindingly, through the room. Coughing, tears streaming from his eyes, Johnny stumbled to the door and threw it open.

As he turned back inside he stopped cold.

Jesse had been playing possum. Watching his chance, he'd lunged to his feet and caught Nan, his arm bent in a choking hug around her throat, the muzzle of his gun pressed to her temple. Sweat beaded glisteningly on his face as he backed toward the archway leading to the dining room. Mike and Johnny stood rooted, helpless.

Johnny said huskily, "Give it up, Jess. You're done."

"Not yet, tiger . . . one more hand to fill."

He attained the archway, and for a moment lowered his gun to Johnny. "At least I can take you—" Nan gave a hard twist of her slim, wiry body; it carried them off balance. To keep his footing, Jesse, had to let go, flinging her aside with a sweep of his arm. Then he snapped a wide shot at Johnny, spinning on his heel as he fired and bounding like a cat through the archway. Johnny heard his pounding footfalls echo through the house, the back door slam.

There was a confused outbreak of yells and scattered shots across the yard. He saw the crew, some of them half-dressed, taking cover behind the corrals as they blazed away at the half-open doors of the stable.

Luke Mayerling turned his gaunt head as Johnny came up. "Heard shots," the old puncher said. "The lot of us came pilin' out of the bunkroom, saw this fella makin' for the timber. We cut him off, he run into the stables. Cornered there. . . . Say now, that shooting—"

"Everyone's all right," Johnny broke in to save talk. "Tell the boys to hold fire, Luke. I'll take him."

A sound of running feet brought Johnny around to face Nan Murphy. Breathlessly, she caught his arms. "Johnny, you've done enough. Don't—"

He shook his head like a ringy bull. "You hear me, Luke? Tell them to hold fire. This one belongs to me."

CHAPTER EIGHTEEN

The wild, ugly passion that boiled in him must have shown in his face because Nan pulled away from him, and stepped back. "Is this the way you'd planned to change, Johnny Vano?" she asked almost inaudibly. "You're not thinking now of bringing a criminal to justice. Only of shooting a man in revenge."

"Quit it," he said thickly, doggedly.

"Johnny, Johnny, don't you understand, even now? Making yourself over isn't only doing, it's feeling. If you kill a man for your reason, you'll be no better than a murderer!"

"The order, Luke."

Luke bawled a command, and the peppering of gunfire died. Johnny expected Nan to protest again, but now she held an almost condemning silence as he moved away, gun drawn, into the labyrinthian cross-hatching of corral poles which would give him partial shelter till he was close to the stable. He ducked low and started running down a narrow runway. It brought him to a cornerpost where the corrals ended. Across a narrow space beyond lay the stable, its door barely ajar.

He crouched by the post, watching the murky patch of

shadow between door and jamb, till his vision was spotty and aching. The sun slanted hot against his back. Was Jesse waiting just within the doorway, to put a bullet into whoever came after him? Breath held, he took a cautious step that exposed his shoulder and part of his arm. A purple-orange tongue of flame licked from the doorway. The bite of the bullet gnawed wood-shards from the post.

Johnny opened up, blasting at the muzzle-flash. He heard a rush of feet in the stable: he'd nicked or scared Jesse into retreating deeper into the building. Johnny lunged into the open, reached the door, kicked it wide with a sweep of his leg, and dived through, hitting the floor on his shoulder and rolling across the gangway, into a stall between two partitions. A pistol spoke from the shadows at the other end of the building. Johnny heard the slug boom into the planking: a high miss, and he knew that Jesse was shooting blind.

He sprawled on his belly, his face barely exposed around the edge of the partition. The cedar stock-plates of his gun lay warm and moist against his palm. A stir of wind banged the door shut, throwing the interior into almost complete gloom. Johnny's body jerked, nerve-strung with the sound, and slowly relaxed, constrained to waiting. Jesse and he were on level terms, each alone in the darkness, but Jesse was the cornered one; Jesse would break first, make the movement or sound that would give his enemy a target.

Though the stable was empty of animals, the rank smell of manure filled his nose suffocatingly. A familiar smell, but heavy and nauseating, here on the dank stable floor. *Watch*, he thought. *Watch, and don't think about it.*

About what, then? What Nan had said? All right, he had to face it. But how, how could a man shed the harsh lessons, the warped, deep-rutted feeling-values of a life-time in a few short weeks? Always in his past, there had been only the code of the gang, the law of any wolf-pack. An eye for an eye. But a man has a choice, Sam Vano, dying, had said. Johnny had ignored it then, and a thirst for vengeance had led to the killing of Emmett Gorman. Nan had said it another way: *Making yourself over isn't only doing, it's feeling.*

Restlessness needled him; he steadied with an iron effort. Jesse had more patience than he'd credited him for. How many loads remained in Norcross's gun? He hadn't had time to reload, and he couldn't do so now without making a giveaway noise. He'd fired three times at Johnny. Three expended shells that Johnny knew of, perhaps more. Assume an empty sixth chamber.

Give him a maximum of two shots, then. Make him use those and you've got him. With infinite care, Johnny pulled himself into a crouch, unfastened one of his spurs. An underhand toss sailed it down the gangway. It made a clear, metallic *chink*. Jesse's nerves must have been strained to breaking; he blasted away wildly, firing twice before the futile click of hammer on an empty chamber.

Johnny stood, but didn't stir from his small niche. "Five shots, Jesse. Throw your gun out, you follow. Or I come after you shooting."

Dead, oppressive silence to which Johnny listened uneasily. It was a reaction unlike Jesse. He might have cursed, wept . . . anything but this.

Then, softly, but with a note of harried desperation: "Here it comes, tiger." The gun skidded down the clay floor of the gangway and stopped in a bar of sunlight from a crack in the warped siding. Johnny gave it a spare glance and said grimly, "Come ahead now, Jess."

He caught the tracery of a shadow inching forward, and waited till a faint glint touched gun-metal at midheight on the shadow, snugged in half-concealment against its hip.

Johnny tilted his gun a bare degree to the left, and sent his shot thundering off. The shadow screamed; the gun it held spewed flame into the floor. Then the shadow was gone, and it took a few seconds for Johnny to see that it had dissolved onto the floor.

Guided by the downed man's groans, Johnny moved to his side, gun held ready while he located a match with his left hand, snapped it alight on his thumbnail. The saffron flare showed Jesse on his back, eyes glazed with pain, his hand twisted in his bloody shirtfront: Johnny knew without looking that his shot had only scraped the ribs. A double-barrel pocket pistol, small enough to be concealed in boot or shirtsleeve, lay by Jesse's arm. Johnny murmured, "Crooked hand straight to the last deal, eh, Jess?" as he kicked the little pistol across the gangway, sheathed his gun, and blew out the match.

He bent over, slung Norcross's arm over his shoulder and steadied him to his feet, supporting the groaning, feebly struggling man to the door, which he nudged open with his foot. As they emerged into the glaring sunlight, the crew surged forward, and with them, Johnny saw, lumbered the rolling bear-shape of Sheriff Wolfe. But Nan, running as lightly as a young boy, was the first to reach him.

He pushed Norcross into the arms of the crew and turned to her. "It's over, Nan," he said wearily, "it's over, and I didn't kill him." She leaned against him with a sob of relief.

Wolfe came up, pale eyes snapping below his bristling scowl. Leo Shallis was at his side, with Mike Murphy following, his broad face deeply calm. The sheriff grabbed Norcross's wrists and clamped on handcuffs, and then, glaring at Johnny, snapped his fingers at his deputy. "Loan me your cuffs, Leo."

"You won't need 'em," Mike said softly. "Not for Johnny."

The sheriff drew a long, sighing breath, as though fighting for self-restraint. His face looked nearly apoplectic. "What the hell," he got out, "*is* this? You been protecting Vano—unless Boze gave him a hand last night on his own account, and I doubt that. When I questioned Nan, a while ago, she was too damned evasive to suit me. That's why I came back. So kindly tell me just what the hell's going on."

Mike smiled wearily. "Come on to the house. I won't tell you, I'll show you. . . .

An hour later, Leonard Wolfe was striding up and down the front room, a touch of buoyant elation in his step, his craggy face more than mollified: he'd heard out Mike and Johnny and even Boze, who, conscious now on the sofa, had insisted on adding his bit in a shaky but strong voice. Sam Vano's death was confirmed, the last of his gang rounded up. The Hornes were jailed, awaiting trial. In a wagon outside lay the tarp covered bodies of King and Sayrs, and Jesse Norcross, his torso swathed in bandages, sat beside them handcuffed to the tailgate.

Mike, sitting at his ease by the fireplace, was saying, "Johnny understands he's got to stand trial for shooting that bank clerk up in Rutherford, Lenny. But there was an exonerating fact or two I think you should know. . . ."

Wolfe, hands clasped at his back, swung his gaze onto Johnny and Nan, standing self-consciously by the door. "Yeah. I know. Gorman lived a while. Confessed everything to accredited witnesses before he died. Among other things, that you shot him in defense."

Even in the overwhelming sense of relief he felt, Johnny could not ignore another nagging guilt with which he'd lived these many weeks. Hesitantly, he said, "The little kid Sam rode down . . . it true she'll never walk again?"

"Afraid so, son. Operation by a specialist would turn the trick, but her folks ain't got that kind of money."

Johnny let out a shuddering breath. "I'd given ten years of my life if I could set that right."

"Let's say, all your life," Mike murmured, somberly, but his tight-set lips struggled with a smile. "You'll serve out the sentence right here." At Johnny's bewildered look, Mike grinned, "I'll pay for the operation . . . a sort of jump-the-gun wedding present."

Wolfe reached for his hat on the mantelpiece, saying, "Better get our prisoner to town. Come on, Leo." Shallis grunted to his feet and waddled after him.

Johnny stepped squarely in front of the sheriff as he started past, saying flatly, "You'll be wanting me."

"No hurry, son. Come in when you're ready." He winked soberly. "If anyone asks, I didn't know you."

Mike called after them, "Send Doc Stone out to look at Boze."

"I'll send him back with your wagon." Wolfe followed Shallis onto the high, creaking wagon seat; Shallis took up the reins and shouted the team into motion.

Mike came to his feet and walked to Leonora who was wiping Boze's perspiring face with a damp cloth. She'd been in a state of half-shock for some minutes after the violence had ended, then had roused herself silently and without a word had helped Nan dress Boze's shoulder wound.

"Lee," he said awkwardly.

She looked away from him. "Don't say it, Mike." Her words were low, toneless with a husky remorse. "Mr. Vano was almost killed because I acted like a sulky school-girl. Anything you could say wouldn't say the half of it."

"Lee," Mike said gently, turning her to face him. "You're my wife. We have a duty to understand each other, not condemn. Reckon we can start with that."

"Mike." Her eyes radiant through tears, the old, sulky discontent gone, made Leonora really beautiful, then.

This Johnny Vano noticed in passing. He drew Nan out onto the porch, then, aware of his ragged, filthy condition, let his hand fall self-consciously. Through a haze of exhaustion he considered all that he wanted to tell her, and could not think how to begin.

"So much has happened," she said in a hushed voice. "I wonder if we can forget it."

"Maybe," he said, searching for his words, "we'll be the better for remembering, all of us." He looked at her obliquely. "Your dad wants us to wait. Be sure, he says."

A mocking little smile touched her mouth. "You're not sure, Johnny?"

"Sure I'm sure. I just—"

"Why, then, that's all we need," Nan murmured, and came into his arms.

BITTER GRASS

AUTHOR'S NOTE

Frontier historians, professional and amateur, will recognize *Bitter Grass* as being in large part a highly fictionalized account of the career of Isom Prentice "Print" Olive, a real-life pioneer cattleman of Texas and Nebraska. With a few exceptions—most notably Alex McKenna—the key characters are drawn from life to one degree or another, as is much of the narrative.

However, because my characterization of actual personalities is imaginary, because many of the events are either fictitious or based only slightly on fact, and because the chronological sprawl of a single career has been here compressed into a ten-year period, I have assigned fictional names to most places and all but a handful of historical persons mentioned (i.e., McCoy, Hickok, Shanghai Pierce).

While the vigorous and violent public (but not private) life of the real "Print" Olive is paralleled very closely by that of the fictional Jonathan "Buck" Trask, no aspect of this book should be regarded as the author's opinion of "how it might have been." *Bitter Grass* is a novel, not a speculative work. Both fact and speculation—and two diametrically opposed viewpoints—on the character of "Print" Olive are abundantly presented in Harry E. Chrisman's *The Ladder Of Rivers* and Mari Sandoz's *The Cattlemen,* to which I refer the curious reader.

T.V.O.

I

ALEX McKENNA PAUSED in his restless circling
of the small, grubby orderly room, halting by a window.
He looked out on a bare stretch of dirt compound and,
beyond that, the palisaded wall of a military stockade. Hot
sunlight slatted through the flyblown glass against his face
as, hands clasped at his back, he held his eyes on the
stockade's south gate, curbing a vast impatience. *Four years,*
he thought, *and two of them in this place.* A man was
bound to be changed, even a man like Jonathan Trask.

The prison superintendent's orderly, sprawled in his chair,
watched him with a brash, amused impudence. "Pick up that
leg in the war, Red?"

Alex glanced at the speaker. He was a callow young
weed wearing a corporal's chevrons on his neat tunic, and
Alex easily hid his annoyance which stemmed not from the
reference to leg, after all, but to his hair. There were things
a man learned to live with, and a gimpy right leg was one.

Stiff only from the knee down, its limp was not too noticeable unless he was tired and used up, as he was now.

In most other ways Alex McKenna made hardly an impressive figure. At twenty-two, he stood perhaps six inches above five feet, and he was slight. One might think frail, but his light body was trim with wiry muscle; except for his limp his movements held a spare, relaxed grace. His dark suit was shabby and ill-cut, seedy and stained from days of stage travel, with a rumpled, slept-in look. The only memorable detail of his appearance besides the limp was his hair, thick and bright red, which burred out from beneath his hat in shaggy fantails. His face was thin and angular, its freckles almost lost in a deep weatherburn, and was slurred by a week's growth of fiery whiskers. His eyes were a deep shade of blue that easily took on an engaging if wry twinkle, and his strong Scot's jaw thrust out to a slight forward cant of his head and held a latent stubbornness.

Without reply now, he eyed the immaculate corporal long enough to make his brash grin turn stiff and waxy. Then gave a pleasant answer: "No, not in the war."

"You borned with it?"

"No."

Swinging back to the window, he left the corporal with his mouth foolishly open. A couple of sentries were dragging open the south gate of the stockade, and now three men came out. One was a blue-clad trooper, his rifle shouldered, stepping behind a gaunt, bearded man in ragged homespuns who towered inches above him. Ahead of them marched the paunchy prison super, Captain Bissell.

Jonathan, Alex thought. *My Lord.*

The corporal had come to stand by Alex' shoulder, peering out too. He clucked his tongue mildly. "Boiled-looking, ain't he? Been in The Box, you can tell. That's a dingus the Cap'n thought up his own self. It is like a coffin, sort of, only made of steel with the lid punched full of holes so's the air can get in. Sun too. 'Long about midday a body locked inside starts roasting to a turn. After a day in that, a man ain't got the juices left for kicking up a ruckus, I tell you."

"Shut up." Alex spoke without thinking; he realized that his jaw was knotted with strain. The corporal chuckled agreeably and went back to his desk.

Jonathan was walking like a man in a trance, placing his stiff-legged steps with care; the fingers of his hands were splayed by his thighs as if he were slightly groping at each stride. The captain walked heavily slow, yet twice Jonathan stumbled and nearly fell. But his back was ramrod-straight and his head was high, and Alex thought, *No saying yet whether there is change, but you know for sure what is still there.*

Captain Bissell came through the door now, then Jonathan, and Alex turned from the window to see his face. Jonathan stood tall in the small room; somehow he filled it and washed out any other presence. His ink-black hair was long and matted; his clothes were grimy rags that showed patches of sunburned dirty skin, and the prison reek of unwashed bodies and offal and sickness made a quiet poison in the close room. His face had a red, broiled look; so did his large, big-knuckled hands, and he kept flexing the fingers. His pale gray eyes were slitted and blinking between swollen lids, for coming into the sudden gloom had almost blinded him.

"Jonathan." Alex' tongue felt thick and strange around the name, and he did not expect the quick recognition that came. He was standing in shadow well to Jonathan's right so that the big man had not noticed him on entering.

"Alex. My God, that really you, boy? Why, you red-headed ol' squirt! Alex—!"

Jonathan's black scrub of beard split to his grin as he started for Alex McKenna, but the guard brought him to a rough halt with a rifle barrel across the belly.

Captain Bissell said with a savage officiousness, "You can talk with him here." The captain was a red-faced turkey

cock of a man, short and rotund, who kept hitching up his
sagging belt for comfort. The heavy saber he wore as a
wistful badge of dignity persisted in banging against nearly
everything. "The guard will remain with you. Perkins, come
in here," the captain said, and wheeled heavily into his
office, his saber clanking on the doorjamb, followed by the
orderly.

The guard put his back against the wall, his rifle up, and
Jonathan grinned at Alex and raised his sun-raw hands.
"Don't mind if I don't shake hands. Mine ain't in much
shape."

The room was innocent of furniture except for the orderly's battered table-desk and two chairs. They sat, Jonathan saying quietly, "Hey, boy. God, it's good to see your
ugly face. How is everyone? You heard?"

"Haven't you?"

"Not in a good four months." Jonathan scowled at his
hands delicately palm-flat on the scarred table. "Any way
that bastard super can make life hell for reb prisoners, he
does, and maybe the best way he come up with was
cutting off all word from their families a spell back." His
somber eyes coalesced with little kindling lights as he leaned
forward. "Mercy. How is she, boy? You ever hear that?"

"Mercy?"

"Mercy Killgrew." Impatience came like a shadow and
darkened his gaze. "What about her? Is something happened?"

Alex said slowly, "She's well, last I heard," and thinking,
*Mercy Killgrew. Then he doesn't know. But that was way
before his mail was cut off . . . so they never told him.
Should I, now?*

Thoughtfully he studied Jonathan's face, as if seeking his
answer there. He remembered the last time he had seen
this face, on that June morning when the Matheson County
Company of Volunteers had set out from Katytown, the
county seat, for San Antonio and service in the Army of
the Confederacy. A brave sight in their rough homespuns

and cowhide boots, yet wearing a rakish air with their colorful cow-hunt hats and flanked by their nattily uniformed officers and flagbearers. And Alex remembered standing in the crowd of cheering Texans with the Trask family and watching Jonathan's broad laughing face, smooth with youth and full of the great bursting exuberance of his nature, waving them goodbye with a sweep of his old hat which, though he was only nineteen, had borne the colors of ten years' service in the cow hunts. Beside him the thin, serious face of his brother Paul who at eighteen had been the only one of the three remaining Trask boys old enough for service. And the undisguised lo~~~g in the face of fierce, righteous Gideon Trask, the father, chafing to join them and restrained not by his fifty-eight years but by fortune's hostages of an ailing wife and two young sons.

But four more years and what seemed like another life lay between that morning and today. And that Jonathan had been a smooth-faced boy; this was a man, seasoned by maturity and war. His brow was high and strong above eyes like jagged black pebbles. His nose curved in a craggy beak to a fierce black bristle of beard blurring a bellicose jut of jaw that swept into a short, powerful neck and gaunt, sloping shoulders ridged with heavy muscle. Only his mouth was clearly defined, the long lower lip holding a surprisingly sensitive pout. Paul had the identical tremulous droop to his mouth, but it exactly fitted Paul's morbid, sensitized nature. In Jonathan this hint as of some obscure raw nerve in his personality had always seemed incongruous. Behind all this, his vital and volatile nature seemed to bubble as ever, undimmed by war or prison. He looked older and harder, and no other change was discernible.

Alex roused himself sharply, thinking, *Get on with it*, and took from his pocket the two documents he had carried across half the country, laying them on the table.

"What's those?"

"One is a special order for your release. The other is a

standard military parole slip." Again Jonathan's face darkened, but Alex raised his hand. "Hold up. I know about all that. But your ma could be dying. Mercy said so in a letter to me. I went to a sight of trouble getting this order so I could fetch you alóng on my way home."

Jonathan's glance burned steadily on him. "Could be another false alarm."

"It could be," Alex conceded. 'Liza Trask had been sickly and periodically invalided for many years; the family had long been resigned to the knowledge that any one of her recurring "attacks" might be the final one.

Knowing this, Alex could sense Jonathan's bitter hesitation, but Trask's next words veered the subject with a hard intensity. He dipped his shaggy head at the papers. "How you come by a Yankee army order?"

Alex exhaled a light sigh. "You know I headed North after you left—just before hostilities commenced?"

"I had the news. Said you was going to Boston, to this Harvard. I never did understand it."

"The law was always my big interest. You knew that, Buck."

Jonathan's grin twitched to faint life at the old nickname; then his eyes were pale frost again. "It's the notion of a Texan sitting out the whole war in the enemy camp that rankles me. We're friends, boy, which is why I'm trying to understand this."

Alex was nettled by the conversation's turn. To him, all militant patriotism had always been a childish bravado. Only his stiff limb had spared him a lifetime of maintaining the tiring façade of being indistinguishably a Southerner and a Texan and a Man. Behind all the weighty rationalizations, men hewed to their political opinions for reasons of quite mindless personal or regional sentiment. If not, the vast majorities of each side would not mechanically ally themselves to the prevailing banners. War seemed the consummate stupidity; so few were guiltless. He said slowly,

"I don't see I feel much different about Texas than you, for a maybe."

"You was against the war as I recall."

"I'm against all war is why, but that doesn't change a man's feeling for his home. Look. The South has few arms-making facilities, right? A lot of the weapons your troops used were taken off dead or captured Yankees. Did you object to using Yankee facilities to fight for Texas? Then why object when I turn their means to the benefit of Texas?"

"I don't follow that, boy."

"Buck, the war's all but over. A matter of days. Lee can't break out of Richmond, and he is outnumbered better than two to one. They have won for sure, and they will be disposed to crow on one hand and bear down rough on the other. A pair of pills we'll have to swallow, bitter or not. Your way can't help Texas any more, if it ever did. She is whipped and belly-down, and setting her up proud for good and all will take knowledge and industry, not bullets and bravado. I've always believed that; it's why I went North, it's why I'm coming back with a law diploma in my possible sack."

Jonathan's gaze stayed flinty and remote. "And a Yankee milit: order. Don't forget that."

"I was coming to it. I had graduated from the law school at mid-term, but was staying on as an instructor of prep courses when Mercy's letter arrived. I wanted to leave right away for Texas, but thought I might obtain your release. I have a friend—we roomed together as underclassmates—whose father is high in the War Department. When I had explained the circumstances, that a man had to see his dying mother, my friend's father agreed to use his influence. In a couple of days, this order which officially renews your parole offer was in my hands."

Jonathan nodded gently. "Made yourself some Yankee friends, did you?"

Alex, keeping a rein on his prickly Scot's temper, said evenly, "That was a mistake, those Yankee friends.

Otherwise I could have let you rot in this place while your mother is breathing her last."

"Sorry, boy. Sorry for that."

Jonathan rose ponderously to his feet, which brought the guard alert, watching, as he moved to the open window. The prison stockade was a little distance off, a squat and ugly scab on a land fresh with the emerald glow of spring. Beyond this, the Illinois countryside rolled under a bright young sun; the warm and silky breeze that pressed through the room smelled of growing things. Jonathan hunched his shoulders, and Alex sensed the aching, nameless need in a saddle-raised man, after two years of confinement and unbearable stenches, for the taste of open country and clean air.

Without looking around, Jonathan began to talk in a kind of grinding, savage undertone that was like cursing except for the words. Alex knew some of what he told: that through the early part of the war, Jonathan had fought with the 2nd Texas Infantry at Shiloh, Iuka, Farmington and in a dozen lesser skirmishes. It was at Shiloh by Pittsburg Landing that, hearing the wounded Paul calling his name, he had run out under fire to carry the younger Trask to safety. Paul's arm had been smashed and after surviving a butchery of amputation, he was invalided home.

Then the siege of Vicksburg, when Jonathan himself had taken a Minié ball. He was unconscious through most of the battle, and when he woke in a field hospital the color of the surgeon's uniform told him that Vicksburg had fallen. He had had no contact with his regiment after that, no news of how his comrades had fared, and not till he was on the mend had he learned that he alone of the Confederate prisoners was refusing parole. Hearing that the 2nd Texas was reorganizing its shattered ranks at Galveston, he had hoped to escape and join them, but had not succeeded then or later, after being shipped to Centralia prison in Illinois.

Alex put in mildly, "As I have it, all the rebel prisoners

taken at Vicksburg in '63 were offered parole." He tapped his finger on the oblong paper beside the military order. "Didn't they ask you to sign a parole slip like this one?"

"Make my mark." Jonathan barely glanced at the slip. "You know I can't write. Read either. Does it say like the one a Yankee officer read off at Vicksburg? About them terms of . . . of capitulation?"

Alex raised his brows and picked up the paper, reading aloud: " '. . . give this my solemn parole under oath—that I will not take up arms against the United States, nor serve in any military or constabulary force in any fort, garrison or field work held by the Confederate States of America against the United States of America, nor as guard of prisoners, depots or stores, nor discharge any duties usually performed by officers or soldiers against the United States of America until duly exchanged by the proper authorities.' "

"God damn it, boy." Abruptly Jonathan swung from the window, sweeping his fingers through his matted hair. "That don't leave a man fixed but to swat flies and wish Yankees dead. Fancy ain't fighting, and I didn't hone on signing that away. Meant to bide my time and bust out of this Christ-bitten hole. I give myself a vow I wouldn't take no Yankee parole while Texas was fighting Yankees. Well, they're fighting on now, beat or not."

Almost Alex could smile at that. For if he did not understand why a man would accept the soul-destroying hell of a military prison to make his point with himself alone, he understood Jonathan Trask only too well. Even when they were boys, it had been just so: once Jonathan set himself to any goal, big or little, he would pursue it at all costs, with a savage and insensate determination.

After a moment, though, Alex said only, "Forget your damned pride for once. You've made your point, and the fighting's nearly ended. A week or two more, what does that matter?" More gently he added, "Buck, you would not forgive youself if she dies now and you could have been there."

"Could be it'll turn out another false alarm," Jonathan muttered again, then: "No easier on you, eh, boy? She's 'most as much ma as you ever known, too."

Alex only nodded. Whenever he thought of what he owed Gideon and 'Liza and the other Trasks, words became inadequate and puerile. There was an irony in this, since over the past four years he had set out to expunge the backcountry from his speech, to master the spoken and written word. Yet all the intensity he had applied to his law studies had been toward the end of bending his wit and learning to the service of the people who had made him one of their own.

Jonathan said glumly now, "You knew how this had to go, boy," and stridently lifted his voice: "*Yankee!*"

Captain Bissell exited from his office almost at once, then hauled up with a cold and breathless glare. Jonathan drawled, "Bet the old stockade won't seem the same without me around, Cap'n."

With a wild and harried dignity, Captain Bissell strode to the table, his saber banging on its leg, and glanced at the documents which he had already perused thoroughly. He said as if the words had a bad taste, "All he has to do is sign this parole slip in my presence. I'd say you know some important people, Mr. McKenna."

"Let's say a friend has an important friend," Alex said coldly. "I'm not too conversant with military law, Captain, or I would quote the letter of whatever covers brutality to prisoners of war."

"Brutality—?" Bissell's jowlish jaw sagged and then snapped like a trap. "Damn it, sir! This unregenerate ruffian went out of his way to make a damned nuisance of himself— sabotaging discipline, instigating riots, organizing prison breaks. Why, he tried an even dozen times to break out and succeeded twice, only to be run down by guards and dogs. He forced me repeatedly to inflict the most drastic punishments—and when I did, he *laughed* at me—"

Captain Bissell was floundering in his raging catalogue of Jonathan's sins; and now Jonathan chuckled, a sound full-throated and rolling and hearty. He stood high and spraddle-legged and somehow indomitable in his rags and filth. The captain blanched faintly; his jowls shook. He had done his worst, in a place already befouled by privation and disease and near-starvation, to break this man who would not break.

"Aw shoot, Cap'n. . . ." Jonathan sounded at once good-natured and gently sly. "You-all got to make it down to Texas one time, y'hear? Damned if I don't hone to show you some grand ol' Secesh hospitality."

Older and harder and essentially unchanged: this was Jonathan Trask, laughing away a two-years' experience that should have destroyed him inside and out, spirit and body. But then the real acid test for him still lay ahead, Alex knew, as surely as he knew the depth of Jonathan's love for Mercy Killgrew. Knowing too what Jonathan did not: that for well over a year, Mercy had been married to Paul Trask, the brother whose life Jonathan had saved at Shiloh.

II

ALEX' SMALL HOARD of Yankee gold and greenbacks outfitted them with a couple of tough and rangy nags that were short on looks but to a horseman's trained eye long-stayers, and two scarred and serviceable saddles. A quantity of dried foods, a few utensils, and two good secondhand

Sharps rifles and two Navy Colts completed their equipment. In addition Alex changed his suit, and Jonathan his prison rags, for a cotton shirt, sturdy kersey trousers, a slouch hat, and a pair of stout boots for each.

The two of them made good time as they followed the thaw-rutted roads into Missouri. Here the Yankee patrols were out in force, cleaning up pockets of resistance, the guerrilla bands of Redlegs and Jayhawkers. More than once Jonathan and Alex were halted on the road and forced to produce identification. Jonathan's parole slip was always enough to pass him. From one such patrol they got the only several-days-old news of the surrender at Appomattox. And it was really over. . . .

Ahead lay a homecoming that a man might well wish to put off, a dying woman who was mother to one, foster-mother to the other. Ahead too lay a defeated and impoverished land. But that land was Texas, and for all their somber thoughts a high anticipation gripped them. They talked to while away the hours; they renewed an old strange bond of friendship that was not forgotten, but blurred around the edges.

And finally home was near: the familiar shaggy sedgegrass prairies of the Yegua country; the groves of pecan trees and liveoak; the ancient buffalo wallows filled by the spring rains where the thousands of wild ducks and curlews and whooping cranes from the Dakotas and Canada wintered. Here were the lonely creek bottoms where as boys they had hunted red squirrels and quail, deer and wild turkey, and the maned giant "lofer" wolves; where they had wetted lines in pooling backwaters full of catfish and bream and perch; where occasional alligators still basked in the sun; where wild longhorns ran the brush as always, but seemingly wilder than ever.

Beyond the West Yegua Creek crossing, as they neared the Brushy Creek and home, Alex was wondering, *Should I tell him about Mercy and Paul now?* It might be kinder to prepare him. Alex briefly chased that ragged impulse and

152

let it die unheeded as Jonathan pointed at a prairie island, a liveoak motte isolated to the west. "Remember that, boy? Pa found you hard by there."

Actually he had been barely old enough to remember, but it was a day that Alex McKenna would never forget. . . .

His father, Rob McKenna, had been a Scotch-Irish immigrant whose wanderings had brought him into the piney woods of northern Louisiana, where he had married and quickly produced a sizable family. His thirst for wild and wide-open places was whetted by a talk with a footloose plainsman fresh out of Texas, and in the spring of 1849 the McKennas had pulled up stakes and, looking for a place to settle, had followed the San Antonio Road to the River Colorado and swung north toward the Yeguá Creek country.

They had made night camp at the edge of a grove not far from the creek when six-year-old Alex, off playing in the trees, had heard a commotion. He remembered running toward the camp and falling, his head striking a root, and then for a long time, nothing at all. Coming to, he had found the charred, smoking wreckage of the wagon, the slaughtered oxen, the butchered bodies of his family, father and mother, three sisters and a baby brother. Then a time of blank and muddy shock.

Gideon Trask and his *vaqueros*, attracted by the smoke, found him the next day. After a simple burial and service, Gideon had brought the shock-silent boy home to his ranch on the Brushy. Later it was learned that a half-dozen drunken Comanches had committed the massacre.

The slow, healing weeks as his mind gradually returned from some dark and withdrawn place were an uncertain blur in his memory. Yet here and there he could find patches of vivid remembrance. There were only two Trask sons then, Jonathan being the older by a year and Paul of an age with Alex. He and the younger Trask brother had been friendly almost from the first; it was Paul whose shy, moody ways had struck some kindred spark, and Paul's friendship, as much as the kindness of 'Liza Trask, then heavy with her third child, her warm heart overflowing with more affection than she could lavish on a husband and two sons, had drawn the orphaned Alex into the Trask circle. Gideon, by native manner brusque and austere, was harder to know, but he had treated Alex exactly like one of his sons.

Jonathan was the unreachable one, though he alone of the Trasks had been boisterous and outgoing. The antagonism between him and Alex had never approached hatred or even strong dislike, yet there had been from the first a perplexing, almost instinctive friction. It was like the stiff-backed sidling and sniffing out of two stranger dogs trying to get each other's measure and finding only the chasm that lies between two inherently opposed personalities.

Jonathan had been big and heavy for his years; often and superciliously and quite deliberately, whenever there was no danger of being caught out, he would lay for the slight, bony Alex and provoke him to fights by giving orders which Alex would never obey. He was sly enough never to leave a bruise where it would show, and Alex would never tattle. Always he had fought back with an insensate stubbornness, silent and tearless and tight-lipped, till he was too licked to continue. (Oddly, in this way alone they were alike, and the fact of meeting his stubborn match may have been a red goad to Jonathan, Alex often thought.)

Still, in spite of personalities and a bad beginning, they had become friends. All because of one event in a single day, another day that would always stick fast with Alex McKenna.

The Yegua cow and mustang hunters always rendezvoused at Jim Killgrew's place, located centrally between the Brushy and Yegua creeks. Here they had sunk hardwood posts, lashing them together with rawhide to form big holding corrals. The native longhorns were hell to catch, and hunting them for beef and hides presented little less difficulty. In open country it was almost impossible to get within musket range of these wild cattle, while they were airily at home in the brush. But they provided the main source of meat and, just as important, tallow, and the tough hides which furnished the settlers with everything from *chaparejo* pants to chairseat lacings.

The Trask boys and Alex were participating in the cow hunts before they turned ten, and after a couple years' apprenticeship each was expected to carry a grown man's workload. Paul had nurtured a sullen discontent, for he never did take suitably to range work. Alex, though, had liked the color and excitement of the hunts, and had made up in determination and drive what he lacked in size and strength.

But it was Jonathan who seemed most in his proper element, as much as a duck on water. By the age of eight he had the job of leading the "bell mare," a tote horse that carried all the gear of the cowhunters. By eleven he was popping the wildest *cimaronnes* out of the worst brush, catching and tying like a seasoned hand. He could toss a tight swift loop over a brushrunner's muzzle and one horn, or over a heel, with equal facility. He also used his increased status to bully Alex, who now led the bell mare. In addition to toting gear, the animal provided a gathering point at meals and night camp for the scattered hunters, a row of tin cups strong on its rope being rattled in summons. Jonathan would mercilessly keep him ringing the primitive "bell" until Alex thought his aching arm would fall off.

About this time Jonathan had learned a game called *colear* from the Mexican *vaqueros* who outnumbered the Anglos on the hunt crews. *Colear* was running your horse alongside a bolting longhorn, getting a hold on the animal's tail and taking a swift single dally around the flat saddle horn, then heading off at right angles so that the cow was flipped off its feet in full stride. It was a practice sternly discouraged by Gideon, as too many cattle were lost to broken legs and snapped vertabrae. However Jonathan, undaunted, would often tackle the reckless game when he was alone or only Paul or Alex were around to see.

This was the case on one day during the spring of 1854, when Alex was eleven and Jonathan just turned twelve.

The year's first hunt was almost over, and the bulk of the district cowhunters were engaged in hazing their catches to the Killgrew corrals for the branding, earmarking and, in the case of bulls, castration.

Jonathan, however, had ridden off some distance from the headquarters that day to take a last whirl at hunting down El Rojo, an ancient steer for whom he nursed a particular grudge. El Rojo was a giant bull with needle-pointed horns and slatty flanks furrowed by the crisscrossed scars of a hundred vicissitudes. For years he had successfully eluded the guns and nooses of the hunters; he was utterly unregenerate, totally vicious, and wily as old Nick. He knew the bottoms and draws better than any settler, where the most impenetrable cover was and when to seek it. Jonathan had tried off and on for a year to run him down, with a spectacular lack of success.

Today, determined not to quit until he had secured the wild one, Jonathan was skirting the creek-bottom thickets, keeping his eyes open. To Alex, he had delegated the task of following with the yoke of oxen that would drag the red steer to the holding corrals when he was taken. Now and then Jonathan would take out his mounting impatience on his companion, railing at him abusively. "God damn you, boy," he would shout, "don't hang back on me. Get along behind me and stay close."

Alex was quite close behind him when El Rojo made a sudden dash from a thicket where he had been standing immobile until the two riders were uncomfortably near. He crashed away into deeper brush, but Jonathan knew the terrain too, and he heeled his bay into a run, cutting El Rojo off and swerving him back to the open.

Heart pounding, Alex stood high in his stirrups and watched as Jonathan expertly tailed up the giant running brute, whirling out the plaited coils of his *riata*. And then, as Alex had fully expected would be the case, Jonathan was unable to resist the challenge posed by tailing El Rojo clear of brush on a straightaway run. Discarding his rawhide lariat, he lay flat to his bay's withers and urged him along-side the steer.

In an instant the stringy tail was in Jonathan's grasp and almost in the same moment he had dallied and was spurring offside to achieve the swift, deadly *colear* that would snap El Rojo clear off his feet.

But El Rojo, by chance or design or instinct, broke his straight run at the same time, pivoting in a direction that was sufficiently opposite to Jonathan's turn to offset his move. In the next confused instant, Alex saw horse and boy and steer down in the moiling dust. The squealing bay was struggling with a broken foreleg; Jonathan was crawling to his hands and knees, dazed.

The red steer lunged to his feet snorting; he wheeled off a short ways and turning, charged down on the half-stunned youth. Alex had not even hesitated as El Rojo had scrambled up; already onto the steer's next move, he put his own mount into a hurtling run that would thrust him across El Rojo's path, between the steer and Jonathan.

Proudly worn in the bright sash around Alex' narrow mid-dle was the shiny cap-and-ball Colt that had been a gift from his foster parents last birthday. Now he yanked it free and pumped two shots at El Rojo as he neared him. They did not slow the big steer by a jot, and in the next moment Alex saw that his angle and momentum were carry-ing his mount and El Rojo into imminent collision. A twitch of the rein could have turned him safely aside, but Alex bore stubbornly side-on to the steer. He sent a shot be-hind the bunched muscles of El Rojo's forehock.

Then the surging and savage impact; he felt himself lifted clear of saddle. The earth pinwheeled and smashed him across the back, driving the breath from him. Next the red and shocking agony of his leg being inexplicably crushed and his own scream mercifully throttled by sudden black-ness. . . .

The last bullet that Alex had fired found El Rojo's heart and the great brute had gone into a dying fall even as

Alex's plucky little cowpony lunged into him. The boy had been thrown clear, but his pony had immediately cartwheeled onward over the downed steer. The rawhide-rigged saddle, backed by the pony's plunging weight, had come down across Alex's outstretched leg. The lower limb was crushed between the solid cantle and the hard earth.

Jonathan, to do him justice, could not have done more toward making amends during the pain-wracked weeks that followed. At first only his keen sense of debt had bridged them; from this bond had grown, finally, friendship. Yet to this day, Alex could not think back on that natural friction between their stubbornly differing personalities without realizing that the passing years would have evolved it into enmity, except for the gap being artifically crossed by that sudden and dramatic accident. . . .

Jonathan's soft whoop yanked him from the mood. They had topped a shallow ridge which stretched for a good mile or more parallel to the Brushy's winding course, but set well back on the black bottomlands above its low, willow-choked bank.

When Gideon had first come on this creek bottom twenty years ago, the site of his future home had taken his eye at once. As an Austin colonist, he had been allotted a head-right league of land that comprised a vast wedge between the Yegua and Brushy creeks. Here, about midway between ridge and creek bank flourished a small park of post oaks and walnuts, and here he had cleared land for his buildings. After completing the house- and shed-raising, with the neighbors' help, he had broken up the virgin bottomland with his turning plow for plantings of corn and potatoes and a little cotton. Except for improvements, the homesite had changed little over the years; the grove and the rambling cabin, whose original structure now boasted two flanking wings, were the same.

But Alex' first bursting lift of spirit choked back in his chest. The fields were barren and untilled, overrun with a

rank tangle of weeds and brush; the buildings had a stark
and silent appearance like desertion, as if they had grown
old waiting for the return of tenants who had gone away
long ago.

"There she is, boy," Jonathan shouted huskily, "there she
is all over, by God," his voice hushing away then as his
face sobered to the thought of why they had returned. He
set the spurs lightly and put his rangy nag down the slope
at a swift, reaching gait.

As they neared the buildings, Alex noticed how the whole
place had gained a prideless, rundown look. The corrals were
fouled, fences were broken and gaping, and stray pieces of
gear made a careless litter of the yard. The dark and weathered buildings were intact, built for a lifetime, but the split-
shake roofs were in sad disrepair, and the cabin's stone
chimney was crumbling at the base. Plain neglect had crept
like a shabby fungus over the place.

Dismounting, they crossed the sagging porch and entered
the house. The parlor, with its big stone fireplace and dark
heavy furniture, was still neatly kept. "Pa!" Jonathan called
softly. "Mercy? Cort, Liam, where are you-all? Ma?"

A man came to a doorway, shuffling and halting there.
Once a big man, he was now stooped and gaunt. Alex
felt a bitter shock, for Gideon Trask had aged incred-
ibly in these few years. His granite face had eroded into
a wasted, deeply incised slackness, and his thick mane of
gray-shot black hair was almost white. His eyes, once hard
and bright, seemed to retreat; and now Alex had the
startled realization that Jonathan had matured to strikingly
resemble the man his father had been.

Gideon's eyes faintly questioned, holding no recognition.
"Gentlemen?" he said softly.

"Pa." Jonathan went to him and took him by the shoulders. "It's me—us—me and Alex. I'm Jonathan, Pa."

"Jonathan . . . no. Jonathan was my boy. Dead boy . . .
Vicksburg."

Jonathan said, "My Lord," and let his hands drop. His

eyes moved past his father to the doorway where Samantha had appeared, quiet as a shadow. She was a tall, fierce-natured Haitian whose spirit had never been cowed by whip or chain. Her thin, aquiline features still hinted at the wild beauty that, as an Afro-Indian and a slave, had cursed her youth.

She did not greet them; her face was carved mahogany as she said tonelessly, "He been that way since old Mis'-ress die, but ain't nothing wrong in his head." Watching their faces, Samantha paused; her impassive features did not faintly change. "See you didn't know. It was a good three weeks ago." She nodded toward a window. "We laid Mis'ress 'Liza over yonder under that biggest walnut. The Rev'rend Mister Boggs said some powerful words." Her eyes glittered faintly; she gently nodded her head. "They carried one strong *juju* on them, them words."

Jonathan half-wheeled toward the doorway, but then halted, his head bowed. Finally he looked slowly at his father, then at Samantha with a questioning scowl. "What's that about nothing wrong in his head?"

Wordlessly she pointed at a half-empty bottle of whiskey on the fireplace mantel, as Gideon walked unsteadily to an armchair and fell slackly into it. His head rolled sidelong on his shoulder; he snored. Alex could not believe it; there was nothing about this malleable shambles of a man to remind him of big, vital Gideon Trask, the man to whom he owed more than his life.

"He got started like that when he knowed your ma was dying," Samantha said matter-of-factly. "Now you and Mister Alex are back, maybe he be better."

"Where is Mercy? My brothers?"

"Mister Paul and the boys is out hunting for meat. Wild beef is all this table is seen for a hard spell. Miss Mercy, she out walking somewheres."

Without another word, Jonathan wheeled and tramped out of the house. Alex came to the doorway and watched him swing big-shouldered across the yard, calling Mercy

Killgrew's name. A flash of color near the creek bank, and a woman's slender form stepped from the fringing willows. She came to a halt as Jonathan called again. Her face, now turning his way, went as colorless as the white blossoms heaped in her upheld apron. She let go the apron and all the fresh-cut water blooms fell unnoticed to the ground. Her lips trembled, forming his name. Jonathan, with a glad soft, "Mercy," reached her in a dozen long steps.

Even as his face dipped, his hands on her arms, she began struggling, twisting her face away. "No, Jonathan— no, listen to me, please—" It was a check on his rough eagerness. And Alex, unwilling to be witness to the destruction of a man's dream, turned back into the house.

III

SAMANTHA HAD BEEN standing somewhat behind him, looking on. Her eyes gleamed darkly in her strong, handsome face. "Plenty evil gwine come 'count of this business." She touched the protective *gris-gris* hung on a rawhide thong about her neck. "Best you don't smile, now, 'bout what you don't understand, mister."

"As a respecter of all faiths," Alex said dryly, "I am duly appreciative of voodos. Especially the optimism." He eyed her thoughtfully. Years ago Gideon Trask had -bought Samantha from a brutal wharf overseer in New Orleans, such an act of charitable pity as a Christian man might bestow on any dumb, suffering animal. But neither blows nor charity could make an obsequious, head-bobbing Auntie of Samantha. Because she was an extremely good worker, the Trasks had grudgingly tolerated her uppity ways, as they would those of an ingrate pup or a fool savage unable to learn better.

Alex said mildly, "Santhy, it's long past the time for breaking ground. Why aren't those fields sowed?"

The fine flare of her nostrils deepened. "Old Mas'r, you think he work now? Mister Paul can't plow any more, and that Cort boy, you can lay he won't if he can be running the brush somewheres."

From outside came the lift of Jonathan's strident and angry voice, "All right—all right," and Alex saw him tramp blindly away down the creek bank. Mercy stood looking after him, then stooped and slowly gathered up the blossoms she had dropped. She went on across the clearing and halted by the gravemound beneath the spreading shade of the biggest walnut. Kneeling, she laid the flowers by the crude headboard, arranging them.

Alex left the house and crossed to the walnut grove. For a moment he stood by 'Liza Trask's grave with bowed head, absorbed in a tribute of good memories to the woman who had been his mother in all but fact. And then he had to meet Mercy's gaze; her eyes were large with reproach.

"Hello, Mercy."

"Alex . . . you could have told him, in all those days you was together. I know, we should have got him word sometime, but him bursting in all a-sudden like this . . . you could have spared me that."

Alex shook his head. "About that, I'm sorry. But none of it was my place to say. You and Paul. . . ."

"Are the culprits. Oh Lord God, what a terrible, terrible mistake." She came to her feet and pressed her cheek to the huge walnut. And struck her palm once against the bark, an anguished, helpless gesture. "Oh Alex, the look in his eyes . . . like watching a little boy getting hurt to the quick and trying . . . trying so hard to understand what he can't."

Mutely Alex watched her, hoping she would not cry.

She straightened after a moment, her shoulders back, and he felt relieved and a little ashamed of it.

The Killgrews had been the Trasks' closest neighbors, and Alex remembered how even as children, the attraction between Jonathan and Mercy had been a spontaneous and inevitable quality. As they had grown up, Paul had offered a spirited rivalry for a time, but even then it had been all Mercy for Jonathan, Jonathan for Mercy, a fact nobody else ever questioned. After typhus had taken both Jim Killgrew and his wife six years ago, she had come to live with the Trasks, making her in a very real way Alex' orphan-sister. She looked almost as he remembered, small and pert and wearing a faded crinoline with the grace of a young princess. The smooth black wings of her brushed-back hair flanked an oval, piquant face which was still unwontedly pale. Her full lips were compressed with a sadness that reached and dimmed the old flash of her eyes, and he knew that maturity had not dulled her vivacity: rather it must have faded from the day that the false rumor of Jonathan's death had reached her. And he said gently now, "I never understood exactly how you came to think Buck was dead."

"Declare . . . I never been such a baby before." She brushed a hand across her eyes. "Remember Lige Manigault?"

"That fellow with an outfit just north of the Yegua?"

"Yes. He entered the 2nd Texas Volunteers with Jonathan and Paul, and he was one of them taken at Vicksburg who got paroled on his word not to fight again. Well, when Lige come home, he paid me a visit straight off. Told me he was standing square beside Jonathan at a barricade when this shot hit—just about tore Jonathan in half, he said." She shuddered, blinking her dark lashes. "Lige might of lied a little bit—he was always sweet on me, and I know he hoped—but I reckon as bad as Jonathan was hurt, he must of honestly looked dead. I have seen it in my dreams a hundred times, Jonathan lying all covered with blood and a huge wound in his stomach."

"But you surely waited for word."

"Alex, I waited! . . . day after day for months. All I could learn was that all the dead at Vicksburg were buried in a common trench. A lot of dead soldiers couldn't be identified. And no word ever come that he'd been taken. If he had, we all figured he would of given his parole and come directly home, or maybe gone to Galveston like some others and volunteered for non-combat duty at the supply docks and warehouses. But never a word—never a word."

"He turned down parole, but he sent you word."

"Yes, a good six months after Vicksburg fell!"

"He was hurt mighty bad, Mercy, touch-and-go a long spell. That long before he was even in shape to have another fellow write for him."

"He told me . . . told me all that." She sank slowly down and sat with her back to the tree, dipping her dark head. "Paul was home, getting back on his feet after losing his arm at Shiloh, and . . . we was thrown together a good bit. Me hurting so much from Jonathan, and Paul so bitter—it was his right arm, and you know how he always hankered to be an artist."

Alex nodded soberly. One summer an itinerant photographer had stopped over at the ranch for a week. He had also been equipped with paints and canvas to capture, he had said, the color and drama of the West as no daguerreotype or ambrotype could. Paul had been fourteen, and that encounter had fixed his lodestar.

"He was always moody, and now it was worse'n ever. A body couldn't but be sorry for him. And he needed me so much—was always in love with me, even when me and Jon—" The delicate arch of her throat quivered; she drew up her knees and clasped her ankles. "For a long spell after I was sure Jonathan was dead, it didn't matter. But then I began to need too, and Paul was there. So we was married." She tilted her head, and a pure misery filled her eyes. "Alex, why? Can you tell me why?"

Alex heard a shout then, and looked over toward the

corral. Three riders, just come into sight, were dropping off their horses. A boy of fifteen had whooped out, and he came over on the run, moving with a lanky adolescent grace. Halting, he grinned unabashedly, thumbs hooked in the waist of his butternut pants, then suddenly thrust out his hand. "Welcome back."

Alex smiled. "Didn't know as you'd recall me, Cort."

"Sure thing." Cortney Trask scooped back his hair, which was thick and black with the deep Trask widow's peak, from his eyes. They were pale and bold and restless, not quite insolent; there was a wiry tensile alertness about him. A second boy had sidled shyly up beside him. Cort said, "This here is Liam. Says he recalls you all right."

Alex held out his hand until Liam took it and said, "H-h-hello," stammering badly. Liam was almost two years younger than Cort, but already as tall and reaching for considerable heft. He had never been stupid; he had showed at times any child's bright curiosity. But his attention wandered like a moth; facts and names and faces drifted in and out of his mind, and his thoughts were faraway. In an aged person you would call it senility; in this child it was some nameless, everlasting daydream which to be wholly wrenched from would leave him naked and miserable. The other Trasks had always watched over him with a fierce protectiveness, and at least one of them was never far from him. Gently Alex rubbed the boy's head, then glanced at the grinning Cort and said soberly, "You notice anything unusual when you rode in?"

"Like what?" Cort demanded.

"Like two extra horses in the corral."

"Sure, yours."

"One of 'em's mine," Alex said with a grin, and watched Cort's face alter from puzzlement to comprehension to disbelief.

"Ah, Alex. Hey, you really mean it? Is he?"

"Take a look by the creek. Last I saw—"

Whooping, Cort broke into a run, then wheeled back and

caught hold of Liam and dragged him along, shouting, "Don't stand there, boy! Ol' Buck's back. Buck, hey!"

Paul Trask had come up and now he halted, watching the two boys run toward the creek. He had always stood apart from his family; Cort's blind idolizing of the absent Jonathan would not have helped matters. Now Paul stepped forward, self-consciously extending his left hand. The empty right sleeve of his cowhide jacket was rolled up and pinned at the shoulder. It was a sharp reminder of the cruelest irony of all: that probably only Jonathan's prompt action in risking his own life had saved his injured brother for the girl Jonathan loved. Briefly Alex shared the awkwardness; he had to force his smile. "Good to see you, fella."

"*You* haven't changed." Paul flicked the first word with inflection. He had his brothers' black, unruly hair, but his fair skin that burned and peeled anew each year was legacy of his brave, frail mother. He had his father's height, without Gideon's former weight and hardihood; his sad and scornful eyes that brooded at all the world betrayed a nervous and near morbid sensitivity. Alex shared with him only a wry satirical outlook, yet it had always sufficed to make Paul the Trask closest to him, and Alex had gotten on well with them all while Paul was close only to his mother.

The smile on Paul's lips nearly reached his eyes; he seemed to remember and his grip tightened. "Alex . . . good you're back." His glance shuttled briefly to Mercy. "Was that straight about you brought Buck with you?"

Alex, explaining how he had obtained Jonathan's release, sensed a fretting of cross-tension between husband and wife. Paul and Mercy watched him, not each other, and yet as he walked slowly toward the house between them, Alex had the uneasy feeling that he was talking over and around, not to them.

With his family present to look after Gideon, Samantha took her leave for the log shack beyond the fields, where she lived. Mercy prepared supper, such as it was. Beef was always available when no other meat was, so filling a man's belly was no problem. Otherwise the table she set was eloquent of the hard times on which the Trasks—and Texas —had fallen. Even an ordinary elegance of greens and good coffee was lacking: Mercy boiled up a pot of chicory and made bad biscuits from weevily flour.

They ate with the wordless concentration of hungry men and boys, except for Gideon, who had gone to sleep in his armchair; and halfway through the meal Jonathan entered at last, took his place and began to eat. His manner was dark and subdued, but not forbidding. Alex had been braced for this meeting, but when Paul said a quiet greeting and Jonathan replied in like fashion, he relaxed. The two brothers' relation had always been at best barely civil; it was at least that now.

After supper the family gathering in the parlor seemed as always. Only the old hand-carved rocker, where 'Liza Trask had spent the evenings with her basket of sewing and mending, made an empty place. Gideon had awakened, the whiskey slept off and his faculties clear. He recognized and greeted his eldest son and Alex with pleasure, but then only sat unspeaking, staring at the empty rocker with a musing, wistful indifference. Paul and Alex talked perfunctorily, telling each other of their lives since the war had separated them. Jonathan slumped in his chair, sunk in thought. The two boys were restless because Cort was and Liam followed his example; they rolled on the floor tussling and grimacing, and finally Cort leaped to his feet.

"Hey, Mercy. Can we roast pecans?"

"You ask your pa," she said from the kitchen.

But it was Jonathan, his voice deep and quiet, who said, "Sure Cort. You roast pecans," then came from his chair in a spare movement and stalked to the fireplace. He leaned an arm on the mantel and settled his eyes on an old Doré print on the far wall, not looking at any of them. Yet his big, slouched frame commanded the room. With five words and a quietly assuming posture, he had taken the reins of Trask leadership. Gideon mused on, paying no attention.

The others did, and nobody commented. Jonathan's very stance proclaimed that this was how it would be, and there was nothing else to know.

When he spoke again, his words were deliberate: "Walked for hours. Seen a goodly number of cattle within a few miles, not over a handful wearing brands."

Paul leaned forward in his chair, setting his one elbow on his knees. "There's cattle, all right, running wild over the whole country, what with most cowmen in the Army and the coast markets dead. Me and the two boys been branding what we can run down, but we got no crew and nothing to pay one. We been just hanging on, and I'm wondering if it's worth the candle."

"It is. Will be now hostilities has ceased." Jonathan inserted a twisted cigar in his teeth and bent to light an oak splinter; his gaze was smoky and speculative. "At Vicksburg I seen civilians pay seven silver dollars for a little cut of good roast. Them Eastern cities will be booming from the war. They will want good beef and will pay aplenty for it." He nodded his shaggy head at Alex, whimsically. "This lawyer we all at once know says there is no shame to using Yankee knowhow. I been pondering them words. All right. Yankee gold shines the same as anyone's." Jonathan straightened up, lighting his smoke with the ignited splinter, and he said: "We will burn the old GT brand on every God damned thing we see that moves and wears horns and a tail. When them Yankees quit crowing and start rubbing their bellies, we'll be ready. We'll start a range count tomorrow."

Paul settled back, drumming his fingers on his knee; he wore a satirical smile. "You mean me? Or Alex? You don't count or cipher 'cept on your fingers, Buck, and there is a few more than ten head out there."

Jonathan had dropped his hand, about to toss the splinter back in the fire, and now he paused and watched it smolder out, puffing gently on the cigar. *Damn Paul's mouth*, Alex thought dismally. When, as boys, Alex and Paul had given

obedient if sometimes lagging attention to the studies that
'Liza had laid out for them, Jonathan in stubborn rebellion had refused the books and had taken repeated hid-
ings for it until his despairing parents had simply given
up, letting him attend exclusively to rangework as he
wanted.

Now, after a moment, Jonathan only said pleasantly, "That's
half right, boy. You for one." He paused deliberately. "And
when you made your count, you report back to me."

The quiet challenge went over Paul's head; he merely
nodded, his attention already straying to the kitchen doorway to absorb his wife's movements. He had always been
indifferent to cattle and ranching and now, Alex thought,
with his arm gone, all he had was Mercy; nothing else held
real concern for him.

A hint of the deep slow excitement gripping Jonathan
showed in the abruptness with which he stood and paced
to a window. Hands clasped at his back, he stared into the
night. "The name of Trask will mean something in this country—in Texas. You mark me." He said it calmly and with
no doubt at all, and Alex thought of the inherent dogged-
ness that had let him refuse parole for two nightmare
years in a prison camp.

But prison had failed to scratch Jonathan's big rough
ebullience. The knowledge of losing Mercy hard on the heels
of his mother's death and seeing his father's manhood
broken—these things had scored deeply. The blackness of
his eyes seemed to tunnel back into his soul, yet gave
no clue to his thoughts. Still the change was there. What
was it then?

Already, with an effort of inner violence that was unique-
ly Jonathan Trask, he had made a wrenching acceptance
of the fact that the only woman in his life was lost to him:
already a new vigor and vision, a dream of empire perhaps,
was possessing him. In sum, maybe that was it. In a few
short hours some great and open-handed quality of Jonathan's, call it an innocence, had left him forever. Alex Mc-

Kenna, loving these foster people of his as only an orphan could, knew that the old broken pattern of the family circle would be reshaped around the sudden void in Jonathan's life. Whatever filled that void would seize the direction that each life would take, good or bad.

IV

IN THE MORNING, at breakfast, Jonathan told Paul to take a tally on the range south of the Brushy, while he covered Trask land north of the creek. Cort was boiling to ride with Jonathan, who crisply squelched the idea.

"Be some changes about here, boy. The place ain't fit for hogs. You and Li get to cleaning out them corrals. Ought to take you the day." He glanced at Alex. "Counselor, reckon you could spare time in the evenings to prime these tads with some book-learning?"

Cort almost wept. "You never bothered yourself with that stuff, hey Buck. Why you putting it on us?"

"It's a need is why," Jonathan said grimly. "One I'll be tending to on my own account when I got the time." He finished his chicory and stood, wiping his hands on his pants. "All right, let's all get rousting."

Paul said, "Alex, want to ride along?"

"He'll ride with me," Jonathan said. "The counselor and me got some palaver to make."

Alex was tempted to challenge the assertion, but a glance at the edge of resentment in Paul's face decided him not to say anything that might deepen the quiet rift.

The morning was bright as a blade as Jonathan and Alex rode north from the headquarters. After a while Jonathan said, "I give a lot of study to what you said about a body needing to truckle to the times. All these woollyheads running about free as their betters now will need work, and there ain't no better workers." He paused. "That's the answer to our big problem, which is we're busted. We will take on a passel of 'em and make top hands of 'em. A few dollars and found will keep 'em happy, seeing they never got paid before."

"Not many hereabouts owned slaves."

"We'll drive a few head to N'Awleans for cash and hire us a passel of Nigras there."

As they steadily covered the dense thickets and the open grass between the mottes and bosques, Alex was astounded at the number of unbranded cows running free over the few square miles they had crossed. These longhorns were wild as deer, literally ranging in color across every spectrum of the rainbow, with great curving horns of all conceivable shapes. Most of the animals were a faded orange in color, but there were also browns and bays, duns and slates, blue and black and white and red, speckled hides and streaked hides, dark horns and light. Jonathan's method of tally had a primitive efficiency: he could count as far as ten, and on every tenth head he tied a knot in his saddle string, making every hundredth knot a double one.

The two men ranged north to the bank of the Yegua and made a wide circle back south. At midafternoon, with Alex' help, Jonathan totaled up his double knots. Even he was staggered, and then exultant. "Almost four thousand head this near to home, and not over a few wearing anyone's brand. Boy, this war could turn out the best thing ever happened to us."

"*Salud* to the Trasks, then."

Jonathan eyed him askance, critically. "You're pretty much a Trask, and don't forget it. Brings me to this medicine I meant to make. All the time we was riding I never asked if you got any plans made."

Alex shrugged. "No time to settle any. When word came

on your ma, I was fixing to leave for Texas within the year anyhow, but thought no more on what next. Had toyed with the idea of opening law practice in Katytown."

"Law practice, hell. You're a cowman, same as any other Trask."

"Same as Paul?"

Jonathan's lip lifted off his teeth, laughing. "You ain't talking me down. Paul never cottoned to cattle work. You always liked it."

"I like law, too. Look, Buck. You are dead right that Texas has a future. A man can grow with it, but a man follows his bent. As a cowman I would always be a second-rater; in law, even politics some day, I can make some real sense to myself, maybe others too."

Jonathan thought it over and nodded. "Reckon that shines, all right. But whatever you do, you stick close by us, boy, hear me?"

"No argument?"

"Counselor, I'm that downwind of my own plans that I tell you here and now, you got your best customer already. Me. Plain enough I'll need a good head about me to handle legal and business points till I catch up on a lot of learning. And I will, along with the boys. Meantime you can be sizing your other prospects, but all I'm asking, don't jump in all at once."

"I'd planned on staying close to the home awhile anyhow, if it was all the same."

"Good. That's settled." Jonathan lifted in his stirrups and shaded his eyes, peering across the sedgegrass. "God damn. Don't tell me, now. Well, the word has got to be passed and here's a good place to start."

Abruptly he reined on toward a hillcrest. Alex was puzzled for moments only; now he saw the ribbon of smoke trickling skyward and, as they ranged on across the hill, the brand fire down in a brushy swale, a tied calf and a lone man slapping iron on it. The calf bawled as hair and flesh seared; the squatting man freed the animal before casually lifting his eyes to the pair of riders coming off the slope. Only when they drew rein a few yards off did he rise from his haunches, at the same time tossing the branding iron from his right hand to his left.

Alex was startled by his swift grace, for the man was huge and rawboned. His air of half-caring negligence was deceptive, for his quick movement was purposeful; so was the freeing of his right hand. He wore a .36 Leech and Rigdon in an odd holster that seemed to be riveted swivel-style to his belt. It would be well, always, to watch this man's hand: he could pivot up and fire his gun without clearing leather.

"*Buenos días,*" he murmured politely, but with his wide clown's smile and big square teeth, several missing, and his tough ugly face, the words were oddly comical.

Jonathan watched him a cold moment, then slowly swung his arm north and south. "You *sabé* the creeks there and there, Pancho, eh?"

"The name, she's Chino Lucero," the big man grinned. A half-shredded *cigarita* projected from a gap in his teeth and he tilted the hot branding iron to light it, screwing up his face like puckered leather. This was comical too, and Alex found himself smiling. "Sure, I know the creeks, and all between them is the Trask land, eh? Sure, man. This is Trask land here, eh?"

"My name is Trask," Jonathan said. "Chew this up and swallow it, Pancho. I'm the big Trask, boy, the one all you brush-popping cow thieves that been living on our beef got to reckon with from here on. I'm serving notice. Anyone gets catched hustling beef on Trask land gets outfitted for a rawhide collar and tall branch. You got any friends, Pancho, you pass the word."

"You are push' pretty damn hard, maybe," Chino Lucero said through his gapped teeth, sleepily smiling. "She is no crime, the branding of plent' loose stuff, eh? My brand is in the county book."

Jonathan lifted his fist and pointed his thumb at Lucero,

shaking it gently. "I just made her a crime, Pancho. Cut that calf loose and haze him along. He's the last for you."

He started to swing away, but Lucero called softly, "Hey, Trask. You don't like us, eh, Mexicans?"

"Horse is a horse, greaser's a greaser. I got nothing for the breed one way or other. You got any say, say it."

Lucero slapped the greasy thigh of his *chaparejos*. "Haaah. You think you are big because you are gringo."

"You got it wrong, Pancho. I'm big because I tell you what I'll do, then I will God damn well do it. Just that, *sabé?*"

"You, gringo, who know you?" He snapped his fingers. "You are nobody."

"I will be. I'll have this country in my tote sack before I'm through. Show up at my house by sundown today if you want to work for me. Otherwise I see you on my land again, you're dead."

"Maybe I come," Lucero said with his gap-toothed grin, "to be by when a big rattler like you get stomp' sometime. Haaah."

In the weeks that followed, Alex' unformed plan for a law practice languished and faded into the background as the old free life of the cowhunter claimed him once more. Dawn to dusk he worked and sweated beside the others, feeling his muscles develop from the wrenched soreness of the neophyte to their former hard temper.

During the evenings, by flickering candlelight, he faithfully dredged up effort toward tutoring Jonathan and the two boys. There was a hungry fury to the way Jonathan devoured knowledge; he carried Cort and Liam along on his own dynamic sweep and just as dynamically broke them into his ambitions for the Trask name, letting them frequently side the men in the daily brush-running.

Only Chino Lucero refused to take things very seriously, making a savage game of the whole cowhunting business. A superb rider, full of reckless stunts, absolutely fearless, with an endless capacity for whiskey and women, he saw life as a great joke and lived it accordingly, whether chasing a pretty girl or twisting a *cimaronne's* tail. Yet Jonathan had a gift for bending Chino's primitive, tigerish energies to productive use, and before long the big Mexican was like his extra arm. It was a strange relation, stranger than friendship, between the clowning, irreverent Chino and the grim, iron-eyed man Jonathan Trask was becoming.

Once Jonathan had been much like Chino, but that part of him was eroding away almost as if it had never been. The harder he drove, the more withdrawn and uncommunicative he became. Yet now and again the old Jonathan, with his hearty laugh and rough pranks, would spring out and take you unaware.

When the tally showed two thousand head in the catch, they drove to New Orleans, where Jonathan named and got a cutthroat price for the herd. Afterward he tramped the waterfront, engaging dozens of recently freed and bewildered slaves in talk, sizing each for the qualities he needed to build the toughest, hardest-riding cattle crew the Yegua country had ever seen. They listened with amazement to the big, bearded white man whose words were as hard and sinewy as oak dollops, each one hitting like a club, striking off sparks of manhood and purpose where there had been the apathy of dumb, beaten brutes. Of those asked to hire on, not one refused. Men with women and children were permitted to bring their families, so that it was a black exodus of sorts that followed Jonathan Trask back to Matheson County, Texas.

By now many neighbors had trickled back from the war, men tired and sick and discouraged, flung into deeper gloom by the conditions they found at home. Rounding up and driving the hundreds of wild cattle meant Herculean labors for a meager profit. Jonathan went from one to the next, putting an identical proposition to each: he would round up and drive to Galveston as many trail-broken cattle as they wished sold, dicker the best price available, and turn the entire proceeds over to them. For this service, Jonathan made a novel charge: An acre of land per cow or steer sold on a rancher's behalf. Many scoffed at the suggestion, but a surprising number of disheartened men, caught up by the lure of a new rumored gold strike in California, accepted the offer.

Jonathan promptly set his Negro crew to the task under the blistering tutelage of Chino Lucero, who swore he would make *vaqueros* of each and every one. Jonathan saw that they worked hard, but he left plenty of leeway for them to play just as hard. At the end of each brutal and grinding week, there was a barrel of whiskey waiting; each weekend held a house-raising or two as timber was cut and adzed for sturdy cabins that gradually reduced the squalid tent-camps the families had made along the river.

The circuit rider, Preacher Boggs, was collared one weekend for a camp meeting that lasted three days, during which incredible quantities of food and drink were consumed, nearly twenty souls spoke up for Christ, five unions that had never been maritally blessed became official, and one dozen people were baptized in the Brushy amid a hot debate between Baptists and Methodists over the proper means of the immersion with the Baptist-ordained Mr. Boggs passing a thoroughly partial verdict.

Each night saw an all-night dance where the younger people stomped and swayed barefoot (for shoes would not have survived a single such night) in superb rhythm kept by chanting hand-clappers on the sidelines. It was a wild and beautiful sight that Alex watched for hours on end and never tired of, a highly improvised, life-pulsing promenade somewhere between Africa and hoedown country, with the fireplay of red light on quick lithe bodies and shining black faces.

The third night was climaxed by a bloody dragout brawl over a mulatto girl, Jonathan settling the dispute by having the two participants fight it out with Bowie knives across a handkerchief. However when each had drawn blood, he halted the altercation by rolling out a fresh cask of whiskey and making the two drink each other's health. Within minutes the atmosphere was fiercely convivial, with the whole crew toasting Jonathan, he calling them his gang of crazy God damn burheads and they roaring back at him with affection. Already known throughout the county as "Trask's Niggers," they wore the name as proudly as medals.

Preacher Boggs, a bilious-looking man with a voice like the clarion of judgment, looked on in amazement for a time. Finally he turned to Alex. "Brother McKenna, you know Buck Trask better than anyone outside the Lord that made him. How do you explain him?"

Alex shook his head. "I don't even try, Reverend. I reckon, though, that what really sticks fast in a man's craw when you think on it is that he has just got started."

V

THE TRACK WAS PLAIN: perhaps thirty head had been driven out of a broad river-bank swale clogged by thorny brazil brush and straggling mesquite, then pushed due eastward along the bank. Jonathan straightened up from examining the track and batted dust from his rawhide *chivarras*. His glance, swinging to Chino Lucero, was as tight and hard as Alex had seen it.

"Third bunch in a week," he said meagerly. "Some of your greaseball friends, you reckon?"

"I'm don't think so." Chino's leathery face crinkled as he squinted an eye nearly shut. "I have tell you a few Mexes have live' off your good Anglo beef time to time, but they poor *peons*, all." He nodded at the tracks. "Boots, not *guarache* track. This was work of *vaqueros*, like me, like you. No greaseballs, I'm think. Only Anglo balls. Haaah."

"Watch your talk about white men," Jonathan growled as he tramped to his horse and stepped into the saddle.

Paul hipped around in his stirrups to ease his hindquarters, remarking dourly, "Now what?" Always an indifferent cattle hand, his missing arm made him more awkward than ever; the grind to which Jonathan had put them all in these last months had told severely on him. Paul had shed weight till he was narrow as a plant, and lines of bitter distaste had etched permanently into his face.

"This time we follow 'em up," Jonathan said flatly, "if it takes all day and night," and put his horse downcreek, his brother and Lucero and Alex following.

This was a fresh step in Jonathan's harsh campaign against the seedy handful of cow thieves, American and Mexican, who had foraged carelessly on Trask range through the war. One by one, Jonathan had caught them out and passed his word: any man who was warned once and afterward mavericked on Buck Trask's land would become free game in an open field. Such men were for the most part poor ne'er-do-wells living on one-loop shoestrings with tribes of slatternly wives and small dirty children. The Mexicans had always been here; the Anglos were second-generation trash from the Southern hills. They knew the Trasks of old; they recalled a younger, dynamic Gideon Trask who had been no man to trifle with, and this son of his was his spit'n'image with something added. So far not a one had not wilted like a pricked balloon before Jonathan's casual iron. He was making no threat, only a simple statement of fact, and they knew it.

Alex' first reading of the change in Jonathan had proved out in a year's time. The press and ambition had swept the dust of residual habit from Jonathan's new bedrock. *Don't tread on me,* the bleakness of his eyes and gaunt set of his shoulders seemed to say. *But you can't be that sure,* Alex told himself. *He drives hard, but for a reason always, and I haven't seen him push a man past his depth. Hard on to his breaking point sometimes, and sometimes a man could hate his guts for that, but never past it. None of them do hate him, though—not a man but wouldn't die for him.*

Yet the table stakes were climbing steadily, trying Jonathan's temper harder. By unhesitatingly seizing his opportunities, Jonathan by a bold swift stroke had bought enough land from his disheartened neighbors to more than quadruple his original holdings. *The land*: this seemed to emerge as the key to his vaulting ambition. Men and women were straws in the wind; when they failed to measure up, to what could a man give his confidence but the earth itself which, being neither faithful nor faithless, was dependable forever?

Downstream within a half mile, the creak broadened and quickened to flat sandy shallows broken by the pale fingers of long sandbars with hoofmarks. Without hesitation, Jonathan led the way across, afterward plunging into the liveoak thickets where the broken passage of cattle lay plain. Now they had left Trask land and were moving straight south; but Jonathan's action made clear that from here on, no mavericker's license or boundary line would protect the one who preyed on his cattle.

Presently the brush began to thin away and they dipped onto a stretch of raw sandhills. Ahead now the dust raised by moving cattle made a tawny shroud; the shouts of the three riders, two point and a drag, drifted clearly.

Jonathan reined up, lifting his hand. "All right, hold up. We will move in slow and then fast; just follow my lead. Chino, take the man on right point. I'll take left." His gaze touched Alex and Paul, and grew faintly sardonic. "Reckon the pair of you can handle that drag man?"

Alex' temper prickled, and prompted rebuttal: "Unless you want help with a point man."

The sun-wrinkles edging Jonathan's eyes crinkled with the small humor rarely seen these days. "All right, then. No shooting unless they offer to start it, *sabé?*"

They broke apart and rode on through the increasing dust; it·boiled up in thick billows, obscuring the cattle and riders. Alex tugged up his bandanna around his nose and slipped

179

out his Navy gun. He saw the lean shape of the drag man through the dust and, off to his right, Jonathan's sweeping arm-signal as he broke into a run. Touching spurs lightly, Alex came up at a swift lope behind the drag man. Above the sounds of cattle on the move, the rider heard him and wheeled his mount, clawing at his pistol. Alex fired above his head, the shot heeling across a rattle of gunfire from the right flank where Jonathan was.

"Pull up there," Alex said, "and throw your gun away, left hand." His voice was tense with expecting the shots to stir up the cattle, but they were sluggish and heavy-moving, full of summer grass, and already were idly milling to a stop.

The rider stared at Alex with bitter yellow eyes. He was a long bony man with a pinched and predatory face; Alex had seen others of the breed, shiftless and hog-dirty and footloose transplants of a still older frontier that was vaguely Southern. Wordlessly he lifted out his gun and let it fall to the ground.

The moiling dust began to settle, and Jonathan was moving this way with a dark-faced *vaquero* in tow. The Mexican was gripping a bloody right arm and pouring out fluid profanity.

The bony man called him Diego and told him to shut up. He did, and Jonathan looked hard at the bony man. "What's your name?"

"Creech."

Jonathan swung toward Chino Lucero, who now came up herding a slat-lean youth with hair like grimy straw. He looked like a feeble-headed relation of the bony man. Jonathan said, "Know any of them?"

Chino cocked shut one eye comically. "I'm not know them."

"How about the Mex?"

"Not him neither." Chino grinned. "What you think, I'm knowing cow thief?"

"You're damned right. How would you size 'em? Ain't ordinary cow thieves from the look, handy-worn guns and all."

"*Vaqueros*, them," Chino agreed. "They all new around. *Muy mal hombres*. Not so bad as you are, but pretty bad."

Jonathan glanced at Paul. "Be useful once, boy, and look over this stuff. See if there's any GT brands in the lot."

Paul pushed through the herd inspecting their flanks, and soon called, "Here's one."

"That's enough," Jonathan said. "Well, Creech, you have trespassed the hell out of my property and taken branded stock."

Creech, yellow-eyed and cautious, hesitated. "One or two brands taken by accident don't make a man a rustler."

"Boy, till now I only passed the word, but it's had time to get around. You must be pretty strange around here. Chuck your guns and light down."

The dirty blond youth shook his head in a slow and positive way. "Not me. I ain't giving up my gun nowise."

"Slack off, Kamas," Creech said. "You'll suit yourself, mister, but this ain't smart."

The blond youth's face tightened with a mounting stubbornness. "I ain't a-going on foot, Jim."

He pawed wildly at his gun, and Jonathan brought his Navy Colt level and pulled trigger. The cap misfired, and Kamas' weapon was swinging up to bear. Almost too fast for the eye to follow, Chino Lucero moved; his Leech and Rigdon swiveled up without leaving his holster. At the flat bellow of the shot, Kamas was rocked sideways out of his saddle. His horse spooked into a gyrating plunge, but the drag of Kamas' dead weight, his foot hung in the stirrup, made the animal settle down.

Creech dropped to the ground; he kept his voice mild. "He was my cousin. We was damn close."

"I don't mean to keep you apart." Jonathan began to tug loose his coiled lariat, and Alex pulled over to his stirrup. "Wait a minute. Is that what you had in mind all the while?"

"What did you figure?"

"That you would warn 'em and set 'em afoot at the most. I thought when you said no shooting—"

"That's because I mean to hang 'em."

Again the Mexican began to chatter volubly, and again Creech told him in a disgusted and savage tone, "Shut up!" He looked at Jonathan, his manner toughening to a bitter contempt. "Go ahead. I said you wasn't smart. When Mr. Danziger—"

"Who's he?"

But Creech said no more. Jonathan dismounted, as did the others except for the terrified Mexican. "Hah, the brave countryman," Chino said, and dragged him to the ground.

Jonathan ordered, "Tie their hands." He settled a veiled stare on Paul. "Scout over by the crick and locate a sound limb."

Alex sidled off from the others a little. He still had a thin hope Jonathan might be bluffing, but he wanted to be in a position to get the drop if there were no other way to stop it.

Paul, white around the lips, shook his head. "There's law to cover this. I won't be a party."

"Law," Jonathan snorted softly. "That might be what ails the counselor—not you. A man with no belly for man's work should stay where the women are." He suddenly tilted his Navy Colt enough to loosely cover Alex. "Don't move around like that, counselor." Something in his face made the sweat start on Alex' belly, and he thought, *Now you know.*

"Buck, don't. It's like Paul said."

"Don't figure I can get away with it?"

"Not the point. Given the conditions, people can get away with a good deal. The point is, you're wrong."

"Who's wrong?" Jonathan's tone was flinty with self-certainty. "You're wrong? Your fancy-ass court's wrong?" He tapped his chest. "Out here, there's nothing but me. I can name any right, any wrong, because I got the power to make it stick. Ain't nothing else that counts.'"

"Where did your license to decide life and death begin?"

"Right here." Jonathan ground his heel into the dun earth. "I could let off them petty bummers and thieves that was scavenging off us before. I knew that they was and how they could be scared away. A word here and there done it. If there'd been need for more, don't think I would of drawn any line. This's different. You heard how me and Chino size these fellows. You heard this Creech name somebody. This is an operation, a leader and all. I don't know what it means, but I'll find out. The whole country knows my word on rustling, so this had to be a test. All right. I aim to see they don't read me amiss. There's just one answer they can't mistake."

They rode along the upper creek to a line of spindly cottonwoods. Jonathan chose one with a thick limb of convenient height. He and Chino slung their ropes across the limb; Chino's falling noose grazed the Mexican rustler's face and he jerked his head away and began screaming.

Chino said in Spanish, "Be still, boy, you disgrace us," and gave him a cuff across the cheek. The shock of the blow, not the words, silenced the Mexican; he sat shaking, mumbling, as Chino adjusted the noose.

Creech sat still-faced, but he was sweating. "Look. Maybe we can talk about paying you for them."

"Talk all you want," Jonathan said. "You'll pay all right." He slipped the noose over Creech's head and kneed his horse around behind them. He lashed at the speckled rump of the Mexican's horse and it walked away, letting the man's full weight drop and swing. He kicked and writhed and slowly strangled. Jonathan struck at Creech's horse; when it didn't move he swore and struck again. The rope was new, the loop around Creech's neck stiff and loose. Creech, with a vigorous twist of his head, freed himself as the horse stepped forward. He slammed home his spurs and drove his horse into a run.

Jonathan snapped at Chino, "Drop him," and the big man took his time, bringing his gun up and spacing his shots. Creech streaked for the nearest thickets bent low in his saddle; not a bullet touched him. Jonathan cursed and rammed his pistol into his belt, reaching for his Sharps in its scabbard. His aim was swift and careful. He fired just as Creech attained the fringe of the thicket. The horse made a limp, bouncing roll across the rocky ground and was motionless.

Jonathan lowered his rifle. "Why didn't you get him first shot, Mex?"

"Maybe I don' like putting it in a man's back, eh?" Chino grinned and shrugged vastly. "Haaah. Maybe I want to see how you do once."

"You know now. Mex, don't ever again miss that way when you got an order."

Paul was dropping off his horse and then, on his knees, he vomited. Jonathan did not even glance at him. He motioned with his rifle at the two dead men, Creech and the blond. "We'll string them both up along with the greaseball. Leave 'em hang. They got friends will find 'em when they don't show up, and I want my sign clear to every one of them cow-lifting bastards."

VI

KATYTOWN, which Gideon Trask and other settlers had started to develop in 1848 with a crossroads store, had changed little since the war. They had named it by mixing their wives' names on slips of paper in Jim Killgrew's old beaver and drawing, Vad Bristow's Katherine being the winner. Within five years the site boasted a couple of dozen homes, a blacksmith shop, Baptist and Methodist churches, two general merchandise stores, a wagon yard and livery stable, a drugstore run by a licensed physician, and a go-for-the-gut Secesh newspaper. Except for a new flour mill and a growing set of oaks and sycamores along the street, it hadn't changed a lot. Alex liked the town and had once hoped to set up law practice here, but he liked progress too.

This bright Saturday morning, riding in with all the Trasks on the monthly hegira to take care of marketing and minor bits of business, he felt the usual dim touch of guilt. A short year ago he'd returned to Texas full of personal hopes and plans. He loved range life, but the fact remained he'd let at least a modest destiny trickle away from him, along with the use of a mind and talent that fitted him for more than cattle work.

Still the Trasks needed him; he was the friend who mortared together the loose stones of their too-exclusive selves. His presence did undeniably ease the various stains created by Jonathan's ambition, Mercy's weakness for him, Paul's morbid complexes, old Gideon's senility and Cort's wildness and Liam's dim independence.

As they jogged into Katytown, Cort and Liam were leading the rustlers' horses, full gear on their backs. Alex had urged Jonathan to turn over the horses, guns and gear of the three men to the sheriff and tell him everything as it had happened. If charges were brought against him, his initiative in bringing the matter before the law would help his defense. Having made his point by the triple hanging, Jonathan had no objection.

They threaded the mild currents of Saturday traffic with hellos to acquaintances and "neighbors," and slipped their horses and wagon into a vacant place at the rail flanking the courthouse. This was a long frame building with a field-stone basement where the sheriff had his dank cubicle of an office.

The men stepped off their horses, except for Gideon Trask, who got stiffly down off the wagon seat he had shared with Mercy.

During the past year, Gideon had made something of a

comeback. Seeing Jonathan's stiff-handed taking over of the enterprises he'd begun had made him button-popping proud. But the new Gideon was ages removed from the old; once stern and reserved, he'd become a garrulous crony of ne'er-do-wells, bragging up Jonathan incessantly. He'd continued his heavy drinking and there was a childish quality to the way he now followed his son's lead.

Jonathan reached up and clasped his hands to Mercy's waist, and swung her down from the wagon. The gesture was almost suggestive in its easy familiarity and Mercy, as her feet touched the ground, drew quickly back, flushed. A hint of casual affection between in-laws shouldn't have seemed particularly offshade, but Jonathan had made the proprietory gesture with a kind of purposive deliberation that brought the heavy blood crawling into Paul's face.

Jonathan was already swinging away; he said, "Do what you-all want; it's a holiday." He slapped Alex on the arm. "We'll see Mapin right off."

Cort moved around his horse, an old Paterson Model Colt that had been his father's strapped to his thigh. He imitated Jonathan's walk, a solid and slightly rolling gait that went with his older brother's bulk but with Cort's wiry frame was mildly ludicrous. Still you didn't feel like laughing. Liam, his dark eyes timid and furtive as he looked about, held close beside Cort.

"Needing me, Buck?"

"No. Here." Jonathan dug out a pair of coppers. "Get some horehounds."

Cort said softly, "I ain't no kid, Buck. I ain't big like you was at sixteen, but I outgrowed candy." His eyes were hot with resentment.

"Did you?" Jonathan said with his heavy-handed irony. "Never did, myself." He flipped the coins to Liam. "Here you, Li, get some for us all."

As he and Jonathan went into the store and down a rickety stairs, Alex remarked, "You ought to take that thing away from him."

"Who? What?"

"Cort. The gun."

"Jesus," Jonathan said. "I'd swear you never come back from the East. Got to outfit like a man to make a man. Here a man ain't dressed without a gun."

"I don't argue that, but the outfit doesn't make the man."

Jonathan halted at the bottom of the stairs, his look grim and quizzical in the basement gloom. "You think he's growing up too fast?"

Alex shook his head. "You know better. In Texas you can't grow up too fast. I've no idea what sort of man Cort might grow into otherwise, but he'll never be your kind, Buck." He paused, and Jonathan said nothing, grimly waiting. "He's trying to follow you, Buck, and he'll never cut it. Cort has your ambition and your temper without your strength or your way with men. As for his judgment, he has none to speak of, not even as sorry as yours."

Jonathan's face darkened; his right fist lifted a bare inch, then settled and unclenched. "No man under the sun but you could say that to me, boy. No man."

Alex only nodded, and then Jonathan wheeled and led off down a moldy corridor to the room at its end. Sheriff Mapin, a string bean of a man with a long and mournful face, was at his rolltop desk reading the county mail. After an exchange of greetings, Jonathan sat down on a creaking crate which, upended by the desk, served as a visitor's chair. "Lou, you ain't been out our way in a coon's age."

Mapin said, "It's a big county, Buck," but Alex, folding his arms as he leaned his back against a damp wall, knew that Mapin never outdid himself in making the rounds of his territory. He listened without expression till Jonathan had told his story.

"Well"—Mapin took out a pocket knife, opened the small blade and began paring his nails, frowning—"that was playing hell, you know, Buck. I don't blame you none, though ever'body and his uncle is picking unbranded strays out of the brush—"

"Not on Trask land they ain't. There was branded stuff mixed in, and I don't call that kind of drive-off any picking up strays."

"Don't either. Point is"—Mapin expertly flicked off a hangnail with the razor tip of his blade—"you should of hung the bastards and kept quiet, particular to me. Law's law, Buck. If you wanted to go after 'em off your own land and let the law know, should of come to me˙ and I'd of deputized you to bring 'em in. Could·be dead or alive, I wouldn't much care." He sighed gently, closing the blade. "Only now you'll be standing trial."

"Good," Jonathan said grimly. "I want the whole country to make my sign out clear. Give me a cowman's jury and I'll tell you the verdict now." He veered the subject. "Lou, there's more to this than three out-at-the-heels bummers picking up a few odd cows. It was the whole look of things. You know anything at all about 'em, Creech or that Kamas or the Mex?"

Mapin scratched his chin. "Nothing but their names and how they look. They'd be James Creech and Kamas Mobley and Diego Montoya. Couldn't of told you that much before a month ago. That's when they started coming to Katytown, them and some others. Drift in and out a few at a time, but the way you see different ones together, clear they're all tied in. Upwards of a dozen or so, and a hard crew. This one big fellow seems to be the leader. Man named Danziger."

"Creech said the name."

"Has a funny first name like a woman's, Alice or Alvina. I rec'lect—Alvah. Word has it he was with them Redlegs˙ and Jayhawkers up in Missouri in the war."

"Guerrillas," Jonathan said tersely. "What else you know, Lou?"

"Ever hear of the Notchcutters?"

Jonathan and Alex exchanged glances. The Notchcutters were a loose federation of cow- and horse-thief gangs who had preyed on the Texas cattlemen for years. Since the war's end, their operations had become swollen and sprawling as their ranks were augmented by deserters and scalawags, the flotsam of both armies. It was rumored that they had friends among state legislators and local officials in various county seats, men who quietly fattened in their service by twisting the law to criminal advantage. Men who had simply defended their rights as citizens had been framed and jailed on the flimsiest of charges. The Notchcutters took their name from a dangerous but proudly flaunted habit of carving a notch on their gunstocks for each murdered victim.

Jonathan said only, meagerly, "We brought in the horses of the ones we hung, all their possibles too. You'll find the pistol grips hacked up some."

"Same with the live ones," Mapin said. "This Alvah Danziger is likely one of their top men. Looks like a big dirty hog, dresses like one too, but is a schooled man and well-spoken. Appears they've pushed operations into Matheson County and Danziger is sort of the district manager." He hesitated. "They approached me and Judge Sharpe. Likewise Williamson, the new county attorney. I can answer for me and the judge, but won't be sure how Williamson stands till a Notchcutter gets brought to trial."

"Hell's blood," Jonathan snapped. "Why ain't you bringing 'em in, Lou?"

Mapin gave a faint, wry shrug. "You're the first they hit, Buck. First that's complained, anyway. And you took your own step." He paused thoughtfully. "Means now they've sized things up, they're starting their moves."

They talked things over with Mapin awhile longer, then took their leave. Jonathan was scowling and thoughtful. The harsh justice he'd dealt to three of the gang would have about as much effect on their total operation as a handful of snow on a prairie fire.

"Where to?" Alex said.

"Blacksmith's," Jonathan growled. He slipped his Navy Colt from its homemade holster and broke out the cylinder.

"This thing misfired on me yesterday. Time I had her converted for metal cartridges."

They crossed the street to Judd Farnum's smithy. Alex, unfamiliar with the new metallic shells, listened with interest as Farnum explained how he converted percussion-cap pistols to fire cartridges. With the old percussion guns you had to load each chamber with powder and ball; then you primed the nipple located behind each chamber with percussion caps. The hammer hitting a cap caused fire to flash through an access hole to the powder in the chamber. What Farnum did was shear off the rear of the cylinder along with the nipples and affix a disc with holes to insert the one-unit cartridges containing primer and powder and bullet in the chamber. He also modified the hammer by adding a firing pin to hit the cartridge primers. "Seems everybody's bringing in their guns to be fixed over," Farnum observed. "I'm getting a mighty sure hand for the job."

"That's good," Jonathan said. "You can have it ready by four this afternoon."

"Well, there's all kinds of jobs ahead of—"

"Four," Jonathan said. "This afternoon."

He watched Farnum's eyes as he spoke, and Farnum, as big a man as Jonathan, shifted his gaze to the forge. "Sure." He spat delicately. "All right."

As they left the smith shop, Alex reflected that the men Jonathan put down could be weak or strong; it was all the same. They might look equal to dealing with him; somehow they never were.

Jonathan halted and took out a cold cigar, half-smoked; he mouthed it with a wry look and struck a match on his heel, shaking off a sulphurous flare of sparks before holding it to his cigar. "See what Lou meant?" He motioned along the street. "More'n a few strange ones in town."

Alex saw him stiffen, and followed his glance. Mercy was proceeding down the street, her arms full of packages, and a bearded, dirty-looking man was weaving toward her. He was drunk. Jonathan flung away his cigar and moved forward, but too late. The drunk collided with Mercy hard enough to spin her lightly against a wall, knocking all the packages to the ground.

A dozen running steps and Jonathan was on the man; he caught him by the collar and whirled him, driving his big fist into the middle of his face. The man skidded on his rear in the dust; lying there, he shook his head, drew the back of a hairy hand across his broken lips, and then started for his gun. Jonathan took a long stride and another, and on the second one, let his boot sweep on in a savage arc that caught the bearded man's wrist as he brought up the gun.

Alex heard the bitter crack of bone breaking; the man shrieked.

"That's enough!"

Alex, hurrying after Jonathan, came to a stop as the words whipped out. He saw a tall man braced in the middle of the street some yards off, hand on his gun. It was he who'd spoken. He was smiling, but his eyes were cold as death. He was lean and long and elegant with a rust-colored mustache; he wore neat range clothes and was no cowhand.

Alex had never seen a killer before; not a man, that was, who had killed and gotten a taste for blood and was ready to kill again. Jonathan was facing the man fully now, tensing, and Alex wanted to cry, *Don't*, at him. Then Jonathan, remembering in time, sighed and slowly straightened his great frame, raising his hands enough to pull back his coat and show his holster empty.

The elegant man smiled under his mustache; he even laughed gracefully, like ice tinkling. Had Jonathan been armed, Alex knew, he would be dead this moment.

Standing beside the elegant gunman, a little behind him, was a great hog of a man in a stained and wrinkled suit. His red hair was matted in a dirty tangle; his several chins sparkled with golden whiskers. His wide bland eyes and the tilted tufts of his brows gave him an air of faint surprise.

He moved heavily forward now, saying quietly, "What a pity, Mr. Trask."

Jonathan raked him with a cold glance, said, "Danziger, eh," and nodded down at the groaning man by his feet. "One of yours?"

Mercy, as if out of a mechanical need to do something, stooped and began gathering up her littered packages with trembling hands. Alex moved over to help her, keeping his eyes on the huge, hoglike man.

Alvah Danziger doffed his shapeless rawhide hat with an amost courtly sweep. "My apologies, dear lady"—his voice was warm as summer butter—"for this incident. You've been pointed out to me, sir; your companion, Mr. McKenna, as well. This is my brother, Lat." He indicated the elegant gunman. "Shall we waste words, Mr. Trask? Or, seeing that we went to the trouble to learn one another's identities, shall we consider all's known that needs to be?"

"I never waste words," Jonathan murmured. "Three of your boys found that out." He turned his head and spat across his shoulder toward the hitchrail, at the horses of the hung outlaws. "You want to claim their stuff?"

Alvah Danziger looked carefully at the three horses; his eyes lidded down sleepily. "Three of my associates had been missing. I'd wondered, till we found their bodies. Dear me, you're a forceful young man. We'd merely been engaged in branding wild steers."

"Meaning any and all, mine included."

"Is that why you murdered my poor friends? You've left me no choice but to request a warrant sworn out for your arrest on their behalf."

Jonathan stared at him. "You've got your gall, by God!"

"Not really, sir. Murder is murder, even if you can show that a few animals wearing your brand were accidentally picked up by Messrs. Creech, Mobley, and Montoya. Lat, see our friend with the injured wrist to a physician, would you? Good day to you, gentlemen, and you, ma'am. I must build a small fire under Mr. Mapin."

VII

AN HOUR LATER Sheriff Mapin, not a little embarrassed, handed Jonathan a warrant for the murders of James Creech and Diego Montoya. He also had a warrant for Chino Lucero, who had shot Kamas Mobley.

"Ain't no hurry," Mapin said. "I'll fetch it out to your place tomorrow or sometime."

"Hope there's no notion afoot of holding us till trial," Jonathan said ominiously.

"Hell, no, not even with bail. Judge Sharpe knows cowfolks in these parts well enough to bend the book when need be. A man's work don't take care of itself. I'll fetch word when your trial is set, and you come in for it."

Late that afternoon, promptly after Jonathan had picked up his converted pistol at the smith's, the Trasks and Alex headed back for the GT, the wagon bed heaped with supplies. Jonathan rode in a kind of grim brooding, shredding a cigar between his teeth, humiliated by being jostled into a legally defensive position by a thief and scalawag like Alvah Danziger.

"Well, lawyer. Suppose this puts a tally on your string."

"Let's say that what's happened hasn't made me wrong."

Jonathan shuttled a grim glance at him. "How would you a-stopped that dumb boy, Kamas, when he throwed down, chucked a lawbook at him?"

"How will you stop Danziger in court?" Alex countered. "The law hereabouts would have looked the other way for your hanging those rustlers, but with Danziger making himself the local gadfly, the matter won't be left to simmer

down. Everything I've heard indicates he's already gained
the county attorney's loyalty. He's no ordinary cow thief,
Buck. Just a gun or a noose can't stop him."

"Stopping him in court's your job. Chew it hard."

Alex did considerable chewing well into that afternoon,
when he and the Trask brothers and some of the Negro
hands were engaged in building new gather pens for the
upcoming cow hunt. Hardwoods from downstream were
being felled and trimmed, cut into lengths, and conveyed
by post wagon to the prairie flats north of the ranch layout. The posts were sunk three feet in the earth and lashed
together with strips of green cowhide, forming corrals that
experience had shown would restrain the fiercest and most
powerful longhorns. Theirs was a one-outfit team now; the
GT had become too big to make its cow hunts a neighborly
operation. So Jonathan had ruled, and made his word firm
by having the new hunt pens constructed on home ground.

Toward midafternoon, as he and Paul were driving the
post wagon back from the groves with a fresh load of
trimmed lengths, Alex snapped his fingers. "Might be," he
murmured. "It just might."

"What?" Paul asked.

"A way for us to handle Danziger brothers and company." They were nearly to the new pens, and shading his
eyes, Alex saw a man leaving the work detail, heading for the
house across the flats. He was carrying a couple of buckets.
"That's Buck . . . looks like he's going for water. Well,
he'll want to hear my idea right away."

Alex dropped off the wagon when they halted by the
pens, then left the others to unload and headed for the
house at a saunter, still thinking over his idea and pleased
as a boy with it. He came up along the flank of the
house to reach the well at the back where Jonathan
would be filling the buckets. The half-absent thought came
to him that water-toting was the sort of chore Jonathan
would ordinarily leave to one of the boys, Cort or Li.

Perhaps the thought gave a wary jog to his preoccupation; at any rate he came to a dead stop as a low drift of voices came to him from around the corner of the house. Mercy's voice, and Jonathan's. They were talking over by the well.

"I wish you wouldn't," Mercy was saying unhappily. "Stealing back here like this to see me."

"Seeing you is all I asked for so far," came Jonathan's deep mutter. "I'm getting mighty short-strung with just seeing."

"You mustn't, oh you mustn't," she was almost crying. "I'm trying to make Paul a good wife—"

"Sure you are," he said with bitterness. "You was mine first, Mercy, and no preacher's word can gainsay it. I ain't ever going to feel different on it, not ever. You hear? Not ever!"

The harshness that had grown on him had slipped momentarily; hurt and hunger and a painful yearning were in his voice. Mercy said with a soft, choked misery, "Oh—don't. Find another girl and marry her and let me alone, Jon, please!"

"You're my girl. Won't ever be any other. Mercy!"

"No—no—" There were muffled sounds like a small struggle; Alex let his weight come forward, then settled back on his heels with a dismal futility. The sounds were different now, and he turned and walked back the way he'd come, feeling more sorrow than disgust, more helplessness than anger.

He could not help, he could only hurt by speaking up; he could say nothing to Paul. And trying to sway Jonathan would be worse than useless.

The next day, after a talk with Jonathan, Alex rode to Katytown alone. Enlisting the help of Sheriff Mapin, he spent the next several days asking questions, sifting bits of information, learning all he could about the Danziger brothers and the gang of riffraff that followed them. When he'd thanked Mapin for his help and left town, Alex had a complete list of names of the gang members and all that was known about each one. He returned briefly to the ranch for another consultation with Jonathan, and within a couple of hours was riding away again. This time he was packed for a longer trip and a longer stay.

He returned from Austin two weeks later, tired and worn but wearing a jubilant grin that said things had gone well. Jonathan's and Chino's trial was two days away; by now word had gone around and half the county would be there to witness the first open clash between cowman and organized outlawry. The outcome could determine local politics for years to come, a fact that was seeping strongly home to the citizenry.

From the moment court convened, it was clear that the county attorney, Williamson, was pressing hard for a conviction. Alex scanned the room while Williamson was questioning a prospective juror, noting the many Notchcutters packed among the spectators. Alvah Danziger was on a rear bench, fanning himself with his hat, stoic as a large toad; his brother Lat slumped loose-jointed beside him, eyes cold and unblinking.

Jonathan had said, "No jury in Texas will convict a man for hanging his own rustlers," but Williamson did a fair job of isolating jurymen that were at least professedly impartial.

When prosecution and defense had made their statements, things moved quickly. Alvah Danziger fanned himself complacently; he appeared corpulently amused by Jonathan's utterly factual and incriminating statement of his action and intent. Chino, it was clear, had fired defensively and would secure an easy acquittal, while Jonathan, it seemed, was miring himself hopelessly in his own straightforwardness.

But through Alex' skilled drawing-out he was doing more; he was making every manjack in the room—or within earshot, since the windows and doorway were crowded with craning spectators—aware of what he had taken on himself and why. He had given an answer for all of them to Danziger and his ilk, an answer they understood and applauded to a man. Literally, for Judge Sharpe had to rap for silence several times to quell bursts of cheering.

Danziger's smile began to stiffen on his cheeks; he fanned himself harder. Whether he won or lost today, an aware public opinion was forming against him. He was watching it harden before his eyes.

Patiently, using what was ostensibly Jonathan's trial, Alex built his case against the Notchcutters. All of Williamson's attempts to quash Alex' line of defense were unsuccessful. His last objection was voiced when Alex introduced a pocket of papers containing evidence on the characters and legal statuses of the men Jonathan had allegedly murdered and requested the court's permission to read it aloud. Judge Sharpe placidly overruled the objection; the court would decide for itself whether the testimony was relevant and would instruct the jury accordingly.

For the next half hour Alex reeled off information on the robber alliance called the Notchcutters, its history, its leaders, its methods. And above all, the kind of men it recruited. He branded the three dead rustlers as killers and thieves of the worst stripe, documented his case exhaustively with the facts he had garnered from the state authorities in Austin. Diego Montoya was wanted in Arizona for breaking jail after being arrested on suspicion of the knife-murders of two women. Jim Creech and Kamas Mobley were wanted in northern counties on different charges of robbery, and Creech was also wanted for murder in Kansas. Alex did not stop there; he went on to state with biting exactness the record of every outlaw in the courtroom. "The jury has a duty," he concluded, "to absolve the man who rid them of three jackals and scavengers who resembled men. They ought to pay him a bounty."

It was thorough and damning, and the jury did not even retire; one phrase rippled from man to man, and the foreman stood up. "Not guilty, y'r honor."

The courtroom erupted with cheering. Alvah Danziger

stood ponderously, his face holding a mottled darkness, and shouldered his way back through the crowd toward the door. Lat Danziger, moving behind him, gave brief nods right and left, signaling the others. The Notchcutters detached themselves from the crowd and filed out after their leaders.

Jonathan, grinning, clapped his arm solidly across Alex' shoulders. "Come on. I want to read my sign to Brother Danziger before he leaves town."

The two of them pushed out past the crowd and went to the long hitchrail at the side. Danziger's men were mounted, and the big man was heaving his own bulk into saddle; he danced his short-coupled brute around in a tight arc, then held it in as he saw the two of them approaching.

"Most thorough of you, Mr. McKenna. But a legal victory is not a military one, Mr. Trask; a skirmish is not the war."

Jonathan's big hands spraddled his hips; his beard was jutting. "That's all right. I won't be fighting with my hands tied, like you hoped. If I can catch and hang three curly wolves, I can hang twelve. Or a hundred. The law just said so. Cut your wolves loose, fat man, or run for your holes."

Danziger nodded slowly, gently. "We'll run—for now. After Mr. McKenna's moving statement in the courtroom, I shouldn't want to take on your whole county."

"You don't need to worry about the county, fat man," Jonathan said grinning. "All you got to worry about is me, because I'll be enough. You got to walk over me first, and you won't never make it."

Danziger's wattles shook; the mottled anger deepened in his face, and he flung his horse half-around and rode away with his men.

Alvah Danziger was true to his word. For a week nothing happened, but meantime it was noted by Katytown citizens that Danziger's crowd was purchasing huge stores of grub supplies, buying up in one swoop all the cases of new metal cartridges stocked at Old Montrose's store.

Jonathan learned as much when he tried to buy a supply for his crew. He'd given his men orders to have their old sidearms converted or to acquire one of the new Smith and Wesson revolvers made for jacketed shells. Seething and worried, he doled out to the crew from his own cartridges.

Alvah Danziger hadn't been seen since the day of the trial, and abruptly, as if their plans were laid, their supplies safely cached, all his men ceased to show themselves. It was the signal for a thieves' offensive that spared the cattle and horse stock of no ranch in three counties. They hit according to the tactics Danziger and his kind had perfected during the war, making swift, small night raids in a dozen different places in lightning success throughout Lee, Matheson, and Bastrop counties.

A substantial loss was often not discovered for several days, and once trackers picked up the sign, they could rarely follow it far. The thieves clung to watercourses and thickly brushed areas where trailing was next to impossible. They made quick, break-up camps, changing the sites every few days. The Austin newspapers warned travelers to hold to open country and avoid trails through trees and thickets. A man could never tell when or where he might ride into the guns of encamped killers; those who did never lived to describe the meetings. . . .

Repeatedly Jonathan set up ambushes at different spots along the thicket-matted banks of the Yegua and Brushy creeks. They made contact with thieves only twice, and on both occasions the quarry got clean away in the dark. It was like boxing with shadows, while the Pig (as Jonathan had dubbed Danziger) bled the range of three counties of the stock that was life itself to people who had made a slow, grueling comeback from the war years, only to find their hard-won gains being nibbled away. Something had to be done, and soon.

One morning Jonathan called Alex into his office. Paul

was already there, seated at the desk and looking blankly at an open ledger. Chino had also been summoned; he sat on the edge of the desk, swinging a spurred foot. Jonathan shut the door behind Alex, then settled his shoulders against the wall and lighted a cigar.

"We're in trouble," he said without preliminary. "The pinch is getting bad, and we're riding on credit. Too many irons in the fire."

Alex, who handled the ranch bookkeeping, said with a trace of irritation, "Well, I warned you long before this trouble started about tying up all your money. By now even your credit is getting tight."

Jonathan pinched out his match. "These thieving bastards got to be stopped. Dead. Now."

"That's fine," Alex said. "You can't even dig out this rumored 'underground' system whereby they're supposed to be moving the stolen stuff in night drives down to the crooked Gulf Coast buyers. And nothing else has worked."

"God damn it—" Jonathan pushed away from the wall, scowling. "Don't tell me again what ain't worked. Put your heads into it. Show me an idea. Kick it around."

Nobody said anything for a minute, and then Paul ventured, "If we knew for sure where they were going to hit once and just when and how, we could lay an ambush so smart they couldn't wriggle out."

Jonathan gave him a disdainful stare. "Just two things wrong with that. We got no way of telling for sure where or when and if we did have, we wouldn't net more'n three or four and likely not Danziger at all. We got to get the lot, and we got to smoke out the Pig."

Paul's thin fingers turned white gripping a pen. "Don't ride me, Buck. You wanted ideas; we have to start somewhere."

"If we had something going," Alex put in quickly, "something big enough to toll the whole crew into the open— well, say a cow hunt to end all hunts. A lot of cows together make a big target. One nobody would try for with just a handful of men."

"*If* they tried for it," Jonathan growled, then snapped his fingers and wheeled toward Chino. "Mex—!"

Chino said, "I'm listen', man," as he finished building a shuck cigarette and inserted it in a corner of his grin.

"You said once you thought these Notchcutters might of made a few friends hereabouts. Was that a windy, or do you know something?"

Chino had taken out his steel *eslabón* and tinder cord; now his hands grew still. "Maybe," he said guardedly.

"If you're working for me, don't maybe me, boy. Be sure."

Chino began idly striking sparks into the tinder with his *eslabón*, and he said finally, "There is a cousin of mine. I ain' tell you his name. I think maybe he know som'thing. I don' think he's in it, but he knows some who been helping them an' how they are doing things."

"God damn," Jonathan said wickedly, and leaned almost into Chino's face. "You been holding out on me?"

"Ain' that." Chino was utterly calm; he lodged a spark in the tinder and blew it into flame, then held it to his cigarette. "Might make my cousin trouble to say som'thing. I don' have that, Trask."

Chino had his own peculiar brand of respect for Jonathan, but he was not afraid of him; Chino feared nothing alive. He took insults and gibes lightly, shrugging them aside with inexhaustible humor, but beyond a point nobody prodded him.

Jonathan teetered back on his heels, nodding. "Well, Mex, there won't be no trouble for your cousin. Don't even care what his name is. What I'm asking, could you get him to help us?"

"Haaah." Chino displayed his gap-toothed amusement. "For why, hah? Why you think he should help you?"

"For money."

Chino's hand, returning his cigarette to his lips, made a

mild shrugging gesture. "Maybe—for money. She's all depend on what you want."

"I'll tell you," Jonathan growled. "Pay attention now."

VIII

Two DAYS LATER Chino reported that his cousin was willing to pass along all he could learn about the Notchcutter activities. He would do this for two hundred dollars. "And considerations," Chino added, winking at Alex, "like the lawyer fella say. Haaah." Jonathan wanted to know what considerations. "When you round up these *ladrones* he don' want to get picked up too," Chino explained. "And the two hundred, she must be in gold."

With a spy in the enemy camp making regular reports through Chino, Jonathan went ahead with the rest of the plan based on Alex' suggestion. The cow hunt, the biggest the county had ever seen, began the next day.

The enlarged Trask pens, stout postoak fences secured together by iron-hard rawhide lacings, now covered twenty acres. Headed by Malachi, Jonathan's big Negro *segundo*, a *corrida* of thirty men worked out through the dense mesquite and chaparral that cloaked the bottomlands.

Jonathan's new-fangled branding traps, the first in the region, enabled them to brand with three times the speed and ease of the old rope and throw method. In a short time the pens were loaded to capacity with road-branded and somewhat gentled cattle.

The Notchcutters had still made no move, and their informant had nothing to report yet. Chino meagerly revealed that his cousin had ingratiated himself into the circle of rustlers, proving himself by accompanying them on several raids, but neither he nor any of the minor outlaws had the confidence of the leaders and he couldn't tell exactly what was brewing.

"Got to carry through," Jonathan said. "Hadn't planned to ship so many cows this spring with all them Kansas and Missouri sodgrubbers bitching about that fever they say we been spreading to their stock. Be lucky to get any through without shootings and stampedes. But we got the cows and we can't send 'em all to the hide and tallow plants. Can't turn 'em loose now without the Pig knowing we was setting up a target for him."

"What's the difference," Paul said, "if he don't make a move?"

"Difference is, we hold out a mite longer and he might just move yet. I allow he's suspicious and careful; so far he's made these little strikes. If we get the cattle moving north, a big herd on the move might toll the Pig out of hiding."

"Way too many for a herd."

"Not for two herds. Start 'em out a day or two apart. If we don't push 'em no farther'n Baxter Springs, Kansas, we might not even run afoul them farmers."

"There's no shipping facilities at Baxter Springs," Alex pointed out.

"Well, a whole lot of trouble has been them God damn freesoilers purely hate Texans. I figure we can dicker a fair price out of a Yankee buyer who's willing to gamble he can move 'em over the fort road to Kansas City or St. Joe."

The first herd started out the next day, Jonathan trailbossing. Malachi was to start the second herd moving in two days. Each herd contained three thousand head, the maximum Jonathan considered safe; other cowmen gave arguments favoring both sides of that figure. Fifteen riders to each herd, with the cook and his roustabout driving the two *carretas* piled with grub and the crew's gear. Alex, along with Gideon Trask and Paul, accompanied the first herd. Chino was to remain at the ranch to receive any information relayed by his cousin; if anything developed, he was to carry word to Jonathan as fast as horseflesh would take him.

A few days later, south of Belton, where Jonathan planned to swing onto Jesse Chisholm's trade road, Chino caught up with the first herd. His horse was blowing and lathered, and the big Mexican was reeling with exhaustion. They had to lift him out of the saddle, and Jonathan produced a bottle of whiskey from the cook's stores.

"That's medicinal, Mex," he warned. "One jolt to prime your pump, then you talk."

"Haaah," Chino said, and drank deeply. "The word is out to the crowd, my little cousin say. All of them, they will meet together and ride north. They will hit this big herd tomorrow night. They will drive off what they can, but mostly the Peeg, he want to ruin you, Trask. So they all are saying, my cousin says. As long as Danziger ruin you, he don' care how many cattle they get. To wreck your drive is what he want."

Jonathan muttered, "Hoped he would," and gave his orders. In minutes the herd was on the move again, and Jonathan pushed hard through that day and well into the night. A halt after dark, grub, nighthawks assigned, and a few hours' sleep. They were out of their blankets at false dawn and had rolled up a full five miles before sunrise broke on the paling prairie.

Jonathan clearly had an objective in mind, but he confided in nobody, not even his father or Alex. He was hard to talk to, brooding, muttering under his breath; that meant he was stewing out the problem from every angle, and nobody questioned him.

The character of the country was slyly altering, broken now with dry canyons and shallow rises. Soon Jonathan himself moved out on scout; he returned within the hour and ordered a slight swing to the northeast. This might be to detour the herd around impossible terrain, but more likely

he was pointing them toward a specific place. That idea
was confirmed when, shortly before sunset, they came to the
low beetling cliffs called the Cibola Breaks, an upheaval of
canyon-cleft ridges that disturbed the prairie running east
and west. The cattle could be run through some of the
canyon passages, but not without difficulties.

At one point the ridges cupped a broad well-grassed vale
shaped like a bottle, with wide canyons offering access at
each end. Jonathan had them sweat the whole herd into the
large end of this valley before he called a halt, ordering
camp pitched in the tapering end of the bottle.

The exhausted men wolfed their food as the washed
blue of the prairie sky grew smoky with day's end. The
first crewman to finish eating loudly clattered his utensils
into the cook's wreckpan, and Jonathan roundly cursed him
for it. Sound carried in brittle waves between these walls,
and the cattle were edgy from being pushed too hard. Alex
ate with the three Trasks. As they were drinking their coffee, squatting on their haunches, Jonathan broke silence at
last:

"If they hit us tonight, they got to hit us where they
find us. I want 'em to find us here."

"That's clear enough, but why here?" Alex made a wide
circle with his hand. "We're in the open, surrounded by
ridges. We'd be cold meat if men got above us with
rifles. They could pin us on all sides while they cut us to
pieces."

"Oh," Paul said half-viciously, flinging out his coffee dregs.
"Our leader wouldn't overlook a little thing like that."

Jonathan nodded gently, almost sleepily. "That's what'll
happen, but not to us. We'll be the ones up there. Waiting for the Pig and his friends to get under our guns."

Alex said skeptically, "What makes you think he'll be so
obliging?"

"I been ticking off how I'd do it. There's different ways,
but I was him, I don't reckon I'd send men up there to
shoot down at our camp." Jonathan pointed with his thumb.

"See that canyon to the south? We drove in through there, so following our tracks, he'll come on this valley from that direction. He'll see the herd bedded down on the wide end, and our camp at the narrow end. Fires, and what look like sleeping men. Brother Danziger just can't help himself; he's bound to want to stampede them cattle this way. Way the valley bottlenecks down, they can't go anywhere but over the camp. We'd never know what hit us. Safe and sound, and he needn't lose a man. *Sabé?*"

"Good thinking, son." Gideon waggled his white head. "Blame good."

Alex said quietly, "That's how you'd do it, Buck?"

Jonathan gave him a look of thoughtful irony. "Uh-huh. Barring my conscience, boy. That's you. You're my conscience."

"One you don't often listen to."

Jonathan chuckled. "But sometimes. Makes it worth it, huh?"

Alex said with a faint acridness, "I'd have to think about that," and folded his arms on his knees, rocking slowly on his heels. "I think it's too neat. A man could almost smell a trap, the way you have it set up."

Jonathan grinned, his eyes half-lidded with a cruel wisdom. "All he's a-going to see is a herd and a sleeping camp spread out for him. He's going to see how he can run that herd over the camp, and then he's going to come hellfire."

"Why?"

"Because it's that way, him or me. Got to be." Jonathan picked a burning twig out of the fire. "There ain't no bleeding hearts going to understand. No God damn pacifist like you. With you, everything's in the head. You ain't going to savvy how two men can look at each other and hate clear through, so hard it don't leave their guts till one is dead. That's the way with Brother Danziger and me. We both knew it from the start. Why, the Pig can't keep his hate from leaking out; even his men talk about it, or how'd Chino's cousin know?" Jonathan carefully pinched out the flaming twig between a calloused thumb and finger. "So what he'll do is what I'd do to him. He'll spot us and he'll ride straight in. If he was one step ahead of me, knowing what I know, shoe'd be on the other foot. But he ain't ahead; he ain't even nose and nose. No reason not to ride in, he'll think. It'll be"—Jonathan sighed and dropped the twig— "just like shooting fish in a barrel. Just like."

When twilight was fading the dun rocks to dust-gray, Jonathan put his plan into motion. The fires were built up; the men arranged their gear and blankets about the fires in a manner that from a small distance gave the impression of men soundly sleeping, dead tired from a long day. All of them were, too, but Jonathan's orders roughened them all to cool alertness; everybody had a part in tonight's work, and he wanted no mistakes.

A few men were to remain by the fires; he wanted them kept stoked to a high, steady flame so Danziger would have no doubts of a sleeping, unaware camp when he first saw it. The rest of the crew was pulled back from the valley onto the circling ridges, all of them armed with cartridge-firing rifles. Each man dug himself into good shelter with a view of the open valley below; their positions were sprinkled loosely on the slopes, but Jonathan placed a tight concentration of men around the mouth of the canyon where he judged Danziger would come through. Once the thieves were aware of being hopelessly trapped, escape would be their first thought. Nobody, Jonathan stated, was to escape.

Alex stayed by one of the fires, now and then feeding it with pieces of mesquite. He didn't want to think about what would occur, but he could not stop it. Here at least he would have no part of the shooting; all he had to worry about was getting out of the way fast if the herd actually flared into motion and thundered onto the camp. It could happen, even if Jonathan didn't permit Danziger's people to get a push started; the trail-skittish cattle could be set off by the first shots.

Among the men stationed by the canyon were Jonathan,

old Gideon, and even Paul. Alex wryly reflected how Paul, even more than himself, disliked violence; but Paul lacked his stubborn individualism and self-determination. Paul was still a Trask, with a duty to meet in his own eyes and those of his family if living were to be halfway tolerable. Different as his nature was, his ways were dependent, so he yielded to the demands of family pride.

The boys, Cort and Liam, were with the second herd two days behind them. Jonathan had overridden Cort's hot insistence on accompanying the first herd, which was the more likely to run into trouble. Alex supposed that his warning to Jonathan about Cort's wildness had taken to a degree. Jonathan was like that: he sometimes heeded Alex' advice where he would nobody else's. In small ways he'd lately curtailed Cort's activities with an eye to blunting his wild side and instilling an appreciation of hard, sober work. Yet Cort was still wearing his gun; his cocky manner had not been dented, and Alex had the feeling that at best such minor restraints were only a goad to his impatience. The only thing that would cure Cort with a fair certainty was a sound horsewhipping. . . .

Even the knife-edge of tension couldn't overcome a dead weariness, and Alex dozed time to time, elbows braced on his knees; but repeatedly jerked awake enough to keep the fire bright and high. Toward midnight he drew more alert, the restlessness of animals in herds at this hour being a notorious fact. It would be a likely time to launch an attack. . . .

The faint-drifting roar of a voice, Jonathan's, came from the heights upvalley. That meant, all of a sudden, that the raiders were in the trap, that the signal had been given. Then the crackle of rifle fire, echoes slamming between the rocky walls; whoops and cries of men in pain and battle lust carried across the herd, which began to make ponderous, ominous stirrings in the night. A wash of starlight frosted the soaring cliffs and gave a solid definition to the milling heads and horns of hundreds of cattle; otherwise there was little to be seen.

Hurriedly, along with the other men tending fires, Alex came to his feet with an armload of brush, heaving it on the flames. Hopefully the increased firelight, along with the handful of nighthawks, would hold back the restless cattle. A heavy ripple of motion coursed through the animals; panic was overcoming indecision, but so far their milling was aimless.

The steady pound of shots continued to shatter the night, but already the battle was shredding into more occasional shooting. Over the other sounds, a man was screaming with a high, inhuman rhythm, as if wounded unmentionably. And a few horses were running—some Notchcutters breaking out of the trap or trying to. Alex had the obscure, startled thought of how millions of minutiae had to flow together for eons to converge in a climactic moment and how these crucial instants, for all their flurry and fury, were seconds in duration. Then they were history, the process reversed to an eternal diverging, affecting whatever they touched forever, like outcircling ripples. . . .

Jonathan Trask's fight with the Notchcutters was decided in less than five minutes, and with it the future of a vast piece of Texas.

The shooting ebbed off; Jonathan was booming and bellowing orders. From this Alex knew the remaining outlaws were throwing down their guns in surrender and the GT riders were closing in around the prisoners.

In a few minutes they had herded the handful of remaining outlaws into the firelight. Jonathan was hatless, his face like brown granite, and a bandanna was twisted around his bleeding left hand. His right hand still held his Navy Colt; he didn't train it anywhere in particular, but his fist continued to flex around the butt, relaxing and gripping, as if he could not let it go.

He sent a flinty glance across the men standing by the fires, then said tonelessly, "Build 'em higher."

They threw more brush on the flames; the orange flicker rolled across the GT men, the four prisoners, and Jonathan's big form, spraddle-legged by Alex' fire. To Alex' remark that he didn't see all the crew present, Jonathan said meagerly that the rest were on burial detail.

"Danziger?" Alex said.

Jonathan's beard jutted; he shook his head. "Him and his brother broke out. They got clear away. I think the two of them and one more man, couldn't be sure."

Slowly he moved over to stand before the biggest outlaw, a ragged, red-bearded man. "Where's Danziger?"

The man shrugged. "Don't know any Danzig—"

Jonathan backhanded him solidly before the last word was quite out; the big man took a step back, rubbing his mouth as it bled into his beard. "He was there," Jonathan said matter-of-factly. "Couldn't no more mistake a pig squealing. Tell me where you boys usually rendezvous at."

"I wouldn't kn—"

This time the smash of Jonathan's fist knocked the man to his knees. He stayed that way, shaking his head slowly. "We got all night," Jonathan said mildly. "I can last a sight longer than you. Figure on that, then figure how much it'll get you in the end."

"Iffen I talk up, I would count on goin' free."

Jonathan shook his head. "No. You're going to hang, the four of you. Only question is how hard you want to go. There's an easy way."

Jonathan tilted the Navy Colt a half-inch; he fired. One of the other three outlaws, kicked back by the bullet's impact in his chest, fell by a fire. His legs twitched; his outflung arm touched an ember and the sleeve began to smolder. A GT man took a couple of steps and toed the arm away from the fire.

Jonathan's words dropped like stones in the silence. "Your friend now, he got it easiest way I know of. Hanging like I do it is a sight harder way. Man's neck don't break and he cuts a mighty sorry figure dying. But there's a sight worse ways."

He lowered the pistol slightly, cocking it. "Here's one, Red. Elbows first. One at a time, no hurry. Then the knees, same way. Plenty other bones in a man's body to get busted. Never done it to a man yet, but I reckon he wouldn't cut half as sorry a figure dancing on a rope."

The red-bearded man did not argue at all. He told them where Danziger would probably go; he spat the words like venom. He gave the appearance, at least, of being more angry than scared, and his defiant fury did not relax as his hands were tied behind him and he was hoisted into a saddle. He cursed them with a steady, bitter monotony as he and his companions were herded on horseback over to a dead, gnarled tree at one end of the valley away from the fires.

The horses were quirted from under them; the three men kicked awhile in the reaching firelight. Jonathan watched as their lives were strangled away, and Alex forced himself to stand by and watch too. After a while he said, "That was damned raw, even for you."

"Three of ours was killed by the canyon. Pa was one."

Alex started; a coldness filled his belly. He'd assumed that both Gideon and Paul were with the burial detail. He turned his head slowly toward Jonathan, who continued to stare at the spastic dance of the three outlaws.

"Some ways I reckon Pa really died a long while back." Jonathan's eyes had squinted nearly shut. "Paul is back by the canyon with him. He went 'most crazy. Said he would shoot me if I even touched Pa's body. By Christ, I won't take no blame for that."

"For that—no," Alex said. "It was the shock, Buck. He had to take it out on somebody."

"A funny thing. We never got on, but I never knew till tonight that he purely hates me."

Alex said nothing for a full minute, then: "I don't have to ask if you mean to go after the Danzigers—say at first light?"

Jonathan nodded, echoing, "First light," as he spun on his heel now, walking toward the nearest fire. Alex fell in beside him, pointing out, "Probably he won't go to his favorite rendezvous, even if he hopes some of his men got away and would join him there. He'd figure somebody you captured might give him away."

"I allow that, but a man gets habits. I allow he'll still head for his general bailiwick. And I mean to keep on his tail, him and them other two and any more I get wind of till there ain't a Notchcutter left in them parts. Not a live one."

"Suppose he runs fast and far and doesn't stop?"

"Then I'll hunt the Pig clear into hell."

This was the single token of Jonathan's grief anybody would see. From that alone, a man couldn't doubt that his father would be revenged to the hilt.

IX

JONATHAN ORDERED the men he'd hung cut down and buried beside the others. He had ordered the mass grave to be made deep and filled up with rocks and left unmarked. The GT dead, including his father, would be returned to the ranch and interred there. The cook's roustabout was assigned the task of conveying the three bodies in a *carreta* to Katytown and the undertaking parlor there.

Jonathan broke off the drive to Baxter Springs; he would leave a minimum of crewmen to return the herd to the GT pens while the rest of the crew followed him on a search for Alvah Danziger.

Before leaving, Alex tramped over to the canyon where

Danziger's gang had been caught in the ambush. Paul was by himself under the starlight, sitting on his haunches by a silent, blanket-covered form. As Alex bent over it, Paul said softly, "Don't touch him."

"Paul—you can't blame Buck."

"Pa never thought I was the man I should be, and likely he was right. But I didn't mind so much, for it was the same with Cort and Li. Buck was the only boy of his he could see. I loved him even so, Alex. . . ."

"So did Buck."

"God damn Buck," Paul said in an intense whisper. "He's put the Indian sign on this family. Land and cattle, more land and more cattle—what's it all gone for? Pa is dead. Cort is growing up wild. And Mercy—it makes me sick inside to see how miserable she is. She still loves him. We could of been happy if he'd never come back. Get away, Alex. Now he's got you standing up for him. Get away from me."

More talk would be useless, Alex saw, and he went back to the fire. He now knew for a certainty that Paul could have no inkling of Jonathan's carrying-on with Mercy. Otherwise, hating Jonathan as intensely as he did, Paul's reaction would be not this vitriolic and remain passive.

As a gray glow relieved the night, Jonathan ordered the men to saddle. In minutes they were riding south. The redbearded outlaw had told them of a cave in a caprock ridge a good ten miles north of the Trask ranch. It had been a favored place of Danziger's, though he was too canny to lay low very long in any one spot.

The night dwindled into full dawn. The sun was high when Jonathan, Alex, and the crew came to the ridge the big outlaw had indicated. Here they beat about through a heavy matting of brush till they located the cave opening. The entrance was so low a man had to duck through, but it was spacious inside. Here, by matchlight, they saw stores of food, cartridges, and other supplies.

"He ain't been here," Jonathan said. "But we'll make sure nobody has the use of this stuff. Lug it outside."

"Wait, wait," Chino Lucero cautioned. "Nobody walk around." He had picked up a lantern and lighted it, and now he paced a slow circle of the cave, holding the light close to the floor. "Haaah. He has been here. Him and the two others. Is plenty track in soft sand. The thin man, the Pig's brother, he is hurt. He limps. He is in a bad way, I'm think. The Pig was holding him up. Here he rested a spell while the Pig and the other man, they pack up some grub. Then they all go out. I ain't tell no more; all your big feet, they have tromped out the sign."

"Get outside." Jonathan's words were honed with tension. "Look around. See if you can't pick up the trail."

By beating through the brush, the GT men had erased any sign to be found near the cave's mouth; but after a few minutes Chino found a patch of mesquite where the outlaws had tethered their horses. Here was track enough to show that Lat Danziger, almost unconscious from blood loss, had been hoisted into his saddle by Alvah and the other man. Then the three of them had struck eastward toward a rim of stony hills that ended the sedgegrass prairies.

"They mean to lay up there," Jonathan said with a note of savage exultance. "All they can do now unless the Pig wants to leave his hurt brother behind, and I got a feeling he won't." He raised his voice. "You men get to lugging out that stuff in the cave. I seen some tins of coal oil in there. Douse it with that, all but the ammunition. Divvy that up. The rest I want burned in a pile. It'll be a marker to keep any and all thieves 'minded this ain't their kind of country."

While the men hauled foodstuffs and other goods from the cave, sorting out only the boxes of shells, Chino followed up the tracks the three outlaws had left, Jonathan and Alex moving behind him. Chino rode slowly, bent from his saddle to study the ground.

"They go pret' slow," Chino grunted. "The thin gringo,

he drop plent' blood. They have to stop soon, I'm think, or he ain't last."

"How far ahead?" Jonathan asked.

"Two, maybe three, hour."

They rode on. Looking back, Alex saw the pyre of Danziger's supplies erupt into billowing smoke; seconds later the men caught up with them. The sun climbed higher and they sweated and groused, chafing with impatience.

At the edge of the hills, the sign left by the three horsemen began to thin away on rocky, treacherous ground. From the way Danziger had often switched camps, it was a fair guess that by now he knew the country well enough to possibly elude his hunters a long while yet.

Jonathan, shredding a cigar between his teeth, said in disgust, "Christ. We should of packed along some of that grub."

Chino swung a long arm. "Just across them hills is where my cousin live, the one who help us. You like beans and coffee?"

"Not the way a peppergut likes it. Forget it. Keep on the trail."

"It goes that way."

They crossed the low range of hills, and a wide valley dipped away below. There were patches of good grass down there, and a herd of sheep was being hazed along by two men, one of them on horseback, the other afoot. "Ho," Chino murmured, and put his gaunt nag down the slope. They reached the bottom and approached the flock. The man on foot, a thin Mexican, raised his staff and said, "Good morning, cousin."

"Good morning, Sandal," Chino said. "What a pity you are not a *vaquero* and I must always look down on you from a horse when we meet."

Jonathan snapped, "He talk American?"

"Haaah," Chino said. "Sure, but not good like Chino, I'm think."

"Then leave off the spick so we can make you out."

Jonathan was staring hard at the man on horseback, who had reined in a few yards away. He had apparently been idly trailing the Mexican, giving him little if any help with the flock, and that seemed curious. He was dark and narrow with a wind-chapped face, and there was a nervousness about him.

Jonathan said, "What's your name, mister?"

"Jess Mandel."

"Mostly we don't ask a stranger his business, but this is a different case. Better tell what you're doing about here."

"Been riding the line for my grub," Mandel said. "I stopped over at this Mex's place last night. Am helping him with his woolies to pay for my food and keep."

Jonathan clapped his stare on the Mexican. "That so?"

"Is so," Sandal nodded, beaming. He had a clown's face that was even uglier than his cousin Chino's. "Plenty so, fella."

Suddenly Chino murmured something in Spanish, the words so low and brisk and fluid that Alex, who understood the tongue well, could hardly follow. What Chino asked his cousin was whether the gringo was what he claimed to be.

He was not, Sandal replied with the same liquid swiftness. There were two others in his house, one of them wounded. They were . . .

Mandel understood something of their talk, or else he sensed the gist of the exchange. His hand stabbed to the percussion Colt thrust slantwise through his belt, but he had barely yanked it free when Chino's bullet smashed his shoulder. Grunting, he tried to bring the weapon level, and Chino's next shot drove him out of the saddle, dead before he struck the ground.

Scowling, Jonathan said, "What the hell? What did that greaseball say?"

"The Danzigers are in his house," Alex said, and spoke in fluent Spanish to Sandal, who nodded and replied at some length. Alex translated during the pauses. Sandal said that three had come to his house very early this morning, one of them half-dead from a bullet wound. They were on the run and had come to Sandal Rojas because they did not yet realize it was he who'd betrayed them. His place was isolated, and it was known that his wife, who was part Choctaw, had skill with medicinal herbs. She had treated the wounded one, Lat Danziger; but his fat brother, who gave the orders, was suspicious and careful. When Sandal had asked to drive his sheep across the valley to graze as usual, Alvah Danziger had sent this one, Mandel, along to watch him.

"The Danzigers are in his place?" Jonathan did not keep the heated exulting from his voice.

"They'll have heard those shots," Alex observed.

"Don't matter. The Pig won't leave his brother. Where's the place, Mex?"

Chino jerked a thumb eastward across the valley, and Jonathan kicked in his spurs and headed away. Sandal shrilled something, and Alex wheeled back. "What did he say?"

"Eh, his wife," Chino grunted. "Don't be afraid, little cousin; I will not let her be hurt." He heeled his mount after Jonathan, and Alex and the crew fell in behind. As they neared a motte of scrub oak, Chino cautioned them to go slow; the trees ahead hid the house of his cousin. To take the quarry by surprise, they should dismount and go through the trees on foot. At the edge of the timber, Jonathan halted and dismounted; he motioned them to do the same.

"Buck," Alex said quietly, stepping to the ground. "Rojas' wife is in there. Go easy now."

"Not for any squaw I don't." Jonathan said it between his teeth, his eyes like black stones.

Chino Lucero dropped out of his saddle like a great cat, light on his feet, and his posture was ominous. Alex said swiftly, "Buck, don't make any mistake here. Do anything to endanger the woman, and you'll have more than a couple Danzigers to worry about."

Jonathan looked at Chino, then scanned the brown-black faces of his crew. All of them stared back, waiting, and Jonathan was no fool. His teeth flashed in his beard. "That's how it's to be, then. But don't make a mistake of your own, which would be you got thinking I give a damn what anyone thinks. I don't."

"Why," Alex said dryly, "that's a mistake nobody could make."

The men glided into the trees, Chino leading the way, slipping from trunk to trunk. The morning was still; percolations of sunlight flected the brush-clean floor of the motte. Then they came into view of the house, and Chino sliced the air with his palm to call a halt. It was a small but well-built cabin of green logs nestled low in the sheltering timber along a creek bank. Off behind it a rambling fence enclosed the sheepfold; there was a small corral with several horses inside.

Dropping to his haunches beside Jonathan, Alex murmured, "We can probably make a deal for the woman's safety, if—"

"No deal," Jonathan interposed flatly.

"Wait. Haaah." The whispery chuckle escaped Chino as the door of the house opened a stealthy crack. A moment later the stocky form of the half-Choctaw glided out, moving noiselessly for all her ungainly bulk. She was making her escape, Alex realized, just as Alvah Danziger shouted from inside, "Woman—you!"

She began to run across the brief clearing, and then Danziger's massive form filled the doorway; he was swinging a rifle to bear. Without a moment to lose, Chino palmed up his pistol in a lightning movement and sprang out of the brush to meet the woman. He shot hastily, spoiling Danziger's aim, and with an astonishing quickness the huge outlaw leaped back into the cabin. Chino pulled the half-breed woman to the shelter of the brush.

Jonathan, swearing luridly, pumped a shot into the puncheon door. Then the flap of oiled paper that half-covered the window was torn away; a rifle barrel nosed across the sill. Danziger fired, the bullet clipping off a leafy twig that dropped on the brim of Alex' hat. Jonathan grated, "Now. Pour it in," and opened fire again.

A salvo of rifle and pistol shots ripped into the cabin. Alex held his Colt in hand, but did not shoot; he coughed against the reek of burned powder, squinting at the cabin. He heard a brittle crash of crockery. The gunfire would be playing havoc with the Rojas' meager belongings. "For God's sake, Buck," he heard his own voice; and then Jonathan's order: the shooting slackened off.

Jonathan roared, "Danziger—come out, you fat bastard! I want to show you where my pa took a bullet in him!"

There was no answer. The cabin had a gutted, empty look, the door hanging wide open, one thong hinge shot in half so it hung crazily askew.

Alex heard a crackle of flames and a faint, gurgling scream. Smoke began to gush from the door and window. Not waiting, he left the trees and crossed the clearing at a run.

Stepping into the cabin's single room, Alex was half-blinded by the pouring smoke. He heard the scream again and saw a man thrashing weakly on a narrow bed at the end of the room, the bedclothes afire.

Alex plunged toward the bed; he strumbled over something and nearly fell. Catching balance, he took a recoiling step back. Alvah's monolithic body, the lower jaw blown nearly away, lay on its back, the eyes wide and sightless.

Alex stepped across the body and reached the bed, whipping off his coat to beat at the flames. Realizing the futility of trying to smother the fire, he tore at the burning blankets tangled around the wounded man. He ripped them away barehanded and rolled Lat Danziger off the smoking mattress to the floor. His clothes were starting to burn, but Alex smothered the smoldering patches with his coat. He tried to lift the writhing, shrieking man, but Lat's struggles made it impossible. Catching him under the arms, Alex, choking and half-blinded, dragged him across the floor.

Mercifully then, Chino and a couple of men were beside him; hands relieved his burden and other hands were guiding him out the door.

For a time after sinking to the gound outside, he could only cough and hold a bandanna to his watering eyes. Finally he could see again. The crewmen were running buckets of water up from the creek and into the shack. Sandal Rojas had arrived and was speaking to his wife in a low fury. Evidently she had left a lamp burning, the flame turned low, at the head of the bed. A shot had shattered the lamp, sending a spray of burning oil across the prone body of Lat. That did not concern Sandal, but it might have burned down their house, he pointed out furiously. As it was, the GT crew had gotten to the fire before it could spread; there was plenty of smoke, but little damage.

Jonathan ordered three men to carry Alvah Danziger's vast corpse from the cabin. Lat Danziger lay groaning on the ground where the men had left him. Despite a great weariness and the pain of his blistered hands, Alex got to his feet and went over and knelt beside Lat. His skin and clothes were so caked with soot and dirt and dried blood that Alex couldn't tell where he'd been wounded or how badly he was hurt. His face was swollen with livid weals, the hair and eyebrows singed completely away, and he was in considerable pain.

Alex started toward Sandal and his wife, intending to ask if there were any lard or grease available to coat Danziger's burns as well as his own hands. Just then he heard Jonathan harshly ordering someone to bring a rope. Alex pivoted in mid-stride, walking over to Jonathan.

"Did I hear you right? That's for Lat Danziger?"

Jonathan nodded, a wicked light in his black eyes. "Told you what would happen to these bastards when I caught 'em."

"But Buck, my God, the man's nearly dead now, wounded and burned—"

"That's just fine. He won't need but a nudge. Trouble is, it's most like doing the son of a bitch a favor."

Feeling a sickness that went beyond disgust now, Alex said, "Then don't. God, Buck—I didn't save a man's life for this."

"Then why did you?"

"A good dozen years ago," Alex said, making his voice calm, "I saved your life and got a leg ruined for it. Does that count as a debt in your scheme of things?"

Jonathan ran a hand through his thick beard, the heavy lines of his face settling in a wry squint. "It does. Get it out."

"All right. I claim a life from you, Lat Danziger's life. If he spends the rest of it in prison, even your tender sensibilities should be satisfied."

"Done. But you mind that squares us."

Alex said edgily, "You can put it in writing for all I give a damn," and walked away from him.

X

THE POWER OF organized outlawry in the region was broken with the demise of the Notchcutters. Lat Danziger's long and painful recovery terminated in a life sentence in the penitentiary. There were still the usual trifling brush-runners and ne'er-do-wells around to scavenge off honest men's hard work, but they were in the category of everyday and unavoidable nuisances, like nits and taxes.

There was still plenty for Jonathan to do outfitting his ambitions, and he set his teeth directly into the job. He had said accurately that the future of Texas depended on two things, the vast increase in longhorn cattle and the demands of a hungry public in the East. The northern ranches had a crying need for beef stock too, a mature high-grade animal fetching up to fifty dollars on the current market. But the obstacles between the Texas cowman and that market were brutal and discouraging. The northbound drovers who swung east ran into the fever quarantine and the plowed fields of angry farmers, while the warlike Comanches made a westward swing just as perilous.

Following his father's funeral, Jonathan again set out for Kansas with his two herds. He got them both through to Baxter Springs, but lost a total third of his cattle to Indians and Jayhawker stampedes. Two of his men were killed fighting off the raiders.

He sold them at a skimpy profit to a Yankee buyer, got drunk for a week of nights, and was preparing to start back for Texas when he met a Midwestern entrepreneur named Joseph McCoy who talked of rosy times just over the next rim.

McCoy, it seemed, had friends among the officials of the Kansas Pacific railroad which was building west, eventually to Denver. There was a good chance he could persuade them to build shipping pens and a siding at a Kansas station by stressing the big payroll spending in any trail town and the freighting boom of transporting cattle to Chicago. McCoy had his eye on a Butterfield stage stop at Mud Creek about a hundred fifty miles southwest of Kansas City. The Texans would have a ready and reasonably handy railhead market for their herds. No farmers, no quarantine, only a warm welcome, a fair shake, and cash on delivery. He wanted to promise the railroad that no less than a million cattle would be shipped out the first season. He was asking every cattleman to spread the word far and wide through his own district, up and down the trail, of a sure market and a square deal.

Through the year that followed, Jonathan bought all the cattle he could in anticipation of a tremendous market boom. Meantime he turned his hand to other financial concerns —and even civic duty.

Though organized outlawry was wiped out in the region, the maverickers who had been rounding up and trailing unmarked stock north since the war were making appreciable inroads into the unbranded cattle still running wild on ranch-owned range. Jonathan, like every ambitious cowman, had done his own share of mavericking; but he was instrumental in having the driving of stock from its native range punishable by a fine and jail sentence unless the drover could prove ownership. Because enforcing the "Act of '66" was almost impossible on the vastness of the Texas plains, Jonathan urged his neighbors to roadbrand all their trail head, a practice he had followed since the war.

His reputation widened as a champion of progressive methods; but the innovations he prompted meant more gold in the Trask pocket. He built picket pens by Chisholm's trade road south of Belton and charged fifteen cents a head to roadmark northbound herds, often slapping a common brand on large herds which already bore the brands of a half-dozen ranches. Biding his time, Jonathan made no trail drive during the fall of 1866, but he turned in a solid profit branding thousands of head for other drovers.

By next spring, he felt less confident; most Texans had cause for jitters. There was a depression in the East; the newspapers reported long queues of unemployed being fed at the Tombs in New York City, and the food was not beef nor even beef broth. The demand for beef was greater than ever, but there was little money available to buy it. By midsummer, with McCoy's new town of Abilene a reality, the sunken market had many cattlemen bitterly declaring their decision to make no drive this year.

Jonathan, always ready for a calculated risk, threw two large herds on the trail. He was hoping that if enough cattlemen stayed home, the tight, limited market that did exist would offer bonanza to the drovers who arrived first. He could command his own price.

It was a shrewd gamble, but it fell through. A cholera epidemic that began among the soldiers guarding the Kansas Pacific tracklayers had spread through the state like wild-fire, even to the drovers on the trail. Half of Jonathan's own crew came down sick, and three of them died. He was stalled on the trail for several weeks, and when he finally reached Abilene it was to learn that the first trainloads of longhorns had already reached Chicago and the depressed East; prices had plummeted.

Jonathan wrote it off as the kind of bad break a man could never take account of, setting his sights on the year to come. And the 1868 season, to be sure, got off with a bang. The Chisholm Trail was overhung with a blanket of dust on all its now-meandering branches, and Abilene was chockful of waiting buyers. Cattle poured in by the thousands, destined for the stockyards and feedlots in Illinois, for the stocking of ranches as far north as Montana, for the quotas of agency beef the government had promised the northern tribes. Abilene itself was, of course, roaring and wide-open; drovers' wages flowed into the town coffers like water; whiskey and blood flowed the way they always did.

It went that way throughout June, which saw a thousand cars full of cattle rolling toward Chicago. Then, early in July, a new Texas fever scare swept Kansas and other states where Texas beef had touched. Out of the seventy-five thousand cattle that reached Abilene that year, a full three-fourths found no buyers, and as with the year before, the all-over season proved out unprofitable.

That was no concern of Jonathan Trask's; he had been among the early arrivals, and he returned to Texas with a gold-laden pack horse, surrounded by his well-armed crew. Along the way he told a number of northbound drovers the bad news about the tick-and-fever scare dropping the bottom out of the Abilene market. Most of them simply changed their destination, but a few, fed up by one too many years of miserable returns, sold out their herds to Jonathan for next to nothing, and he hired enough men from their crews to drive the cattle home.

Promptly on his return, flushed with success and more exuberant than anyone had seen him in years, Jonathan threw the biggest and best celebration the country had ever seen.

Though it was still summer and the weather mild, sleeping tents were set up for the guests. An area was cleared for dancing and a platform raised for a five-piece band. All the calf wagons were put to use hauling supplies from town, including cases of bourbon and rye; mostly staples, for the women from the surrounding ranches would provide the delicacies such as cakes and pies and jellies dear to the palates of working hands and sorely missed on the trail. Preacher Boggs was invited to officiate at a camp meeting for those who wished to attend one. With all arrangements made, riders were sent out in all directions to welcome the ranchers, their families and crews. The women of the Trask ranch kept busy scrubbing clothes and children; the men scraped away or trimmed their beards and washed themselves raw in the creek, and shined their boots with lampblack.

Mercy and Samantha were busy till the last minute making ready. The old house had long been a headquarters for Jonathan's far-flung and constantly enlarging range of activities, and the increasing weight of her duties as hostess and house-keeper was wearing Mercy to a wan shadow. Temperamentally and physically, her tolerations for daily stresses were sharply limited; more and more she was leaning on the sturdy and indefatigable Samantha.

Being childless, the former slave lavished all the love and loyalty of her fierce, protective nature on her mistress. Mercy gratefully accepted this reversal of roles, for her gentle, dependent nature could hardly bear up under what it was carrying already.

Though Mercy's clandestine affair with Jonathan had been going on a good three years, Alex was fairly certain that nobody outside of Samantha and himself was aware of it. Samantha could always be depended on to see everything and to say nothing. Even he was sure of what was going on only because his accidental knowledge of one meeting of theirs had kept him uneasily alert to small signs in their behavior that indicated nothing had changed between them.

Otherwise he wouldn't have paid particular notice to Mercy going off on what seemed like a casual stroll by herself. Not long after, Jonathan, who was helping Alex dig some barbecue pits not far from the house, sauntered off in the same direction. He needed to stretch his legs, he said.

Surprisingly, he returned inside of ten minutes, and went back to work without a word. He looked faintly stunned, even bewildered. Something had hit him hard; he might be boisterous or harsh depending on his mood, but he was never retiring; it was his nature to roar his feelings. Yet through the rest of today he spoke only when necessary, and his face continued to hold a bemused, faraway look that was not angry, not happy, just the look of a man not sure what he should feel.

XI

THE GUESTS began trickling in early next morning. The Trask brothers and Alex personally welcomed each new arrival and assigned each rancher and his family to a tent. Beef ribs bubbling in grass-fat suet in a barbecue pit sent a delicious aroma across the camp that honed every appetite, lifted every spirit and set the mood for the three days of feasting and dancing that would follow.

Samantha, heading up a retinue of Negro woman, wives

and daughters of the crew, took efficient charge of all the culinary activities. She also had the task of seeing that all the colored people—a good many freemen having settled in the Yegua district since war's end—were made welcome in their own part of the camp. No tents were provided for them, but there was straw for pallets and an abundance of food and drink.

The first night was a gala one, with eating and drinking, talking and laughing; two squares of dancers swung before the campfires; the men talked over mutual problems of range and trail, and the women chatted endlessly. The Reverend Mr. Boggs moved from group to group, exchanging pleasantries with the ladies, having a single glass with the men and a warning stare for the heavy quaffers: his mere glance showered brimstone.

Alex, alerted by Jonathan's behavior of yesterday, had had a watchful eye on both him and Mercy throughout today's proceedings. Jonathan was drinking heavily, something he was rarely known to do. Mercy had a nervous and abstracted air; and finally Alex saw her break off talk with some women and walk over to Preacher Boggs.

The circuit rider had paused in his gregarious rounds and, gently nodding in time to the music, was watching the dancers. He glanced at Mercy as she said something; he gave a genial nod, and the two of them walked off a short distance. Again Mercy spoke and even a good thirty yards away, the flickering firelight showed the agitation in her face. Quite unexpectedly, Preacher Boggs wheeled, lifting his long arms; his millennial voice boomed for silence.

"Brethren, now leave off your merrymaking and listen a spell. Listen!" Mercy plucked desperately at his sleeve, her lips plaining forming, "No—no," and her expression at that moment was one of clear, agonized fright. Boggs was not looking at her; beaming at the gathering, he boomed, "She's retiring and modest as becomes a woman, is Sister Trask; but this is a proud time in a woman's life. And a man's. Brother Paul Trask—where is he?"

Someone shouted for Paul; Mercy seemed to quickly recover, or rather gain a resigned composure, but Alex understood that the preacher had mistaken what she'd meant to impart. *A confession?*

Paul, smiling but bewildered, came over from a barbecue pit, men slapping him on the back and passing jovial quips. The Reverend Mr. Boggs threw one arm around his shoulder and the other around Mercy's, his long face shining with a happy benevolence as he told the assemblage what everybody was already onto, that Sister Trask was with first child.

Paul gave his wife a swift and searching look. Then he was shaking hands to right and left, smiling and nodding to a score of well-wishers. But a troubled shadow lurked behind his face, as if he were putting together a hundred minor, once-unrelated observations.

In Alex' mind there was no doubt at all, not even before he noticed Jonathan heading away by himself toward the dark grove along the creek bank. His steps were unsteady; he detoured enough to scoop up a double-eared jug of corn from a table loaded with homemade potations. He tilted the jug and pulled deeply, and moved on into the night, jug swinging from his fist.

Alex' concern at the moment was for Mercy. Sickly and overwrought as she was, she was probably close to a breaking point after what had just happened. He waited till the crowd pressing about her and Paul began to break up, then edged over toward them.

Paul, still nodding absently to the congratulations, detached himself from the group and started away, his brow clouded by uncertainty that a casual onlooker would take for mere preoccupation. He passed Alex at three yards' distance without even a glance at him. Feeling a small alarm, Alex halted and followed Paul's progress across the camp. But he did not seem to have anything particular in mind; he simply walked away toward the house till the darkness swallowed him.

A couple of minutes later, Alex was able to catch Mercy alone. She had gotten off by herself behind a deserted wagon. She was standing there looking across the prairie, a worn *reboza* hugged tight round her thin shoulders though the night was warm.

"Mercy."

She came swiftly around, her eyes dilating in the starlight. He said, "You all right?"

"You know . . . Alex?" Her whisper turned almost inaudible as he nodded. "I thought you did," she murmured. "You're always trying to help us, all us poor weak fools. Nobody can help us any more."

"Couldn't be mistaken, could you?"

"No. Samantha knows about these things. She said—"

"Wasn't my meaning."

"Oh . . . no, there's no mistake. Don't you think I'd know if there was? Even Paul—poor Paul—has finally guessed the truth. Did you see his face?"

"I saw it."

"But he can't be sure. Dear God, he can't be. He hasn't a way of knowing how far gone I am. Not yet, but when the baby is born so long after—"

"Mercy," Alex broke in. "It's time you braced up. No more of what's been. The baby can make all the difference—"

"I'm weak." The words wailed softly from her. "You can't know how weak I am!"

"I know. That's why the baby can make all the difference in the world. It can be like the strength you never had."

"Every time I look at its face—every time, Alex!"

"No," he said flatly. "It won't be that way unless you let it be. Mercy—if you could do for your baby what you never could for yourself alone, it could mean a new life. For you, for Paul. Make him believe the child is his—you can make him believe it because he loves you, because he'll want to believe. God knows it's a white enough lie." He paused grimly. "As for Buck, he'll leave you alone from now on."

"Oh, you know how he is!"

"Maybe I know better than you. Will you ask me to be the baby's godfather?" She looked at him in bewilderment, and he said, "As godfather, I'll have a stick to wave at Buck. I'll tell him in so many words he's to stay the hell away from you, and if he doesn't, if he ever does anything that might hurt my godson, I'll load up a shotgun with scrap iron and empty it in his belly."

She continued to stare at him, incredulously now, and he said wryly, "That doesn't sound like me, I know. But Buck knows me better than you—a sight better than anyone. He'll know it's no bluff. He knows I'd never say it unless I meant it."

Alex left her with that thought; she needed time to assess her feelings. Meantime Jonathan needed to be told a few things; if he weren't too far gone in drink to listen, there was no time like the present. Alex headed for the woods, in him a quiet surprise at his own hard-handed interference. He was reluctant to meddle, but there was no other way to head off disaster. After he'd talked to Jonathan, he might do well to hunt up Paul and josh him a bit and urge him to have a drink or two. It might somewhat allay his suspicions till Mercy could speak to him.

Through the trees ahead, the stars gave a sparkling sheen to the black creek water. He could hear Jonathan, guttural with drink, tunelessly bawling a song. The trees ended by a steep cutbank, and Jonathan sprawled against it on his back, knees pulled up, heels dug in the wet gravel at the water's edge. Alex dropped down beside him.

"Listen, Buck."

"Call me Paw, you sonuvabitch. Gonna be a paw soon." Jonathan hooked a finger in the jughandle and swigged deeply. Then in a haze of drunken fury, he swung the jug at Alex' head. Alex moved nimbly aside, the jug thudding on the turf. With a vast, alcoholic sigh then,

Jonathan rolled quietly on top of the jug, clasping it to his belly, and dropped his bearded head against the bank. Alex took a handful of his hair and lifted his head and then, seeing he was out cold, let his head settle back, turning it enough to keep the sand from shutting off his air. He was tempted, though.

Alex stood and brushed the sand from his trousers, gazing speculatively down at the sodden man. All he could do was let him sleep it off and try again later. He started to ascend the bank, but had taken only a step when there was a harsh crackle of brush as someone broke free of the woods.

It was Paul. He stood on the bank above them, his eyes wild in the murky whiteness of his face. He held a heavy Army Colt in his hand; it was lifting from his side, and Alex felt a thickness of fear clot in his throat.

"That's what I thought," Paul whispered. "That's why I went after the gun, so I could put the question to him and make him answer. I heard him just now. So I don't have to ask. . . ."

The time for words, any sort of bluff, was past; Alex did not waste a word even to divert him. Now he would be lucky to prevent murder. Having no gun, Alex threw himself up the bank as Paul started to cock the pistol. He dived and grappled Paul around the legs, and felt Paul smash downward viciously at his head. The blow missed, the gun barrel slamming across his shoulder. With a savage heave, he lifted Paul clear of the ground and threw him.

They tussled back and forth, fighting for the gun. Alex was the smaller, his trim-muscled body the lighter, despite Paul's gauntness of frame. Paul's physical condition was never much to brag on, but he had enough Trask size to use his weight where it counted, smothering Alex with his trunk and pinning him. They were teetering on the edge of the cutbank; Alex heaved sideways with all his strength, rolling them off the brink. They hit the water on their sides with a shallow splash, but Paul fell in deeper water; his face went under; he coughed and strangled. Alex wrenched the gun away from him. He jammed the muzzle against Paul's ribs, hissing, "Quit it—quit it now!"

In his rage Paul paid no heed; he reared wildly up, upsetting Alex, and for a moment they thrashed around in the muck. Then the pistol made a muffled bellow against Paul's body. He jerked as if broken in two; his mouth came open and the light died coldly in his eyes. Still holding onto Alex, he slumped slowly against him and the strength ebbed from his grip.

In horror Alex shoved him away and watched him roll limp as a rag in the dirty shallows, his head lolling.

"God—Paul?"

Jonathan groaned and mumbled something. He was still dead to the world, and Alex gave him a moment's blank regard. Then he floundered to his feet, bent and caught Paul under the arms and dragged him up the bank. He straightened, feeling a chill bite through his wet clothes; the enormity of what had happened hit him fully. He hadn't meant to pull the trigger; he hadn't even realized that sometime in the struggle the gun had gotten tripped to full cock.

There was a savage, stunning irony here; he'd tried to stop Paul more for Paul's sake than to protect Jonathan. But well-intentioned action or not, Paul was just as dead.

He was not sure how long he sat that way, wet and cold on the bank beside a dead man and a drunken one, before the sound of someone's approach through the brush roused him.

Chino Lucero stepped onto the bank; his black glance stabbed and weighed the scene in one restless glance. He dropped on his haunches beside Paul's body. "He try for kill the big Trask, I'm think," Chino said very softly. "Haaah. Chino watches things and sees much. But I'm think the big Trask was too drunk to do som'thing like this."

"I did it," Alex said hollowly. He made the explanation brief.

"I'm hear the shot," Chino said then. "Nobody else pay much attention; I hear only the one shot, maybe fired in play, I'm think. But I been watching things and I'm not so sure. So I come look."

With a wrenching effort, Alex shook away the numb shock gripping him; he met Chino's stare across the body. "Can't let the truth of what happened here get out. Do you follow me?"

"Maybe I know, but maybe you better say it plain, hah?"

"If what really happened _and_ what led to it gets out, a lot worse will follow. For Miss Mercy. For her unborn child. You know what the word scandal means?"

"Haaah."

"I'm not concerned for myself, Chino—the shot was fired accidentally, and we'll tell it that way. But a little differently. We were clowning, the three of us here, me, Paul, Jonathan, passing the jug back and forth. The horseplay got out of hand. I was fooling with the gun—it went off by chance. That's how it happened. You agree?"

And Chino nodded, his eyes blank as smooth china in his coffee-dark face.

XII

PAUL TRASK'S DEATH put a sudden period to the celebration. He was buried two days later in the walnut grove beside the graves of his father and mother. A dismal rain fell during the brief service. The weather matched Alex' mood, but both would pass in their time, he knew. He was no Trask; he might be enmeshed in their problems, but he was master of his passions as no Trask could ever be. And he could live with what had happened.

As for Jonathan, he'd been too far gone in liquor to be even dimly aware of the truth. Alex was tempted to throw that truth in his teeth, but knew he never would. It would do no good; nothing would ever humble Jonathan, not even guilt, and he must be bearing as much as he could feel. The brother he'd cuckolded for three years was dead, and for days Jonathan was ugly and unapproachable with the weight of his thoughts.

Then, Alex allowed, there was the welfare of Mercy and her baby to be considered. With the woman he'd always wanted free at last to wed him, there seemed a good chance Jonathan would pull out of his doldrums, soften his nature, and do his best to become a good husband and father.

Within the month Preacher Boggs said the words that made them man and wife, but even before this, Jonathan's surly anger at life evaporated as if it had never been. He bent every effort toward building a new kind of life for himself and his family-to-be. He bubbled with plans for his unborn son (always for a son). He hovered around Mercy with the outsize presence of a mother bear, seeing that she didn't exert herself, that her least wish was not neglected. One had the feeling he was engaged in a constant effort to suppress a shout of sheer exuberance in living.

Yet the new state of affairs had a tainted undercurrent. When Jonathan was with her, Mercy showed a quiet happiness, full of her love for him and letting him see nothing else. But several times, catching her alone, Alex saw her staring into the distance, her whole manner vacant and withdrawn.

He supposed she had reasoned out a fair approximation of the truth, that Paul had been killed in an attempt on Jonathan's life and that she and Jonathan shared blame for his death. Perhaps the strength of her love for Jonathan let her hold the ghosts of shame and guilt at bay, if she couldn't wholly exorcise them.

Thought of her approaching motherhood also furnished

Mercy with a happy distraction. She spent her days sewing on infant garments and letting Samantha handle the ordeals of hostess and housekeeper. She ate well and got plenty of sleep to build up her strength.

Everything seemed to be going well until she went into labor weeks ahead of time. All that day she fought waves of excruciating agony while Jonathan paced the parlor muttering over and over, "If she dies . . . if she dies . . ."

Alex was with him when Samantha, her magnificent stamina frayed by hours of vigil, came into the parlor at last. "We lost the baby," she said in a flat, faraway voice. "Mrs. Trask, she well, but she's weak, her. Now she's sleeping."

Jonathan stood tall and heavy-shouldered in the center of the room. Alex was struck anew by the unconscious power the man exerted, his presence dominating the moment with an intensity that overwhelmed. Without a word then, he turned on his heel and tramped from the house. Minutes later he was riding away from the ranch. Watching from a window, Alex saw his quirt flailing up and down.

First of all, when Mercy awoke, she called for Jonathan. He had not returned, and she began to sob weakly, hurt to the quick by his desertion. Strong and soothing, Samantha's words had a calming if not reassuring effect on the girl; she slept again.

Jonathan did not come home that night, or the next, or the night after that; and then word drifted in that he had been involved in various drunken brawls at one roadhouse after another. Alex realized then how large a part Jonathan's plans for the child had played in briefly remaking his character. Jonathan Trask was an empire-builder; like all such men, he saw his ambitions in terms of dynasty.

When he returned a couple of weeks later, he did not seem greatly changed at first. He was even chastened and apologetic, and Mercy quickly forgave him. Still both of them had been changed in ways barely perceptible; as time went along, the variables became sharper, more apparent.

Jonathan had never been more than an occasional drinker.

After a doctor told him that any future pregnancy would put Mercy's life in jeopardy, he took to drinking a good deal, not enough to impair his efficiency, but enough to keep insupportable thoughts in their place. A good many men, some of them great men, did as much all their lives, Alex knew; semi-alcoholism was something a man could live with, but the shame of it was that something had gone out of him forever, a part of courage.

Physically, Mercy's recovery was complete; but more and more frequently she slipped into those spells of mental absence. Sometimes, busy at a household task, her fingers would grow idle; her eyes would turn vacant and she would begin to speak in a soft, toneless way, at times to herself or to the dead Paul, but usually to nobody in particular. She might be alone or with others, it made no difference. If, to snap her out of it, somebody gently spoke to her, she would jerk guiltily back to the present.

Gradually she became fixed in two worlds, separate and distinct: one the sane, normal world of any ranch wife where she functioned perfectly, alert if not happy; the other a dim limbo of her own into which, unbidden, she might cross at any time.

After a few months she got no worse and no better either. And that was how matters remained with Mercy Trask.

Jonathan, meantime, reverted back to the callus of an ambition which dictated that no amount of success was ever success enough. In this regard, at least, all things went his way.

It was another boom year in 1869 for McCoy's Abilene; the number of cattle shipped had doubled, one hundred and fifty thousand head going out in two thousand cars.

The following year the number doubled again, and three hundred thousand were conveyed out by the railroads, which were now engaged in a bitter rating war. These were growing times; and riding with the tide, Jonathan tripled his fortune. To carry home his yearly bonanza in Yankee gold coin (in accordance with the general Texan distrust of paper

money since Confederate currency had turned worthless)
he had a special chuckwagon built to his specifications;
it contained a false floor with a hidden compartment beneath. Some of his money stayed in Kansas, invested in a
variety of mushrooming enterprises.

Despite rumors of growing unemployment in the East,
everybody predicted that 1871 would be the greatest year
the cattle industry had known. But Jonathan, too many
irons in the fire claiming his attention, got a late start north
this year. Not long after his departure, word came down the
trail that Abilene had been shut down. Alex, left in charge of
the ranch as usual, wondered if Jonathan's luck had run out
at last.

But Jonathan returned as always, in a flush of elation. As
soon as he'd gotten wind of the rumors, he had left his
herd and hurried on alone to Abilene. He'd met Shanghai
Pierce just leaving, and got the story from that angry old
wolf of a cattleman. Abilene's own delirious boom, of loose
money and easy sin, had choked off its young life. Antagonism between the Texans and the Abileners had mounted
to fever pitch, and the city fathers had worsened matters by
hiring Wild Bill Hickok as marshal. The town had become
a cynosure for tough and cocky gunmen from all over.
When brash young Wes Hardin took the redoubtable Wild
Bill's guns away from him, it was a red flag to all the
tough ones. Wild Bill downed Phil Coe in a gunfight, then
accidentally killed one of his own deputies. The upshot of
the matter was the town council declaring a hasty termination
of Hickok's job, and Wild Bill just as hastily departing Abilene for reasons of health. The Texans simmered down then,
but proceeded to depart in droves, feeling the town had
given them the raw end of things.

It was clear that Abilene was finished, and old Shanghai
said he was sending word to his own herds down the
trail to swing southwest to Ellsworth. That had also seemed
the best alternative to Jonathan, and he'd turned his own
herds along the same route. But buyers were scarce in

Ellsworth; Shang Pierce decided to hold his cattle there until he could dicker a deal with somebody, and he managed to peddle a few head to the government.

Jonathan was more fortunate; making the rounds of Ellsworth's saloons, he fell into talk with the Yankee representative of a British firm who was looking over prospects for his company. He'd already bought some prime acreage near Fort Kearny, and intended throwing mixed stock on it. Inside of an hour Jonathan had him out sizing up one of his own three herds; he'd made a deal on the spot for all three for a gross profit of one hundred and fifty thousand dollars.

All this was well enough, but Alex had news of his own and it wasn't good. Every sign pointed to a new wave of rustling in the area, the first since Jonathan had cut the ground from under Alvah Danziger's Notchcutters five years ago. But this operation was of a different nature, so scattered and small-scale that it probably wasn't organized.

The quickness of Jonathan's fuming wrath at this news surprised Alex; he said: "Nothing to throw a fit about. I thought you should know, is all. If a man owns the whole dog, he doesn't rile over a few nits who stake their claim."

"That don't make a God damn bit of difference. Nits make lice. Let a few of 'em start up and get away with it and you got a hundred to deal with before you know it. What the hell've you done about it?"

Alex shrugged. "Not a lot. Put out trackers and had Lou Mapin look around. Most we can tell in a general way is the trouble is coming from the Bittercold Creek bunch. What can you do? Some are guilty, some aren't, but blood's thicker than water and the honest ones will cover up for the others. Try taking direct against anyone on his home ground among friends. Even with irrefutable evidence— and we have none—I wouldn't care to take on a whole countryside."

Jonathan chewed his dead cigar and paced the office floor. "What's behind it all? Them Missouri rawhiders been settled around the Bittercold country a good three years now, and we had no trouble till now."

"I have an idea why," Alex said dryly, "but I don't know there's any making a big, successful man like you understand it."

Jonathan halted, eying him with annoyance. "What's that?"

"Well—eking out a bare living isn't enough. A poor man may steal, even when his need isn't quite pressing, out of a pure desperation and defiance. By preference, the man he'll steal from is the man who has a hundred times his own needs. In these parts, that's you. It's the price you pay for being big."

"The hell it is!" Jonathan spat out the cigar butt.

Alex sighed. "Well, I told you."

"That I wouldn't get it, huh? It's clear as glass, counselor. A pack of lazy, do-nothing jackals who can't stand seeing a better man top 'em because he shows 'em the guts and spirit they ain't got."

"That pretty well sums it up. But I don't see what you can do except ignore it."

"I'll show you what." Jonathan stabbed a blunt finger at him like a knife. "That old bastard Cady is the one. Speaks for the others, don't he? Somebody got this business started, and it had to be him. They follow his lead."

"You're wrong," Alex said patiently. "That old man is as honest as they come."

"You know him all that well, eh?"

"By sight only. Beyond that by reputation, and his is a sound one. Everybody who's had dealings with Cady says as much. If his whole bunch isn't all wool and a yard wide, why blame him?"

Rufus Cady, from what Alex had heard, had held a battlefield commission in the Grand Army of the Republic. Before that he had been a supporter of the late John Brown. His position and vitriolic frankness had made him less than beloved among the native Texans since he'd moved from Missouri with his sprawling clan to see if he could raise the family fortunes in the ranching business. All the ranchers north of the Bittercold Creek had two things in common: all were Missourians related by blood in one way or another, and all looked to Rufus Cady for leadership. In spite of Cady's ruffling many feathers, everybody grudgingly conceded his integrity to be dead center.

"We'll see," Jonathan said grimly.

"Cinch up," Alex said. "I told you there's no evidence against anybody. You can't pass sentence without proof—not even you, with due acknowledgment to some of what you've gotten away with. Not and stay out of prison."

Jonathan said dourly, "You ever get tired of being my conscience?"

"Yes," Alex said flatly.

Jonathan's disproportionate anger at the petty thievery did not slack off as time went by; he was careful not to go too far, but he took steps. If he had suspicions about a particular Bittercold neighbor, he would hazard a guess as to his own loss, and that neighbor was likely to find that an equal number of head wearing his brand had been mysteriously shot. Alex knew that Jonathan was giving several of his crew, hand-picked by Chino Lucero, secret orders through Chino as to what should be done where against whom.

By the end of the year, Jonathan's increasing toughness against the continuing depredations had churned up an undercurrent of public resentment. It did not build quickly, because plenty of people who resented Cady's outspoken federalism were willing to believe the worst of him and his people, but Jonathan's harsh retributions were alienating many more, especially after his mathematical slaughtering took in stock of several ranchers not allied with the Bittercold crowd. Even his friends were finding a reason for fearing him.

Jonathan reacted to the public criticism and resentment with even harsher moves. Alex protested in vain: the loss of a few cows could not be worth a fraction of this snowballing antagonism. He was talking against the wind; in

Jonathan's eyes the least act against his interests was a
challenge flung in his teeth. It was a question of time as
things got worse before they became intolerable—then something would have to break.

XIII

WHEN THE 1871 cattle season swung around, Jonathan's
cattle had weathered well one of the bitterest winters in
Texas memories; he threw his biggest herds yet on the trail
for Ellsworth, full of expectations.

Cortney, now twenty-two, and Liam, turning twenty,
stayed behind at the GT for the first time in years, despite
Cort's hot objections. As usual Alex was left in charge of
the headquarters, and Jonathan took him aside before leaving.

"Watch Cort," he said tersely. "Hear me?"

Alex eyed him skeptically before saying, "You know,
I've had the feeling something happened on last year's drive.
What was it?"

Jonathan glowered and hedged, but finally came out with
the story. One night in camp Cort had quarreled with a
new man; they had pulled their guns together, and Cort
had killed the other. To all appearances it had been an
even play and Cort had been the faster, that was all. But
the incident had set badly with the crew; to a man they
felt that Cort had crowded the other to a fight, and one or
two voiced the opinion he'd done so deliberately. Jonathan
didn't give a damn what they thought, but a reaction had
showed in their surly obedience and fumbling work, and
tongue-lashing them till his throat blistered hadn't helped.

Probably the feeling would carry over if Cort accompanied this year's drive, so he was staying home.

"What you're not quite saying," Alex said dryly, "is there could be a repetition of last year's trouble."

Reaching his seniority had only worsened Cort's wild and vicious streak; little about him reminded Alex of the bright-natured youth he'd been. Ironically, the pliancy that had once made Cort almost too agreeable, too willing, had proven the weakness which had led him to take a harsh-natured older brother as his idol, his example.

"What the hell," Jonathan did not quite shout, "do you mean by that?"

"You know what I mean. I told you years ago when I said, take the gun away from him." Alex paused, then added flatly, "I won't be responsible for that kid, Buck. I can't control him—nobody but you can. Most of the time, at least. And I won't be responsible for what happens if you leave him here. He hasn't been far from you at any one time in years. If you want to take the chance, I can't stop you, but it's on your head. He needs looking after more than Liam."

Jonathan glowered some more and cursed, and then said he'd leave Chino behind to look after Cort. Chino Lucero was the man with enough presence to exert command over even Cort, Alex had to admit, but whether Chino was a wise choice in any other respect was debatable. Chino had an unbridled streak of his own which had been tamed only minimally from answering to Jonathan for so long. But Alex couldn't think of a better solution, and it was settled that way.

After Jonathan's departure, Alex kept the three of them busy with a full roster of assignments—Chino, Cort, and Liam, who could handle most range jobs well enough if he weren't left alone. Chino accepted any work cheerfully; Cort groused a good deal and called Alex a slaver, but Alex thought grimly, *Idle hands and the devil,* and kept them hopping.

Since the house had been enlarged, Alex had a whole wing to himself: a bedroom, a study, a room for storage. He liked the time when the ranch was almost deserted for the annual drives: the ranch books were up to date and there wasn't much work to handle. He gave the skeleton crew their assignments each morning and had most of the day to himself. Best of all, the house was quiet. Only the two women were about, and Mercy was as subdued as a mouse; Samantha went about her household duties like a shadow.

One morning some weeks after Jonathan had left for Ellsworth, Alex was looking forward to the day with a special pleasure. A new Zola novel and Thoreau's *Cape Cod*, two books he had sent for months ago, had arrived late yesterday. After he'd issued the day's orders, he intended to retire to his study for a few hours' good reading—till the day's first problem came up. One usually did before long, but maybe he'd be lucky.

As always he took breakfast with Mercy and the two Trask boys; Samantha served them. Cort dawdled over his food and Liam followed his example. Alex finished eating, pushed back his chair, and with a peremptory word to both to get a move on, left the house and headed for the corral where the crew was assembled to receive the day's orders.

Halfway across the yard he saw a horseman coming through the east pasture gate, and in a few moments identified him as Lou Mapin. The sheriff was not coming from the direction of town, and at this early hour that seemed curious. Some business or other must have taken him out in the pre-dawn hours.

Alex halted and waited, and Mapin put his horse directly over to him. "Morning, Lou. Light down."

Mapin said, "Morning, Alex," making no move to dismount. "Don't reckon Buck's back from Kansas yet."

Alex said no, he was in charge, watching Mapin's expression with mounting alertness. The years hadn't touched Mapin to speak of; he was still ambling, just competent, and given to a mild favoritism toward the Trasks. That was why Alex noticed at once the set weather lines around his eyes and the tightness of his jaw; his whole manner was unlike Mapin.

"Better get it out direct, Lou."

"Well, there ain't no other way." Mapin leaned forward, crossing his arms on his pommel. "A couple Bittercold men are dead, and it was pure murder. It looks like something that was ordered done, and the look points this way. Mind I ain't saying I believe it, Alex."

"That's good," Alex said hollowly. "Killed how, Lou?"

"Happened up by Redemption Creek, northeast o' here. A couple of them Bittercold boys, Tris Drucker and Morton Gant—they both are shirttail relatives of old Rufe Cady and work for him—was found just this side of your line, or close to it." Mapin hesitated. "The sign round the place looks like they'd made off with a few GT steers and somebody caught them skinning out the carcasses."

"I asked you how."

Mapin pursed up his lips and turned his big right hand over, regarding the palm blankly. "Well, these GT cows they taken was skinned out like I say. Drucker and Gant was trussed up and wrapped in a couple of the hides. I make it happened early yesterday sometime, and the sun was at 'em all day. You know green rawhide when she gets drying."

"God," Alex whispered in disbelief. "You don't mean they were put inside—alive—"

"They was alive, and I reckon for a good while. Takes a spell to die that way. You see the looks on their faces they died with, you'da believed it."

Alex lowered his chin and scrubbed a hand slowly across his face, then looked up again. "I'd like to know who brought you the word."

"Rufus Cady's boy, Struther. Cady was worried last night when Drucker and Gant didn't report in. Thought they might of gone for a whoop in town, but when they wasn't in by first light this morning, he and his son went out for a look. They knew where Gant and Drucker had been ordered to work out yesterday, so they went along the Redemption and found 'em directly. Then the old man sent his boy in to fetch me. Went to see for myself before comin' here."

"Look, Lou—" Alex paused, trying to frame what he wanted to say. "You won't say you believe we did it. All right, what do you believe?"

"Don't know what to, yet. It was all tramped up around the place, no sign a man could make out. I want to ask was any of your men working out that way yesterday morning."

"Cort was," Alex said slowly. "Li was with him. Chino Lucero, too."

"They always work together, the three of them?"

"Lately, yes. Since Buck—" Alex broke off; the explanation would worsen the implication. "Since Buck left," he finished lamely.

"Alex, you hear me now. I looked the other way for plenty from the Trasks. They been my friends since Gid rode me on his knee when I was a tad. I recall how you and me and the Trask boys would cut up sometimes on the cow hunts and old Gid would roar. Me and Buck and Paul, we-all enlisted in the Matheson County Volunteers same time. Anyhow I allus figured there was plenty justice on Buck's side when he went after the Notchcutters with his own sort of law—there wasn't no other kind could of done the job. And I know this Bittercold bunch has been putting on him with penny-ante thieving." Mapin stopped abruptly, shaking his head. "But Jesus, Alex. No decent man can look away from this."

"Nobody's asking you to, Lou. And nobody knows better than me how hard Buck can crowd. But he's always made a point of never concealing his actions, and he's always seen to any job of that nature personally. He didn't order this done, and neither did I."

"Well, somebody took it on themselves. I want to talk to Cort and Li, Lucero too."

"Right away." Alex glanced toward the corrals where the crewmen were waiting their assignments. He told Mapin to wait a minute or two, then went over to the men. He gave them their orders casually, making no mention of the trouble. He told Chino Lucero to come with him and went back to where Mapin waited as Cort and Liam came sauntering out of the house.

Mapin repeated for the Mexican and the two Trasks what he'd told Alex, and Cort's response was prompt and hot. He threw down his cigarette and heeled it into the earth. "If I'm accused of killing a couple men, I want to hear it said out!"

Alex watched Cort's face carefully; he could detect nothing but honest outrage and his usual temper. With his full growth Cort was only a hair shorter than his brothers. He closely resembled the late Paul at the same age; trim and lean and wiry, almost slender, with intense, nervous features that reflected every feeling. That far, the similarity was striking; from there on you noticed only the differences.

"Nobody's saying it," Mapin murmured. "Just want to hear what-all you boys done yesterday and where you went."

Chino and Cort gave easy, consistent replies to Mapin's queries. Liam couldn't get out much that made sense, but that was to be expected. Liam had grown into a young hulk, somber and heavy-browed. His eyes were intelligent, though the rest of his face was not, and its dullness was deceptive. Nature had left something out of Liam, call it a social vitality, but he was not stupid. Though he could rarely express himself coherently except by writing his thoughts out, his understanding was clear as a bell. He was almost inseparable from Cort, but he knew the difference between right and wrong; he could never had faked the shocked, bewildered effect Mapin's words were having on him.

Finally, impatient with Mapin's line of questioning, Alex

put in, "I'd like to ask something, Cort. Was Li with you the whole time yesterday?"

Cort gave him a bland, easy glance. "Not every minute, no. Is that important? We all split up now and again and fanned out. We was turning out the brush along the creek for calves, and it went faster if we broke up."

"You didn't keep in sight or call of each other all the time?"

"Not all," Cort said in a mildly ruffled tone. "Alex, don't tell me I got to swear to you I'm innocent?"

Alex said flatly, "You'd do better to worry what a grand jury'll believe," then swung around on his heel, hands rammed in his pockets. He scowled at the ground, absently listening to Mapin drone more questions. Cort's facile, unworried air, his touch of injured irritation, left Alex unsure. He told himself, *You don't know anything yet, so go slow.*

He swung around again as Mapin grimly said, "I want y'all to ride out to the Redemption with me. I want you to see this business with your own eyes. You too, Alex, so you'll have no doubts. After, if any of you is hiding something, any old thing that might help find the killer, he'll maybe change his mind."

They rode northeast across the rolling sedgegrass. The wind undulated the grass in gentle waves; the morning was quiet except for the stir of horses, the creak of leather.

Alex gave Chino a thoughtful, lid-narrowed glance—the Mexican's dark, ugly face was sober, maybe a shade bored, exactly as you would expect an innocent Chino to react to a possible murder charge. His carefree manner was sloughed, and that was all. Alex was less sure of Chino than he was of Liam, yet he couldn't believe that Chino had taken part in the grisly killing. His streak of Spanish devilry might make him capable of it, but Cort's good behavior had been entrusted to him, and the more he thought about it, the more he believed Chino would take that trust seriously. He couldn't blame Chino for not feeling he'd had to watch Cort every minute, yet suppose Chino had reason to suspect

Cort of covering up something—would he speak up? For in the muddy uncertainty of the situation, one thing stood out starkly: Cort was the only person at GT whom he'd unequivocally believe capable of unprovoked, cold-blooded killing.

The Redemption was a muddy straggle whose banks were matted and overgrown. As they rode, Chino and Cort pointed out the different places they'd split up to divide the work, guessing at how long they had been apart each time. On at least two different occasions early yesterday, they'd been apart an hour or more. *Long enough,* Alex thought.

Mapin said at last, "There's the place." He pointed at a liveoak motte set back from the creek, and swung his horse that way. A wagon and team were pulled up by the trees, and two men were standing by it. "Old Man Cady and his boy," Mapin explained. "They brought the wagon out to take the bodies home. I told 'em to leave 'em be till I could fetch you out."

Alex glanced at him. "This could be trouble, Lou."

"I reckon not. I made it clear to Cady I won't stand for any. No need to tell you too."

"No." Alex shot a warning look at Cort, who faintly smiled and shrugged his shoulders.

Alex had seen Rufus Cady only once or twice, never without the Spencer repeater he always carried, usually on his saddle but never leaving it in his boot when he left his horse. It was not a killer's weapon; what it seemed to grimly declare was that Cady wanted trouble with no man, and the rifle was to prevent trouble. He was a medium-tall man in his late fifties, pared down to bone and lean muscle. He wore plainest linsey clothes; his beard was a frosty bristle, his face brown as old oak leaves after frost and deeply troughed by time and weather. He stood with the rifle in the crook of his arm, hipshot, and looked over each of them as they rode up. He said, "One of them?"

Mapin said, "You give your word," as he stepped to the ground.

"It'll be kept. We'll wait long enough to see what kind of justice we get from you, Mapin."

"That could be up to a judge." Mapin moved forward into the grove, Alex, Chino and the two Trasks following.

The wrapped corpses in their hide covering lay in the tall grass. The hides had been slashed open, probably by young Cady when he'd found them. The bodies inside were enough exposed to leave no doubt how they died. They had been bound hand and foot with pieces of rawhide *riata*, doubtless their own; the hides had been wrapped tightly around them and stakes driven through the hides to anchor them fast to the earth. They were far enough from any tree so that the sun, broiling down all day, had gradually and excruciatingly drawn the green hides hard and tight till their iron embrace had tightened off wind and circulation. The brands on the hides had been turned plainly up: each was a GT.

Alex forced himself to look for a full half-minute, then he turned away, the muscles in this throat knotted. "Death of the Skins."

Mapin looked at him sharply. "What?"

"Death of the Skins. I've heard of it. A Spanish trick."

"Ever been used hereabouts?" Cady demanded. Mapin shook his head, and Cady's hawklike gaze pounced on Chino Lucero. But he said only, "You find out anything from these rich people, Mapin?"

The sheriff told him what little he had learned. Rufus Cady listened in silence while Struther Cady, fingering one of the new repeating Winchesters, moved up beside him. He was about twenty-five, a black-haired young man inches taller than his father; he was rawboned and lean as a hound's tooth. He had dark eyes that were quick and feral. As Mapin finished, he said swiftly, "That's enough to arrest the three of 'em on."

"Like hell he will," Cort murmured.

"Shut up, Cort!" The flat coldness of Alex' voice rang startling in his own ears, but its sharpness cut through the moment's tension. "Lou, you have Judge Sharpe set a date for a hearing. We'll come in then. I want this thing cleared up."

Mapin stroked his chin and said in a moderate voice, "Reckon that's how it should be."

Alex swung a glance at Cady. "These boys have any family?"

Rufus gave him a long stare, as if debating whether to answer. Finally he said, "Mort was an orphan. Tris, he had an old pap and mam he was sending all he made. The boys was both kin, and I had 'em in my care. That's a trust."

Alex nodded, then dug a roll of bills from his pocket. "Money can't pay for a life, but Drucker's father and mother will need this. Two hundred and fifty dollars, all I have. You can send them two hundred; the rest will pay for a funeral."

Struther Cady said hotly, "Don't take it, Pa! He's trying to buy us off their backs."

"Watch your mouth, boy," Mapin put in flatly. "I don't know how much of what's his Alex McKenna has give away over the years to folks in need, but it's plenty. Everybody in these parts knows the kind of man he is."

"I heard." Cady nodded. "McKenna, you and me ain't met formal, but you're one man I never heard any but a good word said of."

"I can say the same."

"You heard me cussed for a God damn nigger-lover, ain't you?"

Alex smiled faintly. "Could be if we're different there, it's because you roar."

"Maybe you whisper, but I got an idee you make yourself heard all right." Cady tipped his rifle downward as he hooked both thumbs in his jeans. "We can bury our own, McKenna. But Tris's folks can use the money, that fifty too. I'll put in some of my own and see they get it all."

Alex handed him the money, and again Struther began a furious objection, but his father cut him off sharply: "I ain't taking a cent for us, just for this dead boy's old folks. And I'm taking it from this man where I wouldn't from any damn Trask because I know by God when a man means it. You dry up all that jaw, boy, and go fetch the wagon here." Rufus bent with his knife to cut the dried hides and ropes from the two bodies, and Struther tramped sullenly away to the wagon.

As they started back toward the GT, Alex felt Mapin's thoughtful glance. "Alex," he said, "you ought to talk up more often. Could of gone bad back there, Cort and the Cady boy kicking up their spurs, if you hadn't put Cort down fast."

Chino was amused—"Haaah"—but Cort was not, and he reined angrily over to Mapin's stirrup. "He didn't put no-body down!"

Mapin only eyed him a trifle wearily, and Cort flushed and said defensively, "Well, Buck left orders I got to do what Alex says, but that don't mean nothing. If Buck was here, you would of seen things really handled."

"Yeah," Mapin said dryly. "Nobody needs to second-guess how Buck would of handled things. Only thing I can't be sure of is how many men would of come away from this slung across their saddles."

XIV

MOST OF THE Texas drovers who had followed Shanghai Pierce to Ellsworth after Abilene's demise in '71 hadn't been as fortunate as Jonathan Trask in finding an immediate buyer. More than forty thousand cattle wintered in the region next winter, so that when the 1872 season came in full swing, Ellsworth succeeded Abilene as the leading shipping point on the Kansas Pacific. It was another prosperous year for everyone concerned, the only disgruntled note coming from the wintering drovers who had not only had to bear a heavy expense for the use of holding grass, but had to settle for less than top prices, their steers having aged past prime.

Jonathan returned to the Yegua country in the late summer after the usual successful drive and sale of his herd; he was becoming phlegmatic about success. He was in excellent physical condition from hard work straining the booze out of his system, and trigger-tempered because he hadn't taken a drink in weeks.

Learning about the bizarre murder of Drucker and Gant made his wrath flare like sparked gunpowder. He raged around the office a minute or so, then wheeled to confront Alex, who was patiently waiting for his anger to taper off. "I suppose *you* think Cort done it?"

"I don't know," Alex admitted. "I know Liam didn't, and I doubt Chino knows anything."

"Jesus. Only a God damn Injun would kill like that. Look, suppose'n them two had enemies among their own kin. If somebody taken out a grudge on 'em, a good way to throw off suspicion would be to wrap the bodies in a couple hides with the Trask brand."

"That's possible, of course." Alex' tone was skeptical. "Lou Mapin would have covered that angle in his investigation, I'm sure."

Jonathan snorted. "Wouldn't make no mind how many questions he ast, those people would stick together for each other."

"Not Rufe Cady," Alex said positively. "If he had sound reason to suppose any of his people guilty, he'd turn 'em over to Mapin, kin or not."

"Why you so almighty sure of Cady?"

"It's an impression you get of a man—not something you can explain. Look, Lou hasn't turned up a thing that says guilty about any party. The hearing next week will set out the known facts and show we have nothing to hide. The grand jury won't indict and it'll never go to trial."

Alex, Chino Lucero, and all the Trasks but Mercy, who hadn't been off the ranch in years, rode in for the hearing. These days Katytown was showing the flush of a mild prosperity. A steady flow of Yegua longhorns up the trail had brought back a steady flow of Yankee gold; people had money and they wanted to spend it.

Riding in this morning, Alex saw all the signs of new businesses on the way in; he felt the old twinge of guilt that hadn't troubled him in a long time. He took special note of the professional building that was going up alongside the courthouse, and the old daydream of a law office, a practice of his own, gripped him in a musing that held as they all dismounted at the livery and turned their horses over to the hostler.

Court wouldn't convene for a good hour, so the Trask brothers headed for a saloon while Alex sauntered around, still musing as he watched the carpenters at work. Finally he drifted into the general store and looked over the saddles, falling into a friendly hassle with Old Montrose, the proprietor, about the price of a secondhand one. "You damn' Scotchman, why don't you cut loose and buy a new one?" Montrose was saying good-naturedly, then looked past him with his old face pinching up into a bland stiffness that barely masked disapproval. "Do something for you, Miss Cady?"

Alex stood by a counter resting his palms on the saddle he had been eying. For a moment the name barely registered; then he turned his head quickly. The sharpness of his reaction brought the girl's head around too. It was surprise that had made Alex look; something else kept him looking;

he was vaguely aware of this and he knew he shouldn't stare, and yet couldn't stop.

She was nineteen or a little more, and she wasn't pretty by any stretch of fancy. She was tall for a girl, not quite the height of an average man but able to face Alex eye-to-eye. Her figure was on the thin and wiry side, almost boyish but for the fullness of breasts which gave more than demure roundings to the loose drabness of the homespun dress she wore. The skirt was neatly patched in several places.

Her face was arresting in a way; he couldn't say how unless it was a composite effect, because every feature was distinctly wrong. Her mouth was too wide and full, her straight nose too long, her face too thin, angular as a boy's. Her eyes were a fine level gray under straight tawny brows, but her gaze was direct as a man's—very unbecoming, or was it only disconcerting? He disapproved anyway; she was too sun-browned and her hair, streaked almost white by the sun, was done in a careless blond braid that hung down her back nearly to her waist.

She met his stare indifferently, then looked away. She was a rawhider girl, and Old Montrose treated her with the cold politeness her place deserved. *Cady.* Alex frowned at the saddle, still wondering about the name, when Struther Cady came in. He glowered briefly at Alex, then moved over by the girl. Then Alex could be sure; she was as fair as Struther was dark, but their features were almost twinlike.

Old Montrose began filling the order, most of it bulky staples he had to drag from a storeroom at the rear. Struther hoisted a heavy keg to his shoulder and carried it outside to a big freight wagon. The girl bent to wrestle up a heavy sack of flour, and Alex said unthinkingly, "Here, let me help."

She gave him a very level look and said, "Thankye," and surrendered the sack. Alex grabbed two corners, lifted it with a practiced knee, ducked his shoulder to take the weight as his arms swung it back, and started for the door. He almost collided with Struther whose angry look shot to the girl, then back to Alex. "Give me that!" He took a rough hold on the sack and knocked off Alex' hat swinging it to his own shoulder. He said hotly then, "You keep a distance from my sister—any of our women, you hear me, McKenna?"

"McKenna," the girl said in surprise. "Is he—"

"He's a friend of them Trasks!"

"Struther, didn't Pa mention him? Pa said—"

"I don't give a damn what Pa said! Dammit, Jo, you been told and told to put down any stranger that talks to you!"

"By you, nobody else," she said heatedly. "If you figure I'm a little kid needs protecting, it follows I ain't old enough to be trusted with buying supplies. Do it yourself, sorehead—you can load it all up too." Her face was colored with anger as she marched to the door, pushed her brother aside, and went out past him.

"Ah, JoAnne—Jo!" Struther cursed as he tried to wheel through the door after her. He was overbalanced by the heavy sack which hit the doorjamb, burst open, and splashed flour across the floor. Struther stood swearing bitterly; he looked at Alex and swore again, then tramped out the door.

Alex bent and picked up his flour-spattered hat; he dusted it off carefully and set it on his head, then looked gravely at the speechless proprietor. "Don't guess you're in the mood for any more small talk, Monty," he observed, and left the store.

The courtroom was crowded, and the crowd flowed out around the veranda and windows of the courthouse. It was only a grand jury hearing whose outcome seemed foregone, but the grisly murders of Drucker and Gant had excited a good deal of attention. It meant a welcome break in the humdrum of a long summer, besides which just about everybody was convinced that the Trask boys and Lucero had done the job, and that Buck Trask had ordered it done before he'd left for Ellsworth. Despite the recent swing of public opinion against the Trasks, an approval of drastic measures against rustlers had put a surprising number of people in the Trask camp. A lot of them found no moral objection at all in an act which had disgusted even Jonathan—and that took some doing.

However, the testimony by Sheriff Mapin, by Cort and Chino Lucero and Alex himself, by Rufus Cady, became matter-of-factly dull with repetition. Liam, inarticulate with excitement, was excused from testifying. Only Struther Cady threatened to lend a heated note when he took the stand, but Judge Sharpe kept him sternly in hand.

Watching Cort's cocky blandness, Alex was strongly tempted to call him back to the stand and tear his story to pieces. A glib, tough cross-examiner could have shredded his facile defenses—assuming that he had anything to hide—and Alex was angry with the court for not providing a better one. He had to forcibly remind himself that he was present for the defense, that he wasn't only expected but obliged to stand solidly for his client's interests. Above all, he must not let his private dislike for Cort influence his objectivity. Sift it as fine as you pleased, there wasn't a ghost of tangible evidence except the thinly circumstantial against anyone.

No indictment was handed down; the court adjourned and the crowd outside broke up as the spectators began filing out. On impulse, Alex pushed his way to the side of Rufus Cady, who was moving toward the door with his son and daughter. When Cady turned to him, though, Alex found he didn't know what he wanted to say. He finally stated lamely that he wished Mapin had been able to learn more.

"So do we," Cady said, his eyes hawk-irised. "But I wonder why you feel called on to tell me so, McKenna. Ain't got a doubt about the men you defended, have you?"

"If he ain't," Struther snapped, "he damn well ought to—"

"Just shut your jaw," Rufus cut in with a tired note. "I want to go by the law, McKenna. I got an outspoke way that puts folks in mind of a fire-eater, but the fact is otherwise. Fire's no diet for making a life on. The war taught me that. Me and mine got a chance here, and I don't want to have to fight for it. But don't think because I made myself swallow this business, I can be pushed a lot further. Trask better not make that mistake. You tell him."

"I will," Alex said. "Anything you want me to tell him about the cattle he's been losing?"

Rufus lowered his head a half-inch. "I have got wind a few of my people was responsible, but I hate reading Scripture to any man. I talked soft to the ones I suspect, and it ain't helped. Now I'll bust them if need be and bust them hard. That's my promise."

He nodded briefly and moved on, Struther too, his face sullen. JoAnne Cady gave Alex that very direct, disturbing look, and he thought she might say something, but she followed her father and brother without a word.

Alex went to a saloon with Jonathan and the others for a victory drink, then went to the livery to claim his horse. This whole business had left a sour taste in his mouth, and liquor would not kill it. He was glad to leave the town behind and get onto the prairie under a clean hot sun. He went slowly on the road, presently coming over a rise to see a heavy wagon bogged in mud in the swale below. It was a marshy place badly filled when the road was graded, and after a thaw or a heavy rain it was always a treacherous crossing for a loaded wagon.

Alex rode down to the wagon and pulled up by a front wheel, touching his hat. JoAnne Cady was alone on the seat, talking quietly to the horses. Her handling of the team was strong and steady; she did not fight the reins or get angry, but the back wheel had sunk almost axle-deep into a pothole and she was mired solidly.

Again her level, appraising stare. "Reckon I'm hung up in here good. Don't want to take nobody out of their way, but reckon you could give a hand?"

In this country it went without saying that nobody in

trouble went unhelped, particularly a woman, but there was a stiffness in her tone. For a moment Alex thought this reflected a hostility over how things had gone in court, then realized quite suddenly it was only the backwoods shyness of a girl to whom strangers were almost unknown. Even her direct gaze that he'd thought almost bold was only ingenuous; yet she was uncomfortable and did not want to show it.

"Certainly," he said, and swung to the ground. "Have to lighten the load in the wagon bed somewhat, though."

"I'll he'p." She fixed the reins to the seat and stood, setting a foot on the wheel. Alex stepped over and put his hands up to her waist, bracing himself because she was all of his size; she set her hands on his arms and started gingerly to let him take her weight. In that instant, he started to swing her down, her foot slipped on the wheel—she simply dropped fully onto him. Alex' boots skidded and he went down flat on his back in the mud, JoAnne Cady on top of him. She made a muffled, mortified sound and fought in a half-panic to push away from him, her hands and knees getting no purchase on the slick mud. He groaned as her weight smacked squarely down on him again. With that, though, he had a brief wild awareness of the young, wiry life of her, the writhing warmth and squirm of quick thin muscles.

They got disentangled finally and floundered to their feet. Both of them were smeared with black muck from head to foot, and standing ankle-deep in mud, snapping it from his hands, Alex felt his temper come up—damn such a big clumsy horse of a girl. Then he saw the almost horrified mortification in her young face as she stared at his mud-plastered suit.

"Oh, I—I just can't say how sorry I am. My God—er, goodness. I sure didn't mean—"

"No harm done." He smiled with a great effort. "Let's get up on dry land and see what can be done about it."

They slogged out of· the mud and tore up handfuls of dead grass to rub away the bulk of the mud. "What you grinning at?" she said with a hot and abrupt resentment.

"I was grinning *with* you, Miss Cady, if you'd been grinning, that is. It's kind of funny."

"It ain't funny at all!"

"All right," Alex said moderately. He supposed it wasn't at that, for her. Her wet, muddy dress was probably the best she owned.

They set to unloading the supplies stacked in the wagon, which took awhile because each heavy crate or keg had to be carried through the lake of mud that surrounded the wagon to dry ground.

"Leave the lighter stuff," Alex said. "See if you can ease it out now."

He held out his hand, and she eyed him a guarded moment before taking it, supporting herself as she stepped onto the wheel and up to the seat. Alex swung back on his horse as she gave the team a sharp hooraw. The horses leaned into the harness and the wagon stirred forward, but it was going deeper in the mud, the whole stern canting abruptly as the right wheel sank halfway to the hub.

"Whoa up," he said, and unslung his *riata*. Reining his mount around to the other side of the wagon, he shook out the coils and twirled out a huge loop, flicking it easily over the hub of the rear wheel on this side, the one less deeply mired, then over the wagon box'. Alex spurred his horse away to take up the slack, then gave her a nod. JoAnne's shout sent the team surging into the harness, and Alex put his horse's straining weight into dragging the lariat taut. Slowly again the wagon budged and, as the sagging offside heaved suddenly up, the heavy vehicle rumbled free of the mud.

In a few minutes, working with a paucity of words, they had the wagon loaded again. Alex picked up his rope and coiled it as he walked to his horse. He felt the familiar heavy ache that always attacked his leg after it had taken a heavy exertion, and then he felt JoAnne Cody's stare. Ordinarily his limp was barely noticeable; now it was stiffly pronounced, and he felt a sudden fury of resentment against he wasn't sure what.

Again he stepped into his saddle, only then looking at her. He did not want to; he wanted only to say a quick goodbye and leave. She spoke first, saying swiftly, "That was right fine roping—way you handled the wagon too. I never seen better. You give me a start there."

Alex eyed her narrowly, his reins lifted. "Why?"

"Well, Pa said you're a lawyer fellow, and I could see today you're right at home in a court of law. And so fine-spoke and all." She smiled, and he could see her faint embarrassment. "Way you handle a horse and rope give me a start, that's all."

Alex settled his hands to his pommel, feeling about as sheepish as any damned fool. She had stared, then seeing he was offended, had quick-wittedly covered with a compliment that was not supposed to deceive him, only salve his abraised pride. "Well, I grew up with a horse and a rope and I'm still with them."

"I should of guessed that's how you took a bunged-up leg," she said seriously. "A body can't work horses and cows all his life without getting stove up now and again. Least-ways I never knew anybody did."

Alex was surprised by her quick, sure wisdom. Seeing he was mollified, she hadn't hesitated an instant in bringing the disquieting point back into the open where it belonged. He had to grin. "I guess that's right." He glanced back toward Katytown. "Where are your father and brother?"

"Pa has some all-day business to tend to. Struther says he is going to drink up a storm, so I left him to do it. There's only three of us now, Ma being two years gone, and somebody ought to be on the place." She swung up unaided to the high seat, quick and sure-muscled, and picked up the reins. She sat the high seat straight-backed, her hair a honeyed nimbus with the sun at her back, taking a man's eye without meaning to. "Hope they don't have a run-in with them people of yours, I supposed they stayed to get lickered up too. What you stand up for a man like that for, anyway?"

"I stood up for three of them."

"I mean the big Trask, one they call Buck. They say you're his best friend. Now I met you, it just don't make sense."

"Sometimes you don't choose friendship—either of you. It chooses you."

"Is *that* s'posed to make sense, now?"

"Maybe not," he smiled. "But if you have a friend, you take his side when he's right and try to turn him right if you figure he's wrong. I haven't turned him much, but I've slowed him down now and again."

"When has he been right? I'd admire to hear what you can say for a man like that, Mr. McKenna."

"A man like that," Alex said slowly. "A man too big to play it small. You didn't know him as he was once, Miss Cady. I did, and I saw what changed him. If he was to blame for letting himself be changed, then all men but a few saints should be -blamed for being no less pliant when the chips are down. And God knows he's no saint. The thing is, his mistakes had to be giant-sized because his nature wouldn't let him do anything in a small way."

"But that ain't right," she said angrily. "It's like you're saying nothing he ever done was his fault."

"Faults? He has a wagonload. But the wrong he's done doesn't make the people he's dealt with right. He never set out that I know of to get anybody who hadn't wronged him. I hate war, Miss Cady; almost no war I've ever read of or heard of was justifiable by either side—yet a few were, because there's such a thing as one-sided aggression and you have to meet it or go under. That's the kind of war Jonathan Trask fought for this whole country a few years back, and because he did, it's a decent place for men to live and raise their families. I railed against his methods, but rattling an empty scabbard would have been just as wrong. And yes, the way he bulls ahead hurts the wrong people sometimes—but why not reserve a little of your indignation for the right ones, Miss Cady? I'm thinking of several of your good neighbors. Because whatever else Buck Trask may be, he's never been a thief."

JoAnne Cady said glacially, "I'll say good day to you now, Mr. McKenna."

Alex nodded with a chill dignity, saying, "I'll bid you the same, Miss Cady," and made an ironic gesture of touching his hat. A clod of drying mud caked on his sleeve crumbled away and thudded on his shoulder, which didn't lend much to the support of dignity.

XV

WHEN HE GOT HOME, Alex avoided questions by slipping unseen into his quarters and changing his clothes at once. The brothers returned quite late. Liam looked miserable, but not from drinking; he hated liquor. Jonathan was half-drunk and wearing a vicious stare that dared anyone to cross him. Cort was barely able to stand, and booze wasn't all to blame; his clothes were torn and dirty, and his face had been chopped to raw meat. It seemed he had run afoul of Struther Cady; a few hot words were exchanged and subsequently Struther had beaten him to a pulp. It was the fact of Cort's defeat, not his sorry condition, that had Jonathan upset. He shredded an entire cigar to rags between his teeth while he was talking about it.

Cort didn't appear for breakfast next morning. Jonathan's brooding anger held, and nobody had much to say. Halfway through the meal Chino Lucero entered the house unannounced, with the news that he'd found a piece of fence broken on the east side of the horse pasture this morning. He judged that six prime saddle horses had been driven off, and the sign said that a single night rider had done the job. Jonathan promptly reached for his hat, and Alex decided to ride along.

The three men struck eastward along the bank of the Yegua, Chino picking up the trail. Though the area was heavily brushed, the rider seemed to have driven his steal across the most open and sandy places; track was plentiful, and that seemed curious, as if he'd wanted to be quickly followed.

Within an hour they came on the horses on a sandbar projecting from the bank. But the sight of them was enough to make a strong man sick in his guts.

All the animals were alive, but each one had been brutally, senselessly mutilated in one way or another. Two had been hamstrung in both hind legs. Two of them had their tongues cut out. Two had their eyes gouged clear out of the sockets.

They must have been tied and thrown down and the dirty work done, Chino observed with the true Spanish indifference to cruelty. Jonathan simply stood and cursed, and it was clear that what angered him was having good saddle stock ruined. Alex could not say anything—he did not want to look at the pitiful sight, and he could not look away. The wanton shame of this was more than he could bear, and his eyes stung with gratitude when Jonathan, still swearing steadily, yanked his Winchester from its boot and, walking from horse to horse, ended the suffering of each.

Jonathan whispered, "God damn," staring down at the dead animals as the last rifle echoes died away in the morning. "What sort of an evil bastard would cut up fine horses like this?"

Hard on the heels of his words a heavy slug cut through the brush and slapped into the hindquarters of his mare; the animal screamed and half-crumpled, then went down. The three men broke into motion at once, lunging for the thin cover of brush along the bank.

They waited pressing against the earth, their guns out. Alex hadn't seen a thing, not a trace of powdersmoke or a stir of leaves. There was not the shadow of a sound. Close to the ground he could smell earth and green plants and the odor of waterside rot; the insects took up a broken humming again and the sun moved on the water—everything was normal.

After a while Chino eased onto his haunches and looked at Jonathan, who nodded, squinting at the wall of greenery. Chino faded into the thickets. Finally he whistled sharply, and the two of them rose and walked through the brush to where he was squatting.

"He was on foot and he is gone," Chino reported. "Eh, he's plenty good in brush, this fella. Ain't no Injun, I'm think, but he don't leave enough track to follow." He pointed at some shallow scuffs in the ground. "He is squat here and get a clear shot."

Jonathan growled, "That God damn Struther kid?"

"Haaah," Chino snorted. "I'm not think so. He is hothead; he come straight on, he don' think something through. This fella here, he take plent' time and think her clear through, eh? Then he don' shoot at none of us, jus' the horse, an' he is gone."

The assailant's thinking had been patient and thorough all right, Alex reflected, but it was like the thinking of a crabbed, twisted mind. Why drive off a half-dozen horses and leave plain sign, inflict senseless mutilations on the animals, lay up to take a shot at a man's horse and afterward fade enigmatically away?

Somehow the only explanation, a retaliation by some wronged settler, seemed unsatisfactory. Even Jonathan's usual bluster was absent as, after dispatching his crippled mount, he doubled up with Alex and the three men headed back for headquarters.

In the days that followed, Jonathan and his ranch were the brunt of one savage depredation after another. Until now his cattle had sometimes simply dropped from sight, rustled, or

were found butchered for the meat and hides. Now time
and again their carcasses turned up by the dozen, shot for
no apparent reason and left to rot for buzzard bait. One day
the crew might have to disperse in several directions to
smother several grass fires that had suddenly, mysteriously
started at the same time in different places. The next night
they would have to rouse out to wet down a blazing shed,
with never a sign of a prowler.

Jonathan was shot at twice again, or rather shot close
to; there could be no doubt he was the object of this weird
war of nerves. Once his horse was killed under him while
he was riding home from town at night. Another time he
was caught out on the prairie and pinned for two hours
in a swale by a hidden marksman located on a nearby
ridge.

Again and again Chino took up the track of the elusive
enemy, but with no success. He had a fair idea, from what
sign he found, of the man's size and build; the tracks of his
horse were also distinctive; and always, to all appearances,
he worked alone. This was all Chino could learn. The man
handled himself with a wily ease that put Sheriff Lou Mapin,
who lent his services with equal futility, downwind of a
notion.

"I figure he's a professional, Buck," he observed. "There's
men who hire out for the cattle wars who ain't regular
'warriors.' They're pure assassins and they work alone. They
come as a drummer or a grubline drifter or suchlike, all un-
suspected, to size up the situation. Or maybe not a soul
will see 'em till they're ready to strike. Well, I would say
this boy of yours has been about. He's done this kind of
thing before."

"You saying he's been hired?" Jonathan scowled. "The
Bittercold bunch, by God."

"Don't jump all that fast," Mapin cautioned. "Not without proof. There's a lot don't make sense, even if I got this
bugger pegged right. A killer of that stripe don't play with
a victim. He's a professional who plays it safe as he can,

and he finishes the job clean as a whistle. I take it this fellow is in no rush. He has made a game of it and has took some long chances doing so."

The "game" was clearly getting under Jonathan's skin. His surly ways worsened. Where he had once roared, he began to snap, his temper fraying more with each fresh assault by a lone, wraithlike enemy, an enemy he couldn't touch.

His outbursts fell on the hapless crew, the loyal core of which was the group of ex-slaves he'd shown the way to manhood and who had stuck by him through the years. Inevitably his insults acquired a highly personal tinge that no man worth his salt could swallow long. For these were proud men; Jonathan had given them a pride to live for, and till now the admitted racism in his affectionate roaring at his "God damn burheads" had been stingless. Remarks like "Christ, next you niggers will get the notion if you take on white airs a spell, the color will rub off," were something else.

Men who had built homes and raised families on the ranch began to quietly pack and depart. The ones who stayed, men who had made the Trask crew the envy of every rancher in the country, went about their work with a sullen, almost ugly indifference. The solidarity that had welded together the GT people like a family was ended. An essential something in the Trask empire, something that couldn't be measured in money or herds, was gone. Everybody at GT was glumly aware of the change.

Then there was all the trouble with Cort. The signs of his drubbing at the hands of Struther Cady had faded to a faint limp and a few yellowish-green bruises, but the undercutting of his pride had left him raw where it didn't show. Even Jonathan was no longer a drag on his wildness; he went on one mad escapade after another, always involving whiskey and women, always leading to brawls and jail. Jonathan no longer listened to Alex' warnings; he de-

fended Cort with a stubborn fury, putting up bail money
and paying for all damages.

Alex, just to get away from things awhile, went to Katytown alone one Saturday when nobody else did.

After completing a few minor errands, he loitered along
the street. Almost at once he spotted the Cadys' big freight
wagon; it was drawn up in front of Old Montrose's store, just
as he had first seen it the day he'd helped JoAnne Cady
extricate it from a mudhole.

Alex sauntered over by the wagon and took up a careless stance leaning against the hitchrail. Not that he was
really curious, but he wondered if the girl were in town
today. He could hear Rufus Cady's voice from inside the
store. He was commencing to feel pretty foolish standing
there, when Cady came out of the store toting a heavy
crate which he heaved into the wagon bed.

Straightening, he gave Alex a civil nod. "McKenna. My
girl told me how you helped her that time. I'm beholden."

Alex hesitated only a moment before mentioning the campaign of terrorism against Jonathan by a mysterious loner.
Cady hadn't heard about it; he seemed genuinely disturbed
by the news, and more so on learning that Jonathan believed someone had hired the man to dog him, and that it
was probably some of the Bittercold bunch who had sent
for him.

"What do you think, McKenna?"

"I don't know what to believe," Alex said truthfully.
"But I don't believe anything of the sort was arranged
with your knowledge. I told Buck so."

"But some of my kin might of taken action without me?"

Alex did not reply, and Cady shook his head. "I don't
reckon. I give the ones I figured was helping themselves to
Trask cows some harsh warnings. I figure what I said taken
pretty good. But I'll put my ear to the ground and see if I
can learn something. You be in town a week from today, I'll
let you know what I found."

Alex gave Cady a hand loading the supplies he had

purchased into the wagon. Afterward, he stood watching Cady drive away, his thoughts sober. He had liked this man from the first and knew that under different circumstances, they'd be friends. Certain that Cady was innocent of any intrigue, he was determined to see that Jonathan's temper-bleak suspicions brought no harm to the man or his family.

Alex did not start home till late in the afternoon, timing his arrival for the supper hour. When he rode into headquarters, woodsmoke was curling from the chimneys of the still-occupied cabins along the creek; a faintness of talk reached him, and a drift of laughter.

A sudden depth of loneliness that shocked him welled high in Alex McKenna. Half the men on the crew had wives and children while he, busying himself over the years with Buck Trask's responsibilities, had hardly had time to think of any life for himself. Not yet thirty, he was in a deadly rut of habit which, because of the demand it had placed on his energies, had never seemed a rut.

A discontent sharper than any he'd known was gnawing in him as he rode to the corrals. Then he forgot it, seeing Jonathan pacing back and forth by the corral gate, the cigar between his teeth in shreds. That was a sure symptom of his temper, and Alex could only wonder what now.

Jonathan gave him a red-eyed look. "You see Cort on your way in? Li?"

"Should I have?"

"All the crew that should be in is in but them, and I warned Cort his work ain't to take him over a mile from here."

"That was days ago," Alex observed. "With Cort, a message like that one bears repetition. You should have left Chino in charge of him after you got back, too. But then that didn't do much good while you were gone, did it?"

Jonathan stared at him. "That's almighty sharp talk, boy. What the hell's eating on you?"

Alex said, "Nothing, forget it," and set about turning in his

268

horse. Finished, he joined Jonathan by the gate again. "We might as well go eat. You won't hurry anything standing about here."

"He ain't back in an hour, I'm sending men out to find him," Jonathan muttered. "Wait. Someone coming there."

Two horses came into sight from beyond the walnut grove. Cort's horse and Liam's too, but only Cort was mounted, his fist clenched around a leadrope. A body, inert and loose and lifeless, hung bellydown across Liam's saddle.

Cort pulled up before them. His eyes were dark-pitted, and his mouth worked blindly. Then he choked out, "It was them Cadys done it, Buck. Them Cadys killed Li."

XVI

THEY WERE PUTTING out rock salt as Buck had ordered when he and Liam had come on the clear sign, Cort said. A trail had been broken through the brush where somebody had pushed a small bunch of cows along the creek bank, moving upstream.

The track was too plain to resist following, so the two of them had taken up the trail at once. It ran steadily northeast, and unlike the other cattle thefts, the track did not peter out. Soon they'd come on a barranca where the steers had been butchered for the hides, their raw carcasses left in the dry gully.

From there Cort and Li had followed the trail of the lone horseman to the Cady ranch. Cort had reasoned that the hides were hidden in one of the outsheds, and after reconnoitering to make sure they wouldn't be seen, they had stolen in for a closer look. They had uncovered the fresh hides under some cordwood in the first shed they searched.

Cort had promptly gone to the house and yelled for Rufus Cady to come out. He did at once, his son Struther too, and both of them had gone for their guns the instant Cort made his accusation. In the exchange of fire, the Cadys were driven back into the house, but not before Li had taken a bullet in the chest.

He was hard hit, coughing blood, as Cort got him back to their horses. They headed back for the GT, but within a half-mile Li had fallen from his saddle. He was dead in less than ten minutes.

Jonathan said not a word as Cort talked. He stood by Li's mount, listening, his face strangely wrenched, and now and then brought his big fist down against the cantle. When Cort finished, Jonathan whirled on him.

"Why'n't you come back here soon's you trailed them beeves to Cady's? Why'n't you fetch me?"

"Buck—"

"I'd a-gone in there with twenty men and cleaned out them rawhiding bastards, and Li'd be alive now."

Alex saw the agony seared into his face, a driven wildness that was more than raw grief; a tension and inheld rage were finding focus too in this moment, exploding with all the feral bigness of his nature.

"*Li'd be alive*. I'll talk to you later," Jonathan added with an abrupt and terrible calm, his eyes fixing Cort like gunmuzzles. "Right now there's a job to be done."

Alex did not even try to remonstrate with him—not then. In fifteen minutes the whole crew was in saddle, riding out in a body toward the Bittercold range. Jonathan rode ahead of them all, his chin like a bearded crag; his face was ironlike in the fading light of day. He never looked to left or right, and finally Alex, riding nearly at his side, edged over to his stirrup.

"Buck. Don't do this."

Jonathan's stare seemed to go through him.

"I talked to Rufus Cady in town today," Alex said. "He didn't know about anybody being hired to gun you, and he promised to look into the matter." Still Jonathan said nothing and Alex tried again, a desperation crowding his words, "Buck, look, anybody could have planted those hides on Cady's place. Doesn't it strike you as strange that trail was so clear?"

"It don't matter," Jonathan said meagerly, "if someone planted a thousand hides. Cady killed Li. Him or that whelp of his did. I'm going to string 'em both up, and let the buzzards plant 'em."

"If Cort hadn't gone and—"

"They opened fire first!"

"That's what Cort claims," Alex said dryly. "Anybody who's met both Cady and Cort and doesn't happen to be Cort Trask's brother just might not buy that for a moment. On the other hand, I wouldn't put it past Cady's son to fire first, but I'm sure his pa would keep the boy in check."

"That's a fancy guess to make Cort a liar on!"

"One thing I needn't guess about Cort, whether he were right or wrong. He'd tell about anything that happened so he was put in the right. And," Alex said deliberately, "you know damned well he would."

A deadlock of silence stretched between them, then Alex burst out, "Buck, for God's sake—do you want to hang?"

"I stretched plenty of cow thieves' necks and still got my own."

"Those were different circumstances, and you'll find out what the difference is if you go through with this—"

Alex talked on, but he might as well have talked against a blue norther. They were getting close to Cady's, and he began to wish he'd ridden to Katytown to fetch Lou Mapin. But then, what could Mapin have done?

The westered sun was livid at their sides and backs; the day was retreating fast, but there was enough light to show a rider coming across the brow of a hill ahead. Instantly, spotting them, the horsebacker switched course, wheeling away to the northwest.

Jonathan issued a flat order to Chino Lucero and another

crewman, in the same moment that Alex made out the rider's wind-blown skirt and yelled, "Buck!—tell 'em not to shoot! It's a woman."

"Head her off," Jonathan told them. "Bring her back here."

Chino and the Negro rider cut in a straight line toward a point well ahead of the woman. Before they intercepted her, she had veered due north. She rode ahead of them for a while, but it was a matter of a minute or two before they overhauled her.

Jonathan grimly held his men where they were, waiting. Shortly the three reached them, Chino and the other flanking the girl. It was JoAnne Cady, her eyes bright with anger; she was riding like a man and her fair hair was more disarrayed than ever.

"I seen her before," Jonathan muttered. "Couldn't say when."

"In the courtroom a few weeks ago," Alex said. "Cady's daughter."

"That right? Your pa know you're out, Missy?"

"He knows. He didn't like it, but I told him I was going to town for the sheriff, like it or not." She jerked at the reins Chino was holding. "You'll let me go if you know what's good for you."

"Now I'm scared," Jonathan grunted. "If your pa don't want a sheriff, and I can see why a cow thief don't, why you fetching one?"

"My pa's no thief." Her eyes were a blue steady blaze; she pulled sharply at the reins again. "He knew as soon as one of your brothers was hit in that shoot-out, you'd be coming to our place, just like you are. Him and Struther won't budge a step off it, they're waiting for you, but I got no foolish man pride. I'm fetching the sheriff!"

"You was," Jonathan said. "You better come with us." Abruptly he reined forward, and the others put their horses in motion behind him. JoAnne Cady rode at the rear, help-lessly holding her pommel, Chino's grip firm around her reins. After a minute, Alex fell back beside her.

"I tried to talk him out of it, Miss Cady."

"Oh, you did." She looked at him in wild appeal. "How hard did you try? Can't you do something? Why didn't *you* go for the sheriff?"

"Because if he could get there in time," Alex said slowly, "it wouldn't change a thing. Except one, and I don't want Lou Mapin's death on my hands."

She moved her head in disbelief. "No . . . you don't mean that. He wouldn't kill no sheriff."

"Likely not," Alex said bitterly, "if Mapin came too late. Then Buck would likely give himself up—he believes he can get off easy. But if Mapin got there before he does your pa and brother any harm, and Mapin tried to stop him . . ."

JoAnne was still slowly shaking her head, but he could see she believed him. She whispered, "You know that, don't you?"

"I know him."

"Please." She leaned toward him, a horrified pleading in her eyes. "Stop him somehow, can't you? Please try."

Alex did try. He could only rehash every argument he had already pushed, but he made a running harangue of it till he saw he was merely jogging Jonathan's temper to a tighter boil. Then he desisted.

Sunset made a spreading stain of gold-red as they came into first view of the Cady ranch. It was a hardscrabble place on a griddle-flat plain dotted by a few blackjack oaks. Even the comparative newness of the peeled-log buildings and the tidy look of the yard could not disguise the raw-hide poverty or the pride it had nurtured rather than beat down.

No sound came from the house; nothing moved behind the windows. The whole place looked quiet, almost deserted, except for a few horses stirring in the corral. Jonathan raised his hand for the others to halt, then set his jaw and rode in alone between the buildings. Suddenly he careened his horse to a stop, roaring, "Cady, you got plenty gall holding

273

on here, but it won't get you a thing. Save a sight of trouble and give up."

Cady's voice lifted at once in reply; he was inside the shelter of a trackshed. "You got nerve your own self, Trask. That's why I ain't cut you in half yet. But turn your men and get out o' here or I will."

Jonathan spoke quietly in the clean silence: "Go to hell and shoot, you murdering bastard."

He turned his mount with contemptuous unhaste, then idled back to where his men waited. He gave swift orders that took them out of their saddles and sent them fanning out on the run around the outbuildings, surrounding them. At the same time, not trusting Alex, he had Chino relieve him of his pistol and left a man to watch him and the Cady girl. Jonathan himself joined his men, motioning them to close in on the outbuildings. They knew which shed Rufus Cady was in, but his son might be stationed elsewhere.

Then somebody fired a rifle. It might have been Cady or his son, or one of the GT men Alex couldn't spot. The way things were breaking, it didn't matter a lot who opened the shooting. That single shot rang in brief isolation; then the gunfire broke out in earnest.

In seconds it was apparent that the Cadys had forted up in separate sheds set well apart so that rooting them out would prove a bitter job. No matter what approach the GT men took, they were exposed to the rifle of one Cady or the other; several times a hapless runner was caught in the crossfire. This much was clear enough; otherwise it was like any battle, a chaos of unleashed savagery, of powderstink and yelling men and screaming ones.

The end was a foregone conclusion, but still Rufus Cady surrendered only when one of the wild barrage of bullets the GT men had blindly poured into the sheds found his son. A heavy slug went through Struther's right arm, reducing the bone to splinters, and he could not keep the agony of it voiceless. When Rufus realized what had happened, he thrust his rifle out of the shed door and followed it, hands over his head. Struther had no taste for surrender, but reduced to sobbing pain, he had no choice.

Jonathan checked over his men; they had paid a brutal price for his fury. Two of them were cold dead, another would be dead in an hour or less; five had serious wounds of one sort or another. There were a number of minor injuries, Jonathan himself taking a nicked wrist.

"Was it worth it, Trask?" Rufus Cady shouted, the misery and rage in him trembling his voice. "Did you figure we'd just let you walk over us? Was it worth it?—don't ask yourself, ask them—your men. Ask the dead ones too."

Jonathan did not look at him, only turned his head and jutted his beard at a large oak a hundred yards from the house. It stood in ancient, gnarled isolation, like a frozen troll, in the slow twilight that was cloaking the plain.

"Take 'em over there."

"No—no!" The cry was torn from JoAnne Cady, and Jonathan snarled, "Tie up that damn' girl and stuff a gag in her mouth and put her in the house. Get to it."

A couple of riders moved slowly to obey. The girl's cries were muffled, and she was carried away. Alex sat his horse like a man in a nightmare, watching the men pull off toward the big oak. He could see the Cadys side by side under the tree as their wrists were tied and the nooses dropped over their heads; somebody was leading two horses over there. Alex' guard gave him a hesitant look, then left him and headed for the tree so as to miss nothing.

Alex blinked and straightened, coming to his senses. Now the Cadys were being lifted onto the saddles—while he sat here unguarded. He reined over to the nearest horse with a booted rifle on its saddle, and yanked the weapon free of leather. He kicked in his spurs, lunging his mount forward.

The knot of men broke apart as he raced down on them, and the way was clear to the tree where Jonathan was moving behind the horses the Cadys sat, quirt raised.

"Buck—" Alex savagely yanked his horse to a sliding

halt with one hand, bringing up his rifle with the other. "Buck, let them—"

He was aware of Chino Lucero coming up on his right like a lean ghost, and twisted a quick glance at him. A shot came, but not from Chino's gun. The Mexican was reaching for Alex' rein when something like an armored fist, unseen, smashed Alex in the shoulder and drove him sideward out of the saddle.

Vaguely he knew that Chino caught him as he fell, then was easing him to the ground on his back. He felt the massive, sledging pain in his shoulder, but set his teeth and held onto consciousness.

"*Amigo*," Chino was saying, "I'm plent' sorry this happen. It was not me fire. Chino is only mean to stop you before you get yourself hurt, that is all. Then Cort, he shoot."

Cort. A wilderness of pain and rage took hold of Alex, and then he turned his eyes just as Jonathan's quirt fell across the rumps of the two horses. They walked away, and the two bodies hung and kicked. Alex shut his eyes to the sight.

When he could look again, he saw Jonathan coming toward him. The words tore from him with the hoarseness of revulsion: "Get away—keep away from me, damn you!"

Jonathan came to a halt, staring at him, and Chino said then, "I'm think he out of his head."

"The hell I am!" Alex shouted, ignoring the throbbing pain the effort of speech cost. "Get away from me—you too. All of you bastards!"

"Do like he says," Jonathan said quietly.

"He's hurt pret' bad. I'm think—"

"I don't give a God damn what you think. Leave him be."

Chino eased his head and shoulders gently to the ground. Everything began to swim in his vision, but he heard the clear chink of Chino's spurs as he stood up, saying, "I'm go untie the girl. Someone got to see to him."

Jonathan's reply was lost as the red pain surged high, then ebbed into blackness. The next thing he was aware of, as if from a febrile distance, was the noise of riders going away, all but one.

There on his back, unable to move a muscle, his head turned sideways, Alex saw a rider sitting his horse by the dangling, twitching bodies. The man's head was back, a bottle tilted high in his fist; his throat moved. Then he lowered the bottle, and in the dimming light Alex saw he was Cort Trask. Cort saluted the two corpses, then lifted the bottle to Rufus Cady's mouth.

"Have a drink on me, you sorry ol' sonuvabitch—" The liquor splashed darkly off the white beard and spilled down Cady's clothes.

Cort reined back a little then, chuckling to himself in an inspired way. Now he stretched his arm high, upending the bottle over the heads of the dead men, pouring all the whiskey over them. Afterward he fumbled out a match and scratched it into flame. Alex raised his head an inch; a cry sighed weakly in his throat, and he dropped his head back, watching helplessly.

Cort's hands lifted, cupping the spoon of flame till it touched Cady's whiskers. An aura of blue flame grew around Cady's bristling beard, polishing his stony eyes and weathered face with an eery glow, spreading down to his drenched shirt. Cort's horse began to dance nervously, and Cort pulled back a safe distance, watching in open-lipped fascination as the fire quickly consumed the alcohol and ate into cloth, the blue flames turning to livid orange. Already the blaze was enveloping Cady's head and shoulders, and creeping downward. Struther's liquor-soaked clothes had caught by now, and he too was quickly turning into a human torch.

The last thread of Alex' consciousness was raveling off when, in a kind of blurring remoteness that seemed faraway and faint, he heard a woman's scream. He saw Cort jerk half-around in his saddle, looking backward; then he spurred swiftly away in the growing dusk. For Alex then, the dusk fled into sudden darkness, total and merciful.

XVII

A WEEK PASSED before his world took on meaning again. During that whole time, usually unconscious or out of his head, he was dimly aware that JoAnne Cady did what she could for him. Alone she had gotten him into the house, installed him in the big bed that had been her father's, and dressed his wound. She had brought the doctor from Katy-town too, she said, but Alex had no memory of that, only of JoAnne always nearby, always tending his needs.

He had the uncomfortable knowledge that he had pre-sented the same problems of care as an infant or an invalid, and the idea of cutting such a figure before the eyes of this backwoods girl dismayed him, as if his dignity and literacy had been stripped away with his clothes. Then, wondering how well any soft, effete woman could have done in her place, he felt ashamed of himself. But all the same, now that he was rational he saw to his own private needs, though he was still weak as a half-drowned cat and ran a risk of tearing open his healing wound.

That what had happened had changed the girl did not surprise him. She spoke only when spoken to, and then an-swered tersely and curtly. The briskness of her manner saved it from surliness, and a sharp woman was better than a sullen one. All the same he felt concern over the change in her. It was some time before he could bring himself to inquire about her father and brother.

"They hung and burned," she said in a flat monotone. "There wasn't nothing I could do. The ropes burned through pretty soon and they dropped to the ground, but they kept on burning. I was a spell getting the fire out, for all I tried, and they was burned so I was hard put to recognize 'em. After I got you inside and fixed you up, I went to town for the doctor and the sheriff. They come back with me. They took Pa and Struther to town for a coroner's inquest. Some of my kin brought them back here and we buried them."

It was the longest speech she had made; behind the deadness of her words, he felt a complex of feelings that held him uneasily silent.

Finally he asked about Jonathan. She knew only that Sheriff Mapin had served a warrant for his arrest, and Judge Sharpe had directed the grand jury to meet at a special term the first of next month in order to secure a quick indictment.

By the end of another week, Alex could sit up in bed and take solid food, but he felt dizzy and nearly fell when he tried to walk a little. He knew from JoAnne Cady's terse, distant attitude that she'd like to be rid of him, and the sooner the better. He had taken the bullet trying to save her menfolk and she felt obliged to pay the debt in full, but he was convinced that in her mind, though she said nothing, his long association with the Trasks was like an indelible taint.

He didn't improve matters by mentioning that Jonathan had been harrassed for weeks by an unknown assailant, nor by adding that on the day of his death, her father had promised Alex he'd try to learn what he could about those mysterious attacks.

She listened in icy silence, then said briefly, "A Cady's word binds his kin. If Pa says so, it'll be done. I'll do the asking myself."

"Look," Alex said in perplexity. "I didn't bring it up to make you feel obligated—"

"Pa's word was give. It needs to be kept." Without another word she left the room.

Early next morning she rode away from the ranch, setting the team toward town at a brisk clip. She did not return till well after dark. Entering Alex' room, she dropped a pile of newspapers on the bed without a word. He went through them quickly, feeling an unexpected stab of dismay. They were all out for Jonathan's scalp, the Austin papers in particular. Editorials branded him a blood-stained ogre, and a typical headline blared MAN-BURNER HELD FOR TRIAL.

Alex swore, throwing the papers down. "They all play up that the bodies were set afire. That was Cort's doing, not Buck's!"

JoAnne eyed him bitterly. "My pa and brother are just as dead."

"What Buck did was barbarous enough, all right, but they've worsened it to sell papers." Alex went through the tabloids again, scowling. The grand jury had indicted Jonathan Trask for murder in the first degree, while Cort and the GT crewmen who had assisted him had been indicted separately as accessories before the fact. "Not a mention that it was Li's death that set Buck off," Alex muttered. "Not a one."

Standing by the doorway, Jo Anne stiffened; her eyes began to smolder. "I suppose in your fancy lawyer's thinking, that makes a difference."

"It might, if it got brought out in a court," Alex snapped. "I don't see a mention here of a word of it getting into the indictment."

"I don't doubt it would of if you'd a been there!"

"The facts would have gotten in, I can assure you. Something less than half of them were printed here as you can read for yourself—if you can read."

An instant after the words left him, he would have given anything to take them back. She watched him a moment, the color ebbing from her face, then she turned slowly away from him, dipping her face away from the lamplight till he couldn't see it for the cling of shadow. He realized that though he hadn't spoken with calculation, nothing he might have said could have hurt her more deeply.

At last she said almost inaudibly, "I know I don't talk fine. Not like your kind of people. I can read, and I can print a fair hand."

"I'm sorry I said that. Sorry, and more ashamed than I can tell you."

She would not look at him for a while, and then she said quietly, "You got a way of making a body know when you mean it. I believe you're 'shamed right enough. But you thought it or you wouldn't of said it."

"You can say a good many things when you want to hurt. It's wrong, but that hasn't often stopped anybody." Alex spoke wryly, and he added, "I was your age, just about, before I learned the first thing about proper speech. It was plain luck that I had that chance. It's not your place to apologize—it's mine for hinting that you have the least thing to apologize for. You haven't."

"How 'bout a gift for talking yourse'f out of corners with that fancy gab? You learn that too?"

Alex decided her tone was tart but mollified. He grinned. "I suppose so."

"Hmf. You want to hear about this fellow who taken shots at your friend Trask?"

"You learned something?"

"Never mind where," she said guardedly. "I made the rounds of some neighbors and I bent a close ear in town, too. Ever hear of a man called Tigo?"

"Tigo?" Alex frowned and shook his head. "What's his other name?"

"Just Tigo, they say. He first come around maybe a month ago. He made an offer. But I got to have your word my friends won't get hurt by what I tell you."

"You have my word. What was the offer?"

"My pa wasn't ever told about it. They knew he wouldn't go along. This Tigo said he would see Buck Trask was put out of the way for a thousand dollars, and some of 'em talked it over and thought they might scrape up the cash between 'em. Ever'body hedged when it come to saying whether the money ever got paid over, but I reckon it did." She hestitated, then burst out, "Can you blame them? Most of 'em are good men, but they've got too scared to think! That's your friend Buck's doing. Can you blame them for being scared?"

Alex leaned back on the pillow, saying wearily, "No, I guess I can't blame them," as he let his eyes shut. If Tigo were a professional assassin, why was he playing with his victim like a cat with a mouse? Why would Rufus Cady, a man in whose honesty he still believed, steal GT cattle for their hides and leave a transparent trail? He'd considered the possibility that Cort might have faked the theft himself to retaliate for the beating Struther had given him, but now began to wonder if there were a connection between the assassin's strange behavior and the stolen cattle. Wondering got him nowhere, though.

JoAnne's abrupt words made him open his eyes. "I suppose you'll be goin' to court to defend him—Trask."

"That's what you think, eh?"

"I don't know," she said a trifle sullenly, watching him from the corners of her eyes. "You got a bullet trying to save my kin. T'other hand you have stuck by him since you was kids, folks say, and you took up for him plenty fierce a minute go. Like you can't get off a notion he is God or something."

"I wasn't sticking up for him that way. He was in the wrong, more wrong than I could swallow. But there's always two sides, and the newspapers left his out. That's wrong, too." Again he hesitated. "I want you to understand this. My people were killed by some drunken Comanches when I was six. Gideon and 'Liza Trask—Buck's pa and ma—took me in and brought me up like their own. And Buck and I—well, we were different, so different we hit sparks off each other from the first. But this bad leg of mine—I took that saving Buck's life when a wild steer nearly gored him, and that changed things between us. I don't mean we changed; neither of us did, and that's what made it a strange friendship, I reckon. It's been the kind of closeness you see between flint and steel. They can't help rubbing up fire when they come together. Then it's as I told you once before—I never thought Buck was more than half to blame in anything he did. Not until he did what he did—to your pa and Struther. He was riled about Li, but that was no excuse. It's his side of it, but it was no good excuse. Do you understand me, now? Why I've stood up for him in the past—and why I won't any longer?"

JoAnne stood listening; the hardness had gentled out of her young face, and she did not take her eyes from him as she nodded. "I reckon I do, now. Thank you for telling me."

It was not until she had left the room to prepare supper that Alex realized he'd told her feelings of which he'd never spoke to anyone. He thought, *There never was anyone before.* And lay quite still, watching the ceiling, restless with the unexpected thought and not wanting to be.

After cleaning up the supper tray she brought him, he read the newspapers awhile and finally drifted off to sleep.

A sound brought him sluggishly awake. He was lying on his side, and his eyelids twitched in reflex as the light grew strong. Drugged with sleep, he saw through his lashes that JoAnne was bending over the lamp on the commode, turning it up.

She was wearing a long night gown, a poor girl's gown of white sacking; and straightening, she turned toward the bed. The light behind her cutting through the gown limned for one moment the young body, the wiry and almost boyish slimness, the quick leggy grace that was not boyish, no more than the breasts whose round fullness mocked the loose folds of the demure gown. She bent again, above him now, tucking the blankets around his shoulders. He was motionless, but no longer sleepy; he felt the heavy thud of

283

his heart against his arm, and then his heart and time and everything in his world seemed to stop. He turned his head up and opened his eyes.

Her hair was loose, full of tawny tints from the lamplight which smoothly bronzed her face. He raised his hand and wonderingly touched her face, cheek and lips and chin, feeling the sculptured delicacy of arched and hollowed bone beneath, the sharp bloodwarmth under the velvet skin. Momentarily she quivered; then her face turned and twisted to his touch. He said nothing and she didn't, but she murmured in her throat and brought her mouth parted and awkward down to his. His hands were gentle on her shoulders and then, as he felt her warmth and weight grow against his body, became less gentle.

Suddenly she pulled away from him with a quick-muscled yank and came to her feet. Her breasts were rising and falling quickly; she crossed her arms beneath them and rubbed her palms over her arms where he had gripped her. She shivered and said resentfully, "You're a sight stronger than you look." As quickly as it had come, her cool sureness evaporated; she dropped to her knees by the bed and laid her hot cheek against the quilt.

"You can do 'bout anything you want," she whispered. "I'll let you if you say so. But please—don't."

He touched her hair and cheek again, feeling her trembling against his side, feeling the wonder of this seize him. And he smiled: she knew even less about a man than he did about a woman, and he was finding just how little that was.

"It cut me so—when you said that about if I could read," her lips whispered against his neck. "If anyone else had said it, I would of got mad, maybe laughed depending who said it. But from you it just hurt—I can't tell you how much."

Alex stroked her smooth hair, though he felt foolish and awkward. He said his thought: "I'm just shy of thirty. How old are you?"

"That ain't old. I'll be nineteen next month. I don't see it's all that big a difference."

"Maybe not," he said slowly. "But—"

"I'll learn your kind of mannered talk if you want. I will. I'll study every day, every minute I can find to."

"Not that." His smile was sober. "I wanted to say this is for always with me, JoAnne. I'm the one-woman kind of man. When you're young, ten years makes enough difference so I've got to be as sure it's right for you as it is for me."

"My gran'ma married when she was fifteen. My ma wasn't much older. A woman knows. Leastways our women do. There ain't no mistake." She said it just that simply, as if there were no more to be spoken on the matter.

But of course there was, and they talked for an hour, though it was too early to form many plans. Alex' break with the Trasks had freed him for a new future; during his convalescence he'd busied his mind with his old notion of starting a law practice in Katytown. He wanted JoAnne to hold onto her father's ranch; both of them had their roots in country soil, and probably the most satisfying life would be to keep one foot in town, one on the range. But the need for money might upset any definite plans they laid.

"Plenty time to figure out all that," she said at last. "Time you was asleep."

Alex grumbled, "You sound like a wife already." But he liked it.

XVIII

ANOTHER WEEK had gone by before he was fit for the wagon ride to Katytown. They came in on a Saturday morning, and Alex, usually economy-minded, insisted that JoAnne go to the dressmaker's and have a dress fitted for the occasion. He'd see about getting the judge to perform the wedding that afternoon. First, though, he went to a saloon to enjoy a self-congratulatory drink or two.

The saloon crowd was heavy for a morning, he noticed at once, and there were a number of strange faces. Bending an ear to the talk, he soon gathered that the town was thronged with pilgrims come for the trial which would begin on Monday. There were journalists, the curious, the thrill-seekers, even a tithe of religious fanatics and their ultraliberal foes.

At first so much bustling activity over a cowtown trial puzzled Alex, then he began to realize that the bitter newspaper tirades against Jonathan had merely reflected a rising public clamor. A reforming zeal, reaction against the crime and terrorism that had plagued Texas since the war, had reached proportions of near-hysteria. The time was ripe for the red-eyed zealots to find a focal point for their indignation, and Jonathan, because his lynching of the Cady's had been attended by atrocity propaganda—thanks to Cort's firing the two corpses—made a convenient target.

Almost overnight, Alex was stunned to learn, Jonathan had become the symbol of every barbarism committed since Attila, to whom he was compared by a brassy-voiced journalist from Kansas City. A murmur of lynch talk here and there told as plainly as words that Jonathan Trask would get no fair trial in Katytown. All of Alex' training and personal beliefs told him a man deserved a decent trial, no matter what; and he thought of many things then.

Of the savage action that had sickened him into repudiation of Jonathan and all he stood for. Of what he and JoAnne Cady had found together and how it could be destroyed in this fragile first stage. And knowing behind these things what he must do and why. He stared into his glass, thinking, *You knew it all along, didn't you? All right, go be a damned fool.*

He found Sheriff Mapin in his office in the basement of the courthouse. After a brief exchange of greetings, Mapin inquiring after his health, Alex said, "Lou, the feeling hereabouts is running pretty high."

"That's why I got five special deputies taking county pay. They'll make regular rounds about town every hour till the trial's over. They have orders to break up any assembly that don't look peaceable, keep the people moving."

"Good. Should keep the town from disgracing itself any further. Reckon I could talk to Buck?"

Mapin gave him a careful, rather wondering look, but said nothing as he led the way to the cell block in another corner of the basement. Jonathan was alone in his cell, slacked at complete ease on the narrow cot, and he lounged to his feet as Alex came to the bars. Mapin said, "Sing out when you want to leave," and left them alone.

Jonathan leaned his bulk against the bars; there was a lazy amusement in his dark eyes, and though he'd lost a few shades of weatherburn from the weeks of confinement, he looked better than Alex had seen him in years. All the liquor was out of his system; he seemed alert and completely at ease.

"I was going to ask if you need a lawyer," Alex said dryly. "From the look of you, you don't need anything."

Jonathan roared. "Well, by God, I knew you had a bellyful of bein' my conscience. Never figured after what happened you'd be playin' my angel."

"Why, I guess even God needs his angels. You never did make much use of a conscience. What I should have been was your Praetorian Guard."

"What the hell's that?"

"The personal bodyguard of the Roman emperors who, as the crowds cheered, would whisper. 'Remember, O Caesar, that you are mortal.' I thought a spell in the calaboose might humble you, though."

"Thought I'd be trying to crawl up a wall myself, after a week of it. Come to find out, this was what the doc ordered. Been doing nothing but eat and sleep, readin' and thinkin'.

287

You know this is the first rest I had in years? And no hooch, by God. Jesus, I feel like a million dollars."

"You'll be outfitted for a longer rest than you have belly for," Alex said grimly, "if you don't get a good defense."

"Well," Jonathan said somberly, but with his eyes twinkling, "you know I'd want you standing up for me in court, boy, but you didn't show up for some reason, so I sent clear to Austin for a criminal lawyer name of Hazen."

"You got Lamb Hazen to—? If you want me to represent your case," Alex said flatly, "get rid of that shyster. I don't even want his assistance. Drop him."

"Just as you say, boy," Jonathan said agreeably. "I don't figure nobody's going to get me off altogether."

"Nobody is," Alex assured him. "The least you'll get is twenty years in the penetentiary, and I hope you do. In fact, I want to see to it personally."

Jonathan almost sagged with laughter; finally he said, "Where you been keeping yourself? That straw-hair Cady filly treat you proper?"

Alex felt his face burn. "None of your business."

"Why," Jonathan chuckled, "you God damn blue-nosed Presbyterian, you. Next I'll hear you went and married that big kid." His mood sobered then. "I'm grateful you didn't press no charges aganst Cort. Shooting you that way. Damn boy. Only why didn't you?"

Alex shrugged. "All I cared about was calling it quits with the Trasks. I didn't want to do a thing for or against any of you—I wanted to cut it clean was all."

"Clean, hell. Welcome back where you belong, boy."

"Don't make a mistake, Buck," Alex said flatly. "I'll stick by you through the trial because what I heard on the street disgusted me. I'll do my best to see you get a square deal—exactly what you deserve, no more, no less. Otherwise I don't feel a lot differently about what happened. What you did to those Cadys was cold murder—I can't find an argument against that fact, and I won't pretend to. You'll plead guilty and, if you're lucky, get a minimum sentence. I hope you don't get a day less."

An hour later Alex was on his way to the GT ranch for the last time. He wanted to collect his belongings and bring them to the hotel in town, for the trial could be long and drawn-out, and he'd want to be next to all that developed. At the last moment, about to confess to JoAnne that he'd decided to be Jonathan's attorney, he had hedged, explaining that in his quarters at the GT was a good suit that would do to be wed in, and he might as well fetch all his belongings while he was about it.

Slouching on the wagon seat against an angry stitch in his healed shoulder, guiding the team unhurriedly along the road, he let his bleak musings carry to the moment when he could no longer stall off telling JoAnne of his decision to defend the man who'd murdered her father and brother. How could he make her understand that he couldn't do otherwise and justify whatever he lived by, that there was no personality in his position, only duty to a client and to justice? The law, with all its faults, was the mortar that kept human society from flying to pieces. Because he knew just how thin was the civilized veneer over man's raw, warlike instincts, because he feared the unleashing of those instincts, he had made whatever was representative of orderly law into his creed.

He budged his thoughts to the defense he must establish. Jonathan's agreeableness to letting Alex handle everything his way had surprised him. He'd said, "You're the best, boy, and I ain't going to stick at nothing you say," but he had stuck fast at one point. That was when Alex had insisted that, to pare away the aspect of wanton atrocity surrounding the killings, they bring out that Cort, not he, had set fire to the hanging bodies. He was still blindly and stubbornly sheltering his brother, and Alex had given up that argument for the present. A little more friction had occurred when Alex had told Jonathan what little he'd learned about the assassin known as Tigo and then refused, in the face of Jonathan's angry curiosity, to divulge his source.

The GT headquarters was seemingly deserted as he rode in, but he knew from what Jonathan had said that ranch affairs were being conducted as usual, with Chino Lucero in charge. Alex had doubts about his self-control were he to encounter Cort just now, but Cort wasn't around. Samantha answered his knock at the door.

He was surprised to find the parlor floor covered with trunks and crates, and Mercy busily packing them with clothes and other personal things. She looked up as he came in; a gladness touched her face and she came quickly to him and hugged him. "Alex, it's so good to see you. They told me you weren't hurt too seriously . . . but I—I reckon I should of come to visit you."

Alex held her at arm's length and studied her carefully. She was wearing an old dress, her black hair done in a bandanna; behind her gravity he felt something impish, bubbling, irrepressible, the Mercy he remembered from many years ago and whom he'd thought never to see again. That old personality of hers was still subdued like a captive bird, but you could feel it tugging and beating, waiting the moment of release. Even now it flashed in her eyes and quietly animated her small face.

"Why Mercy, you look—" His words floundered, and he weakly motioned at the pile of things on the floor. "What's all this about?"

"I'm leaving, Alex. Leaving the ranch, leaving Texas, leaving—" Her eyes briefly darkened, then sparkled again. "We're going to St. Joe, Samantha and me. I have an aunt there. When all this trouble started, I wrote her and she's agreed to help us. They're moneyed folks, her and her mister, and they can get us started in a dressmaking business or something, show us around to the right people." The rush of her words stopped, and her gaze was level, a little troubled. "Would it sound terrible—I mean with Jon's trouble and all—to say I'm happy for the first time in years?"

Alex shook his head. "Truth is never wrong. If you're happy, more power to you. I'd say you've done your share of penance, if that's the word."

"I hope so." She turned slowly from him, her face lowered. "All that happened—losing the baby, the way Jonathan and me have just been killing off what we felt for each other, all the misery that's been—was God's punishment for what we done to Paul. I'm sure of it—as sure as I am the Lord has pardoned me by showing me this new chance."

Alex said nothing. Mercy's religion was perhaps the only strength she had, and she needed now, as she needed before to use those beliefs in self-castigation, to interpret her blind cry at last for release from her overriding guilt as God's forgiveness. Alex, whose own earliest recollections were tinged with the stark dualities of Scottish Protestantism, understood and sympathized, and thought: *God's will—who knows?*

"I—thought of staying through the trial," she went on. "That would look right, wouldn't it?—and this doesn't. But it's not cowardice, Alex. Everything since the baby died has been a shabby pretense. I have no place with him—he has none with me." She turned fully to face him, and he saw the stir of pain in her face, but it was a pain that belonged to memory only. "What can they really do to him? How can anybody hurt him any more? We was children together, and the children died together—long ago, both of them—on a battlefield at Vicksburg." Her voice sank to a whisper. "They never came back to life or to love. Never, never. A man I didn't know came home to me—and then it turned all dirty, all wrong."

This was how she had talked sometimes in her murmurous, withdrawn periods of self-torture, talked whether there were anyone to hear or not; and Alex saw the anxiety clouding Samantha's face. But the mood passed in a moment; she was the old Mercy again, and she gave him her hand with a soft, bubbling laugh. "Dear Alex—I reckon nobody has to tell you. You always knew things better than anybody."

Alex was only minutes in collecting the clothes, books and other gear he wanted from his old quarters and piling them in the wagon. Then, having said a last goodbye to Mercy and Samantha, he drove back to Katytown.

As he'd expected, a perfunctory check showed that the hotel and several boardinghouses were filled up, but thanks to the generosity of a lawyer friend of his, S. P. Howlitt, he had no difficulty in finding lodging. Howlitt prevailed on Alex to stay with his family as long as he wished. His wife, he added, would like to meet the future Mrs. Mc-Kenna.

Alex hadn't been able to locate JoAnne on his return from the ranch; after leaving his belongings at the Howlitts', he returned downtown to cover the stores.

He found her almost at once. She was in Old Montrose's, glancing over some yard goods, and she barely looked up when he said, "When will Mrs. Hoskins have your new dress ready?"

She didn't answer, and he said with a heavy qualm, "What's the matter?"

"Is it true what I been hearing? You're going to defend him anyways?"

Alex knew then he had made a vital mistake in not telling her immediately. Anybody, perhaps one of Mapin's deputies who'd overheard his talk with Jonathan, could have spread the word, and in a few hours it was public currency. There had been no easy way to tell her, but getting it this secondhand way had compounded the hurt for her.

"Yes," was all he could think of to say.

"Ain't that funny? I told myself and I told myself you was going to say 'no' when I asked. You told me you was through with him and I believed you. I knew what they was saying was only talk and you was going to say 'no.' It's just so funny."

Alex tried to make her listen; he talked about ethics and conscience, and she cut in across his words with a brittle, dry-eyed coldness: "I won't hear no more from you. Your word ain't worth a thing to me. My pa and my brother are dead. Their bodies was set fire to like a pair of wore-out boots. You find anything to say for the men who done that, you go tell a judge. But don't you ever tell me another lyin' thing. Not ever."

She brushed past him going out of the store. Alex stood where he was, feeling as alone as he'd ever been. The difference was that before, he had hardly ever thought about it. Now he would hardly be able to stop thinking of it.

XIX

FROM THE BEGINNING, Alex had a fight on his hands. The state was determined to make an example of Jonathan Trask. Not only did the prosecution assemble an array of the sharpest legal talent in the southwest, the district attorney was quietly shuttled to the rear ranks of proceedings, and a special d.a. pro tem, an orator who had delivered the keynote address at his party's last national convention, was appointed in his place by Judge Sharpe, a leading spokesman for the party in power. The enormous cost was footed by the state treasury through a politico-legal maneuver unprecedented in the history of any state—a special appropriations bill was rammed through the legislature.

This fund had also provided transportation and rations for a company of regular militia brought in ostensibly to keep order but actually, it was widely rumored, to prevent

an army of "Trask's Niggers" from swooping down on Katytown to free their boss. The rumor was just that, a lie neatly promulgated to keep public opinion incited, the militia
being present to give substance to the fear rather than to
allay it.

The raw explosiveness of the situation almost decided
Alex to ask for a change of venue, but he decided against
it. No matter where Jonathan was tried in Texas, the state
politicians could bring their influence to bear. Besides the
affair had achieved so much notoriety that people across the
state were choosing up sides according to their own interests. And in spite of the weight of local sentiment against
Jonathan, stirred up still further by state propaganda, a surprising number of citizens estranged by his actions ranged
themselves in his favor when the chips were down. Rufus
Cady, a Missouri freesoiler and a Union soldier, had been
entirely too outspoken on his positions; a man needn't love
Buck Trask's guts to side him in this instance. He was
still one of them—Cady had been the alien, the outsider, who
had ruffled his own share of feathers.

Time and again over the years, Jonathan's business and
legal interests had taken Alex to Washington, D.C. and other
points East. As often as not he found himself handling a
score of favors for other Matheson County cattlemen;
people not only liked and trusted Alex, they respected his
zest for "impossible" undertakings so much he'd been urged
time after time to run for public office. Though loyalty to
the Trasks had confined his personal ambitions, Alex' original interests had never flagged. Over the years he'd kept in
touch with law school cronies, many of whom had climbed
high in legislative and judicial circles.

Now, with Jonathan's considerable fortune at his disposal,
Alex drew unstintingly on associates old and new to sur-
round himself with a formidable coterie of legal minds that
almost outflanked the prosecuting force.

The first days after court convened were taken up,
thanks to the hot division of opinion in the county, by a te-

dious wrangling over the selection of jurymen. After charges and specifications in the grand jury indictment had been introduced, the prosecution stated that it would show Jonathan Trask had murdered two men in cold blood. There had been nothing at all cold-blooded about the killings, Alex pointed out in the rebuttal by the defense. He meant to hammer at the point that the defendant had been in a highly emotional state. He didn't want to see Jonathan acquitted in any case, only dealt with according to his crime. Since the best defense in the world couldn't have secured an acquittal, he could concentrate without reservation on one goal: saving his client's life.

As the days ground by, the trial settling into a bitter, dragout contest, Alex was satisfied to be holding his own against a powerful adversary. Bit by bit, through success and error, losing a point here and gaining another there, he was building his case and gaining a hard-won wealth of practical experience. But the tension of leading a fight against heavy odds while carrying the daily courtroom grind of issues and personalities was taking a vicious toll of him, mentally and physically.

He became haggard and rundown from a combination of too little sleep and too few meals, these hastily eaten and digested on the run. His nerves were drawn to the breaking point from a constant whirl of work and activity, marshaling evidence and witnesses, arguments and legal opinions, organizing strategy and procedure to a fine degree only to be forced often as not to a hasty retrenching and improvising.

He learned that JoAnne was staying in town at a local boardinghouse, no doubt so that she could follow the trial. He tried again and again, at such odd times as he could spare, to see her and talk to her. She refused to see him, and her indomitable landlady reinforced the edict. Probably for the same reason, she never showed up in court except for a brief hour early in the trial when the prosecution called her as witness to the events leading up to the crime.

Meantime Jonathan rubbed Alex raw on several counts, not the least of which was his monumental cheer in the face of a possible death sentence. It made Alex suspicious and worried. Throughout the trial Jonathan remained almost suspiciously cheerful. He slept well, had his meals catered by the best restaurant in town, put on weight, and despite his imprisonment, cut a figure of ruddy health. He only gave a sad, indulgent little chuckle on learning that Mercy had left him. That grand passion had suffered through too much, grinding down and wearing away till it wasn't worth even a twinge.

The only thing that could upset his cocksure blandness was Alex' repeated insistence that Cort be called to the stand to testify his guilt in the corpse-burning. Jonathan wouldn't budge an inch in his refusal to implicate his brother beyond the charge of accessory already facing him. Nor would any of the GT crewmen who'd been present give testimony against Jonathan's wish. So Alex found, and resigned himself.

Next it came to his ears that Lamb Hazen, the Austin legal counsel Jonathan had agreed to let go, was still around and had visited Jonathan in his cell several times. Alex knew Hazen for an unscrupulous shyster who was still in practice only because he was too shrewd to leave any trail through the quiet webs of his extra-legal chicaneries.

Jonathan insisted that Hazen had only been paying friendly visits, but Alex gave him a flat ultimatum. Either the defense would be handled his way entirely, as agreed, or Jonathan could turn the whole show over to Lamb Hazen. Otherwise he wasn't to see Hazen again or contact him in any way.

Somehow Jonathan's cheery agreement didn't ring quite true, but Alex couldn't smell what, if anything, might be amiss. He had come this far with the case, things were going reasonably well, and he put aside his misgivings and stubbornly set himself to seeing out what he'd begun to the finish. So the trial went on and the weary weeks dragged by.

On the last day, Alex countered the prosecution's summation with a carefully organized analysis of the social, economic, legal, and political motives touching his client's action, couching it all in a rough cow-country idiom his listeners appreciated. He made obscure and complex matters wholly understandable to them, and he was comprehensive. Judge Sharpe kept overruling his sharp attacks on the political machine that was out for Jonathan Trask's scalp, but he successfully interjected quite a · few subtle points that went over the bench's head.

Sweeping the room with his eyes, he caught a good deal of reaction. He mentioned Jonathan's war record, reminded them of the immense debt the county owed Jonathan Trask for his part in making it a decent place to live, and even went so far as to state that many of Jonathan's ways were those of a violent and hardened character, "but not—I repeat, gentlemen—not of an evil man. Jonathan Trask is a product of our times—as much yours and mine as his. When we repudiate his ways, we repudiate our own." To give way to a revengeful passion after the death of his younger brother Liam had been wrong, but the act was neither premeditated nor cold-blooded.

Moreover, though it was Cortney Trask's word against JoAnne Cady's as to who had started the gunfight that ended in Liam Trask's death, it could not be denied the two Trask boys had followed the trail of their stolen cattle to the Cady headquarters. Alex had to force himself to state this part; it was his duty to bring out on his client's behalf every mitigating factor, though he didn't remotely believe Cady had been guilty of either theft or precipitating the fight with Cort and Li.

Later, talking with Jonathan in his cell, he said as much. Jonathan, sitting slackly on his cot, one leg cocked up, only yawned. "That's your duty, boy. You said so yourself."

"Sometimes duty leaves a fairly rotten taste."

"Well, you're dead set in your head against Cort, that's all. Anyway it's all over but the shouting."

"You still could hang. The jury hasn't brought in a verdict yet."

Jonathan waved a hand. "Hell, you talked it up just fine. Most I expect is a stiff term in prison, and Lamb says—"

"Hazen—" Alex pushed away from the wall where he was leaning, dropping his folded arms. "You said you wouldn't see Lamb Hazen again."

"I ain't. We had it all arranged by the time I promised you. Lamb and me went over things start to finish. Thing now, he says, is to get me safe past a noose into the pen. Then he can start things moving for me. In a year, two years, when things have simmered down and the political situation has cooled, Hazen'll ask the state supreme court to review my case. Soon's they grant me a new trial, I should be out in a month."

Alex was speechless for a quarter-minute. He said between his teeth, "What makes you so sure the supreme court'll find grounds for review? If they do, why should they grant a re-trial? And what in the name of hell makes you think a second trial will get you off scot-free? The emotional and political climate will change, but the evidence and testimony against you won't. I want to hear your reasoning."

"Well." Jonathan grinned, and scratched his ear. "You know Lamb. Leastways you say you do. He's got ways of making folks come to taw. If one way don't work, there's always another. I wouldn't be surprised he's got ways he ain't tried yet."

"That's what I know," Alex said thickly. "I wanted to hear you say it. I know his ways. Bribery—blackmail—threats backed by hired thugs."

"Now, boy, you don't know any of that."

"Everybody knows it. The way he works, through other people, nobody can prove it is all."

"Same difference."

"You bastard." Alex could no longer keep the trembling from his voice as he came over to the cot. "Lamb Hazen is only one kind of crook. He has nothing on you."

Jonathan's smile faded. "Look, boy, I never strung you along none. I didn't want nobody but you talking up for me to a home-growed jury. Ain't a soul in these parts don't know you and like you. I needed you to talk me out of a hangrope, and you good as done it. But I ain't going to rot in a prison rest of my life if I can help it. If Lamb Hazen can get me out in a couple years, think I ain't a-going to let him? I said you was running this show, but it's pretty near over. I kept my word, by God."

"No. It was a lie from the start." Alex leaned forward in his intensity. "You and Hazen ran the show. You used me was all, but you planned it so I'd think otherwise. You told me nothing until now because you figured I'd have dropped the case cold if I'd known what would follow."

"Well, God damn," Jonathan said angrily. "You think after how you preached at me all these years, I'd trust you not to cut my throat with your God damn do-good conscience? It ain't your neck on the block, it's mine, and I knew there wasn't nobody but me going to look out for it—"

Jonathan's words had seethed to a roar as he started to his feet, tapping his finger on his chest, but he wasn't fully on his feet when Alex hit him, a full-arm smash to the jaw. The blow knocked him back on the cot and he lay there looking vastly surprised as his mouth bled into his beard.

Jonathan's loudness brought a deputy on the run, and Alex curtly said he wanted to leave. The deputy unlocked the door, and he walked out without another glance at Jonathan.

On the street, Alex' brisk stride slowed; there was a trudging weariness to his steps as he headed for the Howlitt home. *I should have known,* he kept thinking. *I should have known.* He had leaped into this battle with a blind crusader's instinct, and what it had gotten him was a taste of dirt in his mouth. What it had cost him was the larges forfeit of his life—JoAnne.

By midmorning next day, the jury finished its delibera tions and shuffled back into the courtroom. Alex sat at th defense table, palms flat on the scarred tabletop, his head bent. The foreman's voice, as he read off the verdict o second degree murder, seemed to come from a distance. S did the drone of Judge Sharpe passing sentence, imprison ment in the state penitentiary for the rest of Jonathan' natural life. Alex would have laughed aloud, but his edge was too dulled for that; anyway what did it matter?

The sheriff came forward to take Jonathan into custody Alex did not even look at the man, he had defended a he rose, gathering up his briefcase and notes. He didn' want to see whatever expression that black-bearded face wore. He walked from the courtroom, pushing through the eddies of people; some of them spoke to him and he didn't hear them. He had done his duty by his client, had won as much victory as he'd worked for, and there was a feeling like death in his bones. All the way from the court house to the Howlitt home, he felt like a man sleepwalking.

Mary Howlitt said something to him as he entered the house; he fumbled out some words and went on to his room. Standing there, looking around him and slowly rub bing his neck, he felt the everyday world wash back into focus around him. He heard a bird outside the window; he saw the flowered pattern of the wallpaper and a sun square full of lazily swimming motes. A semblance of calm and order came back to things, and he thought wryly, *It's ended, finished, and what's the odds now? That's you all over. You'll be a sight happier when you quit taking your self too damn' seriously.*

Would that ever happen? He smiled again and shook his head, then got his suitcase from the closet and began packing his clothes. He was surprised at the relief he felt that the long weeks filled with work and strain were over; that was a form of self-escape, he supposed, and so was the sudden urge he felt to get away, to be anywhere but here, to let his nerves quietly stitch up while the broken pieces of his life fell into new patterns and he made plans. At the moment he didn't greatly care what direction things took; he just wanted to get far away, to rest and think.

Mary called from the parlor, "Alex, you have a visitor."

Wearily Alex dropped a fistful of shirts in the open suitcase, then went out to the parlor. Mary brushed quietly past him, leaving the room, as he entered. JoAnne was standing in the middle of the room. She looked taller than he remembered, more slender, and he realized this wasn't only because she was actually thinner, her outdoor tan almost gone. She was wearing a well-cut bombazine dress, fresh and new, the skirt rustling in crisp folds as she turned to face him. She was beautiful, he realized—not conventionally, but handsome beyond mere prettiness, the fine bone structure of her face more prominent, her pale hair pulled to a smooth club back of her neck.

She said slowly, "I was in the courtroom today. I spoke to you when you left—reckon you didn't hear me."

"I didn't see you." For the moment he could only look at her with his thoughts blank; he did not know what else to say.

"I hadn't seen you except at a ways off for—for weeks. I didn't know—" Her voice started to break. "Just look at you—fine public figure you cut—all thin and wore down like you hadn't ate a square meal in—and when you been getting any sleep? Answer me that!"

"Well, I—" Something cleared suddenly away in his mind. "Would that be—that wouldn't be your wedding dress?"

To his consternation she began to cry; he had never seen her even close to tears. "Oh, you—lawyer! You damned, damned lawyer."

"I guess that's right." He smiled tiredly and started a step toward her, but she was in his arms before he finished it.

BITTER GRASS

XX

THEY WERE MARRIED that same afternoon. A day that had started as the worst in his memory ended in a new beginning. And Alex McKenna would often wonder, looking back, why he'd ever thought he was contented in that other life. He chose to remain in Katytown, to raise his family here and make his dream of a law practice a reality.

He and JoAnne divided their time between weekdays at their town house and weekends spent at her father's ranch, now kept up by two hired hands. It was touch-and-go a long while, but they managed to hold onto both ranch and town practice, and by the time Alex was getting more clients than he could handle, the pinch was off.

He was too busy to give more than casual note to the deteriorating affairs of the GT empire. The great ranch that he had called home for more than two decades was of no concern to him now; he was no longer handling its legal business and would have refused any that was offered.

He knew what was common gossip: that Cortney Trask, along with the rest of the GT men involved as accessories in the Cady lynching, had gotten off with a few months in prison. Then word came that Cort was back at the GT, trying to get the tangle of Jonathan's affairs in order. Alex smiled at that. Cort's business sense was on a par with his other talents for judgment. However it was soon learned a battery of good lawyers in Austin was working on the legal and bookkeeping end, while Chino Lucero was as competent a right hand for Cort as he'd been for Jonathan. With attorneys to handle the headwork and Chino in effect running the practical side of things, the ranch could almost take care of itself. Alex guessed that even from prison, Jonathan was keeping in a guiding hand through his lawyers and Lucero, while letting Cort have the illusion he was doing important things.

But the year 1873 began with uneasy rumors. The golden boom of railroad building that was to have brought civilization and prosperity to the rude frontier collapsed—construction had outstripped the limited needs of a sparsely populated land. There was widespread speculation, loose credit, a stench of graft in the nation's capital, followed by the scandal of the Crédit Mobilier: the bribery of U. S. Congressmen by the railroad interests. Then Black Friday —the nation's finances crumpled, and banks toppled like dominoes.

Overnight, cattle prices dropped to rock bottom. Many big ranchers with herds of unsold cattle on hand and money tied up with the ruined banks, were wiped out completely. Thanks to adroit maneuvering by the Trask attorneys, an alert ear to whispers on the financial winds, and hasty selling, some of Jonathan's fortune was salvaged though nearly all his interests were gotten rid of at a loss.

Alex shared with other Texans a concern over the course of affairs for his state, county and community. His concern did not scale to anxiety simply because his personal affairs, wife and home and a successful practice, occupied his life so fully. Then, by fall, Robert Gideon McKenna was born, and he was too lost in the pride and pleasure of fatherhood to pay very much attention to any outside matters.

Meantime Lamb Hazen and his associates hadn't been idle. They were testing for a review of Jonathan's case by the state supreme court. They came up with a contention that Rufus Cady's ranch headquarters where the lynching had occurred was just across the Lawton County line; therefore, on the grounds that Judge Sharpe's Matheson County court had lacked jurisdiction in the case, a mistrial should be declared. Admittedly the line had always been in doubt; now the surveyors of both counties went to work and discovered that the line did indeed run a hundred feet south of the tree where the hanging and immolation of the two men had occurred. The supreme court undertook a review and soon announced that the Trask case would be retried in Lawton County. Not long afterward rumor had it the Trask ranch had sold a herd of a thousand prime three-year-old steers to each of the two county surveyors for next to nothing.

Simultaneously with release of news of Jonathan's impending retrial, the GT ranch was shaken by a new wave of terrorism. The depredations by the mystery man called Tigo had ceased on the day Judge Sharpe had sentenced Jonathan to prison for life. Now, a year and a half later, the gadfly was back in the bull's flank. All the earmarks of the one-man terror who had previously plagued the GT were there, but he was no longer satisfied with making the bull grunt and tail-swish at a stinging irritant here or there.

Now his strokes fell bold and swift and savage, one after the other. Mysterious fires were set everywhere; droves of cattle were found dead, massacred by bullets or driven in bunches off canyon rims. Men, too, fell prey to an unerring marksman, always hidden, who shot never to kill, always to incapacitate. These bites were deep and vicious; the gadfly was striking for the heart now, and all the bull could do was stomp and bellow his fury.

Already in a bad way from the '73 panic, the Trask fortune was practically bone-picked to dredge up funds for Jonathan's new defense. Soon it was learned the situation had become so serious that the GT was borrowing heavily against the collateral of its various holdings, even its remaining herds.

By now all but a few of the old crew, the colored cowboys and their families who had once formed the proud nucleus of the Trask pride and power, had left. They were replaced by hard-bitten men who worked for wages, not ordinary punchers but "warriors" whose knowledge of cattle and range was incidental. Bands of these men, well-armed and well-mounted, were out by day and by night, seeing to the safety of ranch property while they kept on the hunt for the elusive Tigo. Such men came high, and their value proved negligible. If their vigilance forestalled some acts of terrorism, Tigo was never at a loss for fresh diversions, hitting unpredictably at any time, any place, in any way that suited him.

None of which held any interest to Robert Gideon McKenna or his proud, delighted parents as they watched him, plump and crowing, taking his first steps.

Howlitt and some of Alex' other friends had prevailed on him to run for the state senate next term. After accepting the draft, Alex felt obliged to follow all important legislative and judicial actions. He was one of the first to hear about Jonathan's new trial, and he followed events closely through the winter of 1874–75. Hazen and others were preparing their briefs, and pretrial wrangling was becoming keen. The trial was set for late March.

On a quiet spring evening Alex sat in his parlor after supper trying to concentrate on a newspaper. At first he thought his noisy son was the reason he couldn't bring his attention to focus, but when JoAnne ended Robert Gideon's romping exuberance by putting him to bed and Alex still felt disoriented, he told himself it was ordinary spring restlessness. Finally, chin on his chest and scowling at his unlighted pipe, he admitted the truth to himself.

Glancing at his wife beside him on the sofa, he permitted himself a moment's satisfaction just watching her. He remembered with pleasure the girl she had been; he saw with deeper pleasure the woman she had become, the young serenity of her face and the fullness of maturity, deep-breasted and round-hipped. Her hair was done in a smooth, pale-gold bun with a silver clasp; she was wearing simple calico now, fashionable and fitted, and sometimes she wore bombazine and silk. She made her own clothes, but someday she would order them made and see to their making with the same care and taste, he knew. The housekeeper and maid who might someday do her bidding would never, for all Jo's supervision, be able to order a household better than JoAnne herself. As a hostess, she was a match for the peerless Samantha who had presided for so long over the Trask home.

For such matters, it seemed, she had almost an instinct; reshaping the speech habits of a lifetime had been far more difficult. She had learned grammar quickly, but had worked long and painfully to incorporate rules of diction into her everyday speech. She did everything because she wanted to; a Cady woman did properly by her man, she had told him seriously. Alex, a little awed by her accomplishments in a few short months, hadn't needed to remind himself that these were small things beside the rest, the love and respect and character that came first, but he was proud of them.

"Jo"—he laid aside his pipe and waited for her to look up from her darning—"I've been thinking. Reckon I'll ride over to Saba City tomorrow."

Saba City was the county seat of Lawton County; with Jonathan's trial opening day after tomorrow, there was no need to ask his reason. But she said, "Is it professional interest, Alex, or just curiosity—or what?"

"Partly the first and mostly the second," he said wryly. "It's been two years and six months, Jo. I'm wondering what that long in prison's done to a man as arrogant as he'd become. He spent two years in a Union stockade, but he was younger then and he still believed in something."

"Himself," JoAnne said quietly. "From all you've said, I doubt he ever believed in anything else, and did he ever lose that belief?"

"That's a point," Alex admitted. "Call it a variance in perspective, then—the world looked a lot differently to him once. Then it all turned dirty."

"With his help."

"Yes. Jo, I don't say he hasn't deserved all that's happened to him nor that he deserves to go free now, as he

possibly will. It doesn't seem likely, but never underestimate
Lamb Hazen. He's a conniver and a crook, but he's also a
gifted orator and a hell of a brilliant lawyer. Suppose he gets
Buck off—what then? What does he come home to? A ruined
ranch, a mass of debts, a slew of people with old grudges,
an enemy whose face he doesn't even know, and not a soul in
the world that gives a damn—"

"Doesn't he have a brother—Cortney?"

"His last living tie. A weakling who's watched the ranch
left in his charge fold up and die. Maybe no man could
have saved it, but only a weakling would fold up along
with it. But that's Cort for you. He came into Katytown
two weeks ago, took a room in the hotel, crawled into a
bottle and hasn't climbed out since. It's common talk. He's
not self-blaming, understand, just self-pitying. And this, my
dear, will prove the unkindest cut of all—Buck set more
store by that boy, God knows why, than anything else. Except for one girl long ago. He'll never come home to nothing, Jo—he'll come home to a good deal less than that."

"Doesn't he deserve to?" Her face held a suggestion of
the bitter tension he remembered too well. "Doesn't he
deserve nothing and less?"

"I don't know," Alex said slowly. "Maybe. It depends on
how much judgment you want to lay. Whether you don't
feel that somewhere, sometime, a man's debt is paid, and
any hardship wished on him from then on is wanton revenge."

"Oh—then if you've stopped judging him, are you judging me now?"

"Only myself," he said soberly. "I didn't lose a father
and brother at his hands, Jo. I can't touch by a country
mile what you've felt. Only . . . I think of what you and
I have had together. And we have Robert Gideon. All of
it a kind of happiness that Buck Trask was never permitted
to know. Don't mistake me—I'll never take up with him or
for him again. But if a man's alone, suffering, and you once

307

called him friend—it ought to be worth a kind word, an outstretched hand, if nothing else."

"Alex. . . ." Her eyes softened. "You're always so—not free and easy, you have that stiff-necked Scot's eye for good and evil. But so ready to return good for harm. So strange to think . . . do you remember that day the trial ended and I came to you—finally?"

"Every detail. I always will."

"It's ironic, I guess. I'd thought I hated you because of your loyalty to Jonathan Trask—and then that day, in court, seeing you worn to a shadow of yourself, all for a principle—I started loving, really loving you. Till that hour, I was a little girl playing at romance." She stood and placed her hands on his shoulders, and bent to kiss him. "You see, I do understand you after my fashion. And I'm proud, very proud, that you're so much more than I can ever be. Go to Saba City and be as much Samaritan as you want. And I'll try—for your sake—not to hate him any more."

XXI

"Is LIKE OLD TIMES," Chino Lucero said, and added predictably, "Haaah."

Chino never changed. Now, as always, he simply watched life go by with a detached, clownish amusement, not caring much how things went. And as always, his lazy loyalty to Jonathan was the only thing that could remotely regulate his careless comings and goings.

He and Alex and Jonathan were a night and day out of Saba City, riding south, and by now they were touching the vast north range of GT's holdings.

The dry grass bent under the wind; a few curlews took wing overhead, going north to their nesting grounds. The sedgegrass plain with its mottes of liveoak and pecan rolled unmarred, changeless, to every horizon, as it had since Alex' earliest remembrance. He sharply remembered another spring day when he and Jonathan had ridden from the north across this same stretch, a day identical to this in more ways than one. Then too, Jonathan Trask had been coming from a prison to a nearly impoverished homeland. But that had been a younger Jonathan, a youth bursting with hope and plans, his muscles still untried. Even if that day's bright promise had soon proved hollow, there had been the hope, the belief; and Alex thought, *Lord in heaven, was that ten years ago?* It was, almost to the day. Well, one thing to be said for all that had happened, good or bad, in those years—there had been hardly a dull moment.

And (somehow it rubbed him against the grain) Jonathan, whatever scars he might carry out of sight, had come off outwardly unchanged. If he'd once looked older than his years warranted, he now seemed younger, for he didn't appear to have aged a day since Alex had last seen him. Often enough over the years, he had been worn and haggard from driving himself, and heavy drinking had never helped. Not that Alex had expected the penitentiary to break Jonathan's spirit—he knew better than that—but it didn't seem quite right for him to come out unscathed, bursting with health and vigor, vital even in the taut bite of his familiar cynicism.

"I'm surprised," Alex had finally felt obliged to remark. "You're looking in fine shape."

"Outside work," Jonathan had explained carelessly. "Good behavior. Spent most of my hitch on the prison farm." He had eyed Alex critically. "You put on a little weight, but you always could of stood some. Married life 'pears to agree with you."

Outside work, Alex dourly reflected, only partly accounted; a man without much of a conscience, lacking even the external one Alex had once provided, didn't spend time brooding on his sins. What did surprise him was Jonathan's air of indifferent calm, with the empire he'd built on sweat and other men's blood drifting toward wholesale ruin. Probably the buoyancy he felt at coming home again a free man let no obstacle look too large to hurdle.

Alex was coming to the wary conclusion that his trip to Saba City had been a fool's errand—two weeks away from his work and family wasted on a man who needed nobody. The fact that of his old circle only Alex and Chino Lucero had come to the trial had produced from Jonathan no particular reaction except a flash of bitter irritation that Cort hadn't bothered to show up.

Typically, though, he had brushed aside Alex' blunt warning of just how far Cort had fallen: "Ain't seen him your own self, have you? Thought not. Hearsay's cheap. If there's anything to it, I'll snap Cortney back to time fast, you bet."

All Alex cared about was getting home to JoAnne and his son. After two weeks of a hotel bed and hotel grub and hours on end in a courtroom watching Lamb Hazen's incredible machinations unfold, he was tired and fed-up. It had been outside the courtroom, when the hours were late, the bottles were low, and tongues were loose, that he had really learned about the devious bends of Hazen's strategy. Jonathan hadn't said a word one way or the other, but Alex knew he'd nearly exhausted the remainder of his fortune paying out massive bribes at Hazen's direction. A heavy price to pay for even freedom, but Lamb had earned his exorbitant fee.

Lawton County people were cattle people. When Lamb Hazen had thundered, "Because one man dared a bold action that served a warning to all potential thieves, the cost of trouble and bloodshed was spared to many," they'd listened. When he'd heatedly declared that "by the Cadys' violation of the Lord's own commandments, 'neither shalt thou covet' and 'neither shalt thou steal,' they brought on their heads a retribution that I say—and bedamned to the mockers of justice who will decry my words—was richly merited," they'd nodded grimly. At the conclusion, when Judge Smyte had promptly discharged the prisoner with "Get the hell out of here, Buck. Time for you to set up drinks over at the Longhorn," they had cheered.

Things couldn't have gone more smoothly, and Jonathan had some small reason for his ebullience, but his mood was wearing thin at last as they rode deeper into GT range now.

The effects of the terrorist's lone-handed carnage were plain on every side. Vast stretches of burned grass cut blackened swaths across the prairie, and several times they detoured so that Chino could point out the clean-picked bones of dozens of cattle killed off one way or another.

It was Alex who first spotted the trickle of smoke lifting above a motte over southeast. The sun was in his eyes, and he tugged his hatbrim down to shade them, and then was sure. He was about to speak when Jonathan and Chino spotted the smoke simultaneously. All three of them reined in with a common thought.

Jonathan said, "Any of our men working over this range now?"

"I'm not know," Chino shrugged. "I'm leave Malachi in charge. I'm not give him any orders, I'm tell him handle things like he want. But I'm got plent' doubt this is fella cause alla trouble."

"Why?"

"We ain' come near catch him at anything. This one smart fella. Every time we find cow kill, fire set, it is long after he come an' gone. He is never letting us get close. This fire, you see, she's just got started."

"Let's get over there," Jonathan snarled, and quirted his animal into a run.

But a caution blunted his haste before he reached the motte; his companions caught up with him, and the three of them advanced slowly into the trees.

In the center of a small clearing they found the fire. It

was untended and smoking badly, and there was nobody around. No accouterments of campsite or branding job were to be seen. There was nothing, in fact, but the smoldering pile of twigs and branches, plainly lighted only minutes ago.

The three men sat their horses in silence, studying the sun-mottled stillness of thickets and trees on every side. There was not a breath of wind, not a movement or a sound, only the heat and drowsing leaves and utter quiet. "Haaah," Chino whispered hoarsely. "We are ducks on the sit, I'm think."

Alex had the same feeling. The heavy verdure around them could hide one man or a regiment of men. Obviously the situation—even to a heaping of green wood to make the fire smoke—had been contrived to pull them in here. But for what reason?

Chino's horse tossed its head and whickered suddenly. At once, from a shield of greenery to the right, came a horse's low whickering answer. Instantly Jonathan wheeled his mount with a heavy hand on the reins; his other hand stabbed to his holstered Colt.

"I wouldn't, Mr. Trask. There is a rifle trained on your heart." The words were followed by a soft laugh like ice tinkling.

Jonathan's hand froze; his glance raked the thickets. There was nothing that Alex could see, not a shadow of a presence; yet the voice and laugh had a startling nearness. And Alex thought, *That laugh—I've heard it at one time or another, but where?*

"Discard your guns, gentlemen. Pistols and rifles, and one at a time. You first, Señor Lucero," the voice went on gracefully. A pause as Chino flipped his gun out gently and tossed it to the ground. He slipped his rifle from its scabbard and dropped that too. "Next Mr. Trask . . . now you, Mr. McKenna."

"I'm not packing one."

"Ah, always the pacific one, sir. You may descend, gentlemen. Keep your hands in sight, please, and step away from your horses."

Each word was a velvet threat, and the three men wordlessly did as they were told. Jonathan growled then, "Where the hell are you? Time you showed your slimy face."

"Behind you, Mr. Trask. I am Tigo."

They all turned their heads. A wiry figure of a man was standing under a large oak. He held a rifle leisurely trained. Alex had last glanced that way only seconds before, and there had been nobody.

The man wore black. His neat broadcloth suit, and low-pulled Stetson were dead black; his tall jackboots were a shining black. A mask of black silk, a dandy's bandanna, covered all his face but the faint slit between his hatbrim at brow level and the bridge of his nose where the mask ended. A breeze fluttered the light silk, but the face remained hidden. There was a theatricality to this whole pose, Alex thought, but the chill it sent up a man's backbone was real. Maybe it was the eyes, palest gray even in shadow, eyes cold as death. And he knew.

"Danziger," he said.

Jonathan clipped a glance at him. "Danziger?—the hell. The Pig's in his grave eight, nine years." He scowled. "His way of talkin', though, puts a man in mind—"

"Not Alvah, Buck. His brother. Lat."

The man in black gave his light, graceful laugh. He moved slowly forward now, holding his left leg rather stiffly. He tapped it with a bony finger. "I can still hinge the knee only with difficulty. Legacy, Mr. Trask, of that tender moment when you closed your cunning trap on my headstrong brother some years ago. The bone was shattered to splinters —beyond repair by the finest surgeon, and as it was, I received something less than solicitous surgical care. This, however, remains of small moment next to a further accomplishment of yours."

Casually Lat Danziger tugged down his silk mask. Alex felt his spine start to crawl even before the disfigurement beneath was fully revealed. It was the mask, actually, that had betrayed Lat's identity. If he had not seen only Lat's eyes and recognized him thus, he would never have noticed his eyes for the gaunt horror below. Not a face—it could no longer be called a face.

It had been obvious on that long-ago day when the bullet-shattered lamp had exploded its clinging liquid fire full in the man's face that the resulting mutilation would be hideous . . . *but this.*

Again Lat laughed; but with full sight of the scarred gap that formed a noise of tinkling grace, the effect was indescribable. "An amusing sight for the post-breakfast hour, gentlemen, eh? My face received even less medication than my leg. A guard at the prison who couldn't bear the sight of me made the sight even more unbearable with periodic clubbings. Once I was on the outside, the result made living somewhat less than hell, but not by much. The ladies, you know, bless their hearts. It was long years, as you may imagine, before I learned to appreciate the ribald opportunities inherent in the situation. Since I had to wear a mask with even the ladies of Cypriot persuasions, the fees necessary to overcome their reluctance were considerable. One night the mask happened to slip." He grimaced with terrible laughter. "Under the circumstances, well, the lady's reaction was understandably extreme. Ah, but gratifying. Gentlemen, I can't forebear these antic qualms whenever I think of it."

"*Dios,*" Chino muttered. "I'm think you do yourself big favor if you laugh yourself to death."

"You're a kindred soul, Mr. Lucero. We are both clowns in life, but my funny face has yours beaten by all odds. But let me satisfy your curiosity, gentlemen—"

Alex, wondering how long they might stall him, put in, "What I don't understand is how you escaped prison without our hearing about it."

Lat grinned frightfully. "No escape, Mr. McKenna. I died there. I was assigned to the farm outside the walls, and attempted a break in company with three others. We were overtaken while crossing a river. Two of my companions were recaptured, one killed by gunfire. I feigned a fatal hit by going under, then letting the current carry me downstream. My body, of course, was never recovered, but to all intent I was killed attempting an escape. That was some six years ago."

"You waited a long time to set this up."

"Not really. Every man needs something to live for. The state of my face precluded any normal goals. That freed me to focus every attention on the matter of destroying Jonathan Trask. While engaging my fancy with delightful possibilities, I was in no hurry and I needed a secure background for the work I had set myself to.

"I became Tigo. The vocation of a hired assassin in cattle wars fitted my talents and my plans, and let me avoid distressing prospects in rubbing elbows with humanity. I kept always to myself, living in the backcountry, developing plainscraft. Meantime I honed my tools on occasional jobs. There was a backwoods store where I purchased supplies; anybody wishing to contact me for professional purposes got a message to me through the storekeeper. A meeting was arranged, to which I always came masked as you've seen me. A suggestion of terror and mystery that helped promote many such a deal. My fees were such that I could have afforded to live resplendently in any world capital, but for—"

Tigo did not have to scowl to make his meaning clear; he only needed to smile. He smiled now, and went on, "When I felt the time was ripe, Mr. Trask, I came here. I learned of your squabble with some settlers and decided to turn your mild feud into a large one. They didn't send for me, you see; I sought them out and offered my services. I promised them only that I would stop you, not necessarily take your life. This dovetailed with my own plans—always collect a fee when and where you can, is my motto.

"To fill you with the taste of personal fear by an occasional ambush was a mere diversion. Every man has his calling. To a man of your gifts, nothing I could devise would stagger you as would the gradual, calculated destruction of all you had built. I started things moving toward that end.

"Then it occurred to me that isolating you from your empire, watching but unable to influence its course, was the way. Prison, of course. You would be helpless as a baby. No—paralyzed man would be better. A paralyzed man in possession of his faculties but unable to stir a muscle. A foretaste of hell to a man of your disposition and energies.

"It was me, as you've by now guessed, who planted those hides on the Cady place, leaving a clear trail there. Then it was only a matter of staying in hiding close by to see what would develop. When your two brothers rode in to find the hides and accuse the Cadys, the hotheaded Cortney drew and fired on them. The Cadys returned fire, but apparently not to kill. I rectified that omission by shooting young Liam. My shot went unnoticed in the general rataplan—evidently Cady believed either he or his son had found the mark, albeit by accident."

Jonathan said, "*You*," and he was swaying on his feet. Alex had never seen anything hit him as Tigo's quiet words did. The blood had run out of his face; he looked gray and stunned, like a fighter on his last legs.

For the first time he was thrown face to face with the fact that he had committed his own raw brand of justice not on a pair of cattle thieves, not on his brother's murderers, but on two guiltless men, men innocent of either thievery or murder. Jonathan had never experienced a small emotion in his life; smallness was not in him, and Alex, seeing a doubt of depth seizing him for probably the first time in his life, thought, *My God—what must he be feeling?*

"You," Jonathan said in a strangling rasp, and cleared his throat. His voice was reedlike as he went on: "You must of done that other thing before—put them two rednecks in them green hides."

"Ah, the truth has bemused you—now you dig for further truth, is that it? Regrettably I did not commit that ingenious atrocity, which predated my arrival. A brilliant and enviable stroke of—"

Jonathan wheeled suddenly, ignoring Tigo's uptilting rifle, hissing at Chino: "Straight now, Mex. Was it Cort? You was with him that day. Was it Cort killed them two in the hides?"

"Haaah. Why for all the sudden you got the taste to hear what really happen? You never want to hear it before."

"Answer me, God damn you!"

"All right, sure. I'm not there when it happen. Like it is told you, we split up to work, me, Cort an' Li. But later I'm come on what's happen. I find the two dead gringos in the hide. I find track all over that is plain. Cort done it. I mess up all the track so nobody know."

"God," Jonathan said.

"I'm ain't cover up to protect Cort. If I say truth, Cort will deny her, hah? Then in gringo court it is word of Chino against a white *Yanqui*. Haaah. I'm think I keep my mouth shut and keep my scalp. Anyway I'm think this is way the big Trask would want it." Chino gave a slight, expressive shrug. "Cort is drinking that day; he bring bottle along and he is pret' high. Maybe it is my fault for not taking bottle away, not keeping him in my sight, eh? I'm think of these things. Besides it ain' so bad killing a couple rustlers that way. She is the Spanish way. But you Anglos look at her wrong. No. Chino is thinking is wise to keep the mouth shut. Now you are ready hear truth, now I'm tell you truth."

"Truth, Mr. Lucero," Lat Danziger said, "is each man's perspective. Knowing what I did of Mr. Trask's, I had no need to hazard guesses as to his reaction. It was a predictable one. Having arranged that he blame the Cadys for his brother's death, I had only to let the law take its course."

Danziger's glance shifted grotesquely to Jonathan. "I was then content with images of you in prison—all perspective, you see? I couldn't guess that you were buoyed up, as surely you were, by a certainty that your release would be effected in a relatively short time. You can guess the rest—my chagrin on reading about your retrial, the resumption of my ravages of your material holdings. The '73 panic had already advanced the attrition of your former fortunes; I had only to abet the process. Then it was no trick of any magnitude to keep myself informed of the progress of your new trial and, when you were acquitted, to arrange today's diversion. You have been watched, gentlemen, since your departure from Saba City."

Alex said, "And now?"

"For you, Mr. McKenna—nothing. You once interceded to save my life. You did me no favor as you see, but your intention was honorable. You are free to ride away from here. I suggest that you do so at once."

"What are your plans for them?"

"You're trying my patience, Mr. McKenna." Danziger's voice crackled suddenly. "If you can look on this face and still ask that, you're a fool. I won't weary you with my plans for Mr. Trask, which involve a considerable detail. Mr. Lucero I owe neither grudge nor favor—I simply cannot afford to let him go. Several times in his dogging of my tracks, he came closer to me than he knew. He is a man of no little skill in shooting and tracking, therefore a danger to me." A pause, and Danziger said gently, "You, McKenna, cannot afford to be a fool. A twice-blessed man should think of his wife—his child."

Alex was thinking of them, and of something else. The pocket pistol he had discovered in his saddlebag at his first camp after leaving Katytown. JoAnne had urged him before his departure to take a pistol, but he hadn't carried one in years, and his rifle should be protection enough. A pistol was an invitation to trouble, he had told her; but she had stowed one in his gear anyway. On afterthought he'd been appreciative; he was inviting no difficulty with a concealed weapon, and it might come in handy.

Without a word now, he went to his horse, stepped into

the saddle and rode slowly from the clearing, not looking back. There was perfect silence behind him, and he
knew that Danziger would be listening to make sure he kept
going.

When a thicket cut him off from view, Alex started un-
doing the flap of one saddlebag, holding his horse to a
measured walk. And a last-minute qualm seized him. Why,
with everything to live for, with a wife and a son dependent
on him, should he risk his life to save two men who had
no claim on his obligations? He remembered wryly his words
to JoAnne, "I'll never take up with him or for him again,"
and thought, *I've got to. It's the way I believe—she knows
that better than anyone. Forgive me, Jo.*

He dived his hand into the saddlebag as he wheeled the
horse on a tight rein; his hand dipped up the small caliber
gun and he drummed his sorrel into a run back toward
the clearing. Danziger would hear him coming, but there was
no time for a stealthy approach. At least Danziger would
not expect him to be armed; but then the little double-
barreled British pistol would be useless as a popgun except
at pointblank range, and probably he would not get that
close.

But Chino, who fed on trouble, could be depended on to
go into action like a blacksnake at the first opportunity. If
he could give Chino that chance, they would all have a
chance.

He raced through the mottled sunlight into the open.
Lat Danziger was waiting for him, calmly swinging up
his rifle. The little gun in Alex' fist spoke twice, like two
flat whipcracks, and threw off Danziger's aim as he shot.

Alex felt the bullet smack into his horse's forequarters,
and the animal was going forward and down. With the
desperation of instinct rather than thought, Alex was flinging himself sideways even as the horse's stride broke. The
world pinwheeled blindly; he struck full on his back with
an impact that sent a wash of blackness across his mind.
The sensation lasted a broken instant—no longer, for his

eyes flicked open in time to catch Chino in mid-lunge, and the big Mexican must have reacted almost at once. He had taken a step or two, then his spring-steel muscles launched him in a hurtling dive toward the guns Tigo had made them discard.

Snake-quick, Danziger had pivoted pulling his rifle around, and in the same second Alex' eyes came open, he shot hastily. A clean miss, and Chino hit the ground on his chest and belly with a savage grunt, an extended hand slapping over the butt of a pistol. He twisted catlike, coming half-up on his knees and elbows to whip the gun into line. Danziger barely got his rifle levered in the interim. The two shots lashed across each other, not merging but not breaking distinctly apart.

Danziger was jarred backward by the .45's impact, slamming against the big oak. His legs were buckling as he tried to bring the rifle up again, his face twisted in frightful agony. He began sliding down along the treetrunk. Sitting, he tried sluggishly again to raise his rifle, and this time nearly succeeded. Then his head canted over and his eyes shaded into glassy fixity—he died that way, cramped against the tree with his knees drawn up.

Chino's face had dropped into the earth after he fired the one shot. Danziger's second bullet had hammered down into his back, killing him instantly.

XXII

IT SEEMED a long time before Jonathan moved, going over to Chino, bending down beside him. He laid a hand on the dead man's back. "Chino," he said. "Mex." There was no particular tone in his voice.

Alex climbed slowly to his feet, moving his legs and arms gingerly, finding with a mild astonishment th t he had broken no bones in his fall. He felt numb and shaken, but that was reaction to the flurry of violence that had left two dead men in its wake. *Two more dead men,* he thought, looking at Jonathan. *Funny he can walk any more, the string of dead men he's wearing around his neck.*

At last, working his legs as slowly and stiffly as a man waking from a long sleep, Jonathan got to his feet. He looked at Alex with eyes that were strangely blank. "You didn't need to come back." He spoke with a distant, fumbling care, as if each word had demanded a conscious effort. "Seems you never could resist taking a hand when you been needed, boy."

Then his thoughts wrenched back to the real object of his concentration. His eyes were still fixed on Alex, but did not see him at all. "Cort," he murmured. "It was Cort really to blame all along, wa'n't it? It was Cort killed them two rednecks with the hides. That was where it started."

Alex watched him, feeling a faint alarm. "No. It started a long time before that."

Jonathan seemed not to hear him. "It was Cort pushed them Cadys into a gunfight, then lied about it."

"You believed him," Alex said quietly. "It was you that went bellering and pawing off after the Cadys. They were strung up on your orders. Give Lat Danziger a vote of credit, too."

"Cort lied," Jonathan went on in the soft, insistent voice of a man working himself toward a focus of intense certainty. "Cort lied to me from the beginning, or nothing Danziger could of done would of worked out. All his life I sheltered him like a baby. I paid off for his skylarkings. I shielded his hide from anyone and everyone who had reason for nailing it up. There ain't nothing left. The GT is ruint, the Mex is dead. There ain't nothing, and all because of that God damn boy."

"Danziger said something about perspective. Did you hear him?"

Jonathan said thickly, "What?"

"The cynic's definition of truth. He said truth was each man's perspective. Your perspective was that Cort could do no wrong. Now, all of a sudden, Cort is to blame for everything."

Talking to Jonathan, he saw, was like grabbing at a greased pig; his words were sliding off Jonathan's frame of mind to no purpose. With a touch of desperation he went on quickly, "But suppose there's a lot more to truth? More than a man can ever know totally, but enough to let him take a long stride past the childish error of settling on any single person or event as a point of origin—fixing all blame there?"

Jonathan scowled suddenly. "You know I never liked that muddy God damn kind of talk."

Alex nodded calmly. "You always were afraid of it as I recall."

"I never been afraid of a God damn thing!"

"No, not of anything you could lay both hands on and tie knots in, whether it was moneymaking or stringing up somebody you decided was in your way. But you were always afraid of a thought, Buck. A thought can topple a thousand bigotries and righteous self-justifications. It can change a man's whole life in less time than it takes to wink an eye. One thought can make it clear as glass that Cort, poor sorry Cort, is just a weak, wild kid."

"That's what I been saying!" Jonathan roared.

"Yes, years after I told you the same thing. A simple, declared fact that you wouldn't see because you didn't want to. Just as now you don't want to see the rest of it— the way Cort just emulated the biggest thing in his young life. You. If his creed became ruthless self-interest, where did he get it from? You. Oh, you never lied or sneaked; you always shot your dogs for the whole world to see. That was your rule of personal strength and pride. But what have rules to do with a weakling like Cort? Man, Cort could never be anything of himself—he could only follow. He could only imitate his big brother's passions, never his codes. Why do you think you always had to stand between Cort and the consequences of his acts? Where does blame begin when—"

"*Shut up!*" Jonathan seemed to tower in his wrath, his great fists flexing open and shut. His eyes were maniacal; an over-powering intensity was bursting in him.

Abruptly he swung on his heel and ran to his horse, throwing himself into the saddle almost before his foot was secure in the stirrup. Turning the animal, he kicked it furiously into an all-out run, cutting west on the sedgegrass plain, straight as a die toward Katytown.

For a moment Alex stood motionless in his dismay. Had he gone too far in his urge to shake Jonathan into a realization, finally, of the whole truth? The answer came to him almost as one with the question. No, he had tried to divert something that was building to a swift, feral head and had failed, that was all.

Jonathan's strength was all of a kind. He could master anything that demanded only a blunt, single decision backed by insensitive force or a show of it. The trouble was, he saw all of life in the same simplistic terms, a wrong set of terms. The complexities involved in realistic living were infinite, and to a perceptive man who could escape the corrosion of cynicism, this same complexity gave life a richness and variance that made it worth the candle. Jonathan had all of an instinctual man's appreciation of the sensual fullness of existence, but he lacked the perceptive man's eye to uncompromising reality.

A single crack in the dyke of his stubborn self-conviction was more than his nature could accommodate. What he had really seen was not Cort's general worthlessness and perfidy—for a part of his mind could not have failed to acknowledge these things all along—but rather the monumental process of his own self-deception over the years. This being more than he could fully admit, he had turned his fury against Cort.

What did he intend doing now? Alex did not know, nor what might be done to stop it, but he expected the worst. With a driving urgency in him, he looked at his own dead horse, then at Chino's mount. Nobody but its late master had ever stayed on that rawboned brute, but he spent several futile minutes in making the attempt. Then, remembering the whicker made by Lat Danziger's concealed horse, he made a hasty search of the nearby thickets.

The animal, a splendid and tractable bay, stood quietly as he mounted, responding beautifully to his touch. In a moment Alex was riding away from the motte and the two sprawled, silent bodies.

He set a swift pace for town, but Jonathan kept well ahead of him. Alex could see the horse and rider, a black static dot on the tawny plain. And the dot vanished at last behind a long swell on the undulating prairie. Only two miles beyond that height of land was Katytown, and Jonathan got there minutes ahead of him.

Alex was on the outskirts of town before he remembered that Jonathan had taken off in his blind haste without retrieving the pistol Danziger had made him discard. Alex thought of Jonathan's present temper, of his probable intention of confronting Cort, and of the quick-triggered wildness that was Cort's typical response to a prodding.

Thinking of these things, Alex didn't slacken his pace as he rode into town. He held the bay to a hard clip as he swerved through three residential blocks to reach the old main street. If Jonathan were looking for his brother, remembering what Alex had said about Cort's recent debauchery, he would head by instinct for the Steerhead Bar, the Trasks' favorite watering place for years.

Jonathan's horse, he saw, was tied at the rack in front; but even as Alex veered that way, the shot came, high and hollow, beating down the midday quiet.

Men were already converging on the Steerhead as Alex

reached the porch, but he was first through the saloon doors.

Jonathan lay face down on the floor, and Cort was sagging against the bar, his back to it. The gun he had used was slipping from his fingers, and it clattered on the floor as Alex stepped inside and halted. Cort's face was pasty with bewilderment and fright. The wildness and marks of low living were momentarily erased for the lost fearfulness of a small boy, but of no boy that Alex could remember.

"He come straight in like a crazy man," Cort said in a thin whisper. "He come right at me, calling me every sort of bad name. I kept telling him to stop—I kept telling—"

Alex walked over to Jonathan, sprawled on his belly in the reeking sawdust. His half-turned face rested in the raw dampness of last night's spilled liquor, his beard touching a gob of tobacco-stained spittle.

So this was how it ended . . . a man who had contained some parts of what men called greatness, who had built one of the West's great cattle fortunes before he was thirty . . . dead at the age of thirty-three on a whiskey-fouled saloon floor. *In this year of grace,* Alex thought with a weary irony. *April 9, 1875.*

"Alex." The word brought his glance up, and he saw the mute, terrible pleading in Cort's expression. "Alex—*help me.*"

Alex said nothing, and after a moment turned toward the door. Lou Mapin had just come in, threading through the gathering clot of the curious, and he said, "Alex, did you see it?"

Alex shook his head and brushed past him, and went out. He stepped off the porch and stood by the hitchrack, gripping it with both hands till the flesh ached. Then he relaxed his hands and shook his head once, gently. He could feel almost nothing. Maybe it would come later, but he didn't think so. When he tried to think back, to remember how the old life had been, it was like a dream savored with a faintness of reality, nothing more.

Mapin had come out of the Steerhead and moved up

beside him, he realized. "Can't get much out of Cort. You can't tell me nothing about what happened, hunh?"

Alex tiredly said that he hadn't seen the shooting, but he told Mapin as much as he could about what had led to it.

Mapin listened in silence till Alex had finished, then shook his head in a glum, abstracted way as if he shared a counterpart of Alex' mood. "Funny. You grow up with a bunch like the Trask boys. You drink and brawl and sky-lark with 'em, and you never once along the way figure it could end like this." He rubbed a hand over his long jaw. "Well, I'll see Cort over to the lock-up, then take a wagon out to fetch in Lucero and Danziger."

"Lou—" Alex paused, considering his next words with no enthusiasm. "Tell Cort I'll defend him. I'll need to talk with him, but not for awhile. The less I have to see of him until the trial, the better all around."

Mapin nodded, and Alex left him, turning off the main street toward the neighborhood where he lived. And the dullness slipped from him with every step. His thoughts quickened ahead; he was coming home to JoAnne and Robert Gideon, and he forgot everything else. For they were his world now . . . all of it.

ABOUT THE AUTHOR

T.V. Olsen was born in Rhinelander, Wisconsin. "My childhood was unremarkable except for an inordinate preoccupation with Zane Grey and Edgar Rice Burroughs." He had originally planned to be a comic-strip artist, but the stories he came up with proved far more interesting to him than any desire to illustrate them. Having read such accomplished Western authors as Les Savage Jr., Luke Short, and Elmore Leonard, he began writing his first Western novel while a junior in high school. He couldn't find a publisher for it until he rewrote it after graduating from college with a bachelor's degree from the University of Wisconsin at Stevens Point in 1955 and sent it to an agent. It was accepted by Ace Books and was published in 1956 as *Haven Of The Hunted*.

Olsen went on to become one of the most widely respected and widely read authors of Western fiction in the second half of the twentieth century. Even early works such as *High Lawless* and *Gunswift* are brilliantly plotted with involving characters and situations and a simple, powerfully evocative style. Olsen went on to write such important Western novels as *The Stalking Moon* and *Arrow In The Sun*, which were made into classic Western films as well, the former starring Gregory Peck and the latter under the title *Soldier Blue* starring Candice Bergen. His novels have been translated into numerous European languages, including French, Spanish, Italian, Swedish, Serbo-Croatian, and Czech.

The second edition of *Twentieth Century Western Writers* concluded that "with the right press Olsen could command the position currently enjoyed by the late Louis L'Amour as America's most popular and foremost author of traditional Western novels." His novel *The Golden Chance* won the Golden Spur Award from the Western Writers of America in 1993.

Suddenly and unexpectedly, death claimed him in his sleep on the afternoon of July 13, 1993. His work, however, will surely abide. Any Olsen novel is guaranteed to combine drama and memorable characters with an authentic background of historical fact and an accurate portrayal of Western terrain.